REJECTS PARADISE

Cover Design: Covers by Aura
Photographer: Valua Vitaly
Proofreading: Danielle Stansbury
Editing: Heather Fox
Editing & Formatting: Sheridan Anne

COCKY
F*ck

To my amazing Street team. We're only a new bunch but you guys already mean so much to me. You keep me motivated and give me all the love in the world to keep going.

To Danielle, my P.A. I still don't know how you do it! You came into my life like a tornado and now I can't even remember how I survived without you before.

Special mention – Deanna Murphy. Your mind is sickly twisted in the best way. She offered a suggestion that helped to shape a particular scene in Chapter 7 which I am now crazy in love with! THANK YOU!!!!!

CHAPTER 1

A heavy bang has my head whipping around to the door of the pool house to find Eli standing proud with a grin across his face. Penis balloons get shoved through the door and fly to the ceiling revealing the penis shaped hat on his head and pant's down around his ankles with his dick staring back at me.

My eyes bug out of my head, but the shock coursing through my veins has me unable to find words. Eli strides through the door with his cock hanging low and in one easy swoop, he starts windmilling it around with his fists pumping into the sky.

"I'M FUCKING SYPHILIS FREE AND IT'S ALL THANKS TO YOU."

What the fuck kind of bullshit have I invited into my life? And why can't I take my eyes off his swinging dick?

It circles at least five full rotations before he reels that monster in and I manage to tear my gaze away. "What the hell are you doing?" I screech, pulling back as he starts racing toward me.

He launches himself across the room and I scramble away but he's too quick. Eli's strong grip curls around my ankle and he drags me back to him before curling me into his warm arms and suffocating me with love. "Get your dirty dick away from me, you skank ass whore."

His groin wriggles against my thigh. "No can do, sweet cheeks," he laughs proudly, his excited grin becoming infectious. "This dick is as clean as they come. Come on, have a good look. I might even let you touch it."

"NO. God, no. Get it away from me."

Eli laughs and finally relents, releasing his strong grip and allowing me to right myself on the couch. He awkwardly gets back to his feet with his jeans hanging around his ankles, and as he goes to bend to hoist them back up Officer Langston steps out of the bathroom and comes to a startling stop.

Eli's eyes bug out of his head and his pants are torn up his legs so damn fast that I start to worry about the likelihood of his dick getting caught in his zipper. I roll my eyes, watching him die of embarrassment as the penis hat swiftly falls from his head.

Langston's eyes narrow and flick between me and Eli, instantly assuming something else is going on here. Embarrassment floods through me even though it shouldn't, and I'm left with bright red cheeks as the officer makes his way back toward the couch.

Eli doesn't care for my embarrassment as protecting me from a threat will always come first. He steps in front of me, blocking me from the cop and knowing damn well that when there's a cop in a room with someone from Breakers Flats, it's not good news. "Who the fuck are you?"

"Eli," I hiss as Langston's hand hovers above the gun at his hip, clearly recognizing the massive black widow spider tattoo on his neck as the mark for his gang. For fuck's sake. I love my boys but they have a way of making matters so much worse. Sometimes it's a gift and other times, like this, it's a nightmare. "Sit your stubborn ass down. Officer Langston was just taking my statement."

"Your statement?" Eli gasps, spinning around to glare at me. "The fuck, Ocean? You know better than to talk to the cops about your shit. Nic said we'll handle it."

I clench my jaw, silently begging him to keep his fucking mouth shut but Officer Langston has a death wish and provokes him. "What's a Black Widow doing in my town? You must be lost, boy."

Eli spins back around, looking as though he just stepped right out of hell. "Boy?" he says, demanding respect. "I'm not your boy. I'm your worst fucking nightmare, and if anyone is lost around here, it's you."

"Black Widow's are not welcome here."

Eli takes a step forward, showing that he's not about to back down. "Black Widows have been running this fucking town since you were in diapers, boy," Eli spits, making my brows furrow and a million questions flow through my mind.

Langston looks around Eli and catches my eyes. "Is he bothering you, ma'am?"

I go to reply but Eli steps aside, blocking his view and making me wonder how this turned into some twisted pissing contest. "She's fine."

Langton's hand flinches at his hip and I let out a frustrated groan before flying to my feet and throwing myself in front of Eli. My arms stretch out wide, blocking as much of his large body as I possibly can. "Okay," I say, hating the fact that this isn't the first time I've had to do this. It's not even the second or third time that I've had to put myself between one of my boys and a cop. "There's clearly been a misunderstanding. Eli is a friend and is more than welcome to barge in here with his pants down whenever the hell he sees fit." I spin around and glare at my friend. "As for you, you need to shut the fuck up and sit your ass down. He's here taking my statement because Charles Carrington was killed this morning … or last night. I don't know."

Eli's brows shoot up into his hairline. "The fuck? Daddy Warbucks is dead?" I nod and he laughs. "No shit. Who would have known? I'm not surprised though. That fucker was a hard ass. He had it coming."

Langston takes a step toward us, his eyes narrowed suspiciously on Eli. "Where were you during the early hours of this morning?"

For fuck's sake.

I groan and turn to face Langston again. "He was home in Breakers Flats."

Langston doesn't move his glare from Eli and it's as though I'm invisible—not that I'm surprised. Before Eli showed up, Langston was respectful and questioned me as if I was hurting over Charles' death. Now that he's seen my connection to Eli that respect has flown straight out the window and it doesn't sit well with me.

"Actually," Eli says with a tone in his voice that has me cringing. "I was sinking deep into Harlow Burberry's pussy all night long. She can verify my story."

I look back up at Eli. "Who the fuck is Harlow Burberry?"

He shrugs his shoulder. "I don't know. I met her at Pony Girl's last night. She was a fucking rocket, babe. You should have seen the way she moved."

"Okay," Officer Langston says, less than impressed. "I think I've heard enough."

With that, he excuses himself and walks out the door, heading back to the main house while most likely disregarding my whole statement. The words of a poor girl from Breakers Flats won't be as valuable as someone born and bred in Bellevue Springs.

I put it to the back of my mind. It's nothing worth crying over, it's just the way things have always been for us and we're more than used to it. So, I focus on a much bigger issue. "You hooked up with a stripper last night?" I demand, smacking a hand over Eli's chest. "No wonder you got syphilis, you dirty man-whore. You're disgusting."

"Chill out," he says, catching my hand before I get a chance to smack him again. "I didn't fuck anyone last night. I wasn't even in Breakers Flats last night, I was here, but it's not like I was about to let that fucker know."

"Sorry," I grumble, shaking my head. "I knew that. It's just been a weird day … and night."

"Yeah, I bet," he says, his voice taking on a more serious tone. Something I'm not exactly used to when it comes to Eli. "So, the old man is really dead?"

"Yeah," I say, glancing away, not wanting him to see the emotion building within my eyes. "He was stabbed right through the chest with a silver dagger."

"A silver dagger?" Eli demands, taking my chin and forcing my eyes back to his. "Your father was killed just like that."

"I know." I tear my chin free and drop down onto the couch. "Trust me, I fucking know. It's all I've been able to think about all morning, but that's not the worst part."

His brows furrow, focusing heavily as he sits down beside me. "How could it get worse? You were fucking raped last night, the dickhead is on the fucking run, and now Carrington is dead."

"The dagger," I told him. "I swear, it was the exact same one that killed my dad. It has the same design on the hilt."

"Nah." Eli shakes his head and drops his arm over my shoulder, pulling me into his side. "That's not possible, babe. Maybe you saw it wrong. You've had a lot on your mind, and I don't blame you after the night you had. That fucker drugged you. You're thinking too much into this."

"It was the same fucking dagger, Eli," I snap, not appreciating being questioned. "I fucking know it. I was the one who walked into that room and saw it sticking out of my father's chest. The image is burned into my mind. It. Was. The. Same. Fucking. Dagger."

"Come on, Ocean. That dagger was taken and put in an evidence locker. This has to be a coincidence."

"Stop talking down at me," I demand, recognizing his tone as the one he uses when trying to reel Kairo in, knowing he's about to kick someone's ass. "I'm telling you, Eli. This is connected. I don't know how or why, I just know it. I feel it in my gut. Whoever did this has something to do with my father's death."

He lets out a heavy sigh and meets my eyes. "Are you sure?"

"I'm positive. I feel it."

Eli studies me for a moment before finally nodding and slipping his hand into his pocket. "Alright, babe. I'll call Nic and get him back here. We'll sort it out."

"No," I rush out. "Don't call him. It's not smart for you guys to be hanging around here with all the cops crawling around. Nic is already a gray area seeing as though he spent most of the night here. I can't have you guys going down for this. You need to stay away."

"Seriously?" He laughs. "There's a fucking rapist with a boner for you running around, and now a murderer who may or may not be the same guy who killed your father. We're not about to let you out of our sight until this is straightened out."

I let out a sigh and look up at him. There's no point trying to fight it. The boys will have it their way no matter what I say or how I feel about it because where they are concerned, all that matters is my safety. I might as well accept it and make the most of the protection detail that's going to be following me around like a bad smell.

"So," I say, wanting to change the topic. "What are you even doing here? Nic will castrate you if he found out you dropped out of the Jude search to come and rub your dick all over me."

"It's fine, babe," he says with a mischievous grin. "Half the fucking Widows are out there searching for the fucker. They'll be alright if I take two minutes to check up on my girl. Besides, what they don't know won't hurt."

"But that's the thing. You walked in here thinking you would just be celebrating your STD-free dick, but now that you have more information, you have no choice but to call Nic, and then you'll be dead."

Eli's face falls and his eyes slowly come back to mine. "Fuck," he sighs. "I didn't think about that, but I guess if I'm going to go down I might as well enjoy myself."

My eyes narrow in suspicion. "What's that supposed to mean?"

"I, uhh … might have made a quick stop on my way here."

The penis balloons float behind his head and I eye them warily. "Why does that make me so nervous?"

His brows bounce excitedly as he strides back toward the front door. "Have you ever walked into an adult store?" he asks, leaning out the door and grabbing a bag. His head reappears and the grin on his face is nearly enough to have me running for the hills. "It's fucking wild, babe. I wanted to cheer you up with a 'syphilis free party' and went fucking nuts."

Eli laughs at his little nut pun and I roll my eyes as he collects his penis hat and fixes it back on his head before dropping the bag on the coffee table. He's quick to start rifling through it, and I watch as a rainbow of suction cup rubber dildos are stuck down on the coffee table. Next penis-shaped straws are pulled out, penis confetti, and naturally, a bunch of penis-shaped candies.

I stare in wonder, having absolutely no idea how his little brain decided that surrounding me with penises was somehow a good idea after the night I've had, but when I see his dorky little smile, it somehow makes me feel a million times better. Though, that mood instantly goes crashing down when he pulls out a penis shirt for me to wear and then tops it off with a crown, declaring me a 'cock dominator.'

For some reason, unknown to me, I let the idiot stay. He drops down beside me with a bottle of tequila, and I find myself grateful for the distraction.

I don't know how my four boys always manage to be there for me exactly when I need them, but somehow, they do and that's one of the main reasons that I love them so damn much.

"So," he says, leaning back into the couch and propping his foot up onto the cock-filled coffee table. His eyes meet mine and before he says another word, it becomes far too clear what he's about to ask. I prepare myself for the worst, knowing I won't make it through this without breaking. "No bullshit, O. How are you really doing?"

I press my lips into a tight line and kick his feet off the coffee table, knowing that even though Mom is inside the Carrington mansion right now, she'll somehow know that someone has their feet on her table.

"Honestly," I start, taking the ridiculous crown off my head and looking down at it. "Not great. Every time I close my eyes, I remember the feeling of not being able to stand properly and calling out for help. I was so scared, Eli. I've never felt anything like it. He just grabbed me and I was defenseless." Tears start welling in my eyes but I try not to break. "He took me upstairs and tore my dress and ..."

"Shhhhh," he soothes, shuffling over on the couch and pulling me into his chest. "Don't tell me the details. I don't want you reliving it."

The tears finally fall and I squish my face into his chest as his arms protectively wrap around me, holding me tight. "How am I ever supposed to forget?"

I feel him shake his head, lost deep in thought. "I don't know, babe. I wish I had a proper answer for you. I'd do anything to be able to take that pain away for you, but someday, somehow, you're going to wake up and realize that you survived. He does not control you, he does not own you, and he sure as hell did not ruin you. You, Oceania Munroe, are a fucking queen. You're beautiful and if I wasn't so in love with being a whore, I know I would have fought Nic tooth and nail until you were mine. Jude may have left you with a scar, but a scar is a story that is only ever going to make you stronger."

"It doesn't feel that way."

"I know," he tells me, rubbing his hand up and down my arm. "But it will."

Silence falls around us and as he holds me, I find the little torn pieces of my heart and soul being sewn back together. I still have a massive mountain to climb before I'm going to feel like myself again, but at least it's a start. Besides, right now, I should be thinking of Charles and figuring out how the hell he ended up with a silver dagger protruding out of his chest. I should be spending time with Colton, making sure he's alright. I should be ... fuck, there's a million other things I should be doing right now, yet I can't seem to find the will to peel myself off this couch and start making a difference.

Instead, Eli and I just sit. Ten minutes pass and it quickly turns into an hour and by the time I'm falling asleep on his lap, the bottle of tequila is almost gone. We're both so lost inside our own heads that reality completely slips away.

A text message comes through on my phone and I glance down and find myself smiling.

Nic - Have you seen E? The fucker disappeared.

"Uh-oh," I tease, showing the text to Eli and watching his face drop while reading over it. I chuckle to myself and start hashing out my reply.

Ocean - Nope. Last I heard he was syphilis free and hooking up with some stripper called Harlow.

Nic - Tell him to get his fucking ass out on the street and start searching for this motherfucker before I leave him there for the West Side Wolves.

Eli's eyes bug out of his head and I look up at him, knowing Nic only brings out the rival gang threat when he is about ready to crack. "I think you better go. He sounds serious."

"Nic is always serious when it comes to you," he says with a heavy sigh. "But you're right. I should go. He only uses Wolves against us when shit is about to go south."

Ocean - He's coming. Don't be mad. I really needed the

company.

A yawn tears from my body and Eli looks down at me before scooping me up off the couch and walking me through to my bedroom. "Sleep it off," he tells me, slipping me in between the sheets and resting my head against the pillow.

My eyes instantly grow heavier and as he leans down and presses a kiss to my temple, warmth spreads through me. "I'm going to find this fucker," he promises me. "I swear, Ocean. We won't stop until this is right."

I nod and watch as he gives me a tight smile before slinking away. As I hear the door of the pool house closing, I allow unconsciousness to claim me, taking me to a place where the pain no longer exists.

CHAPTER 2

The bed dips beside me and my eyes spring open in fear.

"Woah, woah, woah. Wifey, it's just me," Milo says, his tone low and soothing, instantly making my heart ease its rapid beat.

I let out a deep sigh and take a few calming breaths as I meet his eyes, and as I do, his gaze softens and I see nothing but devastation shining back at me.

Shame takes over me. He knows.

"Who told you?" I murmur as he drags me across the bed and into his warm arms. He curls me against his chest and I relax into him. It's not home but for now, it will do.

"I, uhhh … actually, I don't know. It was one of your boys though. He said he was just here and demanded that I come and stay with you while they searched for Jude." His hold tightens around me at the mention of his name and I fight back tears, loving how Eli thought to call Milo to come and be with me so that I don't have to be alone.

"That was Elijah," I murmur, wondering how the hell he had gotten Milo's number, but when it comes to these boys nothing seems impossible.

Milo nods and lets out a heavy breath. "I'm so sorry, Ocean," he murmurs, his tone filled with pain. "I saw you sitting out there by the pool last night and I kept telling myself to go and be with you, but I saw that kiss with Colton and thought you just needed the space to think it over. If I'd just walked out that damn door and sat with you …"

"Don't," I whisper, hating the gut-wrenching pain that rises with his words. "It happened, and there's nothing we can do about it. Saying 'what if' or wishing you'd made different decisions isn't going to change that. I know you're hurting too and that it's eating away at both of us, but I can't have your guilt for not being able to predict the future riding on my shoulders too. It's too much."

"Fuck," he breathes. "You're right. I'm sorry, I didn't think of it that way. I want to take away your hurt, not add to it. I guess I don't really know what to do or say."

"Just be here with me so I don't have to be alone."

"Okay," he says, squeezing a little tighter. "I can do that."

"And perhaps change the topic. I think I'm going to go insane if it doesn't leave my mind soon."

"Alright then," he tells me, sitting us up and dragging me out of bed. "First off, you can explain to me why you smell like a bar, and when you get done doing that, you can tell me why the pool house is filled to the brim with penises. I mean, if you were having a penis party then I'm extremely offended that I wasn't invited."

I glance up to find the most serious look on his face, and for just a brief moment, everything is alright in the world. A smile tears across my face and I run for him, crashing into Milo and spreading my arms out wide. I hold onto him with everything I've got. "Thank you," I laugh, feeling another piece of my soul return to my body. "You're a freaking Godsend. I don't know what I would do without you right now."

"Please," he teases, dragging me back out to the cock-filled living room. "I'm sure you would have caved and would be testing out some of these dildos. Though judging by how much of that tequila bottle is gone, I'd dare say that you'd probably end up in the Emergency Room if you even tried."

I drop down onto the couch and Milo instantly starts cleaning up the mess that Eli and I had made. The need to help pulses through me but I just can't seem to find the energy to help. Milo doesn't say anything, just tells me all about the party and how Colton was standing by the back window, watching me by the pool for most of the night, that is until I got up and left then didn't return to the party. Apparently, he ran out of there and caused a scene, but no one knew why. Not until now.

My heart breaks. Last night was incredible until it wasn't. It was supposed to be my fairy tale night. It was my big ending and Colton and I were finally going to open up and make it work. All I had to do was get my ass from the pool area back to the party but apparently, that was too fucking hard.

Happiness was right at my fingertips. I could feel it creeping up on me and despite the shit that Colton and I had fought through, we were just about at the end of the road. It kills me that the night turned out so disastrous.

Fucking Jude. I can always count on him to ruin a good thing. He's had it out for me since the second I arrived in Bellevue Springs and he finally got what he wanted. Well, mostly. Colton barged in before he was able to finish and I'm grateful for that, but it still doesn't take away those haunting memories.

What worries me is that Jude might want to come back and finish the job. He didn't get the happy ending he was so desperately after and now he's on the run. No one knows where he is and that terrifies me despite how brave I force myself to appear on the outside, and how many times Nic and the boys tell me they'll handle it.

It's become their motto over the past few weeks. *'We'll handle it.'*

It makes me feel as though I'm some sort of incapable fool. They come to my rescue over and over again and each time, I'm left feeling as though I should have been stronger. I feel so weak, and right now, I've never felt so pathetic.

If only I didn't accept those drinks …

If only I didn't run to the pool …

If only I'd stayed with Colton …

Who knows what would have happened. I don't doubt that last night would have been an incredible ending to an already amazing night. He would have spoiled me all night and then taken me up to his room until I was screaming his name, but come this morning when he found out that his father had been murdered, what would have happened then? Would he have still pushed me away? Would he have clung onto me like his only support system? Would he have let me hold him?

I'll never forget the look in his eyes as he stood over his father's dead body. He was devastated but strong. He was an heir claiming his rightful place and taking control. He was the fucking man.

Any innocence that he was desperately clinging onto was stripped away and darkness settled over him. He was hurting, and damn it, I don't doubt that he still is. His warm hand slipped away from mine and whatever twisted emotions had been building between us over the past few weeks burned before my eyes.

Colton looked at me like he could see right through me, like I didn't even exist, and fuck … it was worse than listening to him call me trash or the help. It gutted me. My fairy tale was well and truly over.

There's no salvaging what we might or might not have had. Whatever it was, it's gone now.

He took that dagger from his father's chest and slammed it down on the table. The sound made me jump as I struggled to deal with the memories of my own father's murder flying through my mind. Colton turned those steely hazel eyes on me and just like that, I was dismissed.

I was sent away as though I didn't belong and it tore me to pieces. I don't know what hurts more; Colton's dismissal or Jude's atrocious actions against me.

I guess what it comes down to right now is Charles Carrington. He's what matters now. He might have been a conniving dick with twisted, unclear motives but for the most part, he was nice to me and my mom. He gave us a home when we would have been on the street. He made sure I had an education, a job, a chance for a good life. He gave us salvation when we had nothing. I'll always be grateful even if his intentions weren't exactly pure. I guess his intentions will remain a mystery for now, but in the end, does it really matter?

What matters is that he was brutally murdered in his home while Mom and I were asleep only a short distance away. Hell, Colton was asleep just upstairs. Hearing about random murders back home wasn't such an odd occurrence, but here in this squeaky, clean-cut town, it's unheard of. The fact that the man who lost his life is a name that's known all over the world … well, that just makes it worse.

The cops have been scouring every inch of this massive property searching for evidence all day long. The majority of the staff have been sent home while Mom, Maryne, and Harrison have stayed behind to help out where they can. I'm surprised I've been allowed to stay, but after Officer Langston checked through the pool house and took my statement, he cleared me to remain on the property. I guess being drugged and passed out kinda does have a positive, though that just opened up a whole new round of questions—ones I wasn't prepared to answer.

Since the police first showed up this morning, the whole property has been locked up. After the staff was sent away, it became a no one in, no one out type of situation. Since then, all I've been able to wonder is how Milo and Eli had gotten in here. Though knowing Eli, he probably found a lady cop to flirt with or scaled the massive gates, while Milo most likely paid someone off.

Word has quickly spread and the press has been stationed outside the big iron gates since the early hours of the morning. It's a fucking shit show here. It's one of the biggest stories to hit the media in a long time and somehow, I ended up in the middle of it. From now on, my every move is going to be scrutinized, along with the other staff and Colton. As if I wasn't already dealing with enough shit.

Milo's phone cuts through my thoughts and I glance across to find him standing by the window, staring out at the pool. He answers his phone and as he talks, I'm distantly aware that night has fallen.

When the hell did that happen?

It's been the longest day of my life and while I'm thankful for Milo and Eli spending their day trying to keep me distracted, at some point, I need to face the music. I have to walk into that house and I have to check that Colton is alright.

Every inch of my body is telling me to stay away, but I can't. I'm drawn to him like a moth to a flame and despite all his attempts to push me away, I just keep coming back.

Milo ends his call and as he turns to face me, I give him a small smile. "Hey, babe," he says, speaking before I have a chance. "That was my dad. I have to go. Will you be alright here if I take off? I can tell him no if you need me to stay."

"No," I say with a relieved sigh, happy to not have to be the bitch who kicks him out. "That's fine. I was just thinking that I should go and check on Mom and Maryne. I'm sure it would have been stressful in there today."

He raises a brow and stares straight through me. "By your 'mom and Maryne' what you really mean is go and check on Colton."

"I didn't say that."

"You didn't need to, babe. It's written all over your face."

Fuck.

"It is not."

Milo rolls his eyes and slips his phone back into his pocket before striding over to me and wrapping me in a warm hug. "I'll see you at school tomorrow," he says. "Do you need a ride in the morning?"

I press my lips together and think about it for a second. "Can I let you know? I'm not really sure if I'm feeling down for school right now."

"Okay, sure. Let me know when you know," he says, stepping out of my arms and walking over to the door. He steps out and just before the door closes behind him, he looks back with a smile. "Let me know if you need anything."

With that, he's gone, leaving me truly alone for the first time since sitting out by the pool last night. I'm left with my own torturous thoughts and as every shadow begins to turn into a threat, I know I won't survive here by myself.

CHAPTER 3

I hurry out of the pool house trying to figure out how the hell I'm going to sleep tonight. I wonder how mom will feel about me bunking with her, though that's going to bring questions and I'm not sure I have the strength to tell her about it yet. Maybe I'll just stick with the good old 'leave the bathroom light on' trick.

I reach the back door of the mansion and slip in through the staff quarters before coming to a standstill. I'm not used to it being so damn quiet here. There's not a damn sound. No water boiling on the stove, no washing machines running, no vacuums, or the soft music that plays through the chef's radio.

The cops are gone and the surveillance monitor by Harrison's desk is showing that most of the press from the front gate have started to leave, clearly realizing that they're not about to get any information out of us. Though, it won't do them any good. No one knows anything.

The dagger has been on my mind all day. I don't know if I should go and talk to Colton about it or leave it for a few days. It's a lead and a starting point for the cops to begin searching for whoever did this, but it's also a wound that I'm not sure I'm ready to tear open. Dad only died five months ago and it was horrific. I don't think my heart is ever going to heal.

Desperately needing to get my mind off dad, I start walking through the main part of the house, listening out for Mom, Maryne, Harrison, or Colton. Though, if I was to run into Colton, I'm not sure what might happen. I don't know if I'm ready to face him yet as I know he's going to push me away again, but a part of me is desperately needing to make sure that he's alright.

I've tried to give him space but I'm only human, and the need to feel his arms around me has been pulsing through me all day.

It's so hard to believe that it was only this morning that I was up in Colton's bedroom, listening to him tell me how he can't stay away from me anymore. He explained the reasoning behind the Jade nickname and then in a split second, his lips were on mine and I was ready to give myself to him.

A split second can change it all.

I hear soft murmured voices and I follow them into one of the many formal dining rooms and find myself silently hovering at the door. I peek in, not wanting to interrupt while hoping to find Mom, only it's Harrison and Maryne sitting at the table with papers spread wide and looking more stressed than I've ever seen them.

"I think we should stick with an open casket and have him dressed in that fancy three-piece suit he always raves about," Maryne says, keeping her voice low.

Harrison's eyes bug out of his head as he gapes at her, lowering his reading glasses down his nose. "You want to bury the man in a one-hundred-thousand-dollar suit?"

Maryne gapes right back at him. "That's how much that thing cost?"

"What did you expect from Charles Carrington? If the man was going to splurge on a nice suit, he was going to make it count."

"Good point. I don't know why after all these years I'm still surprised by the man. But I stick with my suggestion, I think he would have wanted to look his best for his final day."

Harrison nods. "I think you're right," he says with a heavy sigh, looking as though he somewhat misses the man despite him being an ass. "I'll arrange for the funeral home to put him in a regular suit when the casket is closed. Colton may want to hang onto Charles' suit for safekeeping."

Maryne's hand falls to Harrison's shoulder and she gives it a gentle squeeze as a tear rolls down her cheek. "That's a lovely thought," she murmurs, her voice barely audible from my position by the door. "Have you seen him today? I don't think he's eaten any of the food I left out for him."

Harrison shakes his head. "No, not since Officer Browning took his statement. He's been hiding out somewhere, but you know what it's like trying to find someone in this house. It's like trying to find a needle in a haystack. He'll emerge when he's ready."

My heart shatters and I fall back against the wall, feeling his pain as though it was my own. My father's death is still too fresh in my mind and it's like it's happening all over again. Colton and Charles had a rough relationship and though Charles was a prick to him and he ran his mother and sisters away, there's still a part of him that always held onto the hope of one day gaining his father's approval, but now that will never happen.

Losing someone you love is one of the hardest things you will have to suffer through. Instead of having the time to grieve that loss, Colton was thrown headfirst into his father's position without pause. Now, as the head of the Carrington family and CEO of many multi-million-dollar businesses, he has the whole world watching him. I don't doubt that he's feeling the pressure.

Ever since I came to Bellevue Springs, I've wanted nothing more than to hate Colton Carrington, and right now, I'm finding it an impossible task. He's a broken soul and my heart is screaming to be the one who gets to fix it and if I can't do that, then maybe he'll just let me be close if only for a little while.

Maryne lets out a heavy sigh and I listen as papers are ruffled around on the table. "Okay," she finally says. "Here are the options for the casket. I'm thinking that he would appreciate the Malaysian 14-karat gold with the red velvet lining."

"I was thinking the same," Harrison says. "It's sophisticated.

Charles would have appreciated that. Now, where are we with the florist and the guest list?"

A phone rings, cutting the conversation short. "Ah, this is probably the funeral home confirming the church." Harrison scoops the phone off the table and steps back. He gets busy with the phone call as Maryne grabs a pen and starts marking off final choices, the same way she does when she's planning one of the Carrington's elaborate parties.

"Ocean?" Mom's voice comes from behind. I spin around to find her walking down the hallway, watching me curiously. "What are you doing, honey?"

"I, uh … I really don't know. I was trying to find everyone but then overheard them discussing funeral arrangements and well … why are they doing it? Shouldn't Colton be involved? Out of everyone here, he knows Charles the most. Wouldn't he want to be the one making these decisions?"

Mom's lips pull into a tight line and I can't help but notice the heaviness behind her eyes and realize just how hard today must be for her as well. She's probably been living Dad's death all over again, just like I have been. "No, sweety. He instructed Maryne and Harrison to take care of the funeral arrangements. Unfortunately, he doesn't want anything to do with the process, but it's okay, he'll find another way to say goodbye. Besides, the poor boy has a lot to do with his mom and sisters not here. Charles has a lot of affairs to get in order and all that has just fallen on Colton's shoulders."

"I …" I cut myself off, not really sure what to say right now, but knowing that if I think too hard on it, I might just break. I'm thrown back in time to when Colton and I were standing in the foyer of the mansion and he was yelling at his dad about not wanting any of this. He didn't want to be some stuck-up CEO, but now it's too late. This empire is his and from here on out, he has to be the son his father always demanded of him. "Maybe I should offer to help with the funeral arrangements? I don't want to be in their way but I can't just stand here and do nothing."

"No, sweety. I offered my assistance this morning and the offer was declined. They don't want to go against Colton's request and would like to settle it quickly and privately using the information they'd gathered from Charles over their time working for him. As sad as it is to say, apart from his direct family, Harrison and Maryne were the closest people he had in his life."

"Yeah but don't rich people usually have all this stuff sorted out in their wills and pre-arranged?"

"WHAT DO YOU MEAN THE CHURCH IS UNAVAILABLE?" comes hollered from the dining room, making both our eyes sweep back into the dining room to find Harrison pacing up and down the length of the table. "DO YOU HAVE ANY IDEA WHO YOU'RE TALKING TO? This service is for the late Charles Carrington and when I say that we want the absolute best for him, that is what I expect to be provided. Now, check again." There's a slight pause before Harrison chuffs. "That's what I thought. Please email me confirmation."

His call ends and I look at Mom impressed. "Wow, I didn't realize that he had it in him."

Mom nods. "Yes, he's surprised me today. I've been hearing him on the phone all day. He's made some pretty amazing deals but what do you expect? This is Charles Carrington we're talking about. No less than perfect will be acceptable."

I nod, knowing far too well just how perfect it has to be. If Bellevue Springs has taught me anything, it's that a man's reputation is everything. It comes before business, family, and love. It's all that matters because without a stellar reputation in this world, you're as good as done.

"Alright, sweety," Mom says, leaning in and giving me a tight hug. "I have to go and make sure the kitchen is in order so everything is perfect if Colton decides to come up for air." I nod and she goes to walk away before stopping herself and looking back. "Perhaps you could go and find him. I know the two of you have become friendly. Maybe he needs some company."

With that, mom scurries off to her duties and as I watch her go, her shoulders slump making me realize just how tired she must be. Mom has been working around the clock since the second we moved here, but the last few days with party preparation, the masquerade ball, and then the massive clean-up that has fallen solely on her shoulders would have almost killed her. Not to mention that she would have heard just how Charles died and would have spent her day struggling to hold it together. She's stronger than anyone I know, but she's also only human.

Mom disappears around the corner and I let out a breath. She's right. Even if Colton doesn't want me to hang around, I have to at least try. The only question is, where the hell is he? Harrison said he'd been MIA ever since walking out of his father's office this morning.

When my dad died, all I wanted was to be alone, but more than that I wanted to forget, and the only way I was able to forget was by drinking until I passed out, and just like that, I know exactly where he is.

I make my way into the Carrington's private kitchen and just like every other time I walk in here, I'm amazed and in absolute awe, but right now, there are more important things for me to focus on.

I walk through the kitchen and come to a stop outside the cabinet that I had stood in front of on my first day in Bellevue Springs with Charles right by my side. A sharp pang slices through my stomach at the memory. I wasn't exactly close with Charles but no one deserves such an awful ending when their story clearly hasn't finished being written.

It's hard to believe that day was only a month ago. So much has happened since then.

I let out a shaky breath, mentally preparing myself for the unknown. My fingers curl around the small, golden handle of the cabinet door and I slowly pull it open to find the private bar that Colton had worked his ass off to install.

The room is in darkness but the light filtering in from the kitchen is enough to see Colton sitting in a lone armchair. His eyes are blazing and focused heavily on mine, intense and lethal, exactly the version of him that I saw in his father's office this morning.

An open bottle of scotch dangles from his fingers. The bottle is near empty and something tells me that it's probably not the only bottle he's worked his way through today.

My heart shatters watching him. I've never seen someone in such pain, but I sure as hell know what it feels like. Colton didn't even like his father that much. He was intimidating, violent, and angry, but he was still the man who raised him. He's responsible for the man that Colton is today and that has to count for something.

The longer we remain in this stare off, the harder it becomes to watch him. I have to do something. I have to help him or somehow make at least a fraction of the pain go away, but when it comes to Colton Carrington, figuring out the right thing to do is always a challenge.

Realizing it's now or never, I swallow my pride and go to take a step into the private bar, but as he stands, I find myself hovering in the open doorway.

His hazel eyes never leave mine and as he walks toward me, my heart starts racing. I've never understood how he can do that. He's just some guy yet whenever he's around, whether it's something good or something bad, he makes me react in a way which I never would have expected.

The closer he gets, the more I'm reminded of our night together and then early this morning before everything turned to shit. Last night was a fairytale at the party. He looked at me as though I was his everything, his whole world wrapped up in golden silk, but right now, he eyes me as though I'm nothing–trash.

Colton steps in front of me and I raise my chin, not understanding why my nerves are riding so high. "Hey, I … umm–"

I cut myself off as he steps right into me, his body pressed right up against mine. My hands naturally fall to his chest but as he takes another step, I'm pushed out, back into the quiet kitchen. He gives me a gentle push, sending me back against the counter but he stays right where he is, his eyes darkening with distaste.

Unease rockets through me and as he reaches the cabinet door and steps back into the private bar, his intentions become clear. The door is slammed between us with a hard thud and as I listen to the lock sliding into place, my world goes up in flames.

Tears begin to well in my eyes at his rejection. I thought this morning could have been forgiven as he'd just found his father dead, but now after hours of coming to terms with it … it hurts. All his rejections over the past month, his taunts, his stares, his hate, they all come back to me and just like that, I realize that whatever I was foolishly trying to build between us is gone.

The Colton Carrington I thought that I was beginning to know doesn't exist. He played me, and despite knowing how much pain he's in right now, something tells me that this is more than just a cry for help. He's done with me and the finality of that tears me wide open, leaving me feeling like a fool, vulnerable and hurt.

I'm left standing here, staring at the closed door between us, and the longer I wait, hoping for it to open, the quicker everything begins to shut down within me.

The fairytale is dead and the sooner I come to terms with that, the better.

CHAPTER 4

"Are you ready for this?" Milo questions as he pulls into the student parking lot bright and early on Monday morning.

I stare up ahead at the students climbing out of their cars and take in the way they all look back at Milo's Aston Martin, knowing I'm sitting right here in the passenger's seat. That's the problem being the only girl in a school full of guys, if even the smallest thing happens in my life, every one of these bastards will know about it.

I shake my head and press my lips into a hard line. "Nope. Not even close, but it's not like there's anything I can do about it."

"Mmhmm," Milo hums. "You just gotta roll with the punches, or you can be a weak bitch and I can take your ass home."

I groan and fall back into my seat as he parks his car. "Have I ever told you how your ability to inspire me is astounding? You're simply one of a kind."

Milo grins wide, knowing damn well that I'm being sarcastic. "What can I say?" he laughs. "You'd prefer me to be a mean bitch than a fake one."

I groan again. "Fuck you. I hate it when you're right."

"Really?" he laughs. "I kinda like it."

The Aston Martin comes to a stop and I watch as all the students turn and start heading toward us. "For fuck's sake," I mutter under my breath as I grab my bag and slip my phone into my pocket. "This is going to be a shit show."

"Just be glad the press isn't here," Milo says, reaching down to the floor space at my feet and grabbing his bag. "It was a fucking joke trying to drive through them this morning."

"I know, but unfortunately, I think it's only going to get worse until they get the answers they're looking for."

"Yeah, but they're not going to find them by stationing themselves outside the front fucking gates. You know, I saw someone had set up a tent. They're sleeping out there, Ocean. It's ridiculous. The last time I saw something like this was when Judge Mackeby was caught with a teenage girl and then dared to claim he thought she was a prostitute. For such a smart man, he is pretty fucking stupid."

My eyes bug out of my head. "Are you serious?" I gasp, wide-eyed. "What kind of messed up perverts do you have living in this town?"

"Trust me, every fucker in Bellevue Springs has the worst kind of skeletons hiding in his closet. The trick is not letting them out, but you know what they say about secrets ..."

I nod. "They always have a way of coming out."

Milo scrunches up his face. "Nope, they always have a way of coming back and fucking you in the ass."

I swing my door open and grin as I look back at Milo. "Seeing as you're already in the closet with all of your secrets, maybe you should let one of them fuck you in the ass."

Milo rolls his eyes and steps out of his Aston Martin. "Ha ha," he says bluntly, looking at me over the roof of his car. "You're so fucking funny, Ocean. I don't know why I haven't kept you around more."

I scoff and meet him around the front of his car so we can start walking up together. "Shut up. You love it."

Milo laughs and throws his arm over my shoulder before leading us up to the massive front gates of Bellevue Springs Academy *for boys*. The nosey students fall in behind us, waiting to see if I know something and will accidentally slip up, and I have to admit, I'm impressed. Usually, when there's a secret around here, the guys forget that they're human beings and get in my face like fucking animals until they get what they want. Maybe they've finally learned to stop messing with me, or maybe they just assume that the help wouldn't know what she's talking about. After all, we are in Bellevue Springs and just as the cops made perfectly clear, my statement and opinions mean absolutely nothing in this world.

Milo and I fall silent while being obnoxiously aware of the crowd gathering behind us. They whisper between themselves, keeping to themselves but it won't be long before one of them grows a pair of balls.

Milo gently knocks his shoulder into mine and keeps his voice low. "Did you see Colton?"

I shake my head. "Not this morning," I say, not ready to hash out the details of last night's rejection. "He's really not taking it well. He's all messed up. I wouldn't be surprised if he locks himself away for a while."

"He can't do that," Milo mutters. "The boards of Charles' businesses will be going crazy searching for ways to get rid of him. I doubt they want an eighteen-year-old kid pulling the strings. He's going to have to get his shit together and show them that he can do it, otherwise, he'll lose it all."

My brows shoot up into my hairline. "Are you serious? Can they even do that?"

"They sure as hell can, and if Colton isn't careful he's going to fuck up a good thing. I know he doesn't want to be the big guy in charge of Daddy's companies, but it's also an opportunity that will never come around again. If one of those board members gets their hands on his position, they'll never give it up and everything that Charles had been working on and had built will be gone."

"Well, shit …"

"Yeah. It's the same for all of us, except we all expect to take over for our fathers in another thirty years when they retire, but even then, they'll still be breathing down our necks. Colton just got thrown right in the deep end without a life raft."

Damn. No wonder he's so fucked up right now. He has the weight of the world sitting on his shoulders and even though I should be hating on him right now for being such an ass, I can't help but hurt for him.

Why am I so fucked up when it comes to Colton Carrington? I should be stronger than this. Hell, I grew up in Breakers Flats. Bullshit like this should have been squished the second it came to light except now I've allowed it to grow into some kind of beast, one that I no longer have the power to tame.

"Yo," comes a voice from the crowded bodies behind us. "Did you do it?"

"Ignore them," Milo mutters under his breath.

The voice comes again, this time with a snicker that has my blood turning cold. "Yo, babe. Did you hear me? Were you fucking around with the billionaire? Couldn't get your claws into Colton so you tried with daddy? Hoping for a payday now that he's gone?"

Milo's fingers curl around my wrist with a strong grip, trying to keep me in check. "Babe," he warns in a low tone. "Don't you dare entertain his bullshit."

A water bottle slams into my back and I stop in my tracks as laughter erupts behind me. "Stop fucking ignoring me, bitch. I'm talking to you."

I spin around so fast that the group of students struggle to stop so suddenly and slam into each other. I find the guy who's been talking by the sick grin on his face while distantly aware of the way Milo releases his grip on my wrist, more than on board now that I've had a bottle thrown at me.

"Oh, fuck," Milo mutters. "Shit's about to get real."

I narrow my gaze on the asshole who stands proud among his group of douchebag friends. They all laugh at my reaction, but quickly sober as they take in my gaze. "What did you just say to me?" I demand, stepping forward and making a few of them take a hesitant step back.

The guy laughs as Milo steps into my back, always ready to back me if I need him. "You heard me. Were you fucking the old guy? Or was Colton in on it? He's had a boner for you since the day you got here. I bet the two of you were in on it, right? You got Charles out of the way so you could have it all. Makes sense for a girl like you."

"A girl like me?" I question, stepping forward again and watching as a weariness creeps into his eyes. "What exactly *is* a girl like me?"

His friends push him on, encouraging him to be the spokesman of the morons, and luckily for me, he takes the bait, giving me every excuse to kick his pathetic ass. "Trash," he says, raising his chin. "Girls like you are fucking whores. You come from nothing and try to take what's ours. You're a fucking leech. Just like your mother. You all are."

I see fucking red.

No one talks about my mother. Period.

If he was talking about just me, I might have found the will power to ignore him and keep walking, but after the weekend I just endured, he couldn't have picked a worse time to fuck with me.

This is more than just me. So much more. Not only did he bring my mother into this—a woman who has fought so damn hard over the past few months just to keep us alive—he's referring to my whole damn community. Every last person I grew up with, all the people who made me the person I am today. He's referring to my boys. Nic. My whole damn world and nobody gets away with disrespecting that.

He will be punished, and I sure as hell will enjoy every last second of it because this is who I am. I grew up fighting on the streets, I grew up fighting for my rights, and I grew up with respect for those of us who are doing it hard. The people in Bellevue Springs don't know what it's like, but this guy is about to figure it out the hard way.

I run at him, throwing myself in the air until I'm coming down over him. His eyes widen with the split second of warning before I'm climbing him like a tree. He tries to push me away, but my hands curl into fists and slam down hard against his jaw as his pathetic attempts of saving himself are rendered useless.

The guy falls back and his friends start howling with laughter, moving away to watch the show instead of helping their friend. Without the crowd at his back, he falls to the ground, and after steadying myself on his chest, I show him exactly what this trash is made of.

My weight sits heavily on his chest and I nail my fists against him as quickly as I can, not allowing him the chance to grab hold of me as he desperately tries to protect himself, just the way Kairo had taught me.

He will not get away with this.

Not only is he disrespecting me and the way I was raised, but he's disrespecting Colton and his father. Who the fuck does that? Back home, no one would dream of speaking ill of a man who was just murdered in cold blood. It's wrong on so many levels.

My fists start to hurt but I keep pounding away for all the times I've been looked down on, for every shitty comment thrown my way, and for every fucker in this place who has constantly underestimated me. I'm back to my roots, feeling like the girl I used to be. I've been on my best behavior here ... well, mostly. I haven't lashed out like this at anyone and to me, that's considered a miracle. The old Ocean is back and from now on, I'm standing tall.

Strong arms curl around my waist and I'm pulled off the king of the douches, kicking and screaming. "Let me go," I demand, clawing at the arm when I realize it's not Milo's.

"Chill, babe," Charlie says in my ear. "You've done enough."

I relax against him and allow him to pull me away while Milo and Spencer follow along. I have no idea where these two came from as I'm damn sure they weren't here when I first started laying into that fucker—though it seems that a lot of people weren't here when this shit started. The crowd has nearly tripled and—not that I give a shit— there are at least twenty cameras on us. Come tomorrow though ...

Charlie doesn't release his hold on me until we're standing in front of my locker and all three boys are crowding around me, making it impossible to escape. "What the hell was that?" Charlie asks. "Do you even know who that guy is?"

I shrug my shoulders. "Should I? He's just another spoiled rich kid who learned not to play with fire."

Spencer groans. "That's Marcus Dawson. His father is on the board for three of Charles' businesses. If you fucked him up, that would mean trouble for Colton."

"Please," I scoff. "Look at me. I'm 5'2. No proud father is about to go and tell the world that his 6-foot son just got his ass whooped by some trailer trash girl from Breakers Flats. Trust me, even with the footage, they'll deny it or call it some sort of distasteful prank."

"Yeah," Spencer scoffs. "To the media, they will, but to Colton, it's a fucking bomb sitting under his ass that he now has to diffuse. He's got enough shit to deal with, he doesn't need you creating more fucking drama all the time."

"Are you fucking kidding me?" I demand, stepping into him. "You better watch yourself. I won't hesitate to put you in the ground."

"Chill out, tiger. Just saying it how it is."

"No. You're being a dick because you're just like the rest of the fucking spoiled asshats around here. Besides, what I do has nothing to do with Colton. If that fucker's moneybags daddy has an issue, then he can bring it to me. I don't need Colton fighting my battles."

Spencer narrows his eyes. "What the hell has gotten into you over the last few days? You're being a fucking bitch."

"Oh, did I miss the part where we became friends?"

"Are you forgetting that little chat we had by the pool?"

"You mean when you came at me during the party and shoved Colton so far down my throat that I'll be shitting him for the next week? The chat where you thought about what was best for him and didn't give a damn about what I might want? Or, maybe it was the little 'chat' you forced on me to keep me outside and allow Jude the time to get to me?"

Spencer's eyes bug out of his head before he grabs me and slams me up against my locker while being careful not to press his body too close to mine, remembering what had happened on Saturday night. "I had nothing to do with that," he spits, holding me tight. "Jude acted alone and don't you fucking forget that. I won't let you bring me down for something that he did. So, despite what you may think, we're the fucking good guys."

Spencer lets out a breath and eases up on his hold but doesn't completely move away. "I don't know what the fuck is wrong with you, Ocean. I thought we were chill. I saw the way you were looking at Colton during that party and I damn well know how he feels about you so stop trying to deny shit. We're here trying to fucking help you."

He releases me and we remain in some sort of twisted stare off. "That's over," I tell him. "He doesn't feel shit for me. Not anymore."

Spencer doesn't dare look away until Charlie finally steps in and looks between us. "Okaaay," he says slowly. "I'm not even going to pretend that I know what the fuck is going on here, but did you just say that Jude was at the masquerade party on Saturday night?"

Fuck. I don't want to go there.

I turn my gaze on Charlie and watch as he retreats from my stare. "Yeah, what about it?"

His brows furrow, unsure why I'm coming at him with an attitude and honestly, I'm a little unsure myself. All I know is that I have a shitload of pent-up aggression and I'd like nothing more than to go back outside and work it all out on that dickhead's face. "Did you speak to him? He's fucking missing. You know that right? No one has seen him in days. Not since ..."

Charlie looks up at Spencer and I can practically read the messages passing between them. Charlie had promised me that they'd handle Jude after he had the whole school sexually harass me, but that was over two weeks ago. What they don't know is that after they were done with him, Nic also paid him a visit and that visit would have been near lethal.

What's clear is that Charlie has no idea what happened on Saturday night and for some reason, I prefer it that way. Charlie is so sweet and innocent. Perhaps innocent is the wrong word but compared to Jude, Colton, and Spencer, Charlie is practically a saint. He doesn't look at me with that same disgust the others do, he treats me like an equal, like someone worth waiting for.

Guilt flares through me. The idea of not being honest with him doesn't sit well in my stomach, but then a lot of the shit that has gone down over the past forty-eight hours doesn't sit well either. In comparison, not telling him this one little detail isn't exactly going to change anything. It'll probably save him from looking at me like the rest of the guys did. If he knew ... fuck. I don't even want to think about that. Charlie and Milo are the only two good things to happen to me in Bellevue Springs and I don't want to ruin that.

I look back at him and shake my head. "No, I didn't speak to him. I just saw him hanging around the main part of the house. I don't think he was actually at the party as a guest."

I feel Spencer and Milo's stares but I tune them out knowing exactly what they're thinking. "Damn," Charlie murmurs, looking off in the distance as he gets lost in thought. "I don't know what could have happened to him. It's not like we fucked him up that bad. I've had his fucking parents calling me and asking if I've seen him. It just doesn't make sense."

Spencer's eyes harden and I'm reminded of Colton's phone call once again.

'Spence, I need your help.'

He knows something and just like I'd suspected with Colton, they know exactly where he is. I just don't understand it. Are they hiding him out or did they help him get away? Why would they protect him like that? All I know is that means that Colton lied to me. He told me that he didn't know where he was and that he'd happily hand Jude over to Nic. Clearly, he didn't quite mean that.

Spencer's stare bores into mine, silently begging me to keep my mouth shut. He knows that I know something. He can see I have all the puzzle pieces, I just haven't been able to put them together. "He'll show up when he's ready," Spencer says to Charlie, all while keeping his gaze locked on mine.

Charlie looks between us again. "What the fuck is going on between you two? Did something happen?"

Spencer shakes his head as I snap. "Nothing happened. He's just a shady bastard." I tear my gaze away from Spencer and watch as he relaxes out of the corner of my eye. I look back at Charlie to find suspicion on his face. "Really," I insist. "We're all good. Spencer decided to take it upon himself to do Colton's bidding on Saturday night and it didn't exactly pan out well."

"Oh, is that it?" Charlie says with a relieved sigh that's also filled with a hint of jealousy. He turns to Spencer. "Thanks a lot, bro. You could have put in a good word for me instead."

"Fuck off, man. You've already sealed the deal with her and seeing as though she's not falling at your feet, I'd dare say that ship has sailed. Move over, you know Colton is going to be her end game."

Charlie rolls his eyes and I scoff at Spencer's remarks. I am so not Colton's end game. I'm not even his half-time game. Besides, any game Colton was playing ended the moment his father's life did.

"Okay, are you guys done harassing my girl?" Milo questions.

"Give up the act," Charlie says. "We know she's not your girl. If anything, she's mine."

I groan and step into Milo, pushing him back away from Charlie and dragging him with me, more than happy to leave the two douchebags of Bellevue Springs behind. "Come on, I'm done with this testosterone-filled bullshit."

"Really?" Milo calls over his shoulder as his hand slips around my waist. "She sure as shit looks like my girl."

My hand whacks out against Milo's stomach and he howls with laughter. "Stop stirring up shit. You're only going to make it worse."

"Please," he scoffs. "Fucking with them is—"

"OCEANIA MUNROE." My name is called from the opposite end of the hallway by a voice that has a shiver running down my spine. I turn around to face Dean Simmons and instantly groan. "My office. NOW."

Well, fuck. I guess news of me beating up one of his precious students has traveled quickly.

I glance up at Milo who scrunches his face, not liking where this is about to go. "You better not keep him waiting," he warns. "The longer he waits, the more time he has to think of your punishment."

"Shit. This is going to be bad."

"Yeah, but kinda worth it."

My hand pumps into a fist at my side and I look up at Milo, meeting his eyes as I grin wide. "Damn straight, it was."

CHAPTER 5

I stand at Dean Simmons' door, gripping the handle with unease. I wonder how much shit I would be in if I were to turn around now and walk away. Surely this is going to be an epic waste of my time. The last few visits with Dean Simmons have not gone well. Not once has he listened to anything I had to say—his conversations were always one-sided. I can only imagine what he's going to say about me now that I'm actually in the wrong.

He's probably been waiting for this moment since the second I walked through those massive iron gates. He's such a dick. I've never been able to wrap my head around how he got this job in the first place. He clearly doesn't belong here. Though, that much could be said about me too.

I let out a breath and push through the door, not bothering with a knock because why the hell would I? It's the little things, right?

Simmons' head snaps up and his eyes narrow as I make my way across his office and drop into the chair opposite of his massive desk. He's clearly overcompensating for something.

"You wanted to see me?" I question, raising a brow.

"Yes," he says, looking unimpressed with my attitude. He scoops up a stack of papers from his desk and shuffles them until they're straight. "We need to discuss your enrollment at this school."

My brows furrow. "What?"

His eyes snap back to mine and I swear, if murder was legal, I'd be dead on the spot. "I said we have—"

"I heard what you said," I tell him. "I'm trying to figure out where the hell it came from."

Dean Simmons groans and leans forward on his desk, propping his elbows against the wooden table. "Would it kill you to show even the tiniest shred of respect, Oceania?"

"Yeah," I nod. "I think it might. I haven't received a shred of respect from any of the faculty at this pretentious school—including yourself—so why should I offer that in return? Respect is earned not given."

"We'll have to agree to disagree on that one, Miss Munroe. Now, let's get down to business so we can both get on with our day."

Less time having to spend sitting across from this prick, now *that* I can agree on. "Right, so what fresh hell are you talking about? What's wrong with my enrollment?"

"Well, now that Mr. Carrington has regrettably passed. I think it appropriate that you transfer to our sister school, Bellevue Springs Private. You will be much happier there and less of a distraction to my students."

"Umm ... what?" I demand, realizing that this has absolutely nothing to do with me kicking that kid's ass this morning and more to do with this bastard's desperation to swing his dick around. "I'm not going anywhere."

"Unfortunately for you, the call has already been made and the papers signed. You will see the week out here and starting next Monday morning, you will be attending BSP full time."

I shake my head, hardly able to believe what I'm hearing. Is this even legal? Surely he can't change my enrollment status without consent and I can guarantee that a call certainly wasn't made to my mother about this. She would have told me, but then, she didn't tell me that I was enrolled here in the first place.

Something has to be done about this.

Anger pulses through me and I fly to my feet, slamming my hands down on his mahogany desk and enjoying the way he startles. "You can't do this," I demand, narrowing my gaze and enjoying the way he shrinks back. "Charles has already paid the fees. I have every right to be here. Besides, without Charles, mom and I would never be able to afford a private school."

Dean Simmons sets his jaw and his angered glare slices to me with disdain. "Sit down Miss Munroe. For the next week, I am still your Dean and you will show respect. As for your finances, they are hardly my business. If you cannot afford the fees, then perhaps you'll be more comfortable in a school suited better to your class."

Oh, he did not just say that. If I was wearing hoop earrings, they'd be out within seconds.

My blood boils and I find my hands curling into fists, stinging with the need to punch out and slam across his sculpted jaw. The idea of knocking him into next week is way too appealing. If I'm getting kicked out of here then I might as well go with style, right?

I take a step to walk around his desk and he leans back in his chair, for the first time realizing that maybe I'm not the bitch he should be fucking with today. After the weekend I've just suffered through, I'll be damned if I allow another rich, privileged man to walk all over me and make a mockery of who I am. I won't stand for it anymore.

"Take your seat," he says slowly. His intentionally low and disapproving tone still not enough to hide the tremor in his voice. I've only been here a month and these past few weeks have been more than enough for these boys to realize who I am.

Everyone in Bellevue Springs has heard of The Black Widows from Breakers Flats and just as I knew they would, the rumors have spread far and wide. They know I have the Black Widows protection, they know Dominic Garcia would move heaven and hell just to get to me, and they know their lives wouldn't be worth living if they were to fuck with me. But unfortunately, there are always a few who think they are the exception. Colton fucking Carrington included.

I take another step and he leans back further. "This is how it's going to go," I tell him, loving being back to my roots. "You're going to reinstate my—"

The phone rings and Dean Simmons launches for it as though it's some kind of lifeline. "Simmons," he says, not once taking his eyes off me.

I go to reach for the phone but a cockiness seeps into his eyes and the terror fades away. I pull back, desperate to know what's going on. From the way his glare shoots back to me, I'd dare say he's just found out about my morning activities.

"Right," he says into the phone, his tone suddenly a shitload chirpier. "I've got her in my office now, it will be dealt with. We do not tolerate violence in this school."

The phone slams down and I swallow my pride. He might not have had a good reason to kick me out before but he sure as hell does now. "Miss Munroe," he starts, tilting his head back toward my seat. "I'd highly suggest that you reel in your attitude before you make matters worse for yourself."

Well, fuck.

I let out a sigh and slink back toward my chair, the fight completely leaving me. I'm fucked.

"Now," Simmons starts. "I'm going to pretend that you weren't about to threaten me and we'll start this meeting over. This time I'm going to speak and you're going to listen. For the next five days, you are a student at Bellevue Springs Academy and it is my responsibility to punish students who step out of line. At 8:45 this morning, you violently attacked another student and behavior like that will not be tolerated in my school. This kind of behavior may have been accepted where you are from, but not here. I can not blame you entirely for your poor morals or lack of discipline, the principal and faculty at your old school have clearly set subpar standards for you and your peers. You have given me no other option Miss Munroe, you have to be punished."

My jaw clenches as I watch him looking more than thrilled to deliver his verdict. My nails press hard into my palms and I take a slow breath, trying to calm the rage pulsing through my body. How did my morning so quickly turn to shit?

"Because you have kindly and happily accepted your transfer, I will do you a favor and not expel you." His threat is as clear as the smile on his face. If I fight him on this, he's going to make me suffer. "However, the school board and the parents will not stand for this. The safety of my students is of the utmost importance and I must remove the threat. You leave me no other choice but to suspend you for the entirety of the week."

Shit.

"I suggest that you make your way to your locker and clear out your things as you will have no other reason to return to Bellevue Springs Academy."

Mom is going to kill me, and not just a stern talking to type of killing me, but the full-on dig a grave type of killing. This is not going to end well for me.

I let out a groan and don't bother saying a word. My back is against the wall and I have nowhere to run. No matter what I say or do, I'm only going to make it worse. I can't afford to go to the girls' school and I sure as hell won't be accepted into a public school after the shit that's listed in my records. BHA is my only option. I won't be able to graduate without it unless I was to go home and go back to Breakers Flats High, but that's not an option, not anymore.

It's already been decided, no surprise there. In this world, the poor girl from Breakers Flats is worthless. I can't fight my way through this no matter how much I want to. It took a Carrington to put this fucker on a leash. Without the name behind me ... I'm finished.

I get up out of my chair and don't miss the way Dean Simmons' eyes tighten, unsure what move I'm about to make, but I'm done. I'm done fighting for equality in this stupid school, I'm done fighting for respect, and I'm done trying to be seen as anything more than just a pussy with a nice set of tits.

I walk out of his office and slam the door behind me without a single word, feeling completely deflated. Despite this school being a complete joke, it was an opportunity that a girl from Breakers Flats would only come across once in a million years. This was my step up in the world, and I blew it. I had the chance of making something of myself and now I'm going to be another statistic. Just another girl who didn't finish school and ended up pregnant, married, and depressed.

As I walk out into the hall, I find it empty and realize that the homeroom bell must have already rung. Disappointment spreads through me. I would have loved to have seen Milo and told him what's going on but it'll be fine. I'm sure he'll have something to say about it and as soon as the last bell rings, he'll be barging his way into the pool house and demanding answers.

Not wanting to disturb him during homeroom, I make my way down to my locker and pull out the few things that I've stored here for the past few weeks. It's not much but I'm not about to leave it all behind.

I shove everything into my bag and haul it onto my back before walking out the gates and not looking back.

I bypass the student parking lot and just as they always do, my eyes fly to Colton's parking space, only today, there's no charcoal Veneno. I wasn't expecting him to show up after everything that happened over the past few days, but not seeing him kinda sucks and I hate that. After the way he pushed me away, I should be hating on him. I should be figuring out a way to make him hurt just like he did to me. I should be angry, but I'm not. I'm sad. I'm sad for all the things we missed out on, I'm sad for the joy I know I would have felt being in his arms, but mostly, I'm sad for the way I know I could have loved him.

I try to put it to the back of my head as I walk out through the student parking lot and onto the main road. I hate walking home, but today, walking is better than waiting around and risking the possibility of running into Dean Simmons.

I can't believe that fucker suspended me. I mean, it's not as though this is my first suspension. This will be my seventh … or maybe it's my eighth. I don't know, but for some reason, this one hits home a little too hard. It's never good news when you're being suspended—I know I completely deserved it—but knowing that this is Dean Simmons taking the easy way out doesn't sit well with me.

I don't know what I'm so upset about. It's not as though I actually like this school. My time here has been complete bullshit. I've been discriminated against because of my gender, my class, and my lack of wealth while also being sexually harassed every fucking day by students and staff. If anything, I should be seeking therapy, but all I want right now is to cry.

If Charles was still here, that wouldn't have happened. He would have been in Dean Simmons' office and put that fucker in his place. Heaven knows it wouldn't be because he had a sweet spot for me, but because it would have been another opportunity to assert his power. Either way, it would have resulted in me being left the hell alone.

I wonder if Colton will now have that kind of power? He already kinda does, but Charles' … wow. When he walked into a room, you knew it. The whole world knew it. He had an air about him that warned people not to fuck with him. Just one sharp glare and you could be on your knees. I don't know if it was a power thing or maybe a danger thing, I never really got the chance to figure it out. Colton sure as hell did though and something tells me that whichever it was, he's going to replicate it in a massive way.

I honestly don't know whether to be impressed, awed, or terrified.

I still can't believe that Charles is gone. It's a tragedy while at the same time, it's something I should have seen coming a mile away. Not the whole same dagger thing though, that completely threw me and left me with more questions than anyone should ever have to ask.

I don't even know where to begin. I guess the main one is who did it? Hell, I didn't even know dad and Charles knew each other, though I could be jumping the gun here. Maybe they didn't know each other. Maybe they both knew someone in common. Maybe they both fucked with the wrong person. Maybe Eli and Nic were right and it's a coincidence and there just happens to be two of the same daggers that were used to kill two of the men in my life.

Yeah … I wouldn't believe that shit either. Besides, I don't believe in coincidences, not ones like this.

What I do know is that there are far too many maybes and not enough solid answers. I don't even know where to start looking for answers, but even if I did, I don't know if I have what it takes to uncover them or even if I want to. The person who did this is responsible for murdering two of the most powerful men in my life.

It just doesn't make sense to me. Where's the connection? Why murder a poor man with nothing to his name and then murder one of the wealthiest men on the planet? No fucking sense.

I let out a heavy sigh and realize that I've somehow made it all the way back to the Carrington mansion and to be honest, I don't remember a damn step I took since stepping off school property twenty minutes ago.

My back hurts from the weight of my bag and every step I take down the long driveway has me desperate to get inside, though seeing the teal blue McLaren 720S parked by the front has me somehow forgetting all about it.

I've never seen that car here before. Don't get me wrong, I'm used to seeing all sorts of fancy cars pulled up out front who are usually guests of Charles' but he's no longer here to receive those guests.

This car is young, it's for someone who cares about their status and likes to show off. It's not for some old, rich businessman. No, this is different and it has curiosity burning through me. It's not my exact dream car like Colton's Veneno is, but damn, it certainly is nice.

I study every aspect of the car as I walk around it, picturing the way the engine would purr beneath me. My dad would be loving this. I can just imagine him rattling off every detail about it as we pass while he reminds me to keep a good few feet away, not wanting my clumsiness to accidentally scratch the expensive paint job.

God, I miss him.

I make my way up the sixty-six steps and put the McLaren to the back of my mind. It's not even 9:30 am and my day has already sucked. All I want to do is climb into bed and turn on Netflix. I'm sure I'll be able to find something that will take my mind off all this bullshit fuckery.

A week. What the hell am I going to do for a whole week?

I could go and visit my boys for a few days, but I'm sure mom wouldn't appreciate that. She tends to be a little stricter on me when I'm serving time on a school suspension. I can just imagine her snapping at me 'You're not on a holiday, Ocean. Get up and clean something.'

She's going to give me hell for this. Though, I guess I could spend my next few days working. Maryne could put a list of things together that could keep me busy though I don't exactly know where my employment status stands now that Colton is the big man in charge. I know before he was kinda my boss but not directly. Now … it's different. I'm not sure how I feel about him actually being my boss or if he's even going to allow me to keep working, and right now, it's not exactly something that I want to go and speak to him about.

I let out a sigh and push my way through the massive front door, instantly dropping my school bag on the marble floors, just the way I used to do when I was back in Breakers Flats and Mom and I had a home of our own.

Shit, maybe I'm getting a little too comfortable here. The other staff would get roasted for walking through the front door like this instead of using the service entrance.

A loud, disgusted grunt has me stopping in my tracks and my head snapping up to find two girls, hovering in the foyer, both staring at me like I'm some kind of piranha.

"Ummm …" I say, taking them in and very quickly realizing that these girls are identical twins and look like the female, much shorter and feminine versions of Colton.

Great. Cora and Casey are home and I've already made an ass of myself.

"Ummm?" The one on the left snaps. "Who the hell are you and what do you think you're doing waltzing into my home and dumping your shit at the door as though you own the place?"

"I, uhhh."

"Can I help you?" the other responds, scrunching her face in disgust. "Hello? Do you speak? Or are you not capable of stringing a sentence together?"

All I can do is stare, although it's probably making matters worse. Are these two bitches seriously Colton's little sisters? They're fucking cows. They're gorgeous though, absolutely stunning but their shitty attitudes make them so damn ugly. It's a shame, I bet they would have gone far in life, though with the money at their backs, I guess their attitudes don't really matter. People would put up with a whole lot of shit just to be close to that kind of cash.

These girls are the exact type of people I was expecting to come out of Bellevue Springs and up until now, I'd been judging my ability to nail down the stereotypes. I've gotten everyone wrong so far, but these two fit exactly where I had predicted. Shallow and mean. Don't get me wrong, a lot of the guys have lived up to that shitty expectation, but they're dudes and they'll never be able to tear a woman down the way that another woman can. These girls … well, these girls could destroy someone with a simple stare. They're exactly the kind of bullshit I was expecting to find here.

I somehow pull myself together before I start making matters worse, yet I have a feeling that there's literally nothing I can do that will make this mess any better. "I'm Ocean. I live in the pool house with my mom, Maria. She's the new live-in housekeeper."

If looks could kill …

"You're the help?" the one on the right screeches, taking a step back as though being anywhere near me could have her catching a disease. "Yuck. What do you think you're doing walking straight through the front door?"

"Yeah," the other cuts in. "You should be using the service entrance out back. Ugh, we're going to have to disinfect everything."

The fuck?

"I …"

"No," she continues, holding a hand up to cut me off. "I don't want to hear your lame excuses. This is a disgusting violation of the rules. We should have you fired for this."

Fired? My eyes bug out of my head and as I go to tell them exactly what I think of their fucked up rules, a throat clears to my left. "Is there an issue, ladies?" Harrison questions, looking as proper as ever.

"Uh, yes, there's a problem," the one on the right scolds. "You've been allowing the help to waltz in and out the front door. She should be using the service entrance like the rest of the staff do."

"No, Miss Carrington, under no circumstances have I been allowing that to happen," Harrison says, meeting my eye and silently begging me to keep my damn mouth shut before I make matters worse. "Miss Munroe, while being staff, is also a friend of Mr. Carrington's and has been welcomed by both your brother and your father to use the main facilities of the property."

They both scrunch their faces in disgust and it's almost comical how it's done in perfect unison. Their glares turn back on me and I swallow as the one on the left takes three steps forward and places herself right in front of me. "I see what's going on here," she says, her voice low and demeaning. "You're not good enough for him and I'll be damned if I allow my brother to be spending his time fucking around with trailer trash like you. He's the head of this family now and there are standards, high fucking standards, that you couldn't reach even if you were a hundred feet tall."

"You've got it wrong."

She scoffs. "Look at you, I don't have it wrong. If anyone around here has it wrong, it's your misconception that you actually mean something to him. Do yourself a favor and scatter away before I'm forced to step in because trust me, bitch, that's not something you want."

With that, she turns and stalks away, and like clockwork, her sister follows behind, leaving an awkward Harrison to slip back into the shadows of the foyer. I gawk at their backs, wondering who the hell these bitches really are. All I know is that they just threw down the biggest challenge and I don't think I have the will power to control myself this time.

Game fucking on, bitches.

CHAPTER 6

Maryne collapses down at the table beside Mom as I push my dinner around my plate. "He's a mess," she says with a heavy sigh, scooping up her fork and looking down into her food.

"Who is?" I question, instantly receiving a glare from my mother who very kindly suggested that I keep my mouth shut for the rest of the day after hearing about my suspension and the bullshit drama with the twins in the foyer. I can't wait to find out what she's going to stay when she realizes that my suspension is just an opener for my transfer to a new school.

"Colton," Maryne says, not noticing mom's silent scold. "He

hasn't been doing well these past two days. The booze wafting off his skin is just ..." she sighs, cutting herself off. "I don't know what to do anymore. I've tried talking to him but he's insistent on heading down this destructive path. His grief is just ... He's going to screw it all up before he even gets a chance to really start."

She trails off and suddenly my appetite no longer exists. I was kinda hoping that he'd be doing better today.

Mom meets my eyes across the table and the silent scolding is gone, replaced with pain. She understands the grief he's suffering through just as I do and it's not easy, even if your father wasn't exactly the idol you'd always wanted.

Mom nods and just like that, I'm out of my chair and crossing through the staff quarters.

I get to the internal door and I can't help but think of the twins. I've remained on my side of the mansion all day, not wanting to start up more bullshit with the sisters from hell, but unfortunately for them, it's time to break some rules.

I push through the door that leads into the main part of the house. It's well past nine at night and with the funeral being held tomorrow and the celebration of Charles' life after, the mansion is a flurry of activity, yet not a single family member can be found.

Harrison is walking around overseeing everything and I don't miss the way his eyes narrow on me as he watches me cut through the main part of the house, a part he and I know damn well that I'm not supposed to be in, but screw him. Someone needs to check on Colton and something tells me that I'm probably the best option even though it means dealing with his bullshit.

I haven't seen him since finding him in the private bar last night and to be honest, I'm not entirely sure that I'm up for a repeat performance of that. Just thinking about it has me cringing with heartbreak. I should never have allowed Colton to get so deep but when I think about it, I don't actually think I allowed it to happen, it just sort of did and that's on me.

I gave him the power to hurt me and last night, that's exactly what he did. I'm a fool because right now, I'm about to let it happen all over again. I must be a glutton for punishment. I should turn around and run back to the pool house as quickly as I can. I should lock the door and chain myself to my bed and not emerge until this bullshit is over or at least until I find the balls that I've lost somewhere along the way. Instead, here I am, standing at the bottom of the massive staircase and launching myself up it, desperate to get to him.

I skip up the stairs, taking two at a time while knowing that his sisters' bedrooms are also on this floor and wanting to avoid them at all costs. I may be a glutton for punishment but I'm not fucking stupid. Okay, sometimes I can be accused of making stupid decisions, but not today, not right now. Actually, I'm sure others would argue that this is one of the stupidest things I've ever done but to me, it feels right.

What kind of person would I be if I didn't try to help him? Who cares if I get hurt in the process? Who cares if he goes running his mouth like he usually does? All that matters is that he's safe and not completely fucked up. After all, there's a funeral tomorrow. It's going to be the first public matter that Colton will have to face as the head of this massive empire and he's going to have to appear as though he has his shit together.

I reach Colton's door and find myself pausing with my hand resting heavily on the doorknob. Am I making a mistake? Maybe I'm about to walk into a trap.

I can't back out. I have to see this through. I want to be able to look back on my life one day and know that I made the right decisions, not just for myself but for the people around me even though it might have been hard. That's the kind of life I want to live. I want to be strong. I want to be someone reliable, and someone that my father would be proud of.

I can do this.

I let out a shaky breath and slowly open the door.

The smell hits me first. It's like a fucking dirty bar from back home in here. Hell, it's worse than that. It's like dealing with the bullshit that comes after one of the many Black Widow parties.

I look around the empty room and find more than just alcohol scattered over his tables. There are empty bottles of scotch thrown carelessly over the couch, spilled drinks on his bed, plates of food fallen off his desk while a little white bag of powder has been broken open, spreading all the contents far and wide. From the looks of things, I'd say there's probably more white powder in the carpet than in his actual bloodstream.

I hear the shower running in his private bathroom and I pray to whoever exists above that Colton hasn't collapsed in there. With the cocktail of alcohol pulsing through his veins, it'd be a miracle if he makes it through the night without getting alcohol poisoning

Colton needs a fucking smack across the head and cleanup crew in here. And unfortunately for me, that job is resting heavily on my shoulders.

I let out a broken sigh and start cleaning up his shit while keeping an ear out for the shower, making sure he doesn't pass out or worse. I hurry around his room, opening the window and hoping that helps to clear out some of the smell, though that probably won't happen until the couch can have a deep clean and the carpets are shampooed.

I strip the alcohol-drenched sheets off his bed and quickly remake it, not doing nearly as good of a job that Maryne or Mom could do but at least he'll have a clean bed to sleep in tonight.

After clearing out everything that doesn't belong and leaving it out in the hallway for the maids to take care of, I find my way into his massive walk-in closet. I can't say that I've been in here before. It's fucking massive. I don't even know where to start.

I switch on the light and watch as the room powers up. There's a rotating wall of suits and I gawk at it. Why am I surprised by this shit? There's a whole section for shoes, ties, watches and then on the opposite side are his normal everyday clothes. It's insane in here. This whole closet is literally bigger than one of the classrooms back at Breakers Flats High. If Milo's closet is anything like this, it's no surprise why he's been hiding out in it for so long.

Hearing the shower still in full swing, I get busy going over the options. I find a nice three-piece suit, match it with a tie, shoes, socks, and a watch before finding the cufflinks and staring. There are fucking diamonds on some of these. It baffles me what kind of money is inside this home.

I find the little cufflinks that I'd seen Colton wearing during the black and white party, the ones that read CC, and I don't doubt his father would have owned an identical pair.

I set out his suit on his clean desk before diving back in and finding him a pair of boxers to wear to bed. I look over the pajama section before quickly realizing that he probably isn't a big pajama wearer. I grab a pair of sweatpants just to be on the safe side and as I walk back out, I find a small plastic trashcan just inside of the closet door and I scoop it up. After all, it's better to be safe than sorry.

The boxers and sweatpants get tossed down onto his made bed while the trashcan goes down beside it, knowing he's bound to need that during the night.

I'm in the middle of placing some painkillers on his bedside table when the shower cuts off and the bathroom door opens with a rush of steam blowing out into his room.

Colton comes striding through with a white towel wrapped dangerously low around his hips, making me wish for a slight breeze to come through the open window and send it sailing down to the carpet.

Nerves rush through me as I watch him walk out of the bathroom. His eyes instantly find mine and I immediately stop what I'm doing, feeling like a kid who's just been caught with her fingers in the cookie jar.

He glances around his room and it takes all of three seconds for him to notice what I've done and even less time to dismiss it all. "What are you doing in here?"

'What are you doing in here?' That's it? The very first words he's spoken to me in nearly two days. Geez, I could be wrong here but I thought I'd deserve a little more than that. A 'sorry for being such an ass' would have gone down well seeing as though the last time we actually had a conversation was when he was telling me how he needs me more than I could possibly know, how he's madly jealous of me being with Charlie, and how the thought of me pushing him away crushes his soul.

Yet here we are not even two whole days later.

I swallow my pride and raise my chin, not letting him see how his dismissal kills me. "Someone had to come and check on you."

"Check on me?" he scoffs, noticing the clothes laid out for him on his bed. "I don't need your fucking charity, Jade."

Jade. There's that name again, the one that holds a power that I wasn't even aware of until yesterday morning, though right now, that power seems more like a curse.

Colton starts crossing the room and I take a few steps back, desperately needing to keep my distance. "It's not charity," I tell him, watching as he drops his towel and grabs his sweatpants. I try not to stare, but damn, I'm only human.

His body is perfection, carved out of the strongest stone, though unfortunately for womankind, that stone went right through to his heart and soul and I'm not sure there's a way to save him. I watch as he pulls on his sweatpants and stumbles on his feet. "Get out of here," he says, turning his back and walking across the room to where he pulls another bottle of scotch.

"No," I say, knowing it's bound to bite me on the ass. "You need to sober up and get to bed. Your father's funeral is in the morning and you can't walk in there like this."

He turns and his glare is sharp enough to kill. "What the fuck is it to you?"

"What's that supposed to mean?"

He comes striding toward me and I find myself backing up a step until I realize what the fuck I'm doing and hold my ground. "What is it to you?" he repeats getting in my face, the anger rolling off him nearly enough to cripple me. "Why do you even care? Fuck off out of here."

I slam my hands into his chest, forcing him back a step and out of my face, hating myself for what I'm about to say. "I'm not going anywhere. Get your shit together, Colton. Look at you. You're embarrassing yourself falling apart like this. It's fucking pathetic. You're weak. This past month, you've gone out of your way to show me that you're the fucking man. You wanted me to see that you're strong, untouchable, and fucking incredible, but right now, you're none of that. You're nothing. Yeah, you lost your father, and yeah, it fucking sucks. Believe me, I know exactly how it feels but it doesn't give you the right to fall apart and throw it all away. Your sisters are counting on you to hold it together, your father is counting on you."

"You don't know what the fuck you're talking about."

Colton lifts the scotch to his lips while his eyes dance with the challenge, daring me to stop him. My blood boils and I clench my jaw, watching as he tries to destroy himself only I won't stand for it.

I fly forward and grab the bottle out of his unsuspecting hands then race straight toward the bathroom. "Hey," he demands, bounding after me. "What do you think you're doing?"

I get to the bathroom sink and manage to pour out half the bottle before he's on me and trying to peel the bottle out of my hands. "Leave it," I demand. "You need to sober up and go to bed. I'm all for you making a fool of yourself here in private, but I won't sit back and watch you destroy everything your father built publicly. Every one of his business partners will be at this damn funeral, every board member, every investor, every fucking person who means anything around here will be showing up and keeping their eyes on the Carrington heir who could potentially fuck everything up. Don't act like you don't know exactly what they're going to do if they don't think you have what it takes to walk in your father's shoes."

His grip on the bottle tightens and he tries to pull it into his chest but I hold on, refusing to release his stare. "Don't think for one fucking second that I won't search every inch of this fucking mansion and get rid of every last bottle of alcohol that I can find."

His stare tightens until he finally releases the bottle. "Whatever," he snaps, spinning around and walking back out of the bathroom. "Keep the fucking scotch if it means that much to you. I don't care anyway."

Well, that's the biggest load of bullshit I've ever heard.

I finish pouring the alcohol down the sink and when I turn around, I find him sitting on the edge of the bed, watching me as though he's confused about something. I place the empty glass bottle down on the vanity and find myself walking out of the bathroom and crossing his room.

I step up to him, putting myself between his open knees. "It's okay to hurt," I whisper, placing my hands upon his strong bare shoulders. "It's okay to be confused and it's okay to want to hate him."

As if on instinct, Colton's hands find my waist and he pulls me in a step. "I don't like you seeing me like this," he murmurs and although he's addressing me, it's almost like he's talking to himself. "You're right, I feel fucking weak. I'm pathetic. I should be stronger. It's you, you're making me weak."

He pushes me away and flies to his feet in front of me. "You make me weak," he repeats. "You're like a fucking leech sucking all the strength out of me. You're going to ruin me."

I swallow back, refusing to show how his words hurt while also struggling to understand why they do. They shouldn't. For a month, I've let his words sail off me like water off a duck's back but lately, they've been sticking like glue.

"You know that's not true," I say, holding back the tears and struggling to get the words past the lump in my throat. "What happened to everything you said to me yesterday morning? Does that just not matter anymore? What about the party?"

Colton steps into me, his stare boring down on my soul. I watch as his red-rimmed eyes blaze with fire before a smirk lifts the corner of his lips. "Fucking weak."

His bedroom door flies open and one of his twin sisters comes barging through with a dress in her hand. Our heads both whip toward her and as she takes me in, fury tears through her eyes. "YOU," she yells, pointing a finger and storming through the room. "You little bitch. You're a thief."

Say what?

I fall back a step, but she doesn't stop until she's standing in my exact spot, her brother right beside her. "You stole my fucking dress."

"What?" I grunt as Colton stares between us. "I didn't steal anything."

"My fucking dress," she demands, holding the black gown up that I'd worn to the black and white party, the very one that has been dry-cleaned, bagged, and hung on the left side of her closet to show that it's been handled with care. "I saw the fucking pictures. You had no right to enter my personal space and take whatever the hell you wanted. That's a disgusting violation of my personal property. Now I have to throw it out. Who knows what kind of diseases you people carry."

"You people?" I demand, my eyes widening.

"Classless scabs," she says, pronouncing every syllable. "Trash who comes in here looking for any way to get ahead in life, but guess what? You're done. You and your mother. You're both out of here. You won't get away with this."

"Excuse me?" I demand, stepping into her and watching as her eyes bug out of her head, proving that she's all words and no action. Hell, she's probably the type to cry over a broken nail. "Your precious dress is in your fucking hand. You can hardly claim that I stole it, and besides, your father was the one who told me I could borrow it. You don't have a fucking leg to stand on."

She throws the gown down on the ground and straightens her shoulder. "You don't want to start with me. I can guarantee that you'll lose."

"Cora," Colton snaps. "That's enough."

I grin, ignoring Colton's warning, the same way he's done to me a million times before. Besides, technically it was her he was warning, he didn't tell me to stop. "You think you have what it takes to win against me?" I laugh. "I get it, you have money bags at your beck and call, but apart from that, you've got nothing, honey. You're just a bitch in Prada. All fucking talk."

Cora's eyes narrow at me and just when I think she's about to explode, she turns on her brother. "Do something," she squeals. "How can you just stand there and let her talk to me like that? I want her fired and out of the pool house by midnight."

"No."

"No?" she rears back, unable to believe what she's hearing.

"You heard me. Get the fuck out."

My eyes bug out of my head. Did Colton just tell his little princess sister to get the fuck out? No way. If I knew shit was going to go down tonight, I would have brought a box of popcorn to help me enjoy the night.

"Excuse me?" Cora demands. "Dad would be rolling over in his grave if he heard you speak to me like that."

"Well then it's a good thing dad isn't in his fucking grave yet," he tells her. "Now get the fuck out. Ocean and her mom aren't going anywhere. Dad hired them for a reason and you'll fucking respect that."

"Like he ever respected me," she spits.

"Maybe if you weren't such a fucking bitch, he might have tolerated you just a little."

My jaw drops as my eyes bounce between them like a tennis match. "Oh, shit. Shots fired," I laugh, though naturally, I'm ignored.

Cora sucks in a sharp breath and her eyes go wide before her hand slaps out hard, heading straight for Colton's face. His reflexes are like lightning and he catches her wrists with the speed of a God, clenching it hard.

There's silence between the two, a mental fight for dominance, and the longer it goes on the clearer Colton's victory becomes. Cora begins to cower under his stare and although he looks terrifying, he'll never physically hurt her.

"Out. Now." His voice is low and it sends shivers sailing down my spine. He sounds just like his father. It's a tone he's never quite used on me and to be honest, I think I'd probably shit my pants if he did.

Cora swallows but they remain staring until he finally releases her wrist. As she scrambles toward the door, she grabs the forgotten dress and turns to meet Colton's hard stare.

"I'm telling mom you're fucking the help!" She lets out an obnoxious squeal as she turns to leave again, disappearing with a sharp slam of the door.

We're left in awkward silence and I look up at him, desperately wanting to diffuse the situation and somehow get the big fucker in bed to sleep off his bad mood. "You didn't need to stand up for me like that. I can handle bitches like Cora and Casey."

He slowly turns his stare back to mine and I feel that same terror that Cora had felt, but unlike her, I'm not so much of a bitch. I was born with a backbone and I'm damn sure that he will never hurt me … physically. Emotionally, that's a different story.

Whatever he's about to say, it's going to be lethal and I know deep in my heart that it's going to destroy me.

I hold my ground as he steps into me, desperately needing to prove myself. He takes two more steps until my back is pressed against the wall and I find myself staring up into his eyes with the need to reach out and hold him pulsing heavily through my veins.

"Get this straight, Oceania," he says, using my full name, knowing it's reserved only for my father. "I didn't stand up for you. I can hardly stand you. My father wanted your mother working here and out of respect for him, that's why I've allowed you to stay. You mean nothing to me. You were a fucking game that's come to an end, a fucking joke, and now I'm done with you."

I shake my head, refusing to believe it. I know what I felt and it was real, so freaking real that it hurt. "You don't mean that."

Colton's lips pull up into a twisted grin, and just like that, he stabs the dagger deep into my back. "Don't I?"

I'm left staring as his low chuckle bounces off the walls and my heart silently shatters inside my chest. They're just words. He doesn't really mean that. I know he doesn't. It was only one night together, but I know it had to mean something. I felt it.

Colton walks away from me and I watch as he pulls open a drawer and reaches in. The lump in my throat tightens and I struggle to breathe around it as another bottle of scotch is pulled out. The lid is opened and as he lifts the bottle to his lips, I feel the tears welling in my eyes.

Do not cry. Do not fucking cry in front of him, Oceania Munroe.

"Get the fuck out, Jade," he says with finality, dismissing me as he swallows another mouthful of scotch. "I'm done with you. So fucking done."

Struggling to catch a breath, I silently walk to the door and push my way out into the hallway, leaving him behind as I slam the door between us. The second the heavy thud of the door vibrates through my ears, I crash against it, feeling the emotions completely overwhelm me.

I slide down to the ground, slamming a hand over my mouth to mask the sound of my sobs as the tears fall free from my eyes, leaving me a complete, broken mess on the marble floor.

CHAPTER 7

Milo's arm loops through mine as he leads me inside the church. I don't know what I was thinking coming here today. Maybe I just needed to see Colton, maybe I had an overwhelming need to say goodbye to the man who used to hit his children and wife, or maybe I just wanted to be supportive of the people around me. I don't know. Anyway I look at it, it's fucked up.

If I had my head screwed on properly, I'd be back at the pool house, keeping myself locked away and out of trouble. I know I can't tell the difference between Cora and Casey but if one of them were to even look at me wrong today, I feel as though I might just break. After the whole suspension thing yesterday, a public scene like that might just throw my mom off the deep end.

As we walk through the church, I can't help but look around. This place is huge. Like not just the Carrington mansion kind of huge, but shopping mall kind of huge. No wonder Harrison was so adamant that this would be the church the service was held in. It's all kinds of fancy with its high ceiling arches, candles, gold trims, and stained windows. It's the kind of place a girl like me would literally have to die to get into. Even then, I'm not sure I'd be worthy.

This place screams elitist and makes me wonder how many times the little donation plate went around and how often the billionaires of Bellevue Springs have had to dip into their pockets. There's no way a church like this would be able to survive on just prayers alone. There's a big financial backer here somewhere and for some reason, the name Carrington is flashing in my head.

There's a woman at the front softly playing the harp and the music fills the church as the guests start pouring in. Milo leads me to a seat toward the back and near the rest of Charles' staff who have been granted the time off to attend the funeral, though not all of them are here. There are still hundreds of people back at the mansion getting ready for the party this afternoon which is being held in Charles' honor. To be honest, I doubt Colton even knows about the party, he's been so distant these past few days.

Yesterday was the worst. It's as though Colton has reverted to the old Colton, the one who existed when I first arrived. He was mean, blunt, and dangerous. He was someone who I didn't want to fuck with, but did because watching him get so worked up was one of the sexiest things I've ever seen. The old Colton liked to torment me, watch me break, and knew that he had the power to do it.

I sat at his bedroom door crying for two hours, unable to pull myself away. I was lucky that the only person to walk by and see my shame was Harrison who actually had the heart to give me a sympathetic smile. He must have been hit badly with Colton's bullshit to have had a reaction like that. Either way, I was grateful.

It took me those two whole hours to work out that maybe he was hurting me just to feel something normal again. The past few days might have been a complete clusterfuck for me, but it's also been that way for him and while his father was lying dead in his home office, he was upstairs in his bedroom, just moments from finally giving in to his desires. The guilt must be eating him alive and his way to deal with that, is to push me away but in doing that, he's not just punishing himself, he's punishing me.

We settle into the back pew and I gaze around the room, watching the people filtering past us. I catch Mom's eye a few rows ahead of us sitting with Maryne, and a smile passes between us.

Just as expected, everybody who is somebody comes striding through the door, not that I know any of them. Milo has a running commentary explaining the who's who of Bellevue Springs. Women in black dresses, over the top hats, and big glasses march their way right to the front while men in ridiculously expensive suits accompany them and look as though they'd rather be anywhere else.

People watch me as they walk by and I don't doubt that had Milo's arm not been around my shoulder, a few of them would be in my face, demanding to know what kind of right I had to be there, and sitting beside a Rinaldi at that.

"Heads up," Milo mutters in my ear. "The bitch twins are coming."

I look toward the door to watch as Cora and Casey come walking into the church, not daring to speak to a single person. Their black glasses sit perfectly over their eyes and if I'd have to take a guess, I'd say it's more of a fashion statement than to cover their tears.

They snub everyone who tries to say hello and I watch as they walk down the aisle, right to the front pew. "God, I hate them," I murmur, doing my best to keep my voice low as I was perhaps a little too vocal about my distaste for the twins on the car ride here. Though luckily for me, it was only me and Milo.

"You and me both, girl," Milo says. "I haven't seen them for a few years but they were bitches then, and clearly bitches now."

The girls have hardly sat down before Colton appears at the entrance of the church. The room falls silent and it's as though he's walking toward his throne, but I guess he kind of is. This is the official goodbye of Charles Carrington and the new reign of the Carrington heir.

Just as I knew they would be, all eyes are on him.

Colton stands tall, wearing the exact suit I had picked out for him last night, right down to the dress shirt and cufflinks. I can't help but feel that this is some sort of message to me, maybe an apology of some sort but then there's also a good chance that he has no recollection of the bullshit from last night. He could have rolled out of bed at the last minute as assumed one of the maids had laid it out for him. I shouldn't think about it as it's only going to mess with my head.

As he walks through the church, he stops and shakes hands with older men who look as though they wipe their asses with hundred dollar bills. He says a polite hello and thanks them for coming before moving on to the next person who's waiting to feel him out and see if he'll crack under the pressure.

I can't help but feel that maybe something I said to him last night resonated within him as this man I'm seeing before me is not the mess I found last night. This isn't the teenage boy who just had the world dropped on his shoulders, this is a man. A real fucking man. The kind of man who dominates during the day and has you screaming for more at night.

This is the kind of man who has me wanting a future that isn't mine to want.

Colton rids himself of the men who are busy feeling him out and subtly shakes off the young, gold-digging women who offer him their condolences by draping themselves over him and giving him a good feel of what they have on offer, you know, as they're saying 'I'm sorry for your loss.'

He breaks free and starts making his way down the aisle but not before his eyes come to mine.

They're dark and intense, certainly not the protective hazel ones that I've come to know. A silent message passes between us and I see his pain. He wants me there by his side but there's no way in hell he's about to come out and ask for it and with this crowd, I'd be a fool to go for it. There's regret in his eyes and I wonder if it's from the hell he put me through last night but this is his father's funeral and it'd be selfish of me to assume his pain is for me.

I need to pull my shit together.

I tear my gaze away and Colton continues to the front of the aisle. He walks right up to the open casket and peers in. Every person in the church watches him. Even his sisters tear their attention away from their phones for a brief second to look up at their older brother.

The priest approaches Colton and they shake hands as I focus on keeping my ass firmly in my seat. *Do not go up there, Ocean. You're only going to make a fool of yourself.*

I watch as they discuss whatever the hell needs discussing while unable to tear my eyes away from him. "Jesus," Milo grumbles beside me. "Don't make it so obvious that you're into him."

I turn my glare on Milo. "First of all, I don't think you're supposed to use that word in a church unless you're singing about how much you love him."

"Honey, the fact that I haven't spontaneously combusted and burned to a crisp yet is already a miracle, don't push your luck, but go on."

I roll my eyes, ignoring his comments. "Secondly, I'm not into Colton. He's an ass. After the bullshit he's been putting me through, it'd be a damn miracle if he ever got close to me again. I'm just curious. I've never been to a big funeral like this."

"For the record, if I can't say 'Jesus' in a church then you can't say 'damn,'" he tells me before dropping his arm from over my shoulder and slouching into the pew as though he's already bored. "Has anyone ever told you that you're a shitty liar? I could see your little lovesick puppy dog eyes from a mile away. You're more than just into him."

I nudge my elbow into his ribs. "You don't know what you're talking about."

"Well, well, here's trouble," a voice says, hovering in the aisle beside the pew.

I look up to find Charlie and Spencer standing beside us. Charlie has a cheesy as fuck grin on his face—which is so not appropriate for a funeral— as he leans against the backrest of the pew while Spencer is staring off into the guests on the other side of the church. His face scrunches in distaste and I follow his line of sight to find his cousin, Jacqueline Vanderbilt, sobbing into a tissue and making a scene.

"What a fucking joke," Spencer scoffs. "I'm going to be hearing about this shit for years. Anyone would think they were star-crossed lovers by the way she's carrying on."

"Maybe they were," I tell him. "I'm pretty sure they were supposed to get hitched and honeymoon in the Maldives for the next few weeks. Poor girl, she's probably mourning her natural suntan. Though, that's considering his 'business trip' was actually for her. Who knows if he was fucking around with other girls."

Spencer scoffs in agreement before looking back at us. "I'll catch you guys later," he says with a grumble.

Charlie and Milo nod while I give him a tight smile and then watch him walk away. I look back up at Charlie to find him also looking out at the guests, only unlike Spencer, he clearly can't find who he's looking for. "What's up?" I ask as his brows begin to pinch.

"Have you guys seen Jude? I don't think the fucker is here."

"Nah, man," Milo says as I go quiet. "Haven't seen him in weeks."

Charlie shakes his head, disappointment wafting off him in waves. "So fucking low," he grumbles. "You'd think he'd show up today of all days. Colton has gone out of his way to keep the guy out of trouble and the fucker can't even show up when his friend needs him the most."

I feel Milo's eyes on my face and I struggle to hold it together. "He'll show up," I promise him, knowing damn well that my boys won't stop searching for him until they have him buried ten feet below. Though, when that happens, I can guarantee that Charlie won't know about it.

"Yeah," Charlie mutters darkly. "Well when that happens, I have a few things to say to him."

"Don't we all," Milo says, his voice taking on a tone that I've never heard from him before. He's usually so happy and chirpy, but not anymore. His joyful little heart has been awakened to the dark side and I don't think he'll ever be able to get back to the innocent view of the world he once had.

Charlie looks down at Milo with a question in his eyes. They hold each other's stare for a short moment before Charlie finally looks away. "Alright, well, my parents expect me to sit with them and play happy family so I'll catch you guys after the service."

"Yeah, alright," I say, giving him a sweet smile.

His eyes linger on my face and there's a weird hesitation. I can't help but feel like he wants to talk, and considering our past, that's not exactly something I feel we should be doing. His gaze drops to Milo's hand that's happily resting in mine and his expression falters for a brief second before he finally starts walking away.

"Oh, girl," Milo chuckles. "You've got problems."

"Don't I know it."

"That boy is going to fall at your feet and when he does, you're not going to be ready for it."

"I know," I say with a groan. "I'm going to have to break his little heart and it's going to kill me. He's too sweet for that."

"Why would you have to break his heart? Charlie is the best kind of guy you could hope for around here. He's sweet, he can fuck like a god, and he looks at you like you walk on water. Why bother waiting around for Colton when it's probably never going to happen?"

An unimpressed grunt comes flying out of me. "Please, I'm not waiting around for Colton. Only a fool would be that stupid. Besides, he's not exactly a knight in shining armor. He's a dick who's intent on making my life hell."

"Exactly. Date Charlie instead. He'll make you happy and have you screaming in the meantime."

I scrunch up my face. The guy is good for a little fun and Milo has never been so right about the fact that he can fuck. He fucks like it's the last thing he'll ever do, it was incredible but … I don't know. Something is missing. A spark? Butterflies? He doesn't make my heart race the way Colton does and he sure as hell doesn't mess me up.

Nic used to mess me up but the more time I spend with Colton, the more I'm beginning to forget that feeling.

The priest bows his head and steps away from Colton and just like that, the congregation quietens down. Colton looks down at his father one more time before turning and facing the crowd. His eyes settle on mine, just as they always do and within the blink of an eye, both Cora and Casey are staring at me like I'm a problem they intend to deal with.

Colton tears his gaze away and walks down to sit with his sisters who haven't stopped staring my way. "Oh, shit," Milo mutters as the priest steps up to the podium. "Those girls are going to make your life a living hell."

"Good luck to them," I scoff. "It already is. There's not much worse they could do to me that their brother hasn't already tried."

Milo rolls his eyes. "For the most part, Colton's kinda been the good guy."

"Yeah … kinda."

The priest clears his throat. "Friends, I humbly invite you to take your seats so that we may get today's service underway."

People start shuffling around and after a few moments, bodies begin dropping into the pews. The room becomes silent and just as I turn back to face the front, a body slides in beside me.

I glance up to give the newcomer a welcome smile but the smile never comes as my jaw falls to the floor. "What the hell are you doing here?" I whisper-yell to Nic as my eyes drop to the suit that dons his strong body.

I don't think I've ever seen Nic in a suit, but I can't even wrap my head around it because I'm still in shock to find the grinning asshole sitting beside me. "What?" he chuckles under his breath. "You think I was about to let you sit through another funeral so close after your father's death without me? Hell no, babe."

His hand slips into mine and he gives it a tight squeeze and for once, I welcome it like I welcome my next breath. I didn't realize how damn much I was needing this but here he is, and I've never been so grateful. "Have I ever told you how amazing you are?" I question. He grins wide and I find my gaze dropping to his suit once again. "Do I even want to know where you got a Valentino suit?"

His grin widens and as he goes to respond, the priest's voice rings clear over the church. "Good morning and welcome to the celebration of Charles Edward Carrington, who was regretfully taken from this world late on Satur–"

BANG!

All eyes shoot to the entrance of the church as the doors violently barge open. Colton and his sister are on their feet while Nic's hand instantly goes to the gun at his back. I dive to restrain him, knowing he's a shoot first and think later kind of guy and I'll be damned if Nic shot up some bastard at this funeral by accident. We'll never live it down.

A woman appears in the doorway and strides through as though she's a model on the Victoria Secret runway. Gasps start sounding throughout the church and before I know it, Milo is leaning into me and murmuring into my ear. "Holy fuck balls. That's Laurelle Carrington."

"Who?" I whisper, watching the woman as she waltzes through the church, covered head to toe in black diamonds that cover her floor-length gown. Her heels are ten inches tall while her glasses rival those of the twins.

"It's Colton's mom. Charles' ex-wife."

My eyes bug out of my head as I take her in. "No shit," I breathe, shooting my eyes to the front of the church to take in Colton who's gawking at his mother like he's seeing a ghost.

She continues down the aisle and the way that she strides makes it look as though she is about to walk into a party. She makes her way right up to the golden casket with every eye in the room, silently watching her. She leans on the edge of the casket and looks down at her ex-husband. "About time someone killed you, you rotten bastard," she says, her voice traveling far and wide through the silent church.

Colton clears his throat and his mother reluctantly steps away from the casket to join her children. Together they sit and just like that, the priest gets started on his service while the rest of the congregation continues to stare in shock.

Five minutes turns to ten and soon enough, half an hour has passed and I finally start breathing easy. Nothing during this service has been anything like my father's funeral and for that, I'm grateful. Feeling me finally starting to relax, Nic squeezes my hand and leans into my side. "The boys are chilling outside," he says. "They wanted to be here for you too."

A warm smile pulls at my lips and I drop my cheek to Nic's large shoulder. "They didn't have to do that."

"I couldn't keep them away."

"You never told me where you got the suit," I murmur, keeping my voice low.

Silent laughter bubbles through Nic and has my head gently

rocking on his shoulder. "I rented it."

Yeah, right. That's as good as saying that he actually put a little thought into being here today. We both know that he was probably just in the area and when he thought about checking in with me, he remembered where I was. Besides, if this was a planned trip, all four boys would be sitting in this pew and I'd bet the few saved up dollars hidden in my underwear drawer that not one of them have a suit with them. "So, by renting it, what you mean is that you intimidated some poor kid out in the parking lot until he gave up the goods."

"Don't know what you're talking about," he murmurs. "Now hush before you get us kicked out of this circus."

Another smile pulls as my lips and I pull my hand free before curling it around his strong arm and holding him to me. I get comfortable against him and he allows me to hold him until the service is finally coming to an end.

The priest wraps up his service and then looks out at the congregation. "I'd like to invite the family to come and say a final goodbye and once they are done, the floor will be open to the rest of the guests." He looks to Colton and his mom and sisters before waving his hand toward the casket. "When you're ready."

The twins are the first to stand, eager to get this over and done with. They adjust their big glasses and make their way to their father with Colton trailing behind. The three of them stand by the casket for a moment until they're joined by their mother.

As a family, they look down at Charles and say their private goodbyes. The twins are the first to walk away as expected and just as they take their seats, Colton turns and lets out a heavy breath. As he walks back to his seat, his gaze lifts to mine.

Nic stiffens beside me, not liking what he's seeing just as Colton does the same, taking me in as I'm pressed into Nic's side and taking comfort in his closeness. Trying to not make himself too obvious, he tears his gaze away and as he does, Laurelle speaks out, loud and so fucking proud, sounding like a survivor who is finally at peace.

"I hope you burn in hell, Charles."

With that, her hand flies toward the casket and in the blink of an eye, the whole thing goes up in flames as she sends Charles to spend an eternity rotting in hell.

CHAPTER 8

The ballroom of the Carrington mansion quickly begins to fill with guests as I stand around with Milo and my boys, still reeling from the shock of what just happened at the church.

She set the fucking casket on fire, and when I say that thing went off like a college girl at her first frat party … damn. I've never seen flames take so fast. It was zero to a hundred in three seconds.

Who the fuck does that? Laurelle Carrington must be suffering from some pretty nasty mental scars to have gone through with that. I mean, I completely understand thinking about it the whole way through the service, but actually getting up there and doing it? I don't know whether I should be terrified of her and her twin spawns or if I should be bowing at her feet.

The woman is clearly a little fucked up.

One second we were ready to wrap up the service and the next it's absolute chaos. The moment the guests saw the flames quickly licking up the side of the casket and taking over, all hell broke loose. Women started screaming, grabbing their shit, and heading for every available exit while men ran toward the fire, desperate to put it out.

The priest stood up on his podium, madly praying as though the chaos was magically going to go away as Laurelle was dragged from the church, kicking and screaming while desperately wanting to watch her ex-husband burn.

I don't know what the hell is going to happen there. Is it a jailable offense or will she get away with it like so many other things get swept under the rug around here? It's not as though her crime was exactly done in private as most of the rich and famous do.

I couldn't believe my eyes as Milo stood beside me, watching the show unfold as though he was watching a midday TV drama. The twins howled with laughter pleased with their mother's craziness while Colton just stared, humiliated, horrified, and completely unsure what the hell he should be doing.

His father's body was burning and the church was quickly filling with smoke, also at risk of burning to the ground.

I started to go for Colton, unsure how I was going to help him but knowing that he needed someone in his corner. Nic had other plans though. The second I made my move toward Colton, Nic clutched onto my hand and pulled me toward the exit, claiming my safety always comes first.

Milo scrambled along with us, not wanting to get lost in the crowd of screaming women all dying to get out of there. Just as I reached the exit, I looked back to find someone with a fire extinguisher, madly trying to save what was left but it would have already been too late. I can only imagine what Charles would look like now.

Harrison and Maryne had gone to all that extra effort of having Charles dressed in his best suit which was then going to be kept for Colton as a keepsake. That won't happen now and the fact that his mother was the one to take that away from him really pisses me off.

Everyone has always said how Laurelle was the nice one, the woman who was all about her children, making memories, and having a good time, but I don't see it. I'm not even going to pretend that I knew what it was like when they were living as a family. I'm sure it would have been awful and I'm damn sure that Charles would have been a terrible husband, but what she did today tells me that there's so much more about Laurelle Carrington that we're all missing. Something much darker than anyone could have anticipated.

Once all the guests were safely outside, it became a waiting game.

Milo stuck by my side as Nic called the boys to come and chill. I have to admit, I've been to a few funerals in my time. Living in Breakers Flats, there's a high chance that you'll lose a friend before your fifteenth birthday. I've seen every different kind of funeral you can see, but today, that shit was all new.

Colton finally came out of the church and told everybody that the party at the mansion was still going ahead and that everybody should head on over there early and grab a few drinks. He was factual and emotionless, straight to the point, and clearly in way over his head. But just as I knew they would, people listened.

I don't know what it is about these Carrington men, but when they speak, people move. It would be nice to have that kind of power.

A champagne flute is pushed into my hand and I look up to find Sebastian grinning back at me. "You look like you could use a drink."

"Thanks," I tell him, noticing the way he looks so damn awkward inside this mansion. "But you look like you could use one more."

"Ain't that the fucking truth," he grumbles as Eli grunts his agreement beside me.

I'm not going to lie, watching these four boys walk inside of the Carrington mansion was kinda comical. It's not something any of us thought would ever happen. Hell, I'm still shocked by the fact that I walk through here every day.

We lost Kairo twenty minutes ago and if I had to guess, I'd say he was upstairs somewhere, checking through the bedrooms and hoping to find a pile of cash lying around. He might find something that can be easily slipped into his pockets and pawned the moment he gets back to Breakers Flats, but cash? I don't know. I haven't come across a massive safe yet and seeing cash lying around isn't something the Carrington's like to do. After all, they didn't end up billionaires by giving everything away.

Nic steps into my side and slides his hand around my waist. "Are you good?" he murmurs, leaning his face into my neck so I feel his breath upon my skin.

I give him a warm smile and lean into his side. "Yeah," I tell him. "I'm fine, just still reeling from that service. I can't believe momma Carrington set him on fire."

"Right?" Milo laughs. "That was fucking insane. I still can't believe it. Laurelle is such a bad fucking bitch."

I roll my eyes as I look at Milo. He's had a lady crush ever since Laurelle showed up to the funeral fashionably late and made her entrance in ridiculous stilettos, not giving a damn what anyone thought of her.

Sebastian sighs, shaking his head in devastation. "I can't believe I missed that shit," he says. "I would have paid to see one of these hoity-toity bitches finally snap."

Milo's eyes sparkle with excitement. "Trust me, man. It was so fucking worth it."

Someone slams into my shoulder, sending my champagne flute flying out of my hands. I screech as the expensive glass goes toppling while Eli does his best to catch it but in doing that, gets covered from head to toe in champagne.

How is it that whenever there's a party in this damn mansion, bullshit always goes down?

Sharp laughter has my head whipping around to the dumb bitch who couldn't possibly watch where she was going. I find the twins, looking down at me and scrunching their faces at my boys. It's impossible to tell which one did it but I honestly don't care. I bet these are the type of girls who would have worked out their little plan together before putting it into action, making them both equally as guilty.

"Ugh, watch yourself," the one on the right says, making me wish I'd taken the time to learn who is who so I could curse them out appropriately. "You're such a fucking mess."

The other laughs and they go to keep walking and although I know I should just let it go, I can't seem to stop myself from launching out and grabbing a fist full of fake, brunette extensions. I pull the one making the nasty comments back to me, spinning her around and loving the high-pitched screech that comes tearing out of her. To be honest, I'm surprised such a small thing can make such a big noise. I should congratulate her.

I pull her up in my face as her sister squeals for me to release her. "What did you just say to me?"

Her eyes bounce between mine and my boys and as they form a circle around us, blocking any kind of escape, she finally starts to understand that I'm not the bitch she wants to mess with.

"I ... I ..."

"No, No," I say, shaking my head. "I talk. You listen."

She looks around again and I watch as her brows crease with fear. I don't see Colton, but I feel him and I know he's watching this bullshit go down, but he's not doing anything to stop it and because of that, I give it my all.

"I'm going to tell you what I told your brother," I say, licking my lips and tilting my face closer to hers, so close that if I was to move another inch, my plum-colored lips would be rubbing against hers. I drop my tone to an intimidating whisper by her ear. "Are you ready?"

I hear her swallow before she nods once again. "We may be in your territory, but this is my fucking game, understand?"

A small squeak pulls from within her and I resist laughing and breaking my concentration. I love the few spoiled girls from Bellevue Springs that I've met so far. They're like cats. Always ready to strike and act like fucking bitches, but put a lion in their path and they scatter like pussies.

The other twin grows a set of balls and grabs hold of my hand that's tangled in her sister's hair. "Let her go," she demands, her voice loud and demanding, getting the attention of every guest in the room.

She pulls on my hand yet all that does is tighten my grip. I tear my gaze away from the twin in front of me and look to the other. "Careful, now. You don't want to be the reason your sister has a bald spot. I've been to the salon here and trust me, they're amazing but they can't do God's work."

She sets her jaw and I'm sure had her daddy still been here, she would have been having a tantrum and running to him right now, but unfortunately for her, she's shit out of luck.

Eli laughs and steps closer to her side, crippling her with fear. "Come on, baby," he coos. "Chill out. We're just having a little fun. Why don't you relax and come over to the dark side? I promise you'll like it."

"Eli," I warn. "Careful. They're seventeen."

"So?" he says with a seductive chuckle, his eyes raking up and down her body. "You were only fifteen when I took your virginity and you fucking loved it. I bet she'd have the time of her fucking life."

"Really?" Nic grunts, shooting his glare at Eli as Sebastian groans. "You want to bring that shit up now?"

"Umm …" the twin in my face says. "Can you please just let me go? I swear, we'll back off."

I raise a brow as I study her, not believing it for one second but to tell the truth, I'm starting to get a little bored. It's clear they've got the message and I have a feeling they won't be fucking with me much longer.

I meet her eyes. "Which one are you?"

"Cora."

Ahh, the one from Colton's room last night. Why does it make me so damn happy that this isn't Casey? "You better watch your back, Cora. I won't hesitate to fuck you up. I don't care who you have at your back. You will not win here. Got it?"

"Yeah, I got it," she says, her attitude firing back up, not appreciating my verbal smackdown.

Keeping my eyes trained on hers, I finally release the grip on her hair and she falls back against Sebastian's chest before he steps away and makes room for the two of them to scurry away. "Hey," Eli calls after them. Casey turns back and meets his eyes and the grin he sends her is more than wicked. "That offer still stands."

Her eyes bug out of her head and they run faster, making the boys buckle over, howling with laughter as Milo stares in wonder, probably wondering if Eli would extend his offer to him.

The boys have hardly finished their celebration when a hard body steps into my back. My body stiffens and as his familiar scent wraps around me and my knees buckle beneath me, Nic straightens.

Colton's hand falls to my waist, keeping me steady as my boys all stop to stare, confusion twisting on their faces. I don't know where the fuck Kairo comes from but suddenly he's there, able to smell the threat from a mile away.

Colton leans into me, his hand slipping further around my waist and doing all sorts of things to me, but the way Nic watches has me ready to duck for a shoot out. He steps forward, putting himself right in front of me to where he can easily reach for Colton's throat. "Take your fucking dirty hands off my girl."

I feel Colton's grin as his hand tightens on my waist. He leans down, dismissing Nic's request. His breath tickles my throat and I keep my eyes locked on Nic's as Colton's demanding whisper sounds right beside my ear. "As of five minutes ago, you were on the clock. If you want to keep your job, then I'd suggest fucking them off and picking up a goddamn serving platter."

Oh, fuck. This is not going to go down well.

My face scrunches as my jaw clenches.

What am I supposed to do here? Tell my boys to go and cause all sorts of shit or lose my job?

I turn in Colton's arm and look up at him, meeting those eyes that have tortured me since the second I stepped through the doors of this over-sized, power-hungry mansion. "Please," I murmur, hating that I'm about to beg, but when it comes to my crew, there's not a damn thing that I won't do. "Don't make me do this."

A grin pulls at his lips and it's clear that he's enjoying himself.

"After the scene you just caused with my sisters at their father's funeral, you're fucking lucky that you're not going with them. Your friend was just up in my bedroom trying to steal my father's Rolex while this other prick just offered to fuck my underage sister. Take your pick, Jade. What's more important to you? A bunch of gang members who have nothing to offer except a prison sentence or a fucking shot at a life after graduation?"

No, no, no, no, no. Why did he have to word it like that?

"Come on, this isn't fair."

"Five fucking seconds. I'd suggest you hurry up and choose."

"Colton."

"Three seconds, Jade."

Fuck.

This is not going to go down well.

I let out a breath and turn to face Nic with regret heavy in my eyes. His gaze tightens and all my boys stiffen, seeing where this is going before I've said a damn word. "You should go," I tell them. "Chill out in the pool house until I'm finished working and we can hang out after that."

"The fuck?" Nic grunts, his face twisting as his brows drop low. "You're turning your back on your boys for this fuckwit?"

"I'm not," I demand, stepping into Nic and feeling the loss of Colton at my back like the loss of a limb. "You're my fucking boys. You always will be, but if you stay you're going to fuck things up for me here. I have a good thing going. You know how much mom and I need this. Colton is my boss now. I have to do this."

"Babe, come on," Sebastian says.

"Please," I say, feeling my heart breaking, seeing the devastation deep within his handsome features. "Just go chill out in the pool house."

Colton scoffs behind me. "What makes you think they're welcome in the pool house?"

I spin around and shoot my glare at him, letting him see just how fucking deeply he's killing me. "I can have guests in the pool house. That's always been the rules," I demand, hating that I'm making a scene right in the middle of the ballroom for Harrison, mom, and Maryne to see.

"They were my father's rules," he says darkly, moving an inch closer and making Nic flinch at my back. "This is my property now."

I clench my jaw and tear my eyes away from his before turning on my heel back to Nic. "Please, Nic."

His hand snakes out and grips my wrist tightly. He pulls me into him. "Come the fuck home with me," he orders, using that tone that I've never been able to deny, the one he uses on his Black Widows, the one that demands respect.

I pull back, everything breaking inside of me. "I'm sorry," I say, tears beginning to well in my eyes. "I can't."

Nic watches me as I silently step back into Colton's chest. Betrayal fills him and I watch as he starts putting together the pieces of a puzzle that I don't even think exists anymore. "I see how it is," he murmurs.

"No, Nic. It's not."

He shakes his head and just like that, he turns and walks away, taking my crew with him and leaving me an absolute mess.

Colton stays right at my back until the last of the boys disappear from the ballroom then scoffs and walks away as though my heartbreak is some kind of joke.

I watch him go but the anger builds within me and I find myself racing after him, intent on … I don't know what. Making a difference? Having a say? Putting him in his damn place? It's lost on me. All I know is that this bullshit isn't over until I say it is.

No one makes me choose between my boys and my future like that apart from me. How dare he force that on me. He knows how much they mean to me. Hell, I'm not even scheduled to work at this party. If anything, I should be free to enjoy my day with my boys the way I see fit.

As if knowing that I'm coming for him, Colton slips out through the back door and keeps on walking until he steps through to a private room, one that I've never been in before, and to be honest, I'm too fucking pissed to even look around to figure out where I am.

Colton closes the door behind me, locking it as I pass. "What the hell was that?" I demand, stepping back into him and slamming my hand against his strong chest as the emotions begin to overwhelm me.

"They're fucking trash and they were causing a scene. They never should have shown up here and you know that. They don't belong."

"Neither do I yet for some fucked up reason that I can't understand, you're keeping me around."

"You're free to go anytime you want, Jade. I'm not fucking keeping you here."

"Please," I scoff. "As if you would have allowed me to walk out that fucking door."

His jaw clenches and his eyes bore into mine. He doesn't respond, but he doesn't need to. We both know it's true even though neither of us can fully understand it.

"So that's how it's going to be?" I question with tears in my eyes. "You're going to keep hurting me, pushing me away and hoping that it can make you feel something inside your dead soul?"

His jaw tightens and I step into him, raising my chin as I rest my hand against his chest and feel his racing heart beneath, unsure why after everything he's put me through, that I'm still here begging for more.

My voice lowers to a whisper as I take him in and realize that he's a fucking mess. He's lost and confused and desperately holding on to our fucked up relationship the only way he knows how—by hurting me. "You're going to break me, Colton," I say, hating the traitorous tear that rolls down my cheek. "Each time you push me away, it hurts a little more and every time you hurt me, you keep chipping away at the little parts I have left of myself, but I see you. I feel your pain. You're confused and hurting and you don't have a fucking clue what you're doing."

"Don't," he warns, realizing I'm climbing the invisible wall that's been erected between us.

I shake my head, refusing to be pushed back down. "It's okay," I tell him. "Hurt me, Colton. Hurt me as much as you fucking need because in the end, I'm not going anywhere. You can't push me away.

Not anymore. I get it, I'm your outlet now. I'm the only person who can make you feel something. So, it's okay. When you need to scream, you scream at me. When you hurt, you hurt me. I can take it. Right till the fucking end, right until you finally realize how fucking amazing you are."

His eyes blaze and within a moment, his lips come crashing down on mine as his hand twines around the back of my neck, holding me to him and refusing to let go.

I cling onto him, melting into his touch and allowing him to take whatever the hell he needs.

His kiss is forceful, needy, and desperate, but so is mine.

His hands slide down my body until they're curling around my ass. He lifts me and slams me against the closed door, keeping me pinned with his hard body. Everything screams within me, my heart, my brain, my fucking pulse. I need his touch more than I need my next breath.

Colton's tongue sweeps into my mouth and my body instantly responds. My arms wrap around him, pulling him impossibly closer.

I'm fucking falling and I'm falling hard. I can't allow it to happen but at the same time, I've never wanted anything more.

He pulls back ever so slightly and meets my eyes. The emotions staring back at me are raw and crazed. He's confused, angry, and has no fucking idea what the hell is going on between us. One minute he wants to hate me, and the next he can't resist my touch.

"It's okay," I murmur again, my voice so low that he may not even be able to hear me.

Colton presses back into me, keeping me pinned against the door and drops his head into the crook of my neck. My arms curl back around him and that's exactly where we stay, holding each other until he finally pulls away and steadies me on my feet.

Without a word, he reaches around me and opens the door. Colton walks out and just like that, he's gone, leaving me a mess of emotions, completely dazed and confused.

CHAPTER 9

I sit at the table within the ballroom, watching the projector screen as it flicks through images of Charles with his family vacationing in the Bahamas, at the Eiffel tower, in Rome, and everywhere this beautiful world has to offer.

A buffet-style dinner has just finished being served and I look around the room. It's well past 9 pm and I haven't heard from the boys or Colton since his little stunt at the start of the party. I don't even know if they're still hanging around. Nic isn't one to wear his heart on his sleeve. He's too proud and he would have shut down the second they walked out of here, but this is me. Surely, he would have stuck around to sort shit out, right?

Fuck. I really screwed this up. No, Colton really screwed it up. I should have called his bluff and told him to fuck off but he would have pushed back harder and there's only so far Nic can be pushed. It wouldn't have ended well, and either way would have broken me.

I look down at my phone on the table and spin it for the billionth time.

To call him or not to call him? That's the question.

I let out a heavy sigh and Milo looks over at me. "It's not just going to magically ring," he tells me after having watched me for the past two hours sulking. "If you want to fix this, then you need to make a move. I know this is all on Colton, but to them, you're the one who chose. You have to make it right because right now, they're all hurting."

"I don't think you understand just how hard that's going to be. We're not the type to sit and talk out our feelings. It's just not the way things are between us. We're the 'rub some dirt on it' type of people."

"I don't think rubbing dirt on it is going to fix it this time. Besides, you know what's going through Nic's head right now?" I look up at him, not wanting the answer but there's no stopping Milo when he has something to say. "Right now, that boy of yours is picturing Colton's hands all over your body and that sweet ass of yours taking his cock deep, just like the way you used to take his."

Fuck. No.

My bottom lip pouts out and I realize that he's right. I have to make a move and I have to do it now before I lose them. Those boys are all I have in this world, apart from Milo, of course. I have a feeling this guy is going to stick to me like glue until our dying days.

I let out a heavy sigh and grab my phone, wondering how I'm going to play this before aiming my guilt trip at the weakest link, the one who's going to cave the easiest. I know he can't resist my puppy dog eyes, and he's the one who is going to cave like a little bitch.

Ocean – Please tell me you guys don't hate me?

There's a short pause before my phone lights up in my hands.

Sebastian – We're in the pool house. Come out and we can talk.

Oh, shit. No cheesy emojis or comments about still fucking me anyway. This is bad.

I push up from the table and look down at Milo. "I'm out. This will probably take a while."

"Take your time, babe. I'll text if I'm leaving. We can chill tomorrow after school."

I give him a warm smile before bending down and pressing a soft kiss to his cheek. I make my way out of the ballroom and cut through the mansion to the back door. I pass through the main kitchen and down into the living area when I find Colton sitting alone in the dark. He leans forward on his knees, his head dropped into his hands.

My heart breaks. I want to run to him, crash into him, and tell him that while the pain may never go away, it gets easier. But if I stop to be with him now, I'll never get back what I had with those boys and I can't lose that. They're too important to me.

Colton raises his head and he watches as I cut through the living room and out the door.

My heart races, desperately begging me to go back to him, but I won't dare. I have to make this right with Nic and the boys. They're my support system and without them, I'm nothing.

As I walk out past the pool, the door of the pool house opens and Nic walks out, his eyes focused heavily on mine. Elijah, Kairo, and Sebastian follow him out and all four of them stare as they slowly make their way toward me.

The walk to meet them in the middle is torture. The looks on their faces are awful.

Nic looks like he's about ready to tear me apart while also somehow looking like a little puppy that's just been pushed aside. Sebastian is weary. He knows how much I love them and is more nervous about how Nic is going to react. He knows I'm heading for a verbal smackdown and he hates it.

Eli, my sweet Elijah. He just looks hurt. Never in his wildest dreams would he think that I would have stayed inside that ballroom with Colton, and I see in his eyes the way he's questioning my loyalty. Kairo though, he just looks pissed. He's not a grudge holder. Out of all of them, Kai is probably the easiest to get along with. He's so simple. All black and white, no grey areas. He'll tell me I fucked up and then we'll move on.

I finally meet them by the edge of the pool and my gaze never moves from Nic's.

I prepare to start groveling.

He stands before me, waiting for an explanation and I see in his eyes that he's ready to blow. Had I been anyone else, I would have already been forgotten. He'd already be back in Breakers Flats with the boys, looking for a replacement or forgetting the bullshit with a good time.

His eyes bore into mine and as I try to reach for him, he flinches away, absolutely gutting me. "Please, Nic. Don't hate me," I beg. "I swear, it's not what you think."

His expression is cold, deadly, lethal. It fucking sucks. "Are you fucking him?"

I shake my head. "No, I … I haven't fucked him."

"Yet," he grunts, reading my unspoken thoughts.

"Nic, please. Don't make this harder than it needs to be. Colton and I … we have a connection. I can't even explain it but it's so not what you're thinking."

He scoffs. "Please, tell me what it is you think I'm thinking."

"Nic."

"Please," he says, sweeping his hand in front of him in a gesture for me to continue. Eli groans as Sebastian scrunches his face, knowing damn well that when Nic throws down a comment like that, I'm not about to hold back. Kai doesn't respond though, just continues staring, probably wanting to hear what it is that I have to say.

"You asked for it, Nic," I grumble, letting out a frustrated sigh but not once tearing my hard glare from his, hoping that somehow he'll understand where the hell he went wrong.. "You think I'm whoring myself out to him like I'm that fucking low. You think I'm getting extra benefits by fucking the boss to get myself ahead in life but what's more, you think he's taking something from you, something that is no longer yours to take because when it comes to Dominic Garcia, everything is about him. Who gives a shit about what I think? Who cares that I actually have a connection with the guy? Who fucking cares that every time I'm around him my heart beats a million miles per minute? No. None of that fucking matters because Nic has his fucking panties in a twist."

Sebastian takes a big step back and sucks in a sharp breath as Eli grumbles under his breath. "Ah, fuck. She went there."

Kairo just continues to stare.

"Yeah, I fucking went there," I snap, "because right now I'm being punished for choosing between the four guys who should have my back and the guy who I might have something real with."

"REAL?" Nic demands, stepping closer. "That's not fucking real. What we had was real. The guy is a fucking loser. He treats you like shit. He'll never love you. You're a convenient fuck to him. Some poor bitch who'll keep her mouth shut."

My hand slaps hard across his face. "Jealousy isn't pretty on you Nic. Fucking pull your shit together. Stop hating on me for wanting to move on. You fucked us up. You slept with another woman. What we had wasn't real. You were the one fucking the poor girl for convenience. Tell me, Nic. Was it nice not having to go out to find some random slut to fuck each night knowing you could just fuck me instead?"

"Don't you try to tell me what the fuck I was feeling."

"Then stop doing the same bullshit to me. I have something real with Colton. I don't even understand it yet but when I tell the four guys who are supposed to love and support me through any decisions I make, whether they think I'm fucking up or not, they should have my back just as I would have theirs."

Sebastian breaks. "Come on, O. You know I got your back. I just … we don't trust him. He treated you like shit from the second you walked in here. He will never have your back like the way we have it."

"Oh, really?" I question. "That's what you really think?"

"That's what we fucking know," Nic says.

I shake my head, stepping right up to Nic and putting myself in front of him. "You don't know shit, Nic. You haven't been here. You don't walk in my shoes. Your possessive asshole act is starting to get old."

Eli subtly steps in between us and stands as awkwardly as possible, knowing if Nic wants to get to me, his ass will get laid out.

"This place has changed you," Nic says.

"No," I tell him. "This place is just offering me more than what Breakers Flats can. This place isn't what's holding me back."

Kairo's voice comes from the back of the group, raw and filled with emotion. "So, that's what you think? That we're holding you back?"

I let out a sigh and meet his eyes. He looks broken and it kills me. I don't think I've ever seen him look at me that way in all the years that I've known him. I walk away from Nic until I'm placed right in front of Kai. I take his hands and look up into his eyes. "Never, Kai. You boys mean the absolute world to me and at the moment, I'm trying to work out how to make room for all these new people coming into my life. I don't even understand what this thing is between me and Colton, but to me, it feels real, and I guess … I guess I just want to know that if I decide to do something about it that you guys aren't going to try to kill him."

Kai shakes his head. "That's not my call to make."

I turn back to the guys and avoid Nic's stare. "I don't want to lose you. I can't. For so long, it's been just us. *No friends* …"

Nic lets out a sigh and something breaks within him. *"Just family,"* he murmurs, finishing off the words that I know mean the absolute world to him, the same words that are tattooed on his skin as a permanent reminder of his deepest belief.

I walk back over to him and take a breath filled with relief as he allows me to take his hand. "Please don't hate me," I beg with a whisper. "I'm not choosing him over you. I'm just opening myself up to more."

Nic holds my eyes, and waiting for his response has my anxiety skyrocketing until he finally pulls me into his chest. "Alright," he finally says. "I'll back off but if he fucking hurts you …"

"I know," I whisper, not needing him to finish his sentence.

"This doesn't change the fact that you're my girl, O. It just means that I'm going to have to try a little harder."

"You know that I love you guys."

"I know," he murmurs.

"And despite making a scene with his sisters and Kai trying to smuggle Charles' Rolex, you were kicked out because Colton is jealous of our relationship, not because you guys are Black Widows."

"Trust me," he says with a scoff. "That's not fucking lost on me."

"So, you forgive me?"

He's quiet for a minute before pulling back and gently taking my chin. He gives me a warm smile. "Mostly. I'm at 80%. I'm still pissed, but calm enough that I'm not about to go in there and whoop your boy into next week."

"He's not my boy."

"He will be though. No one could resist your charm, O. If he knows what's good for him, he'll pull you in and never let you go."

The corner of my lips lift into a small smile, knowing how damn hard that would have been for Nic to say. "Thank you," I whisper, keeping our moment private from the three stooges who haven't dared to look away.

"Come on now," Sebastian says, creeping up behind me and drawing me into his arms. "Share the love."

I wrap myself around him and bury my face into his chest, desperately needing this moment to know that my boys are all good. I squish my face into his chest and breathe him in. I fucking love Sebastian. I don't know where I'd be without him. He's my best friend. He just gets me in a way that no one else does, though I'd never dare utter those words out loud. These boys can't handle themselves when they're jealous and tonight is a perfect example of that.

His hands rub up and down my back as the cool evening air surrounds us, and to be honest, until now I hadn't even realized it was cold. All that mattered was making things right. "So," he finally says in a tone that has me guarding myself. "Are you really sure about this Carrington kid? You saw what his mom did at that funeral and those sisters of his ... crazy runs deep in that family."

I laugh and hold him a little tighter. "Trust me, I've got it handled. I grew up with you four so I'm well-practiced. Besides, no one is crazier than me."

"Ain't that the fucking truth," Eli mutters, joining us and quickly pulling me out of Sebastian's loving arms. He pulls me into his chest and I snuggle in, knowing there's no better place in the world. "Though," he adds. "You're kind of a step above that shit because you come with a nasty fucking bite and a set of steel balls."

"You're damn right, I do."

I can practically feel Nic's eyes roll behind me as Kairo steps into my side. "Come on," he says, peeling my hand off Eli's back and slipping his into it. He pulls me away and the others follow. "We should get out of here," he says, leading me around the side of the house.

"What you mean is that you have a date tonight that'll end with a guaranteed fuck and you want to get your ass back home before you miss your shot."

Kairo scoffs. "Babe, I never miss my fucking shot. I could show up at her doorstep at four in the fucking morning and she'll still drop to her knees."

"Ugh," I say, pretending to gag as he loops our joined hands over my shoulder. "Have I ever told you how disgusting you are?"

"Constantly."

"Good. Just making sure."

The boys chat among themselves as we walk through the massive property, but as we finally reach the front of the mansion, all five of us pull up and find ourselves staring.

Crazy momma Carrington stands on the front steps of the mansion with a small luggage bag held in her hand, and when I say that she looks proud as fucking punch, it's the understatement of the year. She looks like a woman who just cured cancer. All her fucking problems are gone. Her shoulders are lifted, there's a smile on her face, and she walks down those stairs in a way that reminds anyone who's watching that she's the motherfucking boss bitch.

Her twin daughters follow down the steps behind her looking kind of happy but kind of pissed at the same time. It's hard to tell with those two. Hell, they might not be pissed at all. That could just be their usual resting bitch faces.

We watch in silence as the twins reach the bottom of the stairs and slide their luggage into the back of a black limousine before giving their mother a quick hug. The girls chat for a few moments then stride past the limo until their ducking down into the teal McLaren that's been parked out front of the mansion for the last two days.

Laurelle drops down into the limousine and as it pulls away, that's when it finally hits me. They're sneaking out during the middle of a party, and I'm damn sure that they're doing it without even a simple goodbye for Colton.

Pain rockets through me. He might be a fucking boss now, but he's still eighteen years old and struggling with the passing of his father. If anything, he needs his family more than ever. I thought they'd be staying and I didn't question it for even a second. That's the right thing to do, yet there they go, disappearing down the long driveway.

They fucking left him … again, and now without his father around, he's got no one. God, he must be hurting so fucking bad.

"Come on," Kai mutters, seeing the heartbreak and disappointment written all over my face. "It's not your problem."

He pulls me along until we're standing beside Nic's car and by the time we finally made it there, people are beginning to file out of the mansion. It's Tuesday night and every fucker in this place has somewhere to be tomorrow. Whether it's a board meeting or a classroom. Me, I'll be here doing absolutely nothing.

I give each of the boys a quick hug, hating to see them go but Kairo's right. They need to head back home before they can get themselves in any more trouble. Hell, before *I* get them in more trouble.

Nic holds onto me a second longer than necessary and as he goes to drop down into his car, voices from the sixty-six steps of the Carrington mansion draw my attention. I look back over my shoulder and as I take them in, a wide smile spreads across my face.

I can't believe my fucking luck.

I duck down through Nic's open window and look at Kairo. "How important is that date?"

His eyes narrow in suspicion before his low voice comes murmured through the window. "Why?"

I indicate back over my shoulder and all four boys look back. "See those guys?" I say with a grin. Nic grunts, telling me to continue. "They're the five fuckers who crowded me against a car and poured acidic grease over my head until my hair was falling out in chunks."

All four of their eyes darken and as we watch them walk down the drive, the tension gets thicker. To be honest, I'd kind of forgotten about these guys. So much has happened since that day and getting revenge had slipped from my mind after Colton had taken it upon himself to beat the living shit out of all of them. But that was his payback, this is going to be mine.

"No shit," Kairo mutters as they get closer. "They're the same dickheads who were in Breakers Flats a month ago buying drugs from the Widows. Those fuckers thought they could get away from us."

"The same ones from my last night in Breakers Flats?" I question, remembering that night so well, all the way back when my biggest problem was to hotbox Nic's car or not.

"Yep."

Well, damn. I guess these boys really do have a score to settle with the five rich pricks of Bellevue Springs.

Nic looks up at me as the guys pass and grins. "We'll take care of it," he promises before winking and sending my world into a tailspin. I don't know what it is about a man winking that drives me insane but it does and I absolutely love it.

His car slowly pulls out and stalks the five guys and I wait and watch as they realize what the fuck is happening. They start picking up their speed, regretting their decision to park so far up the drive. Their pathetic run is no match for Nic's car. They're fucked and they know it.

With them disappearing into the distance, I turn back to the mansion. I should be heading back to the pool house to drop into bed like a good little girl, but the thought of walking back into that godforsaken place has my feet moving without permission toward its looming doors.

Why am I so good at bad decisions?

Once through the mansion doors, I peer into the massive ballroom. I find Harrison hurrying around, trying to close shit down. This isn't one of those nights where the party will be held into the early hours of the morning. This was a celebration and unfortunately, the reason for celebrating is now gone … literally.

I bypass the end of the party and walk straight through to the kitchen to where I'd seen Colton before I walked out to find the boys. I look down into the open living space and there he is, still sitting in the dark with his head dropped low into his hands.

It's been well over an hour since I walked through here last and he looks as though he hasn't moved an inch.

I go to him.

I don't know what possesses me to do it. Maybe it's that constant need to always insert myself somewhere I don't belong. Who knows?

He doesn't look up as I approach but I know he feels me just the way that I feel him. I walk right up in front of him and he doesn't move a muscle until my fingers trail over his shoulder. Colton sits up and looks up at me and I see nothing but pain reflected in his eyes. It tears me apart. He's done nothing but hurt me since the day I got here but the idea of seeing him in pain kills me.

I move into him, pressing my knee down on the couch beside his thigh and doing the same with the other until I'm straddled on his lap. His arms curl around me and I sink into him, resting my head on his shoulder and just holding him, knowing how damn much he needs me here.

Neither of us utters a single word, as when we do, this will all be over. Instead, we sit in silence, wrapped in each other's arms until the night begins to claim me. A yawn rips though me and his arms instantly tighten around me, somehow holding me even closer.

We sit for another ten minutes before my eyes begin to grow heavy and instead of pushing me away and telling me enough is enough, he simply lifts me off the couch, keeping me wrapped around his body until he's pushing through the door of my bedroom in the pool house.

He puts me down on my bed and presses a soft kiss to my temple before silently walking out and closing the door behind him, unknowingly setting my world on fire to the point where there's now no chance in hell that I'll be able to sleep.

CHAPTER 10

"The fuck?" I demand, staring down at my Kindle as I read over the last page of *Hate* by *Tate James*, desperately trying to flip the page for more because that bitch can't possibly leave me hanging like that. What kind of fucked up ending was that anyway? Where's my happily ever after? Where's the four-way with dicks flying at MK's face?

Damn. Why does she have to play with my emotions like that?

I sit up on the couch, my head still reeling with the epic ending and theories when I realize that it's well past four in the morning. How the hell did that happen? I settled onto the couch at some point after Milo had disappeared, and somehow I'm still here. Shit, I didn't even spare a few seconds to take my ass out to the pool house.

I let out a heavy sigh. There's no way I'll be able to sleep after that.

I pull out my phone and start searching for book two on Amazon and let out a relieved breath as I find it in the recent releases. Thank fuck. I need more of this world and *Archer D'Ath*.

Realizing that starting another book after four in the morning is just a little insane, I put my kindle down and try to find the energy to get up off the couch and make my way to bed, only I can't.

What is it with these authors giving us these incredible books and the BAM, leaving us with blue balls and bullshit cliffhangers that have our tiny minds exploding with insanity? Fuck, if I ever meet that *Tate James* … damn, I'd have a few things to say to her.

Knowing sleep won't be coming anytime soon, I grab the throw blanket off the back of the couch and pull it around myself as I stare off out the back window. The moon shines brightly in the night sky and reflects perfectly off the pool. It's simply stunning. I don't think I'm ever going to get used to this shit.

A noise out in the hallway has my head whipping around and my heart racing. Ever since there was a murderer and a rapist on the loose around here, I've been a little jumpy, but considering the rapist was after me and the murderer may or may not be the same guy who killed my father, it's acceptable to be a little on edge.

I strain through the dark, watching and waiting as whoever is out there gets closer. My fingers curl around the edge of my Kindle. I'm more than prepared to use this bad boy as a weapon, but if it fucks up my Kindle, I'm going to be pissed.

A familiar figure crosses in front of the door and I let out a heavy sigh. "Oh, thank fuck," I say, letting my head flop back to the couch as the relief sails through me.

The figure stops and turns at the sound of my voice. "Jade?" Colton questions, sounding a little unsure if he's believing what he's actually seeing. Though it's not a far stretch, it's nearly pitch black in here.

"Yeah," I murmur into the dark room. "It's me."

He stops and walks into the room, keeping himself at a distance. "What are you doing?" he questions, flipping on a lamp as he passes and spreading a dim light through the room.

"I kinda got distracted reading a book," I tell him. "I only just realized what time it was."

"You read?" he grunts in surprise, his brows flying into his hairline.

"Kind of," I say. "I read to distract myself from the bullshit of the real world. It's not like an obsession or anything. Just something to do when there's nothing keeping me interested on Netflix. What are you doing?" I ask. "It's a little early for you."

He pinches the edges of his grey tank and I allow my eyes to rake over his body. "Ahh, the gym. Right. As if your body needs work," I say with a scoff, feeling like an idiot for not realizing the second he walked through the door.

His lips twist into a proud grin and I roll my eyes at him. He's such a cocky fuck.

His whole schedule has been changing this week. He's been doing some school work through correspondence while spending his days locked in his father's office, trying to wrap his head around everything that he did. It's not as though Charles left Colton a cheat sheet. He's been having to work it all out on his own and honestly, I'm kind of proud.

It's only been a few days since the funeral but so far, Colton has been killing it as a badass CEO of everything Carrington. Hell, I don't even know the business' names or how many there are. I don't even know what those businesses do, but I do know that watching Colton slay day in and day out gets me all kinds of hot and bothered.

"Come on," he says, walking toward me and taking my hand. Butterflies swarm through my stomach as he pulls me up off the couch. "You need to go to bed. You have school in a few hours."

"Oh, you haven't heard?" I question, putting on the brakes. He looks back at me with his brows pinching in confusion. "Dean Simmons called me into his office before school on Monday morning and informed me that now your dad was gone, there was no obligation to keep me at BSA. He had my transfer slips already signed and approved without even thinking of mentioning it to me or Mom."

"The fuck?" he grunts.

"Yeah, I apparently start at the girls' school on Monday morning—not that Mom and I can afford the fees. I'll have to change to whatever public school you guys have around here."

"That's fucking bullshit," he spits, his eyes bouncing around the room, deep in thought. "Don't worry about it. I'll sort it out."

"No," I say, stopping him before he can get too far with that thought. "I don't need you rushing in to save me all the time. It's fine. I mean, the way he handled it was wrong and he should be fired for that shit, but it doesn't change the fact that you guys are a bunch of dudes and I'm a chick. I never should have been enrolled at BSA in the first place."

"I mean …"

"That's what I thought," I grumble, allowing him to pull me out of the room, assuming that he's leading me back to the pool house and sending me off to bed like a good little girl, only he turns in the opposite direction. "Where are we going?"

He doesn't respond, just keeps pulling me along, his fingers laced through mine and doing all sorts of things to me. It's moments like this where I feel we could be so much more but then he always goes and does something to fuck that up.

I don't understand this. Sometimes he's so unbelievably sweet, caring, and overprotective, but other times, he wants to get at me, tear me down, and remind me who's the fucking boss around here. I get it, I really do. It's his way of coping with all the bullshit and trying to keep me in line, it's his way of pretending what he's feeling for me doesn't exist, but it'll get to a point where he can no longer pretend, and when it does … fuck. It's either going to be epic or a colossal cluster fuck. There's no middle ground when it comes to Colton Carrington.

We walk through the house until he stops in front of a set of double doors that look just like the rest, that is until he leans forward and presses the call button. My eyes bug out of my head. "You have a fucking elevator in here and I'm only just finding out now?"

"Jesus," he laughs. "What kind of worker are you? How could you not know this?"

I glare at the magnificent man beside me. "Because I stick to the jobs Maryne gives me and make a point of not snooping around your house."

"Bullshit," he grunts. "I've seen you standing in front of bookshelves tipping books, hoping for a secret dungeon."

My mouth drops. Fuck. Sprung. "I … uhhh. I was just …"

"You were just at the wrong bookshelf."

My eyes widen. "Bullshit. Are you serious?"

He grins. "Dad had to hide his prized possessions somewhere, but don't get too excited. It's just a really big room with all his favorite art, sculptures, and treasures."

"No shit," I laugh. "That's kinda cool."

Colton shrugs, clearly not as impressed as I am.

The elevator arrives and the doors slide open. Colton waves me in and holds the doors open like the gentleman he pretends to be. I step through and Colton follows behind, allowing the doors to close us in.

He presses a button and as the elevator starts taking us up, the tension rises along with it. His hand remains in mine but the need to grab his face and devour it pulses through me. I wonder what kind of alarm system is on this thing and how much jumping around it could take before it broke off the chains and dropped to the ground?

No. Ocean. Behave. I'm not about to have a quickie with Colton in the elevator while dangling between floors. If and when I fuck him, it's going to count and it's going to be so much more than a quickie. It'll be fucking explosive and I can't wait.

There's a soft ding as we reach the top floor and when the doors slide open, I stare ahead in shock. "Holy shit," I breathe as Colton pulls me out of the elevator.

I glance around at the fully stocked library and itch to start searching. It's like a scene out of fairytale in here. It's incredible.

Colton laughs under his breath. "Geez, if you're impressed by this, you should see my dick."

I roll my eyes and glance across at him, struggling to look away from the books on the shelves. How is it that men always have a one-track mind? "I've seen your dick," I remind him, "and although it's impressive, it's got nothing on this."

"Yeah, just wait till you see it in action."

I scoff as I start walking toward the books. "Pretty confident for a guy who practically runs out of the room every time he kisses me."

A low groan comes from behind me as I reach the shelf and run my finger over the titles, taking it all in only to find all of my favorite authors and I realize that maybe I do have a little something in common with the bitch twins after all. "Are you trying to pull some wicked Beauty and The Beast bullshit on me, Mr. Carrington, because it's not going to work."

I look back over my shoulder and laugh at his blank expression. "Please tell me that you understand that reference."

He shakes his head.

Bless his sweet heart. "I meant that … you know what, don't worry," I say, letting out a sigh and focusing back on the books. I take a few steps, scanning over the titles and figuring out what I haven't had a chance to read yet, and honestly, it's quite a lot. "How could I have forgotten there was a library up here? Your dad mentioned it on my first day."

"I know," he murmurs, his voice not so far away anymore. "If I knew you actually liked to read, I probably would have brought you up here sooner."

"Right," I laugh. "For some reason, I can't picture you having done that before now."

A soft chuckle comes from behind me and my warmth spreads through me at the sound and the rare carefree moment between us. "You're right. I would have had Maryne send you up here to clean so you could have claimed that you found it on your own."

I turn around and meet his eyes, stopping as I find him staring right back at me, but not just at my face, right down into my soul. "You would have done that?" I question, lowering my voice, afraid of how it might break.

He nods and slowly takes a step toward me, making the butterflies turn into murderous little bitches, making me feel as though I could throw up. His voice is low and velvety and has me wanting so much more. "I don't want to hurt you anymore, Jade," he murmurs. "But you were right after the funeral. You are my outlet and hurting you makes me feel something, feel part of me that I thought didn't exist."

I take a hesitant step toward him. "I told you it's okay."

"It's not," he says shaking his head. "I shouldn't be hurting you. I shouldn't be constantly trying to push you away. I should be holding on and doing everything in my power not to lose you because you're fucking worth it, Jade. I've never met anyone like you. You're so fucking strong and the fact that you're still standing here, willing to allow me to fuck you up just to make me feel something proves that."

"You've only ever hurt me with words, Colton, but your actions have always spoken so much louder."

He swallows and I see the fear in his eyes, not knowing what the hell is happening between us, and truthfully, I feel it too. This whole relationship is on a level of fucked-up that I've never experienced before and I honestly don't know what any of it means.

He steps into me and takes my waist, pulling me the rest of the way into his chest. His eyes meet mine, heated, wild, and desperate. His tongue slips out and runs over his bottom lip and I instantly become hypnotized. "Maybe I don't need to hurt you to make me feel."

My heart races and before I can say a word or even begin working out what the hell he just meant by that comment, his lips are pressing down on mine and completely destroying me.

My hands slide up his toned arms until they're wrapping around his neck and holding him tight. His tongue sweeps into my mouth and I welcome it like my next breath.

I'm falling hard. Too fucking hard. Colton Carrington is going to destroy me and I'm going to let him.

I need to pull away before I allow him the power to truly hurt me because once I hand my heart over, I don't know if I'll ever get it back. Yet I can't stop. I can't pull away. I can't force myself to let go. I need him like nothing I've ever needed before.

His fingers brush my skin like a caress and my knees instantly go weak. He takes hold of my jaw and tilts my head, opening my neck for him to take. His lips move from mine and he sets every nerve ending on fire as they trail down below my ear.

Colton's thumb brushes over my lips as his other hand trails down my body, claiming every curve until his fingers are flirting with the waistband of my shorts just above my ass. Getting no objection from me, his hand slips inside my pants and he grabs my ass, giving it a firm squeeze.

I press my ass back into his hand, needing more and he obliges just as I knew he would. My shorts are pushed down and I step out of them before he pulls my shirt over my head, leaving me completely naked and free to do with as he pleases.

Needing to feel his body on mine, I go to reach for his shirt but his hand drops from my jaw and he's lifting me before I even know what's going on.

My ass is pushed back onto a high shelf and I find myself sitting among the books. My tits are at Colton's eye level and he's quick to pay them all the attention in the world while my pussy begs to be touched.

I grab his tank and finally pull it over his head, showing off that perfect sun-kissed skin that I've been dying to sink my teeth into.

Colton's fingers trail down my body, leaving a wake of goosebumps and has me sucking in a breath as the anticipation builds.

I feel as though I've been waiting forever to feel his touch and finally, it's happening.

My fingers curl into his hair as his fingers find my clit. He groans low and I feel the vibration against my nipple, sending an electrical pulse right down to my center.

His thumb rubs slow torturous circles over my clit as his fingers begin to explore, finding my center and pushing up into me. I scoot my ass closer to the edge, desperate to get as close to him as possible.

His tongue trails over my nipple and I arch my back, pressing my tits against him.

Fuck, I'd give anything to feel his cock buried deep inside me.

Colton pulls back and raises his head so his lips are back on mine. He kisses me deeply, and just when I think I'm about to get exactly what I've been craving, he drops to his knees between my thighs and throws my legs over his shoulder.

I suck in a gasp, watching as his eyes blaze with need.

Holy fuck. This is going to be good. If Nic doesn't kill me, then I'm sure this will.

Colton licks his lips and everything south of the border clenches. His eyes are filled with desire, but it's the excitement promising the time of my life that really gets me.

He doesn't hold back.

His tongue runs over my clit and I thread my fingers through his hair once again, desperately needing to hold on. His tongue really starts to move. Teasing. Tasting. Taunting.

A thrill shoots through me knowing that at any moment, one of the many staff members could walk through the door and watch as my pussy is eaten like never before, but I don't care. If they want to walk in right now, then let them come. I won't be stopping for anything, not until I've had the full Carrington experience. Hell, if Harrison was to walk in right now, the bastard would just have to close his eyes.

I can't help but look down and watch the show playing out before me. His tongue moves like a snake and I'm completely mesmerized. It's the most erotic thing I've ever seen, so tantalizingly sexy. I can't fucking wait to repay this favor.

Colton adds two thick fingers to the mix and pushes them up into me and a low groan pulls from deep within me. I tighten my grip in his hair and I feel his proud smile against my clit.

He pulls them out before slamming them back in and rocking my world. "Fuck," I grunt, as his fingers rub against my G-spot, hitting it over and over again but it's his tongue that's the real star of this show.

He pushes me to the edge and I feel my orgasm creeping up on me.

Just a little more.

Reading my body like a book, he gives me exactly what I need and within moments, I'm coming hard around his fingers. His tongue is relentless and doesn't stop teasing me until I've completely ridden out my orgasm, only then does he release my legs and straighten up.

He stands before me as I struggle to catch my breath. His eyes are dark and I can only imagine what he has in store for me now, but not before I get to taste his velvety skin on my tongue.

Colton makes a show of licking his lips as his eyes bore heavily into mine, making me more than ready to go again. I reach for him and he instantly steps back into me, keeping his hands on my body.

He lifts me off the shelf and as he steadies me on my feet, his lips come down on mine, letting me taste myself.

I slip my hand down between us and into the front of his low-hanging sweatpants. My fingers curl around his hard cock and the way he groans tells me that he's already close to the edge. My hand pumps up and down and he pulls me into him, resting his chin above my head. "I'm going to fucking regret this but I have to go."

I shake my head, not even close to wanting him to leave. My thumb circles over the tip of his hard cock and I feel him shudder beneath my touch. "You're not going anywhere until I'm through with you."

He lets out a pained moan and I know it's certainly not from what I'm doing, but from the decision he's struggling to make. I look up through my lashes, knowing the exact effect that I'm having on him. "Fair's fair, Carrington," I whisper, biting down on my bottom lip.

He brushes his thumb over my mouth, releasing my bottom lip. "You're going to be the fucking death of me." And just like that, I drop down to my knees, pulling his sweatpants down as I go.

His cock springs free and I have no choice but to grab it with both hands. Colton leans forward bracing himself against the bookshelf and looking down as I run my fingers over his velvety skin, teasing him just as he did to me.

I won't be able to resist long though. I've never been so fucking hungry in my life.

I run my tongue over my lips and watch as his eyes darken as I lean into him. I take him in my mouth and it's just as good as I thought it was going to be. I feel him in the back of my throat but I take him deeper because a man like Colton Carrington deserves the fucking best.

I start moving up and down his impressive length, swirling my tongue over his tip every chance I get. His hand curls into the back of my hair, gripping it tightly as he moves inside my mouth. He grunts low and I continue to work him until I push him over the edge and feel him coming in the back of my throat.

I swallow everything he has on offer and as I raise to my feet, he looks at me as though he just found an angel among demons.

CHAPTER 11

My phone blares to life and I look down to find it buzzing against the cushion of the most comfortable egg chair I've ever had the pleasure of sitting in.

Holy shit. It's already after seven in the morning and I'm still sitting up here in the library after Colton rocked my world with a massive pile of books by my side. This is easily my favorite place in this whole mansion and I'm kind of pissed that it's taken me so long to discover it. I guess that speaks for how big this place really is, and how little I know about it.

I'm still reeling from Colton this morning. I'm kinda in shock while kinda not surprised, but kinda want to do it again. I can't say

I've ever had a secret library world-rocking before and I was down for round two if he hadn't scurried out of here like his ass was on fire.

The phone continues to demand my undivided attention and I scoop it up with a yawn, feeling like an idiot for not having gone to bed the second I was finished with Colton.

"Are you kidding me?" I laugh as I put my phone to my ear. "I didn't realize you knew what seven o'clock in the morning was."

"Look who's talking," Nic says. "What are you doing up? It's Saturday morning. Shouldn't you be sleeping in?"

"Wait. You called me at this ungodly hour even though you thought I'd be enjoying the one day a week I get to sleep in?"

"Please," he scoffs. "You sleep in every day. I've never met another chick who can just roll out of bed and be ready for the day in the three seconds that it takes you, but you avoided my question. Why are you awake? Are you working early today? Is there another one of those bullshit parties that I need to come and chaperone?"

I roll my eyes and slip a bookmark into the page I was reading before peeling myself out of the egg-chair. I'll have to come back after I've slept for a bit and continue exploring this room. I wonder if I could convince Harrison to help me get this chair down the elevator and into the pool house? Nah, that's a long shot. I'll have to do it myself. After all, it's better to ask forgiveness than to be denied permission. Hmm, I bet I could talk Charlie into helping me.

"No," I say, striding over to the elevator and pressing the call button. "There's no party that I'm being forced to work at. I just haven't gone to bed yet."

"What? Why the hell not? What have you been doing all night … who have you been doing all night?"

"Seriously?" I grumble with yet another eye roll. "I've been reading all night. I discovered this place has a fully stocked library."

"Reading?" he grunts, clearly not believing me as the ding for the elevator sounds.

I step into it with a groan. "Yes, you overprotective, possessive douche canoe. I've been reading, and in case you wanted to know, I actually enjoyed this one so you can go right ahead and pull your head out of your ass and stop questioning every little thing I say."

"Jesus. Calm down, O. I was just asking. What's got your panties in such a twist this morning?"

Geez, let's see. It could be a number of things. The ending of that book is one, but then there's also the image of squeezing Colton's head between my thighs as I came harder than I've ever come before. He ran out of here like his ass was on fire, and now Nic is questioning everything I say. Yeah, I have every right to have my panties in a twist, but it's not as though I'm about to start explaining that list to him.

"Nothing," I tell him, riding down in the elevator to the ground floor. "I'm just tired. I don't think I'm working today so I was just about to go back to the pool house and catch a few hours of sleep."

"Wait … you stayed in that fucking house with Carrington all night? I thought you said you were reading."

"Oh, my God, Nic. Chill the fuck out. You're so fucking impossible. I just told you that I was reading in the fucking Library. Where they keep all the goddamn books." I hit the bottom level and the doors quickly slide open. "So no, I wasn't bouncing up and down on Colton's dick if that's what you're really asking."

I step out of the elevator and raise my eyes only to come to a stop.

Get fucked. How is this my morning?

Colton stares back at me with a raised questioning brow and the amusement on his face grinds on my nerves. His body shines with a thin sheen of sweat, and damn it, he looks just as delicious as the first day I showed up here.

He's clearly been working out in the home gym and it shows by the way his arms seem to bulge more than usual. My mouth waters but Nic's voice in my ear has me snapping out of it. "Alright, alright," he says, defensively. "So you were reading all night."

"Good. I'm glad we got that cleared up," I tell him. "But what about our talk the other night? I thought you were going to back off?"

Colton takes a step toward me and reaches for the phone. "Who are you talking to?"

I flinch out of his reach and tighten my grip on my phone just in case. "None of your goddamn business."

"Is that him?" Nic practically roars. "You're fucking with him right now?"

For fuck's sake.

"Fuck you," I say into the phone before looking back at Colton. "And fuck you too."

I end the call before he has a chance to fight back and storm down the hall, barging past Colton before he can do anything about it either. "Woah," Colton laughs at my back, following behind. "What's up with you?"

"Nothing."

"This isn't because I didn't stay and cuddle?"

My mouth drops open and I spin around to glare at him. "Seriously? You're that shallow that everything has to be about you? Screw you."

His hands fly up in defense. "Okay," he laughs, far too entertained for my liking. "So, it's not me then. I have to admit, that's a nice change."

"You know what?" I seethe, "It can be you too."

"What?" he demands as I turn and start storming away again. "I didn't do anything except rock your world. You know you're the sweetest thing I've ever tasted."

Damn him. If he didn't give me the best orgasm I've ever experienced, I'd be in his face saying something about that comment, yet a part of me really hopes it's true. I can't even begin to imagine the number of girls he's eaten his way through and made scream.

I stop in the hallway and spin around. "What is even going on here? You're giving me whiplash. Do we hate each other? Are we secretly something more? Do you wanna fuck? Or are we just continuing to get on each other's nerves only to end up giving in to desires that neither of us understand? What is this, Colton? I need a little definition because I'm so fucking lost right now."

His brows raise and I watch as he truly starts thinking about it. "I ...uhhh"

"Yeah," I scoff, turning and walking away again. "That's what I thought."

"Hey," he says, continuing to follow me. "That's not fair. It's not as though you have any fucking idea what this is either. How am I supposed to know?"

"I don't know, but it seems like you're the one always calling the shots around here. So why don't you leave me alone until you figure it the hell out."

"Fuck, Jade. You're really pissy when you're tired. What happened to all that 'hurt me, Colton' bullshit?"

My blood boils and I turn the corner but as I go to put this fucker in his place, I run into a wall of suits and expensive cologne. My feet bring me to a startling stop as I stare at the six men who hover in the hallway behind me with Harrison, who looks as though he's just been railroaded by whoever these men are.

Colton comes up behind me, stopping with a hand on my waist. His eyes bore into Harrison's. "What's going on?"

"Sir," Harrison says, bowing his head as a sign of respect for his new boss. "The board of directors for Carrington Incorporated have requested an urgent meeting with you. I did suggest that a formal meeting with a scheduled time and date was more appropriate, however, they declined my request."

Colton scoffs and steps out from behind me, raising his chin and squaring his shoulders, looking like the fucking man. "What you mean is that the board of directors, my board of directors decided to welcome themselves uninvited into my home and demand my presence."

Oh, shit. Shots fired.

"Mr. Carrington," an older gentleman says, standing second from the left with a pissed off scowl etched across his face. "We have granted you a week of grieving out of respect for your father but enough is enough. You are a child and we need to work out how we're going to run our business from here on out."

Colton laughs. "You mean *my* business."

Each one of their expressions darken, and it's damn clear that these old men don't appreciate having their futures dictated by an eighteen-year-old high school student who may or may not even want anything to do with this business. For all they know, Colton could be intent on running this shit into the ground.

An intense silence follows, none of them willing to step-up and challenge Colton. They clearly have an agenda in mind and from the way Colton casually stands beside me, he was expecting this.

"Alright," Colton finally says. "We may discuss what is going to happen from here on out. Harrison, please take them through to the formal living area and offer tea or coffee while Oceania prepares the board room."

The fuck?

Harrison nods again. "Yes, sir."

With that, he turns on his heel and gestures for the six intimidating men to follow him as Colton waits, watching them go. I remain right by his side until the men are out of sight before turning on him. "Umm … what the fuck was that about?"

Colton turns and starts heading for the stairs and I follow right behind. "How's that any of your business?"

"Well, you just demanded that I prepare a board room that I didn't even know you had on a day where I'm not scheduled to work and haven't had even two seconds of sleep, so yeah, if you want me to move, then you better fill me in on some details."

Colton reaches the top of the stairs and continues to his bedroom, letting out a heavy sigh. "They're the board of Carrington Incorporated. Dad's biggest business. It pulls in almost triple the amount of revenue of any other business in its field."

"Okay, so what do they want with you?"

"They want to intimidate me to hand over control so they can reallocate the way profits are shared."

"No shit. So, this is a ploy to line their pockets."

"Welcome to my world," he grumbles, pushing through to his bedroom. "But their pockets are already lined. Thanks to my father, their pockets are overflowing but with bastards like that, it's never enough."

"You don't think they just don't want someone a quarter of their age coming in and fucking everything up?"

Colton stops and steps into his closet, heading for his impressive line of suits while peeling his tank over his head. "Listen up and listen good, Jade. Don't fucking doubt me. I'm not going to fuck anything up. Believe it or not, I actually know what I'm doing. You don't grow up with a father like Charles Carrington and not learn how to fuck with a bunch of greedy board members. My father earned this position. Now, are you going to get your ass downstairs and prepare the board room or not? You do work for me, right?"

I scoff and watch as his eyes slice back to mine. "You listen up and you listen good, Carrington," I say repeating his words back to him. "I worked for your father, not for you. If you expect this shit to continue, then you're going to have to make it worth my while. You're not exactly the kind of boss that I'd willingly work under."

He groans. "What do you want?"

I smirk, leaning against the frame of his closet door, knowing all the cards are in my hands. "I want both mine and mom's base rates doubled."

Colton scoffs. "No way. Your mom already receives a high rate.

"And she deserves every cent, wouldn't you agree? I know you've seen how hard she works. She busted her ass for your dad and now she's doing the same for you. Not to mention that you've never once said thank you or even given her a smile."

Colton pulls a grey suit from the line and my face scrunches at his choice. He lets out a sigh. "Fine. Anything else?"

"Yeah, you can double Maryne's as well. She's a badass bitch and has put up with your shit for too long."

"You realize no other housekeeper or staff member in all of Bellevue Springs makes that kind of money?"

"I know," I say. "But the maids all talk and I know that Milo's housekeeper earns a better rate than my mom and has better hours. Oh, and has a boss who isn't an ass and because of that, your dad got a bad rep of being a stingy bastard. You don't want that to be you, do you?"

Colton groans as I step into his closet and pull out a new suit before taking the other out of his hands. "What are you saying, Jade?"

I shrug my shoulders. "I'm not saying anything, just subtly

suggesting that a review of the complete staff wages is probably in order, and considering the whole damn world knows what kind of status and money you have, I'd suggest an increase for everyone. After all, appreciative workers result in a better job done. Though, I'd consider leaving Harrison's right where it is. He could use a few hits to his ego, but I'll leave that to your discretion."

"The fuck?" he grunts. "You want me to give the whole staff an increase? Do you have any idea how many people work here?"

"I do, and I also know that you probably make enough money per second to cover it."

"That's beside the point."

"No, that's exactly the point."

He lets out a groan. "You know what? Don't worry about it. I'll call Maryne in early to set up the board room."

I suck in a breath. "You know damn well that she has her niece's dance recital this morning and that she's been looking forward to it all week."

"Fine. Your mom will do it."

"You're going to get her out of bed on the one day she's had off in nearly three weeks. I know she'll do it but I'll be kicking your ass if you even tried it."

A frustrated huff pulls from within him as he watches me go around his closet, picking out a button-down shirt, shoes, cufflinks, and a Rolex. I lay it all out for him, knowing damn well that he's going to look like a fucking treat. "Fine," he finally says. "I'll have my accountant do a complete review and have her adjust yours, Maryne's, and Maria's rates to reflect a permanent doubled rate."

A beaming smile rips across my face and I step up into Colton's warm body and press a kiss to his cheek, watching as his eyes soften. "Thank you," I whisper. "You have no idea what kind of difference that's going to make in my mom's life."

"Just hurry up and get your ass in that boardroom. I don't want to keep those fuckers waiting."

"Maybe you should keep them waiting," I suggest. "Pissed off men have a way of fucking up when they think someone doesn't value their importance. But just a word of advice, don't be such a pushover in there. I just got exactly what I wanted without even batting an eyelash when I would have done it for free had you just said please."

His expression hardens once again and I step away from him. I get to the door of his closet and look back. "Oh, and maybe take a shower and brush your teeth. You smell like shit."

He walks toward me and without warning, drops his lips to mine. "I'll shower but I'm not brushing my teeth. I want to keep your sweet taste on my lips all fucking day."

Heat floods me and he steps past me, knowing damn well that he just got the last word without even trying, leaving me completely shook. I guess we both got a little something out of this meeting.

Colton disappears into his bathroom, leaving the door wide open as he loses his pants. I tear my eyes away from his smirking reflection in the mirror that showcases every part of his perfectly toned and hard body and stick to my part of the deal.

I fly out of his room and as I'm dashing down the stairs, I find

Harrison walking up them. "The board members are seated in the formal living space," he informs me. "Please offer them a beverage before starting in the boardroom."

I roll my eyes, both of us knowing damn well that Colton had asked Harrison to take care of the tea and coffee. "Alright," I say, also knowing that I'm about to shuffle that job off to one of the maids. "Where's the board room and what exactly entails setting it up for a meeting with the board members?"

For once, Harrison is straight with me and leaves all the bullshit behind, knowing how important this meeting is going to be. If Colton fucks this up, then he could lose everything that his father had worked towards.

I get right on it and half an hour later, Harrison is leading the board members into the room while I quickly finish up. They all take their seats, leaving the head of the table empty for Colton.

A smug grin stretches over my face, knowing that having Colton in that seat is going to grate on their nerves the whole way through the meeting.

Colton strides in a moment later looking like fucking fire. My mouth waters as he wears the suit I'd picked out for him like a fucking boss. He walks right up to his seat and looks around the men sitting before him. "Gentlemen," he says, not bullshitting around.

Colton takes his seat, his eyes briefly flicking across to me as I fill seven glasses of water and begin handing them around the table. "Let's get this meeting underway."

One of the men scoff and I can't help but notice how similar this man looks to Charlie. "I think not," he says. "We will wait until your incompetent help has completed her tasks, but if you ask me, she should have been finished ages ago." he looks at me. "Are you not aware that my time means money? If I'm going to be wasting my time on a girl like you, you better be making it worth my time."

Fucking bastard. I don't give a shit who he is. After what happened with Jude, no one in this world will get away with sexualizing me.

I give him a pleasant smile as Colton's eyes darken at the way he addressed me. "I apologize," I say, reaching for a glass of water to place down in front of him and accidentally spilling it all over the bastard. "Oh, no," I gasp, hurrying for a napkin to mop up the spilled water. "How clumsy of me."

The big version of Charlie flies up out of his chair and the men around him scurry to save the paperwork laid out on the table. "OUT NOW, YOU INCOMPETENT FOOL," he hollers, raising his hand.

It flies toward my face but Colton is there a second later, catching his hand and holding it out like a steel vice. "Touch her and I will end you. I don't give a shit that your son is my best friend." He looks around at all the men. "That goes for all of you. Oceania is mine to deal with how I see fit. If I say she remains in this damn room, then she remains. Is that understood?"

They all nod and I watch in amazement as these executive businessmen fold to his will like little bitches. Colton looks back to Charlie's father with an intense stare that demands respect and has everything south of my border clenching. "Now, I suggest you sit your ass down so I can get this bullshit excuse of a meeting underway."

He narrows his eyes at Colton and after a moment of hesitation, he finally relents and takes his seat.

Colton turns and starts walking back toward the head of the table and as he does, his eyes come to mine and man is he pissed, but there's also a hint of amusement. My arousal is as clear as day and I know he sees it which only makes his eyes flame with need.

'Stay' he mouths as he passes me.

My back straightens. Stay? What the fuck? Why the hell would he want me to stay? It's not as though I can offer anything to this meeting. I don't even know what Carrington Incorporated is or what it does—nor do I care to. There must be another reason he wants me to stay, so I keep myself looking busy for as long as possible.

Colton reaches the head of the table and instead of taking a seat, he leans over it. He presses his knuckles against the hardwood and stares down at his board members, refusing to remain on the same level as them. "Let's keep this short and sweet," he starts, the authority in his tone having me nearly dropping to my knees and ready to submit to his every wish. "You're all here assuming that I've spent the last week mourning my father's death, claiming that you've waited out of respect for my father, but you're going to listen and you're going to listen well."

There's a short pause where his eyes flick to my grin when he uses those exact words. His disloyal subjects stare, patiently waiting to hear whatever Colton has to say and damn it, I'm waiting with bated breath as well. I know Harrison is standing just outside the door listening just as intently, all of us dying to see if our boy has what it takes to truly dominate in this world.

I stop what I'm doing and give him my full attention, listening to every last word.

"You underestimated me. My father spent every spare second he had training me for this exact position. I know every damn business deal he made, every fucked up decision, and every deal made on the side. I know dollar amounts, I know every dodgy lie told to get those deals across the line, including every last thing you bastards have done over the years to keep your positions." he slowly looks around the table, pointing out each one. "Embezzlement. Fraud. Child labor. Prostitutes. Affairs. Perjury. Not one of your hands are clean. Charles Carrington appointed me to be his sole heir to continue what he built, what his father grew, and what my great-grandfather started from the ground up. This business has been in Carrington hands for over a hundred years and I'd be damned to let it go to a bunch of pricks like you.

"You made a mistake assuming that I've spent the last week devastated by the loss of Charles Carrington. I haven't. My father was a bastard and he will rot in hell, but that doesn't mean that I'm about to allow you bastards to come into my home and railroad me out of here. I'm in charge now and things are going to be done my way. If you don't like it, then you can leave. So, tell me," he says, dropping into his chair and relaxing back into it. "Are we going to have a problem here?"

The men look around, each of them equally as unsure as the next. The one who had been accused of fraud clears his throat. "No, Mr. Carrington. There are no problems here."

"Good. Now, as Roderick pointed out, time is money and if you're all done wasting mine, we need to work out how we're going to move forward."

Well damn.

Colton Carrington is a fucking boss and I don't think I've ever had so much respect for him.

CHAPTER 12

I stare down at the Bellevue Springs Private uniform on my bed with a few too many questions running through my head, each of them demanding attention and giving me the worst migraine in history.

One. Where the fuck did it come from?

Two. Who the hell actually decided that I'll be going to that school today?

Three. Where the hell is Colton Carrington so I can kick his stupid ass?

For me to have a uniform would mean that the fees have been paid. For the fees to be paid, it had to have come from one very rich eighteen-year-old, and I don't know how I feel about that.

It's one thing for Charles to pay my fees for BSA, but Colton? I don't know. It's weird. Demeaning almost. There's no way in hell mom and I would be able to afford to pay him back, like ever. It's insane. What kind of shitty investment is that on his part? I hope he's not running his father's businesses like that otherwise he can wave goodbye to those billions that keep him toasty warm at night.

Realizing that I don't have much choice, I get myself dressed and look at myself in the full-length mirror. I hate it. It's similar to my old uniform with the blouse and pleated skirt. But instead of the soft grey that complimented my skin, the skirt is an off-pink with a weird checkered pattern and no damn pockets. What school uniform doesn't come equipped with pockets? Where am I supposed to hide my phone?

I check the time and realize that I should probably get a move on. I'm not exactly sure what time this school starts but if I take my first day at BSA into consideration when Colton had driven by the girl's school and we'd seen them all just arriving, I'd say we're working on a similar schedule.

I walk into the main house and stop by the staff quarters to grab something to take for lunch and find myself smiling as I bump into Maryne who holds out a packed lunch all ready for me to take. "Thank you," I murmur, truly appreciating how wonderful she's been to me and mom since the very second we showed up here.

Maryne nods and gets back to work as though she didn't just soften my stone-cold heart. I laugh it off and make myself a coffee before deciding on one more stop.

I walk through the house, sipping on my too-hot coffee and wishing I had time to go back and add a little more milk to the mix.

I grab hold of the door handle and throw it open to find Colton sitting behind his father's desk, staring at his computer screen. He raises a brow as I walk in and before he has a chance to get a word out, I hit him with it.

"What the fuck is this?" I demand, gesturing down my body at the ridiculous, pocketless uniform. "I told you I didn't want you getting involved."

He leans back in his chair and watches me as though I'm the most entertaining creature he's ever come across. "I told you I was going to sort it out."

"Are you serious?" I screech, throwing my hands up and somehow avoiding spilling my coffee all over my brand new expensive private girl uniform. "Do you not remember the part where I specifically asked you not to do anything?"

His face scrunches as though he's actually thinking about what we'd discussed during the extremely early hours of Saturday morning. Though to be fair, I can't exactly be accountable for remembering shit people tell me in the middle of the night. "You see, I remember a lot of things from that conversation," he starts. "But nothing about you being a whiny bitch. I must have forgotten that part after you showed me what you could do with your tongue."

"Fuck you. You're such an ass," I tell him, wondering how he somehow pulled a smile out of me despite calling me a whiny bitch, but I have to admit, that's not the only reaction he manages to get out of me. Need shoots through my veins and a flash of desperation comes over me as I recall the feel of his heavy cock inside my mouth. I quickly file the thought away for later. If I want to give him a verbal smackdown, then I need to keep my mind out of the gutter, no matter how badly I want it there.

Colton shrugs his shoulders as though being called an ass isn't anything new, and honestly, it probably isn't. "What are you going to do about it?"

I square my shoulders and step right up to the front of his desk. "You need to undo it. I'd prefer to go to the public school."

His lips pull into a grin. "No."

"No?" I demand. "What the hell do you mean no?"

"I mean just that. No. I'm not going to fix it. You're going to BSP now."

"Oh, I'm sorry. I must have missed the part where it became your decision and you were handed the right to decide what's best for my future. Just fill me in on how that happened."

"Okay," he says, his grin stretching wider. "Appease me. Tell me how the hell you think it's going to work with you going to a public school? You do realize that the closest public school is a forty-five-minute drive from here?"

Shit. Forty-five minutes? I didn't exactly know that.

"I have a driver's license. I'm not completely useless."

"That's great. Do you have a car?"

My face falls. I should have thought that one through before throwing it out there like that. "You know I don't have a car."

"So, assuming you're too proud to let me buy you one, what's your next genius plan?"

"Bus."

"Come on, now," he laughs. "Now you're just making a mockery. You know busses don't come out this way, and you can bet your sweet ass that I'm not about to let you walk that far every day."

"Let?" I demand.

"Seriously. That's what you want to argue about right now? You know damn well I'm not going to watch you walk out the door every day knowing it'll take you at least three hours to get to school, and I know you're not stupid enough to assume that I'm going to drive you. You have no other options. Despite the size of the balls you think you have, you can't go to BSA, so your only option is BSP."

My shoulders sag in defeat. He's right. I have no other option. If I want to finish school and graduate, then I have to go to BSP and put up with the bitchy girls. It's only another five months. I can do it. Hell, I put up with the boys for a month, the girls should be a piece of cake.

I drop down onto the chair opposite his desk, the same one I've sat in time and time again when barging in on Charles, and somehow being extended the time in his day to listen to my fucked up problems. I look up at the man who is quickly becoming a massive part of my life. "I really have no other options?"

He shakes his head. "Not unless you'd prefer to drop out."

"No," I say, my defeat starting to get the best of me. "I want to make something of myself."

Pride shines through Colton's eyes and it makes everything tingle within me. He goes to say something when a moronic dipshit comes flying through the door and ruins whatever moment we were about to have.

"Yo," Charlie says, barging through the door and making himself comfortable in the seat beside me. He looks up and down my body before his brows pinch. "What's going on? What the fuck are you wearing?"

"Oh, you didn't hear?" I question, laying the sarcasm on thick. "I'm going to BSP now."

His face scrunches as Colton scoffs. "Fuck off, Charlie. You know damn well that she goes to BSP now. Stop stirring shit."

I narrow my eyes at Charlie and fall against the backrest of the chair. "You're such an ass," I tell him, holding up the mug in my hand. "You're so freaking lucky that I'm halfway through my coffee otherwise your head would be shoved so far up Colton's ass that he'd have to birth you just to get you out."

Colton's face twists with discomfort as Charlie pulls back. "That bad, huh?"

"That freaking bad."

"Damn. You're not even a little excited?"

I wave my hand around my face. "Do I look excited?"

Colton grins. "Who would know? Are you even capable of getting a smile past that resting bitch face of yours?"

I pick up a notepad and launch it across his office, scowling as he catches it with a laugh. "Why don't you try being a decent human being and we'll see?"

His eyes sparkle with the challenge but I'd be a fool to assume he's just going to miraculously learn how to become a decent person overnight. Though, I know he's pretty good at pretending.

"Well," Charlie says, his eyes focusing on my new uniform. "If it counts for anything, you look fucking hot. All you need is a lollipop and your hair in pigtails and you'll look like one of the girls from those sexy schoolgirl porns."

My glare sharpens on him. "You did not just tell me that I look like a fucking whore."

His eyes bug out of his head as he looks back at me. "No. I didn't, at least, I don't think I did."

Colton laughs, watching as his friend grows more uncomfortable by the second. "Ahh, yeah. You kinda did."

"Fuck, babe. I didn't mean it like that. I was just trying to say that you look good."

"Yeah, yeah. We get your point," Colton says, clearly having enough of hearing what his friend thinks about me in uniform, though watching the jealousy creep into his eyes is a little entertaining. I could push the matter but I don't exactly want to start another war while things are just starting to get good.

"What are you doing here anyway? I didn't realize that you knew the clock started before 9 am."

Charlie looks across at Colton. "Thought I'd just check in and remind this bastard that at some point, he's going to have to actually turn up at school. Can't be a fucking CEO if you can't finish high school. I doubt those board members are going to put up with him long if he doesn't even look like he's attempting to get a college degree."

My brow arches as I meet Colton's eyes only to find him mere seconds away from telling Charlie to fuck off. "It's fine, bro, but stop acting as though you're here checking up on my well-being when it's damn clear that you're hoping to give Jade a ride to school."

Charlie has the audacity to actually look bashful and the fire that burns in Coltons eyes is nearly enough to have Charlie dead on the spot. He looks at me with a grin. "I mean, he's not wrong."

"You realize that Milo picks me up every day, right?"

"Really?"

I nod and Charlie quickly pulls out his phone, presses a few buttons, and puts it to his ear. "Yo, Milo," he says a moment later. "I've got Ocean today." There's a short pause before he says a quick goodbye and turns back to me. "Looks like you'll be needing that ride after all."

"So, you're just assuming that I'm going to allow pricks like yourselves to make decisions on my behalf? What if I wanted to walk today? What if I have an aversion to cherry red Ferraris? What if I don't want some guy dropping me off at my new school just so he can shake his dick in front of the whole female student body?"

Charlie's eyes glisten with laughter. "What if I just wanted to shake my dick in front of you?"

The need to look at Colton shoots through me but I resist. "Then I'd be under a moral obligation to say been there, done that."

Charlie's face falls. "No. Don't wound me like that."

"Alright," Colton says, sitting up in his chair. "Get the fuck out of here before your bullshit chatter makes her late for school."

Charlie laughs. "You suddenly care if she makes it to school on time?" Colton's eyes flash to mine and this time, Charlie doesn't miss a thing. "Wait. You do care," he says, looking between us both. "There's something … what's going on here? How are you two sitting in the same room without blood splattered over the wall? Did something happen? Is something going on between you two?"

I scoff as Colton laughs. "In her fucking dreams."

I glare at Colton and this time it's as real as it comes. "Speak for yourself. You're the one who's had a boner for me since the second you saw me."

He rolls his eyes. "Like you can talk. Everywhere I go, you're right there with those fucking eyes on me. I see you. You can't fucking stop. You want to, but you can't."

My eyes narrow. Do I need to remind him that he's always the one who comes to me? He's the one who led me up to the library and he's the one who couldn't resist kissing me. I mean, I've had a few slip-ups of my own where I go seeking him out, but it's usually done in a fit of rage after he's done something to get under my skin.

"Okaaaay," Charlie says, standing and offering me his hand. "I'm going to get you out of here before this bullshit goes somewhere none of us want it to go." I reluctantly take his hand and he pulls me to my feet. "If you behave, I might even stop by Starbucks and get you a proper coffee."

Well, shit. That cheered me right up.

"What are you waiting for?" I question, smiling up at him. "Lead the way."

Charlie grins like he's just won the lottery, but then, I guess winning the lottery wouldn't be as exciting to these guys as it would be to me. I let him pull me along and as we step through the door, I can't help but glance back at Colton who's staring at the way Charlie holds my hand.

His eyes raise and meet mine and a million messages pass between us but as his lips lift into a secretive grin and he winks, I die.

He speaks right to my soul and everything clenches within me. It's as though he just became the pussy whisperer.

Good lord. I've never seen anything so attractive.

I stop walking, needing a moment to recover, and with Colton out of view, I fall against the wall, trying to catch my breath. I fight the need to run back in there and straddle his waist while giving him everything I've got.

"Woah, babe. Are you okay?" Charlie asks, looking back at my struggle in a panic.

"Oh, ummm … yeah." Shit. "Just a little dizzy is all. I haven't had a chance to eat anything yet. It's probably just that."

Charlie beams back at me with excitement sparkling in his eyes. "Well, I guess I get to feed you as well. It can be a date."

I let out a heavy sigh.

Fuck me.

Twenty minutes later, Charlie pulls away from Starbucks and as we get closer to Bellevue Spring Private, he grows quiet. As a general rule, Charlie Bryant is never quiet.

"Spit it out, Charlie," I say as I try to stop dying over the fact that

I'm in a Ferrari right now. I mean, wow. It's got nothing on the Veneno but I'm never going to get bored of this shit.

He looks across at me and scrunches his face before turning back to the road. "It's nothing."

"Charlie. We're going to pull up at BSP in less than three minutes so you have until then to get whatever answers you're looking for, otherwise, it's going to be stewing on your mind all day."

"Fuck," he sighs. "I hate when you're right."

"Get used to it, Hot Sauce, I usually am."

He rolls his eyes but I can't help but notice the grin that spreads wide across his face at being called Hot Sauce, and truth be told, watching him like that makes me want to do it again and again. I wonder what other bullshit names I can come up with that'll make him blush.

"Stop it," he laughs. "If you insist on having a nickname for me, it's going to be Wild Stallion."

"Wild Stallion," I say, testing the words on my lips and watching as his eyes heat with excitement. "I don't know. I think I prefer Hot Sauce."

He shakes his head as though he's never been so offended in his life before taking a deep breath and glancing back at me. "Don't hate me, okay?"

My mood plummets and I narrow my eyes on him. "What did you do?"

"No, it's not like that. I just have to ask you something and I want you to be real with me."

I catch his eyes and it all becomes too obvious. He's giving me that same look that he had during the masquerade party when he was watching me and Colton dance so I start preparing my answer before he gets a chance to let the words fly.

"I just … are you and Colton a thing? Are you fucking him?"

Okay, that's not exactly what I was thinking he was going to ask but at least we're in the same ballpark. Once the shock wears off, I stare at him blankly. "Excuse me?"

He cringes. "I warned you not to hate me."

I let out a sigh and decide to be real with him. "No, we're not fucking," I tell him, grazing straight over the other things that we may or may not be doing. "But how is that any of your business?"

"Because you're my business."

"I'm really not, Charlie. We hooked up once."

He looks away. "You like him though?"

Now I look away, not wanting to discuss this with him. Hell, I hardly wanted to discuss it with my boys. "I might."

"Would I be overstepping a line if I asked you to keep your legs closed for a while?"

Okay, how can I not stare at him now? "You wouldn't be just overstepping the line, Charlie. You'd be fucking bounding over it and pissing on everything as you went."

He cringes and falls silent.

"Just ask me what it is you want to ask?" I challenge as he approaches the front of the school.

Charlie lets out a sigh and pulls up out the front before putting his car in park and turning to look at me. "I want to be with you, Ocean. Having one random fuck on my friend's couch isn't enough for me. I want more. I want to see you every fucking day and it damn near kills me seeing you getting closer to Colton. I've been holding back because I see it in him. He looks at you like you're his fucking sun, moon, and the whole damn sky, but if he's going to keep pushing you away and not make a move, then I'm not going to keep holding back."

I stare at him, not expecting him to have been so forward. "I … I don't even know what to say to that. You know I like you. Apart from Milo, you're probably the nicest person I've met in Bellevue Springs. But we just fucked once. It was for fun."

"I know," he says. "But can't it be more than just fun? I know you've got something happening with Milo, but come on, be real, babe. It's clear that's just some cover-up to keep Colton off your back. You don't belong with him."

"And what? Am I supposed to belong with you?"

"I know a trap when I see one, Ocean. I'm not about to tell you where you belong only to have it blow up in my face because you're the only person who can decide where you belong, but if you want an honest answer, then yeah, I think you belong with me."

"You don't Charlie. I'm just the first girl who isn't interested in all the shiny things you could offer me. I'm the one who could piss off mommy and daddy while also rocking your world. We aren't a forever thing. We were just having a little fun."

He sits back and I expect him to be disappointed but he flashes a blinding smile my way. "I think you're wrong," he says, almost like a challenge. "And I'm going to prove it."

"Oh, geez. Dare I ask how you're going to do that?"

"You can ask but I'm not going to tell you."

"Why? Because you haven't figured it out yet?"

His cocky grin fades away and is replaced with a guilty one. "Maybe. Now hurry up and get out of my car. I'm not being the reason that you're late for your first day."

I can't help but lean over and press a kiss to his cheek. "You can go ahead and try to win me over," I tell him. "My answer is always going to be no, but it's going to be fun watching you try."

Charlie rolls his eyes as I scoop my coffee out of the cup holder. "Fuck off, babe."

I laugh and let myself out of his Ferrari and start making my way into the school, noticing how he doesn't drive away until I step through the front gates.

I let out a heavy breath. It's one thing dealing with Colton and Charlie first thing in the morning, but walking into this school is going to be something entirely different.

The school is big. Maybe even bigger than BSA but I try not to let that intimidate me. I've got this. If I survived through an all-boys school then surely I can make it through this too.

There are girls everywhere and they instantly start staring. The whispers come next and while they're bitchy, they're not catcalls about wanting to fuck or comments on my tits, pussy, or ass, and because of that, I find myself falling right into place.

"Ocean! Hey," a voice calls out.

I spin around, not having expected to know anyone here, and dread instantly floods me. It's the girl from the boat and from Colton's party and I still haven't figured out her damn name. She crashes into me, throwing her arms around my waist and pulling me in for a quick hug. "I didn't know you were coming here now. How are you?"

"Hey," I say, finding myself pleasantly surprised by how happy I feel to see her again. "I'm good. To be honest, I didn't really know I was coming here either. I just found the uniform on my bed this morning."

"Damn, that would have come as a shock."

"You're telling me," I laugh.

She loops her arm through mine and starts pulling me deeper into the school. "Well not to worry. I made this school my bitch on day one. I've got you covered."

She leads me into a hallway filled with lockers on either side, but unlike BSA, these look as though they haven't been tortured by a bunch of raging, testosterone-filled boys and it's kind of refreshing.

The further down the hall we get, the louder the bitchiness becomes and my unnamed friend pulls me closer to her side. "Don't worry about them. The second they realize that you're practically the Carrington whisperer, they'll be bowing at your feet. I swear, Colton has the best parties and these bitches are dying for an invite."

Well, I guess that's good to know. I could use that to my advantage, only I'm not sure how I feel about being responsible for bringing other chicks into Colton's world. Call me a jealous, insecure loser if you must, but I kinda like being the sole torturer in his world.

She brings me to a stop and within seconds, girls are flooding around us. "Hey, Drix. Who's this?"

Drix? What the hell kind of name is that?

"This is Ocean," she beams as though she's introducing her new baby girl to the world for the very first time. "She's practically a sister to Colton. Lives with him and everything."

Mouths drop as I cringe from the term 'sister.' "Ohmygod, ohmygod, ohmygod. You know Colton?"

Annnd … so it starts.

Girls start begging for my attention and just like that, I become the most popular girl in school and I don't know whether I should be happy or terrified about it.

Drix gets rid of the girls and soon enough we're left with just her close circle of friends. A girl leans in and offers me her hand, something I'm starting to realize is just the formal manners these girls have been brought up with. "Hey, I'm Jess. I think I met you at that party. At least, I think it was you. Did you give me a tattoo?"

My eyes bug out of my head. I fucking knew that shit was going to catch up to me. "Ummm, possibly."

"Oh, shit. Don't look so freaked out. I love it."

The bell sounds and Jess rolls her eyes. "Shit, I better go. I have Mrs. Mirran taking over my homeroom this week and if I even think about being late she'll whoop my ass." Drix laughs and Jess looks back at me. "Listen, stick with us alright. With me and Hendrix at your side, you'll be good. We can hook you up."

Hendrix, huh? I kinda like that. It suits her. I had her pegged as a

Katie or a Tara, but I like her originality, it suits her willingness to step outside of the box and be the one girl who was willing to approach the new girl and make my day a little more bearable. She did it on the boat and at the party and for that, I'm grateful.

With that, Jess scurries away and I meet Drix's eyes. "Come on," she says, looping her arm through mine once again. "I'll show you to the student office to get your orientation pack and then you can tell me why Charlie Bryant was dropping you off."

CHAPTER 13

This afternoon has sucked.

I walked through the doors of the Carrington mansion feeling like a complete idiot. Milo and I didn't exactly have a chance to speak today after Charlie intervened this morning, so Milo had assumed I didn't need a ride home.

Big fucking mistake.

Day one of being a private school girl was exhausting, and then getting to the end of the day only to find myself walking was a pain in the ass. I should have called him during the day to say hi and ask if he could swing by to pick me up. He would have said yes and I would have been saved the torture of getting my own way home.

Freaking Charlie. I know he didn't intentionally mean for that to happen, though, maybe he did. Maybe he was hoping for me to call him, desperately needing him to save my ass and give him the chance to be my hero.

Yeah fucking right. I'd rather walk than give in to him like that. Don't get me wrong, Charlie is an absolute sweetheart. He really is one of the nicest guys I've met in Bellevue Springs and not to mention, he's an absolute fireball when making his way around the female anatomy, but apart from that, there's nothing. To me, he's just like one of my boys and I'm not prepared to go and screw up a good thing when I know it's not going to go any further than just great sex.

Charlie needs a little spitfire who's going to put stars in his eyes. He deserves to find the real deal and soon enough, he's going to realize that it's not me. I'm too messed up to be his girl. He's not dark enough, not tough enough. Not that I need a man by my side, but if I had to pick one, it's going to be one who's not afraid to get his hands dirty, a real alpha who's not going to hold back, and who's not afraid to tell me no. I need a strong, fierce man, not a boy who's still playing games.

I make my way around the kitchen, getting everything ready for dinner as mom cleans up after another long day of work. "How was your first day of school?" she calls from the bathroom, speaking over the sound of the water as she washes her hands. "Did you meet any nice girls?"

"I guess," I call back. "They were alright. Though, they're more interested in how I can get them closer to Colton than actually getting to know me."

I hear mom's heavy sigh as she walks out of the bathroom and appears back in the kitchen. "That's a shame," she says, grabbing our plates and taking them over to the table. "Just give it a few weeks and you'll be able to weed out the good eggs from the bad ones."

"I hope so. There was one girl, Hendrix, who I met a few weeks ago. She seems alright. She's no Nic though."

Mom turns her back but not before I see her subtle eye roll. "You can't keep putting Nic so high up on that pedestal. He's just a regular boy, just like the rest of them," she tells me. "One day you're going to realize this."

"I've never really understood your aversion to Nic. He was great until he cheated, but as a friend, he's always been amazing."

"He has," she agrees, coming back to the kitchen counter for the cutlery and soda. "But I want better for you. I want you to have more than a shitty dead-end job, living in a town that's overrun by crime, and coming home each night to a man who has blood on his hands. Do I need to remind you that Nic will be taking over for his father soon enough and I don't want a target like that on your back. The West Side Wolves would do anything to stop Nic getting into power because they know he's a game-changer. Just because he has his head screwed on properly, doesn't make him the right boy for you."

"So, what kind of boy is the right one for me?"

"Someone who is going to let you fly, not the one who wants to keep you caged. The right one for you is not afraid to let you go because if he truly is your soulmate, he'll know that you'll come back to him. A man who keeps you caged doesn't love you for you, he loves what you can offer him. A man who keeps a woman caged sees her as only a possession and not an equal."

I stare at the back of my mother's head as she goes about setting the table and I can't help but wonder if she's right. Is that how she thinks Nic really is? Does he care more about me as a possession than as the love of his life? He tells me all the time that he wants me back, but why? He cheated. Clearly he didn't feel that what we had as a couple was something worth treasuring, so why fight so hard for it?

I put the lid back on the pan to keep the leftover pasta warm as mom drops down into her chair at the table. I start making my way toward her, lost inside my thoughts when a knock sounds at the door, making my heart leap right out of my chest.

I spin around, finding Colton standing awkwardly in our doorway and I gape at him, not because I'm surprised to find him here, but because I was so lost inside my thoughts on Nic's possessive behavior that I didn't even notice Colton cut in front of the massive floor to ceiling windows to get to the door.

Mom flies to her feet, desperately trying to be respectful of our rich prick boss who stands in our doorway. "Mr. Carrington," she says, her eyes going wide with fear, instantly assuming that she's in trouble for something. "Is everything alright? Did I forget to do something?"

"Oh, no. Everything is perfect, Maria," he insists, waving off her worry. His eyes briefly flick to mine before looking back at mom. "I was actually wondering if I could join you for dinner?"

The fuck?

"Oh, of course," Mom says, her eyes going wide before she begins fussing around trying to make space for him. I gawk at him awkwardly as he steps through the doorway and heads for the table, wondering what his game plan is. "Did you not like the meal that was left out for you? I can prepare something else and let the chefs know to remove tonight's options from their rotation. I'll just need a moment—"

"No, no, no," he rushes out, giving mom a warm smile. "It's nothing like that at all. It's just …" he lets out a soft sigh before looking back at mom. "I used to eat with dad every night and now that he's gone …"

"You're alone," I whisper, finishing his sentence.

Colton's gaze comes back to mine and he presses his lips into a firm line before finally nodding.

Mom sucks in a sharp gasp before flying across the room and enveloping him in her arms. "I'm so sorry, my sweet boy," she says, holding him tight as his eyes widen in confusion. "I should have been more thoughtful. It must get so lonely in that big house by yourself."

"It certainly has its moments."

Mom pulls back and gives him some space to move before pulling out a chair at the table and offering it to him. "You can join us whenever you want, Colton. My table is your table."

"Thank you, Mrs. Munroe. It's awfully kind of you to take me in like this. I hope I'm not intruding."

"No, not at all. I'm actually quite used to it," mom says. "With Ocean having her four boys, my dinner table was always filled with hungry bodies. I've actually been struggling to remember to cook less each night now that it's just me and Ocean."

"I can imagine."

"Yes, well Ocean …" Mom's eyes flick to mine. "OCEAN! What are you doing? Don't just stand there. Dish him up a plate. The poor boy must be starving."

The poor boy? Oh, no. She's got this all wrong. Colton Carrington is far from a poor boy. Wicked, lethal, dangerous, cocky, prick, sexy as sin. They're all the kinds of words that I would use to describe him. Definitely not poor. Not to mention, he also wouldn't know what starving would feel like. I bet he hasn't missed a single meal in his life.

Colton looks back at me and his lips pull up into a grin, realizing he's completely won my mother over with a sob story about being lonely in his big mansion. I don't doubt it. He probably is lonely, but the loneliness didn't start because his father died. It started way before that and I can guarantee that it doesn't bother him as much as he's putting on. If he was really that lonely, he could have called a million people who would have jumped at the chance to keep him company but instead, he chose to come here and have dinner with me and my mom.

He's up to something. There has to be an ulterior motive that's either going to embarrass or humiliate me, either way, I'm going to be ready for it. Though, there's also a slight chance that he's here hoping to screw my brains out.

As mom walks back around to her seat, I can't help but flip him off and enjoy the way his brow shoots straight up. His eyes darken and just like that, it's on.

How dare he play the lonely, broken billionaire and come in here and creep his way into my mother's heart. That's a twisted little game he's playing. If he breaks her, there'll be trouble.

"So, Colton," Mom says, giving him a warm smile as I reluctantly grab a bowl and dish up a serving of pasta. "Tell me about yourself."

"There's honestly not a lot to know," he says. "Mom and my sisters left when I was sixteen and never looked back so it's been just me and dad ever since. Well, me, dad, and whatever gold-digger he was sleeping with."

Mom's lips pull into a tight, sympathetic line and she reaches across the table to squeeze his hand. "I can't imagine how confusing and painful that would have been for a young boy. Do you keep in touch with them?"

He shakes his head. "Not really. You saw for yourself just how passionate they can be. Mom had originally taken me with her, but when dad came looking and I went with him, she turned her back on me too. She claims that I'm just like him."

I shake my head as I walk back to the table with his dinner. "You're nothing like your father," I tell him. "It doesn't take a genius to see that."

He looks up and meets my eyes as I slide the bowl down on the table in front of him. "Are you sure about that?" he murmurs low. "Because honestly, I don't know anymore."

I nod, captivated by his eyes, and unable to look away. "Yeah," I tell him, reaching out and dropping my hand to the back of his neck, curling my fingers into his dark hair. "You're nothing like him. He was ruthless and cruel, and yes, often you can be that way too, but under all your layers, you have a heart buried in there and I see so much in it. You've protected me from the bullshit, dark world of Bellevue Springs every step of the way despite the way I've constantly pushed you away. You're a good one, Colton, you just have to believe it."

Colton's hand raises to my lower back. "You're worth protecting, Jade."

Mom's throat clears and our eyes go wide before our hands are torn away from each other. "Is there something going on here that I need to be aware of?"

"No," I rush out as Colton's eyes fall heavily to his bowl of pasta.

His lips press into a tight line before he looks up at my mother. "This pasta looks great."

Fuck me. Could we be any more obvious?

Mom's eyes narrow on Colton before quickly flicking to mine, searching for confirmation, but she doesn't need it, she can see it clear as day. She just doesn't know how deep it runs. Hell, I don't even know how deep it runs.

I hastily scoop a forkful of pasta into my mouth, trying to act busy as mom's gaze settles back on Colton. She raises her chin, somehow becoming the boss. "Are you in love with my daughter, Colton?"

The pasta practically falls out of my mouth as Colton gapes at my mom. His eyes flick to mine before quickly settling back on Mom with a terror on his face that I didn't know he was capable of. "I, umm … No. Look, I'm not going to lie to you, Mrs. Munroe. I think your daughter is the most breathtaking thing I've ever had the pleasure of coming across. She's like a fireball, always ready to throw down and stand up for what she thinks is right, but no, I'm not in love with Ocean," he says before his brows pinch in confusion and he looks at me. "At least … not yet."

"NOT YET?" I shriek, gaping at him. "What the fuck is that? It's a simple no. No, you're not in love with me."

Colton laughs and for a brief moment I wonder if he said that just to fuck with me, but it becomes pretty damn clear that he simply doesn't know what the hell he's feeling, and any chance to mess with me in the process is a bonus.

"Wow," mom says, with a laugh, looking at me. "How could I have not seen this happening?"

"Because there's nothing to see happening," I say, refusing to look his way. "He might have accidentally kissed me once or twice, but it was … it was accidental. Nothing worth bringing up with my mother."

"Geez, thanks," Colton grunts.

Mom looks between us again. "Are you two … together?"

"Yep."

My head whips around to Colton so fast that I fear it might spin right off my shoulders. "What? You're insane if you think we're actually together. We can hardly stand each other and for the most part of the day, you're busy bossing me around while I remind you how much of an asshole you are."

"Don't act like getting all fired up every time you talk to me isn't the best part of your day."

I flop back against my seat and cross my arms over my chest, looking anywhere but at him. "You're impossible."

Colton laughs and casually holds out a hand toward mom. "Could you pass the salt?"

My jaw drops and I whip my head back to him. "Can you pass the salt?" I mimic, copying his carefree attitude. "You go and drop all these bombs at the dinner table and then hit Mom with a 'can you pass the salt?' You really are insane."

"I'm sorry," Colton says, looking back at mom. "Could you *please* pass the salt."

Oh, my God. I swear he's only here to torture me.

"Okay," Mom says. "Both of you need to shut up and eat your dinner before it gets cold, and then after dinner, Ocean, you need to give Nic a call and let him know what's going on before he finds out for himself."

I roll my eyes and pick up my fork once again. "Nic already knows," I tell her with a low groan. "Not that there's anything to know."

Mom lets out a soft sigh. "No wonder that boy's been coming around so much."

"Seriously?" I groan. "Can we just pretend this whole conversation never happened?"

"Yes, but don't think that we're not going to talk about this afterward."

My head drops into my hand and my leg shoots out under the table until it connects with Colton's shin. I watch from the corner of my eye as he jumps and whips his head back to me. "What the hell was that for?" he demands.

I narrow my eyes at him. "Oh, now you want to play stupid?"

"Alright," Mom says. "That's enough out of you two. Shut up and eat your dinner."

I gape at mom, surprised by her audacity to speak to Colton like that. After all, he is her boss, but I guess while she's off the clock he's just the guy who's been trying to put moves on her daughter while also doing his best to drive her insane. Though, from the entertained smirk on his face, he obviously doesn't care.

Having wasted enough time, we get stuck into our dinner and half an hour later, Colton stands beside me at the sink, passing me dishes to wash up as mom clears everything off the table.

His arm brushes against mine and every little touch sends electricity pulsing through my body. "You're an asshole, you know that right?"

Colton chuckles softly. "I know, but watching the panic in your eyes was too good to stop."

I groan and dunk another plate under the water and busily scrub it until it is sparkling clean. We get halfway through the dishes when Mom's phone chimes on the kitchen counter, indicating an incoming email. She scurries across the room and scoops it up before leaning on to the counter.

A soft smile spreads across Colton's face and it has me wondering if he already knows what just arrived in her inbox and I find myself leaning around him to watch her.

Mom quickly scans over the email as I feel my phone vibrate in my jeans pocket. I wipe my hands on the dish towel and am just about ready to pull my phone out of my pocket when Mom screeches with joy. Her loud squeal makes me jump and I look back at her to find her jumping up and down.

"Oh, thank you, thank you, thank you," she says a moment before slamming into Colton and giving him a tight hug.

"What is it?" I demand.

"Oh, Honey," Mom says, her eyes filling with tears and she falls away from Colton and drops into my arms, giving me the tightest squeeze. "Colton has doubled my salary."

"What?" I laugh, meeting his eyes over Mom's shoulder and realizing that there's no point in checking my phone as it's just going to be the same email that mom received from Colton's accountant. "That's incredible. Congratulations."

"Oh, my God, Honey," she whispers into my ear. "The things this could mean for us …" She lets out an emotion-filled sigh and pulls out of my arms before turning and looking back up at Colton. "This is incredible, but I can't accept it."

"You can and you will," he tells her.

Mom shakes her head in wonder. "I … I don't even know what to say. I just … why?"

Colton meets my eyes, both of us knowing exactly why this happened. I shake my head ever so slightly, hoping he's able to put his douchey tendencies to rest, if only for a second and tell her what I need him to, rather than admit that she got a raise because I demanded it on her behalf, risking everything.

He looks back at Mom and I hold my breath, the anticipation burning within me. "Because you deserve it," he finally says, putting me out of my misery. "With Dad gone, I thought it was a good time to review all the finances and decided that all the full-time staff could use a raise. The way my father has treated them over the years hasn't always been great and they should be compensated for that. But there were a select few who are here every day, busting their asses to make my life easier, and what better way to show my appreciation than offering them what they deserve? I see you, Mrs. Munroe, everything you do here. You're the best housekeeper we've had in years."

Tears brim in her eyes and she pulls Colton into another hug. "Are you sure this isn't just because you're trying to impress my daughter?"

"I seriously doubt that throwing money around is something that's going to impress a girl like Ocean."

Mom nods and pulls back. "You'd be right about that," she says. "So very right."

We get back into cleaning up and every few minutes, a small joyful laugh slips out of Mom, and every time it does, Colton grins to himself, making all sorts of happiness sweep through me.

We finish up and it's not long before Mom excuses herself to get ready for bed, leaving me with Colton staring down at me. His hands drop to my waist, just as they always do and I find myself leaning into him, bringing my hands to his wide chest and sliding them up around his neck while wondering what exactly is going on here. Are we more than just two people having a little fun while constantly at each other's throats? Are we together and I just don't know it? No. I don't know.

"What are you doing now?" he murmurs, letting his lips brush across mine.

I shrug my shoulders. "I don't know. I was maybe going to find another book to read."

His eyes darken. "You could always come and chill with me."

"Dare I ask what chilling with you entails?"

Colton laughs. "Honestly, when it comes to you, I have no fucking idea."

I can't help but laugh with him because he's never been so right. When it comes to this messed up relationship that continues to grow between us, every step has been taken in the dark. Something sobers within me and I raise my chin to gently press my lips against his. "Thank you," I whisper.

"For what?"

"Following through with the raise. You could have easily forgotten about it the second I walked out of your room, but you didn't."

"No, I didn't."

"You changed her life," I tell him. "I saw the way you were in the board meeting. You completely dominated it and I realized that you're not the kind of guy who will allow anyone to walk all over you, but I got exactly what I asked for and I hardly even put up a fight."

"Because I wanted that for you, but I needed you to take it. If I had just given it to you, you never would have accepted it. You needed to think that you did it on your own, and besides, you looked so damn proud of yourself. How could I have taken that away?"

His eyes remain on mine and something deepens between us but neither of us are ready to think about what it means. Instead, he reaches up and takes my hand, lacing his fingers through mine. "Come on," he says, pulling me toward the door. "Enough of this serious talk.

If it goes on any longer, one of us is going to accidentally start another war."

I laugh as I allow him to pull me along and soon enough we're dropping down onto the couch in the den before he draws me into his arms and for the first time, I truly feel like that's exactly where I belong.

CHAPTER 14

A grape flies through the air and I watch as Colton catches it in his mouth. He lays at the other end of the long couch, grinning back at me and looking more relaxed than I've seen him all week. "Strippers deserve the utmost respect, don't you think?" he questions with a grin, continuing with our conversation.

I cross my legs under myself as the movie plays on the screen, completely forgotten about. "I think so. Four of the girls I went to school with were stripping just so they could support themselves after their parents were either murdered or left them to fend for themselves. Putting yourself out there to be sexualized by men just to make a little cash couldn't be easy."

"Fair point," he says, raising his chin for another grape and catching it with ease when I launch it across the room. "What about male strippers?"

"Oh, hell. I have all the respect in the world for those guys. They can come through here and show off their talents any time they want," I laugh. "Though, I'm going to need to borrow a few dollar bills so I can make it rain."

"That's fine," he says with a wicked grin. "You can have all the dollar bills you want, but you're going to have to make your ass clap to get them."

I grab a handful of grapes and launch them across the room, every single one of them missing him completely. "I am not your personal stripper and besides, I don't think I'm even capable of making my ass clap."

"Trust me, Jade," he says, scooping a stray grape off the couch beside him and popping it into his mouth. "If you want to make your ass clap, then you can do it."

"I don't know whether to be touched by the faith you have in my abilities or disturbed by how sure you are about it."

Colton shrugs a shoulder and I watch as his eyes brim with joy. He waves his hand to the space in front of him. "Why don't you give it a try and save us all this wondering."

Another grape flies and he barks out a sharp laugh. "Would you quit throwing grapes at me?"

"Quit making crude comments and I won't have to."

His hands fly up in surrender. "Fine," he says. "I'll behave."

Yeah, right. Colton Carrington actually sticking to his word? I'll believe it when I see it. Though for some reason, he has my complete trust. If this was a life or death situation, I'd trust him with my life to stick to his word, but in this situation, not so much.

"You better," I warn him, holding up the bowl of grapes. "I have plenty to spare."

His eyes soften and I'm left confused for the millionth time tonight. Things have finally started to ease between us, but I can't help but keep going back to the comment he made during dinner.

Not yet. He's not in love with me yet.

He left that whole topic wide open and although I desperately shut it down, I can't help but want to know more. It was clear by the look on his face that he was giving me his honest truth and if I have to dive deep inside myself, I'd probably find that I felt the same.

I don't want to love him. That seems like a death trap, but I feel that if we keep getting closer the way we are, I might one day. I certainly have a soft spot for him and every day, it keeps getting softer … stronger.

We're not at each other's throat or desperate to get under each other's skin anymore. Though, if the opportunity presented itself, I'd take it with both hands and never let go. I love that part about our relationship. Now that the anger and distaste have faded away, the bickering and arguments just leave me hot.

Colton's head drops back against the cushion of the couch and a seriousness creeps into his eyes. "Tell me something about you, Ocean. Something I don't know."

I press my lips together, trying to figure out what this guy wouldn't already know from one of the background searches he would have done on me. "I …" I start before cutting myself off and realizing that not only is this way too deep but it's also too soon, especially for him.

"What is it?" he murmurs, never taking his eyes off me.

My eyes drop to the grape rolling between my fingers. "It's nothing."

"Ocean."

Fuck. Why does he have to say my name like that? His voice is low and filled with authority. Why do I want him to know me so badly? Not just the me that I allow the outside world to see, but the version of me that I keep private. The one that only my four boys and my mom know exist.

My eyes raise back to meet his and as they stare into mine, the words start falling from my lips. "Have you ever looked into my father's murder?"

He shakes his head ever so slightly. "Should I have?"

"No," I say. "I'm kinda glad you haven't. It's not exactly something I want being public knowledge."

He nods in understanding. "What are you trying to tell me that you keep dancing around?"

I let out a soft sigh and find the courage building within me. "I was the one to find him lying there with the … you know, and all the blood …"

Colton's brow arches and he watches me for a silent second before adjusting his position on the couch and patting the empty space beside him. I move instantly.

I crawl along the couch until I'm pressed into his side and his lips are firmly against my temples. "I'm sorry," he murmurs. "Finding my father was the hardest thing I've ever done. I can't imagine how bad it would have been had I actually had a good relationship with him."

"Mmhmm," I agree, knowing all too well as I slip the strap of my tank off my shoulder and show him my tattoo. "See the outline of the tattoo?" I ask, watching as his gaze travels over my heated skin and waiting for his nod to go on. "I don't know if this makes me morbid or just weird, but the outline is the same shape as the pool of blood that surrounded him. I never wanted to forget it so I had it tattooed over my shoulder then added the flowers to remind me that he's in a better place now. Knowing that he's up there somewhere, no longer struggling or stressed is the silver lining."

Colton's fingers trace over the flowers and I close my eyes, melting into his touch. His lips press against my shoulder and as I turn to look down at him, he raises his chin to meet mine. He captures my lips and sparks fly, just as they do every time they're on mine.

Colton takes my waist and lifts me until I'm straddled over his hips but the longer his lips move against mine, the more something pulls within me. I place my hand against his chest and feel his heart racing beneath my touch. I gently pull back from him and he looks up at me, his brows furrowing as he takes in the hesitation on my face.

"What's wrong?" he murmurs, his voice wrapping around me like the softest caress as his thumbs roam up and down my waist.

I bite down on my bottom lip, unsure if I should really be telling him this. To know that I've been holding onto this little piece of information might just undo everything that we've been able to get past over the last week. The fear of having him pull away tears at my soul but what kind of person would I be if I kept this from him?

"You really haven't looked up anything about my father's death?"

His brows furrow and his hands stop moving on my waist. "No. Why?"

I glance away, unable to handle the intensity shining through his hazel eyes. "Please don't hate me."

"Hate you?" he scoffs. "What's going on, Jade?"

I let out a heavy sigh, feeling the guilt build against my soul. "My father was stabbed with a silver, 12-inch dagger that pierced through his heart from his back. It was old, and the design on the hilt was intricate and obviously handmade."

Colton's face drops a little more with every word I say until he's looking at me in complete confusion. "What are you saying, Ocean?"

"I'm saying that the dagger that killed my father was the exact same dagger that I saw protruding from your father's chest last week."

"No," he says, shaking his head. "That's not possible."

"I know," I tell him, "But what are the chances that both our fathers were killed the same way by identical knives? Either it was the same knife or whoever did this has duplicates. I don't believe in coincidences, Colton. Mom and I weren't brought here by chance. Something has put us here and I don't know why. I don't understand it but to say this is all coincidental would be a mistake."

"Shit, babe," he murmurs, his eyes going far away as he thinks over the information I just dumped on him. "Are you sure?"

"How could I not be? What are the chances of my mom getting offered a job here and your father being murdered the exact same way as her husband only five months later by the same dagger?"

Colton sits up on the couch, pulling me up with him. "And you decided to wait over a week to come and say something about this?"

"Really?" I grunt. "The day your father died, you pushed me away. Had I even thought about opening my mouth, you would have killed me on the spot. Then you locked yourself away with a bottle of … I don't even remember what it was … scotch, maybe? Then there was the funeral and since then you practically locked yourself in your office while avoiding everyone and everything. I mean, there were those few minutes in the library where I could have said something but my mind was a little preoccupied."

"Okay, okay. I get it," he says, his eyes briefly heating at the mention of the library. "I might have been a bit of a hermit this week, but I have a pretty good reason."

"I never said you didn't," I tell him. "But speaking of your hermit tendencies, did you even go to school last week? You know you have to actually attend to graduate, right? Dean Simmons is a fucking prick. He's going to start failing you soon and those board members won't exactly be happy with a director who couldn't make it through high school."

"I can just—"

"If you say 'pay him off' I'm going to castrate you, Carrington."

Colton's lips twist into a devilish grin. "I wasn't going to say that," he says. "But that might work too."

"Oh, geez! Do I even want to know?"

He shakes his head. "Trust me, you're better off in the dark on this one."

I can only imagine what that could mean when he's talking about a guy like Dean Simmons and I can only imagine that it's the worst kind of awful. Maybe Colton is right. Maybe I am better off in the dark where Simmons is involved.

"You're not mad at me for not telling you about this sooner?"

Colton lets out a soft breath and I watch as he takes a moment to actually think it over. "No," he finally says. "I want to be, but I'm not. What happened to your father is a tragedy but it's also none of my business. You're under no obligation to have to share that with me just because you feel there's a connection, but I'm happy you did. I don't want that bullshit building up on your shoulders and now it gives us somewhere to start looking."

My hand falls to his and he instantly threads his fingers through mine. "Thank you."

A small smile pulls at the corners of his lips before they press into a tight line. "Out of curiosity, did they ever find the guy who killed your dad?"

I shake my head. "It was a stabbing in Breakers Flats. It got ruled as gang violence before his body was even cold but dad had nothing to do with the gangs. He was completely against them and made a point not to get involved. Even when Nic or any of the boys were over, he'd go and hide out in the garage or disappear completely."

"So, you think the same guy who killed your father is the same one who killed mine?" Colton asks, leaning back into the couch.

I shrug my shoulders. "It makes sense, right?"

"It does," he murmurs. "All week I've been thinking it was the DeCarlo family."

"The who?" I grunt, scrunching my face at the unfamiliar name.

"Vincent DeCarlo. Fifteen years ago, his business was going bankrupt and dad helped him out. He bought his business and got the whole family out of debt. That business turned into Carrington Incorporated and once dad got it back on its feet and transformed it into a billion-dollar business, Vincent wanted it back."

"Well, shit."

"Yeah. Vincent and his sons aren't exactly known for doing things by the law. They've targeted all of dad's other businesses, trying to take him down from the outside, but the Carrington's are untouchable."

"What does 'take him down' actually mean?"

"They lit an office building on fire, killing four people. They've planted spies. They've tried to plant evidence and have our businesses raided, even our home has been bugged at one point. They've wanted dad out of the picture for years but every effort has failed."

"So, I guess it wasn't such a stretch to assume it was them?"

"Nope. They're probably cheering that the old man is gone, hoping that I'm going to be an easier target. It's no secret around here that I wasn't exactly Dad's biggest fan. They're probably hoping that I'll use this as my final fuck you to my father."

I shake my head. "They've got another thing coming," I tell him.

"After what I saw in that meeting on Saturday morning, they're going to be sorely disappointed."

"Damn straight. I'm not going anywhere."

I grin down at him, adoring his confidence. "You know, it's kinda sexy when—"

A loud buzzer cuts me off and our eyes widen for a fraction before Colton jumps into action. He practically throws me off him and I scramble to my feet before hurrying after him into the office which holds all the surveillance equipment. "What alarm is that?" I call over the noise, hoping it doesn't wake mom. Where the hell is his security team?

"It's the front gate," he says, looking up at the twenty monitors before him until he finds the right one. "Someone just entered an unauthorized code."

"What?" I demand, my eyes widening as I watch the monitor with the front gate currently letting a driver through. "So, why the hell did it open?"

He shakes his head, putting an end to the buzzer. "I've got no fucking clue."

"Okay, but do you recognize the car?"

"Nope," he says, grabbing my hand and pulling me out into the hallway and leading me in the direction of the front door. "But we're about to find out."

We reach the foyer in record time and Colton instantly hits the front door, tearing it open and ready to face down the threat. He doesn't cower behind the door nor does he try to peek through a window first, just throws himself headfirst out the door, ready to be a man and handle what's coming for him. Honestly, I don't know if I should be terrified for him, or if I should be grabbing him by the balls, throwing him down and riding him until the sun comes up. There's nothing more attractive than a man who stands up and protects what's his, and damn it, Colton has done that over and over again, even when the thing he's protecting isn't his to protect.

I stand at his side, having dealt with more than my fair share of uninvited party crashers, and stare ahead as a black Audi comes to a screeching stop at the bottom of the stairs. The suddenness of it has me flinching, but not Colton. He stands tall.

I can't help but think of the story Colton had just finished telling me about the threat from the DeCarlo family and I find comfort in the fact that there are sixty-six steps between us and the black Audi. If guns are involved though, we're fucked. I have Nic's gun in my underwear drawer back in the pool house, but I highly doubt they're going to wait a second for me to run back and grab it.

The car door flies open and I suck in a breath just moments before a stiletto boot drops down against the driveway.

The fuck? It's a woman.

"That's not your mom's car, is it?"

Colton shakes his head and we watch with bated breath until the woman finally steps out of the car, and confuses the ever-loving shit out of us both.

Jacqueline Vanderbilt.

What the hell is she doing here late on a Tuesday night?

Colton's body relaxes a bit and I follow his lead but I don't relax entirely. He may not see her as a threat, but I've seen the devilish side of a woman and I know for a fact that bitches be crazy. Hell, I can be one of them myself.

She starts making her way up the stairs and as she finally reaches the top and steps right in front of Colton, my claws come out.

"What do you think you're doing here?" Colton spits. "You sure as hell weren't invited."

"Oh, no?" she says, slipping a piece of paper from out of her bag and pressing it into Colton's chest. "You should be welcoming me home, after all, I am your new mommy."

What. The. Actual. Fuck?

Colton stares at her, completely horrified as I tear the paper out of his hands. "It's a marriage certificate," I murmur, scanning over the names.

He shakes his head. "No. There's no way. Dad knows better than to get himself hitched."

I hold the paper up. "It's right here," I say, showing him the proof. "Why do you think he was taking off to the Maldives for two weeks? We were celebrating our honeymoon."

Honeymoon? Well damn. He couldn't have been that fond of her if a billionaire could only afford to splurge two weeks on his new bride. If I were to marry a Daddy Warbucks, I'd want at least a six month round the world complete tour and that's at a minimum. Something isn't adding up here.

Colton's jaw clenches and he refuses to take his eyes from Jacqueline for even a second. She smirks, her sick little plan clearly working. Hell, maybe we have a new suspect to add to the 'who did it' list. "Here's how it's going to go," she starts, her smirk twisting into a wicked grin. "You're going to march that toned ass of yours inside and you're going to give me a nice, thick slice of that inheritance that I know is coming your way and if you don't, I will go to the press and tell them how the billionaire heir is refusing his father's widow what she is legally owed. I didn't suck that old bastard's dick for nothing."

"You're fucking lying," he spits.

"You want to test that?" she questions with a laugh. "But don't worry, I'm not stupid. I know how these things work. I'll give you some time to get your finances in order."

With that, she turns on her black stiletto boots and starts marching her way back down the stairs, but stops when she gets halfway down. "Don't be a stranger, son. The clock is ticking."

CHAPTER 15

I walk through the door after another interesting day of learning about the ins and outs of Bellevue Springs Private. The more time I spend there, the more the girls' perfect attitudes begin slipping away to reveal their true bitchy nature.

Gotta love a spoiled rich girl with her daddy wrapped around her little finger.

Yesterday was more about getting to know the school and my classes, but today was all about the girls. To them, I was still the shiny new toy and the Colton cloud that hung over my head just seemed to get bigger by the second, but to me, they were complicated little puzzles that needed to be worked out.

Once I figured out the first girl, the rest followed suit. Watching best friends stab each other in the back—all while smiling—was pretty damn funny. I'll be sure not to make the same mistake. Everyone at Bellevue Springs Private will be held at arm's length. I'm not interested in having one of those preppy bitches stab me in the back just for a little fun during her day.

It won't be long until they realize that they won't be able to get to Colton through me and when that happens, all hell is going to break loose. I'm going to be public enemy number one but to be perfectly honest, I'm kinda excited about it. In the short month that I've lived in Bellevue Springs so much has happened. All I need is one of those bitches to try to tear me down, I have no patience, and a shitload of pent-up aggression. I'm already close to exploding, and when I do, a bitch is going to get fucked-up.

I get halfway through the foyer before Colton's loud, booming voice tears through the mansion—considering the size of this place, that's pretty damn impressive. "THERE HAS TO BE ANOTHER WAY," he booms. "FIND IT. I'M NOT PAYING YOU BY THE HOUR FOR YOU TO TELL ME THAT SHE GETS WHATEVER THE FUCK SHE WANTS."

Damn. I guess he's still in that meeting with the team of thirty lawyers who all piled in here first thing this morning.

I can't imagine what it would be like walking in Colton's shoes. He's surrounded by corporate wolves, with the weight of the world on his shoulders—growing heavier with each step—all of them watching and waiting for him to fuck it up. It's not fair. He's only eighteen and never asked for this shit, and despite the fact that he's flown through it and dominated so far, he's also suffocating. Colton won't be able to handle all of this bullshit for much longer, it's not physically possible. I mean, the amount of stress he must be under … damn. I can't even imagine.

Making my way through the house, I have no choice but to pass the formal dining hall that Colton is using for his meeting. Last night Colton had mentioned meeting with his lawyers after Jacqueline claimed she was married to his father. I just assumed that it was going to be in the same board room I'd prepared once before. When thirty lawyers showed up, I realized Colton had called in the whole calvary—the board room was not going to cut it.

I can't help but peek through the open door as I pass, finding Colton standing at the head of the table, head dropped between his shoulders. He's looking over the mess before him—all the strength and confidence from over the weekend completely gone now. He looks helplessly at the papers flying around the table and back to the lawyers that are trying desperately to speak over one another.

Jacqueline Vanderbilt coming in here with no pre-nup could potentially take it all. We should have seen this coming. What kind of twenty-something-year-old blonde goddess spends her time choking on old dick when she should be out on some rich dude's fancy yacht, sipping champagne and fucking until the sun comes up? Obviously, she's a gold digger to the most epic standard, but why accept an informal wedding with absolutely no hype? Is she that desperate for the cash?

I quickly pass the formal dining hall, sure as hell that Colton wouldn't want me looking in on this. For them to have spent all day on this and still not have an answer, it's not good.

What the hell was Charles thinking getting hitched to his girlfriend like that? Hell, the last time I'd heard about it, he couldn't even remember the name of the girl who was on her knees sucking him dry. It just doesn't make sense. Why would he do it? I know Colton had a rough relationship with his father, but surely he would have let him know that he was about to bring a new mommy into the house.

Charles doesn't strike me as the type to make spur of the moment decisions like that. He was always calculated, he thought through and evaluated every single risk before leaping. Marrying some bimbo because she gives good head doesn't exactly sit right. The guy had been training his son day in and day out to run his business so that one day, he'll be able to take over. A guy who is that dedicated to ensuring the future of his legacy doesn't just accidentally fall into a marriage. Something more is going on here.

"Right," Colton says, his voice fading as I make my way farther down the hall. "Someone get me the credentials of the fucker who signed off on this. I want to know everything about him, every marriage he's signed off on, every time he's slipped up, and every fucking time he takes a shit during the day."

Well, damn. Colton is pushing every angle to get this shit sorted out and I don't blame him. I can't even imagine what would happen if all of this was taken away from him. Having someone like Jacqueline Vanderbilt in charge would be a disaster. She'd destroy it all within seconds and Carrington Incorporated would be back in the hands of the Decarlo family in the blink of an eye.

I tune the meeting out and get my ass into the staff quarters because the best thing I can do for Colton right now is stay out of the way. Hell, the majority of the words those lawyers were throwing around in there completely went over my head. I'm way out of my element here.

As usual, I drop down at any available table and get stuck into my homework. I know this was Charles' rule and he's not exactly around to enforce it anymore, but what it comes down to is my need to graduate. He might have been a ruthless dick, but he was right about one thing—education is important. And it shows in the way Colton can stand in that room and run that meeting like a boss, completely understanding everything that's been said. Hell, maybe if I had put that much dedication into my education over the years, I'd have a better chance at … well, everything.

After an hour of suffering through my math homework, my brain is fried and I decide it's probably best to put it away for another day. I still don't understand this bullshit, but every day it gets a little easier.

With homework mostly out of the way, I hurry back into the pool house and as I'm stripping out of my school uniform, a thought occurs to me. Charles Carrington was a greedy man. He wouldn't go and get married like that, and this time I don't mean it as a confused statement, but a fact. What if he didn't actually get married? What if this is all some kind of sham and Jacqueline forged the paperwork to cash in?

I pull on a pair of high waisted shorts, tug a black crop over my head, and fish through my bra for my phone that's been stashed in there all day.

It rings twice before Nic's handsome face appears on my screen. "Facetime?" he questions with an exaggerated gasp. "What did I do to receive this honor?"

I roll my eyes but can't help smiling at the idiot. "I missed you," I tell him, my lips pulling into a goofy as fuck grin. "I feel like I haven't seen you in forever."

"I know, babe, but it's just been a week."

I let out a heavy sigh and focus on the way his eyes soften as he watches me through the screen. "A week is too long."

A scoff comes from the background before the phone is wrestled out of Nic's hands and Sebastian's face appears. "What the fuck is this?" Sebastian demands. "Nic gets a Facetime call and all I get is an occasional text message when you remember to actually send one."

"Shut up," I laugh. "You know I love you too. Shit has been a little crazy here."

"Yeah right, you've probably just been distracted by the new boyfriend of yours."

"He's not my boyfriend."

"I'll believe that wh—"

The phone is stolen right back and I hear Sebastian's objections in the background before the screen drops to the ground and I hear the familiar sound of Nic's heavy punch slamming into Sebastian's flawless skin. A loud, pissed off groan sails through my speakers before Nic picks up the phone and his face re-appears. "So, what's up, O? You never Facetime. Is something wrong?"

"No, nothing wrong with me exactly," I say with a cringe, wondering how he's going to feel about me asking to help when it comes to Carrington business. Hell, Colton's probably going to be pissed when he finds out I was talking to outsiders about something that's clearly a family matter.

"Spit it out, babe. I'm about to go on a run."

Shit.

"Do you remember the crying bitch from Charles' funeral?"

"Yeah, the same one who was sucking his dick at that party?"

"Yeah, that's her. She kinda showed up here late last night claiming that she'd married Charles in secret and is wanting, well, I don't exactly know what she wants but it doesn't seem right to me. Something fishy is going on and I was wondering how easy it is to forge a marriage certificate and have a room full of thirty lawyers completely stumped?"

Nic scrunches his face. "Come on, babe. I really don't think I should be getting involved in this shit."

"Please. I just … I don't need you to get involved but can you at least look at the certificate and tell if it's fake or not?"

Nic groans and he stares at me for a long moment before finally giving in. "Fine. Go and get your mom and dad's marriage certificate and make it quick. I've only got ten minutes to spare."

"On it," I beam, hurrying into mom's room and pulling down the box she keeps in the top of her closet that is filled with all our important things. I rifle through it, skipping over my birth certificate and dad's death certificate before finally finding a copy of their marriage license and the original marriage certificate.

"Got it," I announce, holding it up to the phone so he can see.

"Good, now go and get the one you think is fake."

My eyes bug out of my head. "You want me to go into that room and take the one thing they're all fretting over?"

Nic stares at me as though he's looking at some kind of stranger. "Fuck me, O. I knew moving away was going to change you but I didn't think you were going to lose those steel balls that you've always had. That's a real fucking shame."

"Hey," I snap. "My balls are still hanging right where I left them."

"Then what are you waiting for? Go and march that sweet ass in there and take what you need just like I always taught you to."

Fuck. He's right.

I pull up my big girl panties and get the fuck over it. If I'm right, he'll learn to forgive me and if I'm wrong, then screw him because I was at least trying, which seems like a lot more than what his very expensive lawyers are doing.

I march out of the pool house and don't stop until I'm storming my way through the massive door of the formal dining room. All eyes fall to mine and the noisy room becomes silent.

Colton watches me through narrowed eyes and I can tell that he's only moments away from telling me to fuck off out of here.

"I need the marriage certificate," I say, keeping my chin high and demanding respect.

A few scoffs come from the lawyers and I'm instantly dismissed until Colton notices the phone in my hand and the other marriage certificate. "Give it to her," he roars, making at least fifteen of the fuckers jump.

They all scramble—grown ass men terrified of an eighteen-year-old kid. It takes a full minute of searching through the mess of papers until the certificate is finally found and passed to Colton as though it holds the secrets of the universe.

He instantly hands it to me and I step up to the table beside him, sweeping my hand over the papers in my way and watching as they go flying off the table.

Nasty comments are muttered under breaths while Colton cringes, knowing that shit isn't going to sit well with the dickheads around the table. It's Nic's laugh through the phone that keeps my spirits high.

"You better know what you're doing," Colton murmurs beside me, making Nic scoff at his lack of faith.

"Have I ever led you wrong?"

Colton scoffs right back and I decide to get this figured out before it turns into some petty bullshit fight through a phone. "Alright," Nic says. "Hold the phone down at the table so I can see them both up close."

I do as I'm asked and as Nic looks over the certificates, Colton looks down at me. "What the hell do you think you're doing?" he demands, keeping his voice low but with the silence in the room, every ear has a front-row seat to our conversation.

"Thinking like a woman," I tell him, earning myself a few irritated scoffs from the table of men before me, every single one of them a sexist asshole. "You dove headfirst into trying to keep her from getting her hands on your father's fortune that you didn't even stop to think if it's even real—"

"It's real," comes grunted from the left-hand side of the table.

My eyes snap up to the bastards before me. "Are you sure about that?" I question, looking back at Colton. "If it were real, where's the marriage license and why the hell are we only hearing about it now? Not to mention, there's always a delay in getting these certificates. It takes at least six weeks after the wedding to receive it, but according to the date on the certificate, they were married less than two weeks ago. It doesn't add up. Besides, your dad was a lot of things, but he wasn't careless. If he was going to marry some gold-digging whore, he would have done it the right way and he would have had the tightest prenup that money could buy. He cared about money bags, his reputation, and his businesses more than his own children. So no, I don't think he would have risked it all for some girl. Even if she was the love of his life."

"I'm not going to lie," he murmurs, "I haven't been able to wrap my head around him actually doing this but the certificate was there …"

"Are you serious?" a voice says from across the room. "You're taking advice from an uneducated girl who comes from trash? Colton, please think this through. You need to be smart about this."

Colton's stare is sharp enough to kill and the man instantly goes quiet. "Pack up your things and get the fuck out of my house."

"I … I …"

"NOW."

The old man reluctantly stands up and starts packing up his things with a huff, but I don't get to watch the show as Nic's voice comes through the phone again. "O, lower the phone so I can see the bottom half."

I adjust my phone as silence falls across the room again and after a long, agonizing minute, Nic's voice cuts through the room. "It's fake."

"What?" Colton demands, his brows flying up as he steals the phone and looks at Nic through the screen. "What do you mean it's fake? How can you tell?"

Nic lets out a sigh. He's not exactly one who likes having to explain himself but seeing as though this case is a little different from the bullshit he's used to dealing with, he sucks it up and gets on with his explanation. "O, grab the certificates."

I slip them off the table and look down at them, one in each hand. "Got them."

"See the bottom of your parent's marriage certificate?" Nic questions. "There's an emblem and it's really clear, bold lines but the Carrington one has bleeding. The picture isn't as clear. A government-issued certificate wouldn't have that. This was printed by a cheap printer and I bet the paper quality even feels different."

I rub my thumbs over the paper and look up at Colton. "He's right. They're different."

"I'm always fucking right," Nic mutters as Colton hands me back my phone and takes the certificates from me, studying them for himself.

Colton takes all of three seconds to notice the differences between the two and when he does, his hand slams down on the table before he glances up at his lawyers. "We're done here. Come back tomorrow, I want that bitch done for forgery and inheritance fraud."

"Yes, sir," they say then dive into the paperwork on the table, hastily getting it all cleaned up before Colton gives them something else to do.

He picks the certificates up from the table and takes my elbow before leading me out of the room. "You could have said that you thought it was fake hours ago and saved me all that bullshit."

Nic scoffs and I know without a doubt that a sarcastic comment is about to go flying from between his lips. "Yeah, because she's the one responsible for saving your ass. That was fucking bullshit, man. Your lawyers should have picked that up the second they looked at it."

Colton's jaw clenches. He knows that Nic is right but he'll be damned if he admits it. He meets my eyes above the phone before indicating down to it, silently telling me to wrap it up.

He turns away as if to give me privacy and I roll my eyes before dropping my gaze back to Nic's. "Thank you," I murmur. "He'll never admit it, but you just saved his ass."

Colton scoffs, but thankfully Nic ignores him. "It's cool, O. You know I did it because you asked me to, not because that fucker deserved it. I would have slept easy had I said no."

"I know, but still …"

Nic nods. "Listen, babe. I have to go. I'll check in with you later, alright?"

"K," I say with a small smile. "Love you. Tell the boys I miss them."

Nic scoffs and in the blink of an eye, he disappears from the screen and as I look up at Colton, I find him staring at me with jealousy burning in his hazel eyes.

"Do you love him?" he questions, his gaze not breaking from mine for even a second.

I take a slight step back, preparing to hit him with my A-game. "How is that any of your business?"

"Just answer the question, Jade."

I let out a heavy sigh and lean against the wall of the hallway. "Part of me still does while the other part wants to hate him so damn bad, but I just can't. It's complicated between me and Nic."

"Did he ever hurt you?"

"Not in the way you're thinking," I explain. "He cheated."

Colton's lips pull into a tight line and as his eyes remain on mine, I see the exhaustion buried within him. I take his hand and start pulling him down the hallway while sending a quick text to Sebastian.

Ocean - Hook me up.

Sebastian - You sure, babe?

Ocean - Never been so sure in my life.

Sebastian - Give me ten minutes.

"What are we doing?" Colton asks when we reach the private bar in the kitchen and I still haven't said a word.

I look up at him as I open the door and a wide grin slowly stretches across my face. "We're getting fucked up and I don't care what you say about it."

Colton nods, a grin of his own lighting his eyes in a way that has me desperate to kiss him. "About fucking time."

CHAPTER 16

Bodies fill the Carrington mansion and I have to admit, after Sebastian had a contact show up at the door and drop off a few party favors, this party turned into one of the best nights I've ever had in Bellevue Springs.

Sebastian sent enough joints to get all of Bellevue Springs stoned, and after the bullshit Colton's been through, he was the first to shove his hand into the little baggie and light one up.

We were practically inseparable until the crowd showed up. Since then, I haven't seen him. I have no idea what happened to him though. I'm pretty sure he's probably avoiding Spencer because of the bullshit that's going down with his cousin and Charlie ... well, things with

Charlie are a little stressed seeing as though they're both trying to get into my pants.

When will the bullshit end?

Milo curls his arm around my waist and lifts me off the floor as a loud squeal tears from within me. "Put me down," I laugh, grabbing at his wrists and pulling until I'm finally freed.

"Girl," he says as he starts to move his body to the beat of the music. "This party is fucking insane. We should do this every Tuesday night."

"Yeah, right," I laugh. "You're not even going to remember this party in the morning."

"As if I could forge—" Milo's eyes go wide as he cuts himself off. "Let's get in the pool."

"No way. You can go and get in the pool all by yourself."

"Hell yeah." Milo takes off at a run, stripping out of his clothes as he goes. His shirt is torn over his head and thrown across the living room, gaining the attention of every girl in the room. Milo has a body on him, a fucking nice one, and not even I could resist stealing a peek. Next up, he kicks his shoes off and as he approaches the pool, his pants begin to go too.

Girls start squealing for him and his concentration breaks, looking over at them with a cheesy as fuck grin and encouraging them to come with him. Milo's not stupid. He's been playing this game since the very beginning and knows that if the girls strip down to their bikinis that there's a good chance that the guys will join them in the pool and that's exactly what he wants.

Milo continues running and honestly, he looks like a swan preparing for the most spectacular dive into the pool but as he continues calling for the girls to join him, he misses a step and his feet get tangled in pants that are halfway down his shins.

Milo goes tumbling with every last person at the party watching him and my breath catches in my throat. If he wasn't so high and just about finished with his fourth Mudslide, he'd be beside himself with fear, but the alcohol might just do the trick to help him play this off smart.

One second he's tumbling and the next, he disappears into the indoor portion of the pool with a massive crash. Water spits up around him as everyone watches, some laughing while others gasp, worried that he's hurt himself, but in true Milo fashion, he comes shooting to the surface with a loud booming laugh. "Fuck me," he says, his laughs so uncontrollable that I can hardly understand the gibberish that's coming out of his mouth. "Did you see that shit?"

The whole room starts cheering and not a second later, people start rushing toward him, clothes getting thrown all over the place.

Someone presses the button that opens the room into a huge indoor/outdoor space and suddenly the party has doubled in size. I'm reminded of my first day here when Charles had so proudly shown me this feature of his home and a fondness sweeps over me. The music is turned up and booze flows faster than it has ever flowed before, creating the best party Bellevue Springs has ever seen.

"Wow, I always forget just how big this place is. It's freaking huge," a familiar voice says, moving in beside me.

I glance across to find Hendrix's warm smile and Jess close by her side. She's looking out at the pool with a red cup in her hand, filled to the brim with who the hell knows what.

"Right," I say. "I live here and still can't wrap my head around it."

"Holy shit," Jess says, not bothering with a hello as whatever has her attention is clearly far too important. "Who's that guy in the pool? He is fucking delicious. I could lick him up and down and never get tired of it."

I hold back a grin. "That's Milo. He's my best friend and you know what? He's newly single and was just telling me how he wants to let loose tonight and get a little crazy. I think you've got a shot if you play your cards right."

Jess' eyes bug out of her head as she whips around to me, excitement pulsing through her and radiating off her in waves. "Bullshit. Really?"

I nod. "You're just his type."

"Hell yeah," she cheers, throwing back what's left of her drink and then shoving the empty cup into Hendrix's hands. Her shirt is pulled up over her head revealing a skimpy red bikini that has her tits looking as though they're worth a million dollars. Her skirt is shimmied down her hips and before we know it, she's racing for Milo and dropping into the pool right beside him.

The laugh tears out of me as I watch Milo's reaction to her. She swims right into him, throwing her arms around his shoulders and whispering in his ear with a seductive grin as her legs wrap around his waist. Milo's eyes flick to mine and the longer he watches me, the darker they get, that is until he decides to play along. He slips his arm around her waist and locks his lips against hers.

"Holy crap," Hendrix laughs. "They move fast."

I shake my head, enjoying this way too much. Milo's had enough to drink that I really don't think he cares who he kisses. After all, a kiss is a kiss, and no matter where it comes from, it's nice either way. Besides, this is no doubt helping the whole 'gay image' that he's desperately trying to conceal.

The guys standing around the pool start cheering for Milo as though he's just one of the boys about to get his dick wet and just like that, he's saved from their scrutiny and rumors for at least another few months.

Hendrix loops her arms through mine and she starts pulling me out toward the pool. "Okay, don't get weird with me," she starts, digging into her purse with a nervous cringe, hoping I'm down for whatever bullshit she wants to get up to, and honestly, there's not a lot that I'm not down with. "But do you want to get fucked up with me?"

Drix holds out a joint and a laugh pulls from deep within me as I slip my hand into my bra and pull out one of my own. "You're on."

We drop down in the grass and watch the party around us as a guy carrying a bottle of vodka strides past. He looks as though he's already had enough to drink and Hendrix lures him in with a seductive smile. She holds up a finger and indicates for him to come closer and just as she knew it would, it works like a treat.

The guy stumbles forward, excited with the idea of being the object of Hendrix's attention. He falls down in front of us and Hendrix instantly curls her fingers around the bottle. She pulls it closer and the guy comes right along, looking into her eyes as though she holds the secrets of the universe. "Why don't you go and wait for me upstairs?"

His brow raises and he nods furiously before scrambling to his feet and taking off back into the house, leaving the bottle behind as I gape at my new friend. "What the hell was that?"

She grins proudly while uncapping the bottle of vodka. "It's my party trick," she says, bringing the bottle to her lips and taking a quick swig. "Did you like it? Works every time."

She hands me the bottle and I take a drink. "It was inspiring," I laugh. "I need to sharpen up on my own tricks."

"Damn straight, girl," she says. "Otherwise I'm going to be showing you up at every turn and we can't have that now, can we?"

She sure as hell has a point.

Hendrix nods toward the pool to where Jess is busily running her claws all over Milo's toned, sun-kissed body. "Is she really going to get anywhere with him?"

I shake my head, letting the laughter shine through my eyes. "No chance in hell, but it'll be fun watching her work it out."

"Damn," Hendrix laughs. "That's brutal."

I shrug my shoulders. "She'll be alright. It's not as though she isn't going to enjoy herself while she's at it. He'll accidentally give her the wrong number and come tomorrow morning, neither of them are even going to remember this happened. She should think of it as fun, I know I am."

"Geez, I can't wait to see how you deal with shit when someone's crossed you."

"Trust me, you don't want to be that poor bitch."

"I bet."

Half an hour later, we're sitting on the kitchen counter, each with a shot glass in our hands. The ceiling is closed in and the walls are slid back into place after the wind decided to ruin the pool party fun. Bodies are crammed back inside, grinding and dancing upon one another as the music flows freely.

I can hardly hold myself up and I'm ashamed to say that we haven't seen Jess or Milo since they were making out in the pool. The bottle of vodka is down to the last few drops and our heads are spinning, but we're having a good time and we're not going to stop until one of us passes out on the counter or is hurling in the expensive vase. Though, I'm kinda hoping we don't because I'll be the one who has to clean it in the morning.

Colton sits across the room and I haven't missed the way that his eyes linger on me, so intense and full of need that it makes me itch to get him between my legs. If I was smart, we could have forgotten about the party and it would have been just me and him all night long, free to do whatever the hell we wanted, but no. Apparently, when you get fucked up and high on weed after a shitty few weeks, all you want to do is relax and party until you can't remember your own damn name.

"Damn, that boy hasn't stopped staring," Hendrix says, watching my line of sight and clearly realizing that there's something deeper going on here than just two people living on the same property. Hell, she was there on the yacht and would have seen the tension between us that has only gotten worse as time goes by.

"He's not," I say, looking back at her. "Are you ready for your shot?"

"No way," she screeches. "It's your turn."

"Bullshit," I laugh. "I just stood in the middle of the room and climbed on the coffee table to do my own rendition of the robot dance. It's so your turn."

Hendrix's face scrunches. "Shit. Is it bad that I've already forgotten about that?"

I choke back a laugh, wondering why the hell I'm finding every little thing so damn funny.

"Alright," Hendrix says, looking down at the shot of vodka in her hands. "I can't drink another one of these or else I'm going to end up throwing up all over Colton's place and I'll never live it down. What do I have to do?"

A grin pulls at my lips and I slam my hand down on the counter that I'm sitting on. "You need to climb up here, flash those perfect titties of yours while swinging your shirt above your head like a helicopter and screaming 'Spring Break, baby!'"

Her eyes bug out of her head, absolutely mortified by the challenge that's been thrown down, but she doesn't strike me as the type to bitch out. "You're fucking kidding me?"

I shake my head. "It's fine. You don't have to do it, just take another shot instead."

Hendrix groans before handing me her shot and climbing up onto the counter. I throw her shot back, more than capable of handling another few shots before I pass out. Hendrix gets to her feet and I can't help but look up at her as she starts pulling her shirt above her head.

She gets the attention of the many guys in the room and by the time her shirt is swinging around above her head with her tits bouncing softly as she moves, every last eye in the room is staring.

"SPRING BREAK, BABY!" she squeals.

Hands are thrown up in the air and excited cheers flow through the room, begging for more. People laugh, assuming she's so drunk that she doesn't realize that we're not even close to Spring break, while the other half are probably just assuming that she's on something, and way too wasted and fucked up to know what the hell is going on.

Hendrix jumps down with a renewed confidence that has her chin held high. "You didn't think I was going to do it, did you?"

"I have to admit," I tell her, a grin stretching wide across my face. "I thought you were going to chicken out."

She shakes her head. "Not me, baby. I'm the fucking man around here. You better watch out, I know you're a bad bitch, but baby, I just got badder."

"I don't even think that makes sense."

I roll my eyes as she grabs her empty shot glass and gets busy refilling it. "I don't care," she tells me. "All that matters is that you just stepped up the game and I'm meeting you there. Ain't no more bullshit challenges for you."

Damn it. I should have known she was going to throw it back at me.

"What do I have to do?"

Her eyes scan around the room and stop on Colton. My stomach sinks as I follow her gaze and find his eyes already on mine, narrowed and clearly aware that whatever we're doing has something to do with him. "See that lap of his?" she questions, looking at me as though I'm a chicken shit. "It looks very lonely. I bet he could use a dance."

I meet Hendrix's eyes. "You want me to give Colton Carrington a lap dance in the middle of a fucking party?"

She shrugs. "I mean … you could always take another shot."

I look back at Colton and his gaze is like two hazel pits that have me drowning with need. "Fine," I say, grabbing the shot and taking it anyway.

Hendrix laughs as though she just won this round, but when I jump down from the marble counter and start making my way around it she calls out after me. "That's not how the game works."

I turn back to her but keep walking toward my target. "You think I'm about to skip out on a chance at getting wasted and rubbing my coochie all over Colton Carrington? I don't fucking think so, babe."

She shrugs her shoulder while howling out a laugh. "It's your funeral," she tells me, spinning around on the marble counter so she can watch the show without having to crane her neck.

I turn back to Colton, seeing him clearly through the throng of people, and as I grow closer my eyes become hooded. I don't know what it is about this man, but the more time I spend with him, the more attractive he becomes. He's like my kryptonite. I'm the moth and he's the flame.

The closer I get, the more suspicious he becomes, but when I start unbuttoning my shirt, he grows wary. I let the fabric slide down my arms and watch as hunger flashes through his eyes. Colton licks his lips, liking what he sees as I stride toward him in my black string bikini top, wanting it more than maybe even I do.

I step up before him and slip in between his legs, feeling like an absolute goddess as his fingers twitch with the need to touch me. "What do you think you are doing?" he questions, his tone low and cold as if someone had flipped a switch.

My brows furrow. "What do you mean?"

A wall slams down behind his eyes and it instantly puts me on edge, especially as he watches me like a child who's about to break.

A silence settles between us and it's as if he's willing me to figure it out so he doesn't have to be the one to say the words.

What the hell is his problem? He's been more than happy to have my body rubbing all over his since the moment I arrived in Bellevue Springs. What's the difference between those times and now? He was more than into it when we were standing in the library.

It hits me like a fucking wrecking ball. The people. He's more than happy to have me in private, but he's too ashamed to be seen with the help in front of his rich friends.

That fucking bastard.

Everything inside of me shatters. How could I have been so stupid?

I pull back from him and stare into his eyes as every little fiber within me breaks. "So, I'm just going to be your dirty little secret then?"

"Come on, Jade. It's not like that," he says, sitting up so he can get a bit closer.

"Oh, really?" I grunt, watching as his eyes harden, realizing that I hit the nail on the head. "Then please tell me what it's like because I'm fucking dying to know."

Colton stands and looks down at me as a frustrated groan pulls from deep within him, making it appear as though dealing with my drama is some kind of chore. "Jade," he murmurs, trying to keep our conversation private as he reaches for me.

"No," I say, pulling out of his reach. "If I'm not good enough to have in front of your pathetic friends, then I'm not good enough period. Whatever this is, it's through. Nic was right. You're just looking for some bitch who's going to bend to your will, but that's not me. I don't get hidden away."

I turn and go to walk away but he catches my wrist, pulling me back to him. "Jade, come on," he urges, staring down into my eyes but keeping a distance between us that makes it look somewhat professional. "You know what the fuck I'm facing with the board. If they knew we were … you know?"

"If we were what, Colton? Friends? Together? Screwing around? What would it matter? You're the fucking boss, if they don't like it, they can fuck off, but you're choosing your precious reputation over everything else, just like your father always did."

His stare hardens and anger pulses through him, his hold tightening on my wrist. "That's not fair."

"No?" I question, tearing my wrist free. "Then prove me wrong. Kiss me right fucking here for the world to see."

"I can't," he whispers, silently begging me to give in, the way he's so used to the rest of the world doing.

I shake my head. "I don't come second place to anything, Colton. Just forget about it. I'm done."

I walk away and find myself back in the kitchen wearing my heart on my sleeve. I grab what's left of the vodka bottle and throw it back, feeling the burn as it travels down my throat. "Uh oh," Hendrix says. "Trouble in paradise? What happened?"

"Nothing worth mentioning," I tell her, tearing open the door to the private bar and welcoming myself in as my heart sits heavy in my chest. I grab the first bottle I can wrap my fingers around and walk back out, holding it out to her, "Now, are you going to be a little pussy or are you ready to get really fucked up."

Hendrix takes the bottle from me and uncaps it with a tight smile. "You better fucking believe it."

A body steps in behind me and I'm crowded against the counter, a hand on either side of my hips keeping me caged. "Are you alright?" Charlie murmurs in my ear. "That looked rough."

Fuck.

I turn in Charlie's arms and look up into his caring eyes, knowing damn well that a man with such a pure heart is way too good for me, but at the same time, if he wants to play with fire and ignore the warnings, then that's on him.

I push up onto my toes and raise my chin so my lips hover just in front of his. "Dance with me, Hot Sauce."

Charlie's eyes narrow as he stares down at me. He knows there's only one right answer and that's to tell me no. He knows that Colton's going to be pissed and he knows that he's going to come after him the second he steps out of my arms despite the way he denies that there's anything between us. Hell, Charlie even knows that I'm using him just to make Colton jealous, but damn it, he's not pulling away.

"I'm going to regret this, aren't I?"

"So fucking much."

"Then you better give me all you've got."

CHAPTER 17

The afternoon sun streams through my bedroom window and I groan, wondering why I had to go and prove some ridiculous point to Colton last night.

Charlie and I practically screwed on the dance floor while I watched Colton's eyes get darker by the second. Charlie sure as hell wasn't too ashamed of me to show me off in front of all his friends. Though, knowing Charlie, having a rumor attaching him to me would most likely be the perfect 'fuck you' to his dickhead father. After his third time asking me to slip out to the pool house with him, I decided enough was enough.

It was cruel really, knowing how he feels about me and playing on that just to get at Colton. I kinda regret it, but I kinda don't. They all knew the game we were playing and when you play with fire, you're bound to get burned. In Colton's case, that fucker got obliterated. Fingers crossed that he's learned his lesson about playing with my heart. Oceania Munroe doesn't play fair, she plays to win.

I don't know why his rejection bothered me so much. It's not as though I didn't see it coming. At least, I should have. I've always known deep down that Colton was never going to take it any further with me. I'm the goddamn help. He's destined to date Victoria Secret models until he finally gets past that stage and marries one of his friends' little sisters in a bid to close a billion-dollar deal. Dating the help was never in his plans, and fuck, it really hurts.

Nic keeps telling me that he's going to hurt me one day and while I knew that he was right, I thought I was strong enough to have it sail off me like water off a duck's back.

This is killing me. I must have looked so fucking pathetic, walking across the room to a man who pushed me away without a second thought. I must have looked desperate.

Pitiful.

Inadequate.

All this time, I've been pretending. I've been going to their fancy schools, making fancy friends, joining in on their fancy lifestyles, but this isn't who I am. Colton's rejection is a reminder of that. What have I been doing? I should have been working out how to find myself in this godforsaken town, how to live day by day without losing myself to their world but I got caught up. That can't happen again. I won't allow it.

I let out a heavy sigh and throw the blanket off me. The clock up on the wall is telling me that it's just after one in the afternoon and I instantly start hating on myself. It was only a few weeks ago that I made a promise to myself to really try with my schooling so I can graduate and not have the shadow of Breakers Flats looming over me. Then I go and do something like sleeping through the day after allowing myself to get fucked up. I'm not going to lie though, that party was fucking epic … you know, until Colton went and screwed it up for me.

I had every intention of getting up early and taking my sorry ass to school. It would have been a shitty day but I feel as though it would have been a step in the right direction. It would have served to remind me that I'm a strong independent woman and despite the shit going on in my life, I'm still capable of making the right decisions.

Apparently not.

I screwed that up when I fell into bed at three in the morning and then slept right through my alarm, snoozing it for over an hour before throwing my phone out the window and instantly regretting it. I'm going to have to go out there at some point to find it but knowing my luck, it's probably fallen down a drain or been stolen by Colton to use as a weapon against me.

As I lay in bed staring up at the ceiling, I can't help but think over everything that happened at the party. It was supposed to be a celebration of how Colton and I had conquered Jacqueline Vanderbilt. We were supposed to get fucked up together and enjoy our night before screwing on every surface of the house until we finally passed out on the couch, but I guess things never really go to plan in Bellevue Springs. Just ask Charles Carrington, he sure as shit learned that the hard way.

A few good things came out of the party though so I guess it wasn't a complete waste. I mean, Milo certainly had a little unintended fun. I'm going to have to check in with him at some point and get a run down because after he disappeared with Jess, I never saw him again. As for Hendrix, I feel as though I saw another side of her and I think that I actually like it. I'll stick with her from now on. She doesn't seem like the rest of the girls I've come across in Bellevue Springs. She seems sincere while the rest are sheep. They'll show their true colors soon enough and when they do, I'll be ready for them.

After somehow managing to peel myself out of bed, I trudge out to the kitchen and grab myself an orange juice. There's nothing quite like a hangover, but then it honestly beats getting up at 7 am and getting myself ready for another horrendous day at my new school. I'd take sleeping in and a headache any day. After all, it's nothing a quick throw up and pain killers can't fix.

I grab the bottle of orange juice and as I close the fridge, the bright pink sticky note staring back at me steals my attention. I recognize Mom's handwriting immediately and a weight drops in my stomach. It's never good news when Mom goes to the effort of leaving a note.

No school = working. You have a HUGE mess to clean up. I am not happy!

Shit. I guess my good day of lounging around the pool house just went to shit.

Now knowing that there's a big mess being left for me, I bypass the whole drinking out of a cup thing and just lift the bottle to my lips, cringing at mom's voice in my head threatening to kill me if I was to keep doing it. The bottle gets jammed back into the fridge and I dawdled into the bathroom before madly searching through the drawers for some painkillers.

I get myself through a hot shower and after dressing and finding my phone, I push through to the staff quarters to find both Mom and Maryne staring back at me. Scowls instantly spread over their faces and guilt pours through me. It would be so easy to say that party was Colton's idea but they know me well enough to know he wouldn't have done it without the idea being pushed into his douchey little mind.

I press my lips into a tight line and scurry past them before either gets a chance to curse me out. I can only imagine the string of curses that would come flying out of my mother's mouth. It'd be enough to make even the devil blush.

I grab one of the maid's cleaning carts, knowing damn well that the mess in the kitchen, living room, and pool area is going to need all the help it can get. I start pushing and get out into the main part of the house before finding myself following the murmured voices coming from one of the informal living spaces.

Colton's low rumble sounds through the room and I stop just short of the door. I'm all too curious about what the hell is going on in there. "I'm sure he'll show up," Colton murmurs. "He's disappeared without a word before."

Disappeared? Is he talking about Jude? I've been doing a good job of pretending that fucker doesn't exist, but Colton's words have the memories from last Saturday night flooding back to the forefront of my head. My hands are shaking as anger begins pulsing through me.

"Not like this," a woman responds, her tone full of panic. "He's always left a note or at least sent a text when he's going to be gone for a few days."

"It's only been a week …"

"A week and a half, Colton. It's been a week and a half. Something is wrong."

Colton lets out a heavy sigh. "I really think he's alright, Mrs. Carter. I would have heard if something had happened. He probably just took a trip down south with some friends or maybe he's met someone who's keeping him away. You know how he gets. He probably hasn't even realized that he's worrying everyone back home."

Worrying them? The fuck? No one is fucking worried about him. He's a fucking rapist. He should be slaughtered, not searched out because mommy and daddy are desperate to get their little boy home.

Mrs. Carter lets out a heavy sigh. "I guess," she says as I hear the familiar sounds of someone raising off the couch. "He'll come home to me. He always does."

"I'll let you know if I hear anything."

"Thank you, love. You've been a great help in easing my worries, though unfortunately, my fears are still there."

"I know," he says.

I hear them walking out of the room and anger pulses through me.

That's it? Colton isn't going to tell her how her precious son sexually harassed me for weeks until he finally found the courage to drug and rape me? He's just going to let her walk away?

No. I can't let this happen.

"I wouldn't if I were you," Harrison murmurs so softly behind me that I practically jump right out of my skin.

"And why the hell not?" I demand, narrowing my eyes as Colton steps out of the living room with Mrs. Carter and leads her to the front door.

"I'm not going to pretend to know what that boy did to you, but the staff talk, and I can only assume that it was horrendous. But think about who you are and what that boy has gotten away with. Do you think they're going to believe the poor girl from Breakers Flats?"

I clench my jaw, shaking my head as I already know he's right.

"They're going to call you a liar until you believe it yourself."

"Colton walked in. He saw what he did to me. He can back me up."

"Colton has lied for Jude in the past and his parents are well aware of it. They're not going to believe a word he says, especially when the whole of Bellevue Springs knows that you and Mr. Carrington share a … connection."

Connection my ass.

I scoff. "So, you're saying that there's nothing I can do about it? I just have to sit back and let that bastard get away with it? I don't think so."

"I didn't say that at all," he murmurs, stepping away. "The

opportunity will present itself and when it does, I trust you will make it count."

Damn fucking straight I will.

I don't respond, but I don't need to. My confirmation is written all over my face. "That's what I thought," Harrison says. "Now, you've already wasted the morning away. I'd suggest that you hurry along and get started on the Carrington's private kitchen and living area."

I nod and he gracefully slips away, somehow making it seem like he was never there in the first place. I take a few deep breaths, desperately trying to calm myself and pull back the need to chase after Colton and put both him and Jude's mother in their place. I find myself watching his back, keeping my eyes trained on the tight muscles beneath his shirt as he practically pushes Mrs. Carter through the door.

He turns around once she's gone and his eyes lift from the ground, zoning straight in on me and it's almost as though he knew I was here all along. He walks toward me, not once taking his eyes off of mine. I find myself sucking in a breath and holding it, for some reason scared to step out of line.

His eyes narrow with every passing second until he finally passes me and is gone without a single word between us.

Why the hell did that feel so damn intense?

I shake it off, feeling like an idiot for allowing him to get to me. He's probably just pissed and hungover after the bullshit from last night, then add the whole listening in on his private conversation thing. Yeah, I'd probably be a little sour myself.

I try to put it to the back of my mind and take myself into the kitchen and look around. The room is a fucking mess. Like it's not just untidy with a few leftover bottles and scattered red cups, it's trashed. The furniture is out of place, the floors are sticky as shit, the pool looks like it's only half filled, while there's a disgusting smell coming from the back half of the room.

Great. Just fucking great.

I let out a heavy sigh and start working out my game plan before getting stuck into it.

I get halfway through when my phone rings and I glance down to find it well and truly after three in the afternoon. Milo's name is flashing on my screen. "Hey, Husband. What's going on?"

"Ugh. Why are you so chirpy at this time of the morning?"

"Morning?" I question. "It's after three in the afternoon. Are you only just getting out of bed?"

"Uh-huh," he grumbles, his voice filled with sleep. "I, uh … you busy?"

"Kinda. I have to clean up after the party. The place is trashed. You should see this shit. It's freaking insane."

Milo scoffs out a laugh but it doesn't sound convincing. "Welcome to a real Bellevue Springs party. Where the rich pricks have never had to clean up after themselves or bother respecting other people's things."

"Ain't that the truth," I grumble.

"Yeah," he says. "Can you talk while you're cleaning?"

I pull my phone away from my ear and hit the speakerphone before I grab a trash bag and start making my way around the pool, collecting all the littered cups as I go. "Yeah, what's up? You kinda disappeared last night."

"Yeah … about that …"

Milo trails off and I'm left staring down at my phone, desperate to hear what's about to come out of his mouth. "You can't just leave it at that. What happened? One second you were showing Jess the time of her life in the pool and the next thing I knew, you were gone."

"Ifuckedher," he rushes out.

"WHAT?"

"I fucked her, okay?" he says, sounding sick to his stomach. "I fucked her and it was … I don't know. It was fucking weird."

"Wait. Hold on. Go back. You did what to that poor girl?" I demand, unable to keep the laugh out of my tone. "How the hell did that even happen? You know she's a chick, right? With tits and a tight little pussy."

"SHUT UP," he yells. "Stop reminding me. I don't even know how this happened. We were in the pool and so fucking drunk and her coochie was pressed up against my man bits and it was just … ready to go."

"Dude …"

"Don't," he groans. "I don't know what to do."

"Well … did you like it?"

A soft groan sounds through the phone and I hold back a laugh. "I mean, it wasn't awful," he tells me thoughtfully. "It was actually kinda nice, you know, once I started picturing her as a dude. But I just … I don't fucking get it. I'm gay. One hundred percent gay. I like dudes. I like big, veiny, hard cocks springing free from their pants and smacking this bitch in the face. Cock, cock, cock. Every day of the fucking week. Cock for breakfast, cock for lunch, cock for dinner. I don't do coochie. Hell, I even went as far as filing coochie away in the 'never go there' box and then topped it off with a 'Do Not Disturb' sign."

"You liked sliding up into that sweet, tight pussy, didn't you? It felt good."

"You're not fucking helping."

I let out a heavy sigh and give it to him straight. "You can look at it in either one of two ways. One, you were experimenting. I'm assuming you've never been with a chick before but how are you supposed to know what you like unless you give it a try?"

"Two. What's option two?" Milo prompts.

I shrug a shoulder despite him not being able to see me. "Maybe you're not as gay as you thought you were. Have you considered that maybe you like both men and women? It's not a crime to be bi, you know? You don't have to pick a side. You can swing that dick both ways and have love for everybody."

"Bi?"

"Mmhmm."

"I don't know," he says thoughtfully. "I'm pretty fond of dick and when your tongue was down my throat, I wanted to bite it the fuck off just so it would go away."

"Hey," I snap. "You're fucking lucky that you got to experience my tongue down your throat. There's a whole lot of boys lining up just to give that a try."

I can practically hear him rolling his eyes. "You're really not helping me."

"Why don't you get up, take a few painkillers and a hot shower, then think about it when your head is a little clearer. Hell, no one would blame you for thinking chicks are hot. We are hot and our coochies are smooth as hell."

"I'm hanging up on you," he growls through the phone.

"Okay," I laugh, rushing it to get the last word in before he hangs up on me. "Call me when you work out what genitalia floats your boat."

The line goes dead and I laugh to myself, feeling like a dickhead for laughing out loud when there's no one around, but fuck it. I know I shouldn't use Milo's confusion as my daily dose of entertainment but how could I not? He can hate on me later, for now, I need a good laugh to distract me from the memory of Jude Fucking Carter.

That fucking prick.

I can't believe Colton had the audacity to allow his mother through that door to preach about what a good little boy that rat bastard is. God, I hope no one ever finds him. Well, anyone from Bellevue Springs that is. If that fucker is going to be found by someone, I'm hoping it's one of the Black Widows—specifically one of my four boys.

Once the pool area is cleared of all the littered cups and trash, I start making my way back inside only to find Colton standing in the kitchen, staring at me as he leans against the marble counter.

I avert my eyes and keep picking up trash, feeling more like the help than ever before. What is it about Colton Carrington that gives him the power to completely humiliate me?

"So, what?" Colton's voice rings out. "You're just not going to talk to me?"

"I'm busy, Colton. Go find some other pathetic bitch to torture."

"Jade."

"Stop," I snap, turning on him and dropping the bag of trash at my feet. "I'm not your little chew toy that you get to fuck around with whenever you want. I told you to hurt me. I gave you exactly what you needed but last night, that was different. That was your pride getting in the way and I'm not about to sit back and allow you or any other fucker in this town make me feel ashamed of who I am or where I come from. You got that, Carrington?"

His eyes tighten and it's like watching that same familiar wall sliding back into place as he tries to work out what the fuck is going on inside his chest. "You done?" he questions, bringing back the version of himself that I thought we'd already worked past. "I don't give a shit about your little sob story. When will you be finished with this room? I'm expecting guests."

I raise a brow while looking at him, my glare sharper than glass. "Are you fucking kidding me right now?" I demand, wondering what the hell happened to the kindhearted boy who sat across from me at my dinner table the other night and told my mother that I was the most breathtaking thing he's ever seen and then went on to say that he wasn't in love with me ... not yet. I threw grapes at him while we got to know each other better and it was perfect, honestly one of the best nights of my life. How does it go downhill so damn fast?

"Does it look like I'm kidding?"

Anger pulses through my veins and after the bullshit with Jude's mom earlier, my patience snaps. I grab the trash bag from my feet and storm into the kitchen. "Fuck you," I growl, slamming the trash bag into his chest. "Fuck you to the deepest pits of hell. Clean up the goddamn room yourself."

I don't say another word as he stares at me in shock. I doubt anyone who has ever worked for the Carrington's has ever spoken to them like that, but if he wants to keep going with this bullshit, then he's going to have to get used to it.

I walk out of the kitchen with his heated eyes on my back, not even caring if he was to fire me right now. If that's what he wants, then he can go right ahead. There's more than enough rich pricks living in Bellevue Springs. I'm sure one of them can be convinced to hire the broken girl from Breakers Flats.

I get to the door when Harrison comes barging in from the other side, momentarily forcing me to put a hold in my dramatic storm off. He briefly looks between me and Colton and I watch the very second he realizes that I've just said something that I probably shouldn't have. His eyes narrow to slits but before he can say anything, I'm out the door, more than ready to get out of here.

"What is it?" I hear Colton's voice trailing from the kitchen behind me.

"Sir," Harrison says. "I have Vincent DeCarlo on the phone for you. He'd like to make you an offer."

"Fuck," Colton sighs, his voice growing more distant by the second. "I'll take it in the office."

CHAPTER 18

"Oceania Munroe," I hear my name hollered through my English classroom.

My eyes snap up from the worksheet on my desk to find Mrs. Matthews' harsh stare on me, sending nerves pulsing through my veins. Her hand hovers over the phone on her desk and dread settles heavily into my gut. What did I do? I swear I haven't called anyone a rude bitch all day. The only time my name has ever been called out by a teacher holding a phone was when I was about to get my ass handed to me.

"Umm ... yes?"

"You're ten minutes late for your scheduled appointment with the guidance counselor. Why are you still sitting in my classroom?"

My gaze flicks across to Jess who sits beside me before landing back on Mrs. Matthews'. "I'm sorry. Who? I didn't schedule an appointment."

"It is compulsory and you are currently giving yourself a bad name. Now hurry up and attend your appointment before you're forced to reschedule and miss more class time."

"Yeah, okay," I say, pushing up from my chair and grabbing my things. I look back at Jess. "What's this about?"

She shrugs her shoulders. "You can never be too sure with that one, but seeing as though you're new, I'd assume she just wants to touch base and know what your next steps are."

"Next steps?"

"Don't ask. It's her motto. Everything is about the 'next step.'"

My face scrunches in distaste. I don't know whether I'd prefer to suffer through this English class or get stuck with someone wanting to poke their nose into my business, but unlucky for me, I don't exactly have a choice. "Where am I supposed to go?"

"Third door on the right after you pass the student office. You can't miss it. Her name is Miss Davies, it's on the door."

I give Jess a small smile and as I go to leave, she pulls me back. "Hey, Ocean," she whisper-yells. I look back at her, waiting to hear whatever other useful advice she's got for me to help me through this little meeting. "While you're gone, could you check in with Milo? I haven't heard from him since the party."

Hmm, apparently Jess is all out of useful advice.

"I, uh …"

"Oceania," Mrs. Matthews snaps. "Miss Davies has been very patiently waiting for you. You're wasting her time and now mine. Get a move on."

I give Jess a tight smile and scram. The last thing I need is to be the one to have to break it to her that Milo was just using her for a little fun. That's assuming he decides that he wants to go back to eating cocks for breakfast, lunch, and dinner. I mean, I'm all down for that, but it's not an issue if he wanted to have a little coochie for an afternoon snack.

I get my ass down to the student office and start looking for Miss Davies' office and just as Jess had said, I find her name scrawled across the third door on the right. I give a small knock, cringing with the thought of what I'm about to find.

"Come in," a timid voice says from inside the office.

I twist the handle and push the door open to find a young woman staring back at me through thick rimmed glasses. Her hair is down, and without the expensive skirt suit she wears she'd look like a younger, more chilled out version of my mom. "Hey, umm … sorry. I didn't know I had an appointment that I was supposed to attend."

"That's perfectly fine, Oceania," she says, waving me through. "Please, take a seat. We have a lot to cover."

"A lot to cover?" I question, somehow managing to hide my groan. "Like what?"

"Like your future."

"Future?" I say with a sharp, barking laugh. "What future?"

Miss Davies has the nerve to look offended and honestly, I don't think she has the right. She mustn't know who she's dealing with if she thinks a girl like me is about to have some big respectable future.

Her eyes narrow on me and it's as though she's trying to work me out. I wait a moment, suffering through her silence before she sits back in her chair, apparently having exactly what she needs. Though if she knows something I don't, it'd be great if she could share it around.

"Tell me, Oceania. Why does the idea of a future scare you?"

My brows instantly pinch together. Scare me? What the hell is she talking about? I was expecting a lot of things to come flying out of her mouth but that certainly wasn't one of them. "It's just Ocean," I clarify.

Her lips pull into a small smile. "Ocean," she repeats, leaning forward and adjusting my name in her schedule. "I like it. It's very original. Now let's get back to the question, shall we?"

I shake my head. "You've got me all wrong. I'm not scared of my future."

"No?"

"No. You can't be scared of something that you're never going to have." Her brow shoots up and as she silently leans back in her chair, I feel her waiting for an explanation. Realizing that I'm not going to get out of here until we're through, I give her my hard truth, knowing damn well that hiding it has never gotten me anywhere before.

"Did you look me up?" I question, watching as she gives me a small nod. "Then you know that I'm from Breakers Flats, and the kids there … they're not exactly taught to dream big. The majority of my class won't graduate and will be either killed by the time they're thirty or jumped into a gang, and those of us who do graduate might get a job working at the grocery store. That is until the banks lock the doors and we're left selling ourselves just to get by. People like me, we're not taught to dream for a future because it's hard enough just getting through each day. Dreaming is for those who like disappointment. We're taught to survive."

Miss Davies studies me, keeping her eyes trained on mine as she puts to use that degree that's framed up on her wall. "You know what I see?"

"Here we go. Another qualified person here to tell me what's best for me when they don't know anything about my life or growing up like I did."

"Oh really? You're so quick to judge but what would you say if you found out that I grew up in Blaxlands Grove and only just escaped gang life after my brother got jumped in? I worked my ass off, graduated high school, and by some miracle was accepted into college? What would you say then?"

My eyes bug out of my head, I would say her brother is most likely a Wolf. "You grew up in Blaxlands Grove?" I question, not sure if I should be wary of the girl who comes from the rival town of Breakers Flats, home of the West Side Wolves.

"I did," she says. "I made a life for myself. I broke ties with the people from back home who were holding me back and I built a future for myself. I went to college, graduated, and got myself a job. I had to start small but I worked my way up, and now I own my own home and don't need a man to help provide it for me. You can do that too, Ocean. You just have to believe in yourself."

"You say it like it's easy."

"It's not," she says bluntly. "Making it to my high school graduation was a feat on its own, and then to get myself through college while not succumbing to my family who wanted me home was the hardest thing I ever did."

"Then you're the one in a million. It's not going to happen for me so you shouldn't bother wasting your time."

"I think you're wrong," she tells me. "I've been going over your grades and reports, and while the reports are a little rough, the grades aren't so bad. You've already taken the first step by distancing yourself from Breakers Flats. All you need to do is focus on your grades and I don't see any reason why you won't be able to attend college."

"Okay," I say with a laugh. "Have you considered the fact that college costs money? Say some kind of miracle occurs and I do get in, what then? How am I supposed to pay for that? I'm sure as hell not going to take any more money out of my mother's pocket, and I'll be damned if I was to ask one of these rich pricks for a loan."

"It's called a job," she says bluntly. "I worked at Hooters for four years, six nights a week while I studied through the day and look at me now. I have a great paying job, respect from my colleagues, and was able to purchase a home. It is possible, Ocean. It's hard work but you don't need to be another statistic. Make something of yourself. Be the one that got out."

I lean back in my chair, looking at the woman who wants to tear down my complete belief system. "You really think I can do it?"

"I bet you grew up thinking it was impossible to get out of Breakers Flats and look at you now. You've already taken the first step, but now you need to make it count."

Well, shit. Who the hell taught her all this motivational crap? It's dangerous. It's making me want things that a girl like me should never be brave enough to dream about.

"I don't know," I tell her honestly. "My plan was to just try to keep afloat out here and find a job after graduation. I could find somewhere cheap to rent and live, trying every day to not make the kinds of decisions that would see me back in Breakers Flats with the Black Widows."

Her brow raises. "You have connections to the Black Widows?"

A strange tension settles in the air and something tells me to keep my mouth shut about my boys. I shake my head. "No, I just … I figured that's where I'd end up."

"Oh, I see," she says. "My brother is a Wolf and would have a heart attack if he thought I was trying to help out a Widow."

I laugh as I try to figure out who could possibly be her brother. "Oh, no. I've always tried to keep away from the gangs. I've already lost my father, I don't need to lose anything else."

Her brows furrow and she leans forward to look over her papers. "Wait. Munroe?" she says, thoughtful. "What was your father's name?"

Unease settles into me but I can't find a good excuse not to tell her. After all, she could probably just look it up. "His name was Louis."

"Louis Munroe," she says, her eyes sparkling with excitement.

"Your dad was Big Lou?"

I shake my head. "Umm, no … I think you've got him confused with someone else. It's a very common name."

"No," she says. "He was good friends with my father. I remember him saying he had a daughter your age. Why didn't you say you had connections to the Wolves? I would have had your college applications already filled out and sent off the day you arrived."

My brows furrow. "Okay … you've really got your wires crossed. I'm certainly not a Wolf and my father wasn't affiliated with any gangs."

Confusion twists her features. "Are you sure?"

"I'm certain."

"Oh, sorry. I just … I guess I assumed."

I shrug my shoulders and give her a small smile while I'm dying on the inside. I need to get to Nic and I need to ask what the hell he knows. There's no way my father was a Wolf because that would make me one of them and that's just not possible. If I was one of them then my boys … fuck. I need to work this out.

"Alright, enough of that," she says, moving along. "Tell me what you'd like to do with yourself. Do you have any idea what field you'd like to move into or what you'd want to study if you get into college?"

"I, umm …" I try to bring my mind back to the present, but I'm stuck filtering through every last thing I know about my dad and I end up looking back up at her, feeling way out of my depth. "I actually have no idea," I tell her. "I guess I've never actually had to think about it before."

"Okay, that's perfectly fine," she says. "Why don't you think about it over the next few days and come back to me when you've worked it out. Then we can start making a plan for your future. How does that sound?"

She gives me a warm smile and just like that, my whole world has been tipped upside down.

By the time I'm walking through the door after school I'm an absolute mess. I don't know if I should be thinking about my future, my dad, my fucked up relationship with Colton, or if I should be calling Nic to ask what he knows. But then that's probably just going to cause even more problems. What I should really be doing is sitting down with mom and asking her about it. If anyone around here is going to know what dad was into, it'd be her, right? She's always tried to steer me clear of the Black Widows. Perhaps there's more to it than just wanting me away from my crew.

My mind is so clouded with the endless thoughts that I don't even notice Jacqueline Vanderbilt loitering in the foyer until it's already too late. "You there," she calls, looking down at me as my head snaps up. "I have been waiting for twenty minutes. Where is Colton Carrington?"

My face scrunches up in distaste. "How should I know?" I demand, looking at the evil witch who thought she was going to get away with inheritance fraud. Considering she's happily standing here, I'm assuming she still thinks she's about to race off into the sunset with Charles' buckets of cash. "You literally just saw me walk through the door. Am I supposed to be able to read minds?"

"You work here, don't you?" she demands before letting out a frustrated sigh. "Are you stupid? Go and find him."

"Fuck you," I snap. "I'm not on the clock. Go and find him yourself, you daft bitch."

Her eyes bug out of her head and her palm instantly races toward my face, but I'm ready for it. The girls around here only come equipped with the one move. My fingers curl around her wrist and I hold her hand up, refusing to let go. "I wouldn't if I were you," I taunt. "I could fuck you up a million different ways before you even knew what was happening."

"Release me now," she spits through clenched teeth. "Or I swear to God, when I take over this place, your little bitch ass will be the first to go."

A grin spreads wide across my face and I step into her, watching as her eyes widen in fear. She tries to back up, but I move right along with her. "I dare you to try," I beg of her. "Today is the day you do not want to mess with me."

Jaqueline sucks in a deep breath but luckily keeps her mouth closed, and upon realizing that she doesn't have a leg to stand on, I finally start to back off. My fingers slowly uncurl from her wrist and by the time I step back and allow her the chance to breathe, a throat clears behind me. "Miss Vanderbilt," Harrison says, pleasantly pretending as though he didn't just witness me threatening one of our guests. "Please take a seat in the living area. Mr. Carrington will be with you in a brief moment."

Jaqueline huffs and turns so quickly on her heel that her hair whips across my face and I resist the urge to grab hold of it and tear out her fake extensions. She stalks off to the living room and I glare after her before turning and slamming straight into a solid wall of muscle.

Colton catches me as I rebound off his chest and I scrunch up my face, feeling pain tear through my poor little nose. "What the hell are you doing?" I demand, grabbing hold of my nose as Colton's skin burns against my arms. "What kind of idiot creeps up behind a girl?"

"Fuck, Jade," he says, his eyes filled with concern. "Are you okay?"

I pull out of his reach and will my eyes not to well up as the pain rockets through me. *I'm going to be okay. I'm going to be okay. Do not cry in front of him.*

"I'm fine, but why do you care? Afraid I'm going to sue you for a new nose?"

"Jade," he says, his voice lowering with concern.

I shake my head in disappointment, but as I go to walk away a knock sounds at the door. Colton quickly glances around before looking over my shoulder at the living room, finding no trace of Harrison. He cringes. "Am I way out of line to ask you to get that?"

"Are you fucking kidding me?"

"Please, babe. I have to deal with Jacqueline and trust me, you're going to want to see this."

I let out a groan and start making my way to the door, hoping to God that I don't have a bleeding nose. I look back over my shoulder to find Colton making his way toward the living room, and as if sensing my gaze on him, he looks back at me with raw emotion pulsing through his heavy stare.

God. Why does he make it so hard to hate him?

I look back to the door and keep my eyes glued there until my hand curls around the handle and I tear it open. I stare ahead, slightly confused with my heart racing. If these guys showed up on my doorstep in Breakers Flats, it could only mean that someone was dead, or that someone was about to be. Though, considering Jacqueline Vanderbilt is in the other room, it's all pretty clear.

"Ma'am," the officer on the right says, probably being the first person in my whole life to address me that way. "My name is Officer Laney. We were called to assist Mr. Carrington."

Well, well. Maybe Colton was right, I really don't want to miss this.

I step out of the way and wave them through before pointing out the living room. They're quick to jump into action and start making their way toward it with me being far too nosey for my own good and following behind them.

I step into the living room just in time to watch the smug grin on Jacqueline's face drop in horror, realizing that she's been caught.

Fuck yes. That was so damn satisfying.

She quickly pulls herself together. "What is the meaning of this?" she demands, waving her hand toward the police. "This is a private matter."

Colton laughs, his eyes briefly flicking toward me. "You really thought that you'd get away with this?" he questions. "I'm Colton Fucking Carrington. Bitches like you have been trying to weasel your way into my father's bank account for years. You're a snake and you'll never get your hands on a single dime, but it's okay, you won't be needing it where you're going."

Her eyes bug out of her head and a laugh bubbles up my throat.

Jacqueline shoots her nasty glare at me. "You think this is funny?"

"Yeah, actually, I do," I tell her, making a show of pulling out my phone. "You're a fraud who took advantage of Colton while he's trying to grieve for his lost father. You're getting exactly what you deserve, but it's going to be even funnier recording you getting arrested. Do me a favor and make it super dramatic. Throw in some squeals and maybe those crocodile tears that I bet you're so good at. It'll make great footage for all my social media accounts. I wonder if it will go viral?" I pause for a brief moment, scoffing at my own idiocy. "Duh. Of course it will. This is Charles Carrington we're talking about. I bet I could sell it for a good price too."

A high-pitched squeal comes tearing out of her and she runs at me, claws out and ready to go. The two cops dive for her and I quickly hit record. "This is great, by the way," I say as she screams while making sure to keep Colton's face off camera. "Keep up the good work."

Jacqueline is handcuffed and as she's pulled away, Officer Laney begins reading her rights. She's taken outside and we follow the cops to the door, watching as they start carting her downstairs and then all too soon, the door is closed and Colton and I are left standing in the quiet foyer, neither of us knowing what the hell to say.

I look up at him, meeting the eyes that make my heart both race and break at the same damn time. His stare softens and is quickly filled with regret. Although I'm desperate for some kind of apology and to feel him pull me into his arms, I simply don't have the strength to deal with it right now. So, I do what any other self-respecting girl would do and walk away.

CHAPTER 19

I stare up at the graying clouds above as I lay in the thick, manicured grass of the Carrington property. I don't know how the hell Charles managed to make the grass this damn soft, but it's no surprise that he was so proud of it. Well, to be honest, the softness of the grass probably has absolutely nothing to do with him. He probably didn't know the first thing about taking care of the lawn, but he certainly took the credit for it.

Back home, our grass was always brown and kinda prickly and the thought of lying in it sends chills racing down my spine. I think this is the first time in my life that I've ever voluntarily laid in the grass and I'm really starting to see the appeal.

The past month has been hell. I've suffered through all sorts of shit from the people of Bellevue Springs, things that no seventeen-year-old girl should ever have to face. If I could do it all over again, I think I'd try harder to talk Mom out of coming here, but she's so damn happy here. How could I have been the reason she missed out on that?

Mom knows most of the bullshit that's been going on, but if I were to tell her about Jude, she'd pack us up and leave. One part of me screams for it, screams to be released from this hell, to be somewhere that I won't have the constant reminder of what he did to me ... but the other part, the part that desperately wants to be accepted, that part of me won't let me leave.

To be honest, Colton is a massive part of that too.

If I were a smart girl, I would have been out of here after I was cornered by those boys and had acidic grease poured all over me. Hell, if I were smart, I would have left after the first time that Jude welcomed himself into my room. I thought I was stronger. I thought that I could handle it, but I was wrong—so fucking wrong. I knew Jude was a predator and I knew he had me in his sights. Walking out to the pool area was a bad move, but allowing myself to be out there alone, that was just stupid.

The greying clouds become darker and soon cover the late afternoon sky, making it appear later in the evening that what it really is. My eyes close and I take a few deep breaths, trying to release all the tortuous thoughts from my mind. I've been holding onto so much anger and I'm getting closer and closer to the edge. I'm eventually going to break and I don't even want to be around me when that happens.

I take a slow breath in, hold it for two, and then let it out.

Repeat.

And again.

With each breath I blow out, I let go of something that's been weighing me down. The frustration of Nic's protectiveness, the pain at having to let down Charlie, and the way I miss both my crew and the ridiculous boys at BSA. But most of all, I want to let go of the hurt of Colton's rejection, it's just going to take a little more than a few calming breaths to completely lose that pain. His public rejection cut deep but that's on me. I saw it coming and still dove headfirst, practically begging for it.

I go over my new little ritual at least thirty times before I hear thunder rumbling in the distance and for some reason, it's soothing as hell. Is this what it's like to meditate? I don't know, I can't say I've ever tried it before, but if this is it, I completely understand it. I'm chilled the fuck out. Colton can come at me with his bullshit right now and I'd just smile and wave until he walked his fine ass away.

Nothing can destroy this moment.

For the first time since being here, I feel refreshed. I might even read another book tonight or hell, maybe I'll just stay here until the clouds pass and watch the sky move along until the stars come out to play.

The weight on my shoulders seems to have disappeared but I know the second I get back to real life, it'll all start pressing down on me again, so damn it, I'm going to enjoy this brief moment of freedom while I can.

The first raindrops begin to fall and I cringe as they splash on my face. I don't want this to end. I could stay here forever and live a happy life.

What's the harm? It's only a little water.

The soft rainfall splashes down around me until a loud crack of lightning flashes through the sky. Thunder rumbles through Bellevue Springs and within seconds, the rain comes pouring.

My clothes are soaked through within moments and the chill quickly begins seeping through to my bones but I don't dare move, I just continue lying in the grass, soaking in the moment.

There's something refreshing about being out in the rain. I don't even think that I can explain it. It's just me being one with nature and maybe that makes me sound kinda crazy, but I don't care—at least not right now. I'll probably be a little pissed with my decision come tomorrow when my nose is all stuffy and I'm running a fever. For now, I'm chilling and I fucking love it.

Ten minutes pass before I hear him.

Get fucked. Why is he always around to ruin something good?

Colton storms up to me and doesn't even give me a chance to pull away before he grabs hold of me and somehow pulls me right up from the grass and over his shoulder. "What the fuck do you think you're doing?" He demands as he madly dashes back to the house. "Are you insane or just stupid? Can't you tell it's fucking pouring down with rain?"

I start kicking my legs and slamming my hands down over his back as water rushes off me. "Put me down, asshole. I was enjoying myself."

"Enjoy yourself inside like the rest of the human population does when it's raining."

"Fuck you."

"Fuck you right back, Jade." Anger rests heavy in his tone which only manages to piss me off more. He doesn't have the right to be angry with me. I didn't do anything wrong. He's the one who drew me in, made Mom gush about how incredible he is, and then pushed me away the second someone was going to find out about us. Us? Were we even an 'us'? He certainly had no issues telling my mom we were together without actually consulting me about that first.

I don't know. I honestly shouldn't even care. It was like one day of perfectness. One day where I thought I was going to have it all. One day where he treated me the way I've always wanted him to. Maybe I'm overthinking this whole thing.

Colton breaks through the rain and when he finally pushes through the door, he doesn't drop my ass in the closest chair like I'd assumed he would. He keeps his hand over my ass, holding me steady as he silently makes his way through the house. I'm not fooled though, his silence isn't him being calm, it's him biting his tongue and forcing himself not to say what he really wants to say.

"Where are you taking me, dickhead?" I demand, banging my fist against his back, desperately trying to break his silence, knowing damn well that when he does, he won't be able to hold back. The words are going to spill from his mouth and they're going to be exactly what I need to get all fired up. Maybe relaxing wasn't what I needed after all, maybe I just really need to scream and let it all out. Fuck, that would be fun. Nothing gets me hotter than screaming at Colton Carrington and putting him in his place.

His hand slaps down over my ass and fury burns within me. "Let me go."

"NO."

A battle cry tears from the back of my throat and I lose my shit, slamming my hands down over him and trying to wriggle free, only his hold tightens and I'm locked over his shoulder. His hold is unbreakable and it's as though he's physically strapped me down, that is until he races up the stairs and slams through his bedroom door.

He walks right into his bathroom and as he steps through to his shower, he grabs hold of me, pulling me off his shoulder and flipping me the right way up. My back is slammed against the tiles and he holds me still as his other hand twists the taps, sending water shooting down over both of us.

"What do you think you're doing?" I demand, but as the hot water slams down over my skin, it becomes startlingly clear just how fucking cold I am. The water is warm but feels as though it's burning my skin. I try to break free, but he holds me there, his eyes filled with an intensity that I've never seen before. He's filled with anger, but there's also something else … something that I'm not quite sure of.

The water quickly begins to warm me and I feel myself desperately needing more—more heat, more anger, more of him.

Tears well up in my eyes, surprising the ever-loving shit out of me as an emotional overload begins to rock through me.

What the hell is this? What's happening?

Colton just stares, watching me go through whatever the hell this is. He steps into me and my walls instantly shoot up, fearlessly trying to protect myself. My hand slams out, pressing against his chest and forcing him to keep a distance, but he grabs it and pushes it aside, relentless as he grows nearer.

His hand flies to the back of my neck and within the blink of an eye, his warm lips are pressing down on mine. I kiss him back for all of three seconds before my senses come back to me. "No," I demand, pushing against his chest.

Colton shakes his head, his eyes wild with need, ignoring my pleas as though he knows what I need more than I could ever understand. His thumb rubs up and down my cold cheek and he moves back into me, this time not allowing me the chance to pull away.

His lips come down on mine and my will power breaks as I melt into him. His large body presses mine against the cold tiles but I don't even notice it, all that matters are his lips on mine, completely devouring me and somehow making me forget the torturous world around me.

Need slams through me and suddenly he's not the guy who rejected me at the party, he's not the guy who's been driving me to the edge of insanity, but he's the one who could offer a release. He could give me exactly what I need and I'll be damned if I'm going to stop.

I grab the hem of his shirt and tear it over his head, desperate to feel his skin beneath my fingers. He's so fucking warm—warmer than what is humanly possible. He's superhuman, always filled with perfection, always so much more than what I was expecting.

My drenched tank is pulled over my head and as his hands find my skin, everything comes to life within me. I need his touch more than I need to breathe.

Colton's lips come back to mine and we desperately peel each other out of our remaining clothes. We listen to the heavy rush of water spraying against our skin and the sound of our wet clothes dropping onto the shower floor while becoming lost to our most basic urges.

Without another thought, I jump up into his arms, wrapping my legs around him as his arm curls around my waist, holding me steady against the shower wall. I feel his hard, veiny cock at my entrance and without hesitation, he slams it deep within me.

My eyes roll to the back of my head. I don't know how fucking long I've been craving that, needing it with every part of my being. "Holy shit," I pant as a low, drawn-out "fucccck," pulls from deep within his chest.

My arms curl around his neck, holding myself up as I don't doubt this is about to be a wild ride, one that I don't want to fall off of. Colton's fingers dig into my waist and I'm damn sure that it's going to bruise but I welcome it with wide, open arms. I'd give anything to feel everything that he's got.

He starts to move, drawing himself back out of me before sliding back in. I groan low in the back of my throat, getting used to his incredible size as he fills me to the brim. He seats himself balls-deep inside me and it's as though he was made just for me. It's so fucking right. Denying this for so damn long should be a crime.

His lips come back to mine as he pulls back again, a little faster now, really starting to give us both what we've been needing since the day I first walked in here.

Colton fucks me deep, hard, and wild, sending my world into a complete tailspin. Don't get me wrong, I'm no prude. I've slept with my fair share of men, but I didn't know it could be like this. It was incredible with Nic, but this is new level shit. Maybe it's the intensity that comes along with it or maybe it's just Colton, but all I know is that I've died and gone to heaven because nothing is better than this moment right now.

Colton holds on to me, refusing to let me go. His body pressed up against mine and completely consuming me.

I feel that familiar tingle building inside of me, burning and growing with need and I know this is going to be explosive. Hell, the library has nothing on this. Colton moves like a fucking God and damn it, I'm so close to getting on my hands and knees and worshipping him like one.

Flames burst within me and I hold onto him, claiming everything I possibly can. He gives it to me just how I need it, as if reading my body like a book, satisfying every burning desire within me until stars are blurring my vision.

Colton's hand lowers to my ass, grabbing hold and squeezing firmly as his other slips between our bodies and wreaks havoc on my clit.

In. Out. In. Out. It's fucking torture.

His low groan in my ear sends chills sweeping through my body as his heated skin against mine drives me to insanity. I love it—every little thing. The smell of his body, the feel of his touch, the sound of his need. I want everything he has to offer, and damn it, he gives it all to me.

My orgasm builds until I physically can't hold onto it any longer and everything shatters within me. Stars dance behind my eyes and I'm filled with euphoria. My nails dig into his sun-kissed skin and my head falls to his shoulder. "Fuck, Colton," I groan as my orgasm completely overwhelms me.

Colton keeps moving, letting me ride it out as I clench down around him but all too soon, he tears out of me. The need to scream pulses through me as he comes hard which is when I realize that we didn't use a condom. Hell, I didn't even think about it in my desperation to feel him inside of me.

His rapid breaths slowly begin to return to normal as he holds me up in his arms. "Fuck, Jade."

My head falls back against the tiles and I meet his heated stare. "You can say that again," I murmur, still panting from the rollercoaster of a ride he just took me on.

A smirk pulls at his lips just moments before they're back on mine and once again, I find myself melting into him. He pulls me off the confines of the shower tiles and holds me under the warm water. "I can't say that I was expecting that," I rumble as we finally pull away from each other.

"Well, you better expect it from now on because I plan on doing that over and over again. Fuck the bullshit rules. I don't want to hold back from you anymore."

I pull back a little more, feeling myself beginning to sober. "You mean that?"

"Which part?"

"The over and over again part? You and I both know that come tomorrow you'll happily put the rules back in place, but the over and over again part, if you're just fucking with me, that's really going to suck."

"I'm not fucking with you, Jade."

"Good, because it's one thing to push me away altogether, but it's another expecting me to be here for a good fucking time whenever you don't have an audience."

"So," he says, putting me back on my feet and holding onto me as my legs continue to shake. His arm slips around my waist and he pulls me in tight. "Are you saying that we have no other issues?"

"You'd be a fool to assume we had no other issues," I tell him. "There are some things a good fuck can't fix, Colton, but you're certainly heading in the right direction."

His brow arches as my hands roam over his strong shoulders. "Really?" he questions, reaching around me and turning off the water. "So, you're saying that if I were to take you to my bed and do that all over again ...?"

"That I'd *consider* forgiving you for the party."

"Just consider, huh?" I nod and his lips press into a flat line. "And what about everything else?"

"Everything else is going to have to come with time," I tell him truthfully. "But stepping up and being the kind of man who shamelessly goes after what he wants, well that's the kind of thing a woman won't be able to resist."

"Well then," he says, lifting me once again. "I think I have a few things to make up for."

Colton steps out of the shower, taking me with him and before a laugh can slip between my lips, he's throwing me down on his bed and coming down on top of me with a promise not to stop until he's earned every ounce of my forgiveness.

CHAPTER 20

My hands press against Colton's chest as I stare down at him, desperately trying to catch my breath as his cock remains seated deep within me. What is it about being on top of a guy that always seems to make it plunge so much deeper? I could feel him in my throat for most of that, though luckily we remembered to wrap it up before I sank down onto it.

"I could get used to this," I tell him.

A wide grin splits across his face and it blows me the fuck away. It's absolutely breathtaking. If I had a camera right now, I'd be taking a photo to make sure this moment lasts forever.

Colton catches my hand and pulls me down beside him until I'm curled into his side with my head against his wide chest. Contentment settles over me. I'm fucking home. I've never had this feeling with anyone, not even Nic, but with Colton, it just feels so damn right.

I wonder if he feels the same …

Does this mean something to him like it does to me, or is this his last shot at making Daddy Warbucks roll over in his grave? God knows that Charles would never approve of me and Colton together and all of Bellevue Springs would agree with him, apart from maybe Charlie but that's probably because he was hoping for the same thing himself.

Colton's hand starts rubbing up and down my bare back and all those ridiculous thoughts fade from my mind. This has to be real. It feels so right, how could it not be? "You're not running," I comment, all too used to his usual routine of scrambling away from me anytime he gets too close.

"I'm not," he tells me. "Not anymore. The last few days with you pissed at me have sucked. I hated not being able to just kiss you whenever the fuck I wanted."

"To be fair, my mood never really stopped you from doing it before."

A low chuckle rumbles through the room. "That was different and you know it. After the party …"

I let out a heavy sigh, knowing exactly what he's referring to. Every time he has hurt me or tried to push me away, I've always bounced back. I was always ready for more, always ready to fight back, but during that goddamn party, he crossed the line and he didn't just hurt me, he completely shattered me.

"I pulled away," I whisper, finishing off his thought.

"You did," he murmurs, his voice trailing off into the room, sounding more like a distant thought. He clears his throat and holds me a little tighter. "I owe you an apology." Colton's low voice rumbles through the room, somehow waking the butterflies in my stomach as I feel the vibrations of his tone through his chest. His words hit deep and I find myself looking up and meeting his perfect hazel eyes.

"You're going to have to be a little more specific," I murmur, unable to stop the smirk that pulls at my lips. "There are a few things …"

His hand trails lower to my ass and he gives it a gentle squeeze, showing off just how perfectly the size of his hand fits around my ass. "For everything," he tells me. "Since the day you arrived here, I've done nothing but try to tear you down and you just kept coming back, proving over and over again just how fucking strong you are. I thought you were going to be different, but I was so fucking wrong. I underestimated you, Jade, and that's the biggest mistake I've ever made."

"You did," I whisper, sliding my hand over his chest until it meets with his. Our fingers lace together and I find myself gently pressing my lips against his. "I've just never understood why. Why push me away like you did? What's the purpose of being an ass the second I walked in here?"

"Because you made me feel something and it scared the shit out of me. My whole life has been planned out for me. Every last detail since before I was born so when something unexpected comes along, it throws me off course, and fuck, Jade. You didn't just throw me, you fucking launched me. Everything changed when you came along."

"You really mean that?" I question, feeling the emotions beginning to drown me.

Colton nods ever so slightly and rolls us until he's looking down at me. "I do," he tells me. "I'm not going to lie to you, this thing between us still scares the shit out of me. I don't know what it is, what it means, or where we even go from here, but I know that I'm never letting you go. I don't give a damn what Nic or any of those friends of yours say, you're mine now."

"Even in public?"

He nods, "Even in public."

Well, shit. Today took a turn.

"So," I say, needing an escape from the overwhelming emotions that are running so deep that they're starting to make me feel things I didn't know I was capable of. "You think you can give me one award-winning speech and throw in a few apologies and suddenly claim me like property?"

His eyes bug out of his head. "I … no. Fuck, Jade. I didn't mean it like that. I …"

"I'm just teasing you," I laugh as a blinding smile cuts across my face, absolute joy tearing through me.

He stares at me blankly. "What's the chick version of an asshole?"

I shake my head. "I think it's still an asshole, but I guess that means we now have something in common."

He watches me with his eyes shimmering with joy and everything inside of me warms. How is it possible for this to be so damn perfect? I always knew he had this power over me, but I never knew it could feel so pure, so strong, and filled with emotion.

I better not be falling for this guy because when he realizes that I'm just an average girl from Breakers Flats and leaves me, it's going to suck, like really fucking suck.

"You're going to be trouble, Oceania Munroe."

I raise my chin, brushing my lips gently across his and not even caring that he used my full name. All that matters right here is us. "More than you could know."

Colton catches my lips in his and he kisses me deeply, sending my whole body into overdrive. My arms snake around his neck and I feel his heavy cock hardening against my thigh. He slips his hand down between us and within moments, he's sliding back into me for the third time tonight.

He starts to move and my eyes roll to the back of my head. How is it possible for him to hit it so good every damn time?

Colton thrusts up into me and just as his hands lace through mine, a loud alarm tears through the mansion. His body stiffens and fear shines through his eyes. "Fuck," he rushes out, tearing out of me and flying off the bed. "Get dressed."

"What?" I demand, calling over the noise as I sit up on the edge of the bed, feeling panic begin to rise within me, but why? "What's going on?"

Colton rushes into his closet and returns a second later, tossing a shirt and sweatpants at my chest while quickly pulling on clothes of his own.

"Colton?" I demand, stepping into the sweatpants.

He rushes over to me and practically shoves my head through the shirt before grabbing my hand and hauling ass out of his bedroom. "Colton," I yell. "What the fuck is going on?"

He looks back at me and the panic in his eyes is so much more. It's not just fear but absolute terror and coming from a guy who so fearlessly stood up against my crew, that's a big fucking call. "We have to get to the panic room."

"Panic room?" I shriek. "What for? What's going on?"

He shakes his head, his jaw clenching. "I don't know, but my guess is the DeCarlo family is sick of waiting."

"What?"

He cringes, still pulling me along. "I sorta told Vincent DeCarlo where the fuck he could stick his shitty offer, and possibly insinuated that he could go and fuck his own mother in the process."

My eyes bug out of my head. I don't know these people but I know gang leaders and I'm assuming they all work the same. "You disrespected his fucking mother? Are you insane? Do you have a fucking death wish? He's out for blood."

"Just … I know. Okay, I know. It was fucking stupid but you had the shits with me. Jacqueline was trying to do me fucking dirty, and I just snapped. It wasn't my finest moment."

I pull back on his hand, desperate to bring him to a stop, really not giving a shit about his explanation. "My mom is out there somewhere. Harrison and Maryne too. We can't just leave them."

He pulls back, practically dragging me along the hallway. "They'll be okay. They have emergency procedures in place for attacks. This isn't the first time something like this has happened. Please, Jade. Just let me get you to safety."

Procedures? What procedures? I've been here for over a month and this is the first I'm hearing about it, and I can guarantee that if Mom knew something about a procedure that was put in place to keep me safe, she would have told me at the first chance she got.

She doesn't know anything about this.

"No," I scream, hearing a loud banging noise from downstairs, so loud that I hear it perfectly over the alarm. "I have to find her. I have to know she's okay."

Colton groans and as he looks back at me, I see nothing but regret. I try to pull away, knowing exactly what I'm seeing in his eyes because it's the same thing that's looked back at me from my four boys anytime shit went down in Breakers Flats.

My hand is pulled free of his and I take off at a sprint, desperate to find my mom and get her away. When shit goes down, we never leave someone behind. That's just the way it is. That's just what being family means.

Colton's steel grip crushes around me and I'm lifted off the ground. He throws me over his shoulder and I desperately try to get free. "I have to get to my mom," I scream with tears rolling down my cheeks.

"I'm sorry," he says, running through the hall, the alarm so deafening that I hardly hear myself think. "Please forgive me."

Colton runs into a room upstairs that I've never been in before and steps in front of a huge family portrait. There's a keypad on the golden frame and he hashes in a code. The whole wall sinks back, making a door and he rushes into a hidden room before pressing another button and the heavy door slides closed.

"No," I cry, kicking until he lets me down. I run for the door, pressing every fucking button I can find, desperate for it to open. Getting absolutely nowhere, I turn back to Colton. "How could you do that? My mom is out there. Open the door."

He shakes his head. "I'm sorry," he says, hurrying over to a massive computer system and turning it on. "I can't do that."

"You have to," I cry, rushing after him.

"I'm sorry, Ocean. I won't risk you like that," he tells me. "Once the door is sealed, it won't open until the threat is gone. The cops were notified the second the alarm sounded. They're going to be alright."

I slam my hands into his back, demanding his undivided attention. "That's my mom. *My fucking mom.* You're just going to leave her out there to get hurt? Who are you?"

Colton turns around and I instantly slam my hands into his chest, over and over until he pulls me into him and locks me in his steel arms, caging me in. "I'm sorry," he murmurs as the fat tears continue rolling down my cheeks. "Just trust me, please. Your mom is going to be alright. She's a smart woman. They gain nothing from hurting her. They're after me."

"Then let *me* go." When he doesn't respond, I feel myself breaking like never before. "Please," I whisper.

I feel as he shakes his head. "I need to let go of you, Ocean. I have to turn on the camera so we can see what's happening out there. Are you going to be alright?"

I shake my head, not knowing what I'm going to do, but as he releases me from his tight grip, all I feel is empty. I sag to the concrete ground and drop my face into my hands as sobs tear painfully from deep in my chest.

I feel his eyes on me as he steps back in front of the computers but I don't dare look up at him as I know all I'm going to find is his pity. Minutes pass and I hear loud yelling coming from the ground floor of the mansion and I can't help but raise my gaze to the monitors to watch what's happening below.

There must be four or five men storming through the mansion each with a black bandana covering the majority of their faces. They're dressed in all black and if I didn't know any better, I'd say that it looked like there was a gang war going on downstairs.

"Is that the DeCarlo family?" I question as I watch them make their way through the mansion, looking like my worst kind of nightmare. This is the kind of thing that I would have expected to happen in Breakers Flats, but here, I thought we were safe.

"Yes," he says. "They're Vincent's sons. They're bad news."

"No shit," I grunt, pulling myself up off the cold ground and moving in closer to watch as two maids scramble under a table, holding onto each other in terror while one of Vincent's sons takes the room by storm. He's waving his gun in the air and yelling violently at them, their heads shaking in response.

They're not willing to give their boss away and it becomes all too clear why Colton was so desperate to get me in here. These guys are ruthless. They don't take prisoners and they honestly don't give a shit how they have to get what they want. How did Charles keep them at bay all this time?

My gaze flicks to the next monitor to where one of the brothers stands at the entryway of the staff quarters and my stomach sinks. The door is locked and he slams his fists against the wood. Panic rises within me. "Are they in there?"

Colton shakes his head. "I don't know, Jade," he tells me, looking over to the next monitor that shows the inside of the staff kitchen. The room looks empty but I give it a second glance just to make sure.

The guy gets annoyed with the door and with one big kick, the door splinters and flies off its hinges. He strides into the staff quarters and starts looking around, checking under tables and inside of cupboards.

Not finding what he's looking for, he moves on and I try to take a calming breath. They would have gotten away. Harrison and Maryne have been working here for years, they would know every little hiding spot in this place. They have to be alright. They would have taken Mom with them. They're going to be okay.

There's movement on the first screen and my gaze shoots back toward it to find mom dashing across the formal living room. "What the hell is she doing?" I panic, watching as she rushes around, her phone in her hand, desperately searching. Then it hits me, she's looking for me.

"No, no, no, no, no," I chant, leaning into Colton's side, needing the comfort his closeness always seems to bring as he stares motionless at the screens, watching it all play out like some kind of horror movie.

Mom's head whips around, clearly hearing something and dives behind one of the large statues, crouching down low and doing her best to keep herself hidden. "Why can't I hear anything?" I rush out, searching around the computers for a volume button.

"There's no sound. Only visual."

"What?" I demand. "You're a fucking billionaire. Why is there no sound?"

"It's not my system," he tells me. "Trust me, if this was on me, I'd have sound in every fucking room."

My heart stops as a man walks through the formal living room and mom begins silently praying that she will get out of this. Her gaze falls back to her phone and she holds it to her ear. Whoever she's trying to call doesn't respond and she tries again and again.

I pat around my pockets and realize that she's probably calling me. My phone is back in the pool house and she has absolutely no idea if I'm safe. The man walks out of the room and like lightning, mom flies in the opposite direction, continuing her search.

"I have to let her know that I'm okay," I tell him. "Do you have your phone?"

He shakes his head. "It's back in my room."

"FUCK! She's going to get herself killed."

"Check the drawers," Colton says, indicating to the row of drawers that span the length of the room. I practically dive on them, tearing each one of them open and madly searching. There are all sorts of things in there and I realize that each drawer was filled specifically with the intent to keep them alive in here for weeks on end.

I get to the fourth drawer and as I tear it open, I find an old phone attached to a charger and I rip it out faster than Colton dragged my ass in here

I rush back over to the computers and keep my eye on mom as I madly start hashing out a text.

Unknown - Mom. I'm in the panic room. Stop moving around. I'm okay. Go and hide.

Unknown - Where are Maryne and Harrison?

I watch as her head snaps down to her phone and she quickly reads over the text. Relief visibly pours through her and she sags against the wall, needing a moment to catch up with everything that's happening.

I've never wanted to scream so bad in my life but she quickly gets moving and I watch as she dives into the coat closet just outside of the entryway foyer.

She'll be alright in there.

The phone in my hand buzzes and I quickly scan over the text.

Unknown - Thank God. I was so worried. Don't you dare come out of there until they're gone. Do you understand me?

Unknown - Maryne and Harrison are in the wine cellar under the Carrington's private kitchen. They're going to be alright down there.

I let out a shaky breath and step back into Colton's side. "They're in the wine cellar."

"Which one?" he rushes out in a strange tone. "Dad's personal one or under the kitchen?"

"Kitchen."

Colton presses a few keys and within seconds, he brings up the camera for the wine cellar but instead of finding them hiding in there, we find Maryne being dragged out by her hair while a gun remains trained on Harrison's chest.

"Fuck," Colton grunts, flying out of his chair. He instantly begins pacing in front of the screen in an absolute panic, not once taking his eyes off the people who have done more for him than his own parents.

The need to break out of here pulses through me and I wonder just how stupid it would be to race down to the pool house and find Nic's gun in the back of my underwear drawer. I stand no chance against these guys but at least I'd be doing something instead of just standing here and watching as it all plays out.

Maryne is dragged up the six steps leading down to the wine cellar and she scrambles to get free, clawing at the guy's hand in her hair. She draws blood but he's relentless and refuses to release her.

They get to the top and Colton switches the screen so we see them in the kitchen. The DeCarlo son stands over her, yelling in her face. Tears roll down her cheeks but she's strong, whatever he wants, he's not getting it from her. She spits in his face and my eyes widen in fear as he rears back and slaps her hard across the face.

Harrison appears in the kitchen and I've never seen him look so pissed. He rushes toward them but the guy jams the gun hard under Maryne's chin while grinning up at Harrison like some kind of monster.

Harrison comes screeching to a stop, hands up, and looking at

Maryne with fear in his eyes. He pleads with the brother to let Maryne go but in the blink of an eye, a sick grin twists across his face and the trigger is pulled, sending blood spraying throughout the kitchen.

CHAPTER 21

"**N**OOOOO," I scream, racing to the door and banging my fits against it. "You fucking bastard. I'm going to kill you."

Colton races after me, curling his strong arms around my waist and hauling me away from the door. "Shhhh, Jade. Shhhhhh."

I fight against his hold, clawing at his arms, desperate for my freedom. I'd do anything to get downstairs and curl my hands around that fucker's throat. Hell, maybe I'll shove his own fucking gun against his jaw and shoot him exactly the same way he shot Maryne.

He didn't even hesitate, just shot her. She didn't do anything wrong, never hurt anybody, and was always the first person to offer me a warm smile. I need to make this right. I need to get out of here. I need my fucking Widows. I need Nic. He'll know what to do.

"Come on, baby, please. You need to calm down. We're outnumbered. If they find us up here, they won't leave until we're in body bags. Come on, Jade. Please, there's nothing we can do."

"No," I cry, desperately trying to pull free. "There has to be something. I refuse to just sit here and let them get away with this. They can't do this. She ...she ..."

Colton turns me in his arms and crushes me into his wide chest. "I know," he murmurs. "But I'm not going to let that be your fate. We have to wait them out. Believe me, we will make them pay. I will end them, but we can't win like this. We have nothing. If we run out of here right now, we're both dead."

"I ... I ..." He holds me tighter and the fight begins to leave. She's dead. He just took her life as though it meant nothing. Sweet Maryne, gone just like that.

My eyes begin welling with tears as reality truly starts to sink in.

She's gone.

Gone.

My eyes flash to the monitor to see Harrison on his knees with Maryne's lifeless body in his arms. He holds her tight, sobbing for his lost friend as blood pools around his knees. I've never seen someone so filled with pain and it becomes instantly clear—Harrison was deeply in love with Maryne.

My breath catches on a lump in my throat and as the grief comes up and hits me, heavy sobs begin to overwhelm me.

I cry into Colton's chest and he holds me impossibly tighter, resting his chin above my head. I only knew Maryne for a month but in that time, she became so much more than just a supervisor, she was like another mother to me. I can only imagine how hard this is hitting Colton.

Maryne's been the only motherly figure in Colton's life since his own mother left a few years ago and even before then, she was probably still the only motherly figure. After what I saw at the funeral, I doubt Laurelle Carrington has a maternal bone in her body. If anything, it was probably a competition between Charles and Laurelle as to who could be the shittiest parent.

It all becomes too much and as I watch the men storming through the mansion and wreaking havoc on the staff, my knees buckle and I sink to the floor. Colton drops down with me, refusing to let me go as he watches the screen closely, removing all traces of emotion from his face.

"It'll be over soon," he promises me, his hand roaming up and down my back. His tone doesn't match his words and the lack of confidence leaves me wondering if he's even talking to me. It sounds more like he's trying to convince himself.

Ten minutes turns into twenty and then thirty as I watch the men get more agitated. Someone checks the garage and checks for Colton's Veneno, making sure he's even on the property. I watch as they go back and forth in front of the coat closet that mom hides in and every time they do, my breath catches. I can not lose her. She's the only blood family I have left. Without her …

Shit.

The same brother who had shot Maryne walks past Harrison at least ten times, smirking at her lifeless body, and every time he does, my body stiffens with the need to grab one of the many knives in that kitchen and slice it across the fuckers throat. I'll be more than happy to be the one smirking then.

Harrison flinches and holds Maryne tighter and I watch as every time the brother steps out of the room, Harrison drags her body further and further away.

Colton stiffens beneath me and I follow his line of sight to the next monitor to find two of the brothers searching through the bedrooms. One goes through the bedroom I had used when I first arrived here while the other recklessly searches through mom's old room, trashing it as he goes.

They quickly realize that there's nothing in there and move onto Colton's bedroom.

Within mere moments, they figure out whose room they're in and they spend a little more time tearing it apart. They go through his private things, checking over papers, and scanning through any documents they can find. But they won't find whatever it is they're looking for. Colton's not stupid and Charles certainly didn't teach him to be careless with anything important. It would all be hidden away and seeing as though they haven't found Charles' office, I'd dare say that everything is safe.

They spend ten minutes tearing his room to shreds and I find myself glancing at the time in the bottom right corner of the monitor.

It's well past ten at night and we've now been in here for forty-five minutes. Where the fuck are the police?

This should be over. They should have shown up here ten minutes after the brothers first stormed the mansion, the DeCarlo's should have been carted out of here in either handcuffs or body bags, and they sure as hell should have had this dealt with before Maryne was shot and killed.

The two brothers move from Colton's room, continuing to make their way down the hallway and closer to the panic room. They trash everything as they go, tearing priceless artworks off the walls and shooting holes through the family members' faces as they come across their portraits.

Colton's eyes darken with every step they take. I've never seen him like this before. His eyes didn't even look this haunted when we stood in his father's office, staring at his dead body. It's only moments before he snaps. There's only so much patience one man can have.

The brothers move into the room that Colton had only dragged me into a short forty-five minutes ago, the room that hides the secret door.

Colton goes stiff and the silence in the room becomes eerie.

We watch them make their way around the room, tearing shit off walls and destroying everything that the Carrington's have built over the years. Colton curls my head into his chest so I don't see the screen and holds me as still as a statue. "Shhhhh," he whispers so softly that I barely hear him.

My eyes close and I focus solely on my breathing.

"It's going to be okay," he soothes. "It'll be over soon."

It feels like a lifetime before Colton's body relaxes just a fraction, wordlessly letting me know that they've moved on.

They continue to harass the staff, taunting and terrorizing them until finally, they walk out the doors, leaving nothing but disaster behind.

We wait until they've gotten in their cars and are flying through the broken iron gates before Colton lifts us off the cold ground. He places his hands on my shoulders and looks into my eyes. "Are you alright?"

I shake my head. "Nothing about this is alright."

His lips press into a tight line and I finally see the devastation behind his eyes. "I know," he tells me, taking my hand and pulling me toward the door. "But we have to find a way to make it alright, otherwise we'll never find the strength to move on."

"There's only one way to make this alright," I insist.

Colton nods, meeting my eyes with nothing but rage. "I know."

He keys in a code and the door quickly unlocks. We have to take a step back as it opens toward us and as we do, we get our first real glimpse into the room. It's completely torn apart. I could see the damage done on the monitor but it certainly didn't do it justice.

We start making our way out of the room and everywhere we go is pure devastation. Colton is going to have to get people in here to completely redo the mansion. The beds are torn apart, the walls have bullet holes, the artworks are completely trashed. It's heartbreaking.

We reach the stairs and as we walk down them, I start to pick up our pace. "MOM?" I call out with desperation, my voice traveling far through the broken mansion. "Mom. They're gone."

I hit the bottom of the stairs and race toward the foyer only to meet Mom halfway there. She crashes into me, flinging her arms around me and crying into the crook of my neck. "Oh, honey. When I couldn't reach you …" Her words are cut off by a broken sob and it tears right through to my soul.

"I know," I tell her, holding her as tight as humanly possible. "I tried to go back for you, but Colton wouldn't let me. I had to know you were safe."

"He did the right thing," she tells me. "I would have killed him myself had he let you go."

Her use of the word 'killed' has my stomach twisting with pain and my eyes instantly fill with tears. "What's wrong?" she demands, her eyes roaming all over me, starting from my head and not stopping until she reaches my toes.

Everything inside of me aches. "They killed her," I cry through the lump in my throat. "He just … he shot her and she didn't do anything."

"Who?" mom demands, grabbing my shoulders with force, her eyes wide and fearful. "Who are you talking about?"

"Maryne."

A pained wail tears out of Mom and she drops to her knees as she grieves for her lost friend. I go down with her, holding her the same way Colton had just done for me. Mom and Maryne had gotten close over the last few weeks. They were more than just colleagues, they were friends, really good friends. There was no one quite like Maryne.

Colton appears at my back, protectively hovering over us. He leans down and takes my mother's hand, helping her to her feet. "Come on," he murmurs. "We need to go and check on the other staff."

Mom wipes her tears as Colton meets my eyes, knowing that breaking that news to Mom couldn't have been easy. He reaches for my hand and I take it instantly. Mom lets out a shaky breath. "You're right," she says, trying to be the strong adult of the group. "Are you sure all of them are gone?"

"Yes," Colton says. "All five were counted as they made their escape."

"Right," she says formally, looking back to me, her bottom lip quivering as she tries to hold it together. "Where is Maryne's body?"

"Private kitchen."

With that, we all start making our way to the kitchen, bringing along the staff we find on the way.

I remember the day I walked in and found my father's dead body. I didn't know anything had happened to him and walking in to find him like that … nothing could prepare a daughter for that sight. The same had happened when I saw Charles' body and I had assumed that it was because of the shock, but walking into the kitchen, already knowing and already prepared for what I'm about to see, it doesn't change just how horrible it is.

I walk into the kitchen and instantly suck in a shocked gasp, stumbling over my feet and catching myself before I fall. Blood covers the kitchen and is sprayed all over the cabinetry. Silence falls among the staff as we take it all in but upon taking another step and seeing the smeared blood from the kitchen to the media room, everything inside of me sinks.

We follow the tracks, being careful not to step into any of her spilled blood and disturb the murder scene. As we get to the open door, we find Harrison silently weeping as he holds onto Maryne's lifeless body, refusing to let her go.

Tears flow down my cheeks as my chest really begins to ache. "Oh, Harrison," Mom cries, rushing into his side and placing a gentle hand on his shoulder, offering him all of her support and comfort.

As I watch them together, I can't help but wonder if Colton and I are cursed. Every time we finally climb over a hurdle and open ourselves up to one another, tragedy strikes. Is this our doing? Should we just stay away from each other to ensure the safety of our friends and family?

As the torturous thoughts roam wildly through my mind, I look up at Colton to find his broken gaze already on me. "I'm going to make this right."

I nod, trusting him wholeheartedly to stand by his word.

More of the staff begin to crowd around and I don't miss the way that Enrique the gardener has been messed up with cuts and dark bruises forming on his face or the way one of the maids looks as though she's been thrown around.

I've never lived through such tragedy, not even in Breakers Flats, though that could just mean that I've had it good. Hell, I wouldn't be surprised if Nic's dad made his new recruits perform home invasions just as an initiation into the gang. Nic has never really opened up about that part of his life, he's always tried to protect me from it but I know that whatever it is, it wouldn't be good.

A silent ten minutes pass before Harrison is finally able to be pulled away. A maid grabs a white sheet and gently lays it over Maryne, giving her the privacy she deserves.

We all walk out of the den and everyone sits around the massive dining table either staring at their hands or finding a way to blame themselves, wishing things could have been different. I find myself looking at Colton, watching as he makes his way around the staff he's known all of his life, gently soothing their fears and letting them know that they can take some time off if needed.

He's such a generous boss, so completely different from his father. In some cases, Colton is just like him, but then he goes and surprises me in a time like this. He's compassionate, kind, and caring. I don't think Charles even understood the meaning of words like that. He had times where he would show concern for me, but I quickly came to realize that it was all to fit his own agenda and that my struggles were being used to his advantage. Colton would never do that.

As his hazel gaze sweeps back to mine, silently checking for the millionth time that I'm not about to break, I remember how he was telling me that he provoked Vincent during their phone call the other day. He said things that he knew he shouldn't and this was their retaliation.

That thought would be sitting heavily in his mind and realizing this only makes me want to run into his chest and hold onto him for as long as I can. It's not his fault but I don't doubt that he'll never forgive himself for the role he played in Maryne's death. That will forever plague him and the fact that he's standing tall and putting aside his own grief for those around him just shows what kind of an incredible leader he is.

Colton Carrington really is everything.

I tiptoe across the kitchen and find everything I need to make tea and coffee for everyone before bringing it over to a section of the kitchen which is safe to spread out. I don't know where the hell the cops are but once they get here, everyone is going to be questioned and for those who were up at the crack of dawn, it's going to be a very long night.

I get busy and am halfway through when Harrison's voice rumbles over the silent conversations. "Who did this?" he demands, speaking very out of character as he addresses Colton. "Was it the same bastards who killed your father?"

My gaze snaps up just as everyone else's does. Colton shakes his head. "No," he says, his eyes briefly flicking to mine before settling back on Harrison's. "They're not connected. The man who killed my father was a professional. His weapon was delicately chosen and the way he struck my father with his blade was done with accuracy. He was a trained killer—careful and precise." Colton waves his hands around the destruction of his home. "The men who did this were reckless, randomly shooting, and leaving DNA on everything. These men weren't concerned with hiding their identity. They just wanted to cause havoc and send a message."

Harrison narrows his eyes at Colton. "You know who did this."

Colton nods. "Yes," he says, speaking clearly and giving it to him straight. "This was the DeCarlo sons and I can guarantee that the go-ahead came from Vincent himself."

Gasps sound through the room and I don't doubt how every one of the men and women in this room are remembering a time or two where they have catered to the DeCarlo family through the many meetings they would have had over the years. Not one of them had expected this, but the proof is all around us. We have security footage from the moment they destroyed the front gates, them terrorizing the staff, and the very moment the trigger was pulled, killing the most beloved member of this dysfunctional family.

Harrison stands. "We can not let them get away with this."

"We won't," Colton assures him, slipping his phone out of his pocket that he'd had a maid retrieve for him earlier. He presses a few buttons and holds it to his ear while keeping his determined stare locked on Harrisons.

There's a short pause before Colton's deadly tone cuts through the room, sending chills spiraling down my spine. "You will not get away with this," he warns. "You sent your sons into my home to cause havoc. They took an innocent life and terrorized my staff. They destroyed the home that my father built and for that, I guarantee that each one of them will go down. I'm going to pick them off one by one and I'm going to leave you for last. You are not untouchable, DeCarlo. I'm going to destroy you."

CHAPTER 22

I stand in the full-length mirror, staring at the black dress that hangs from my body. How is it possible that I'm about to attend the second funeral in as many weeks? This isn't right. Is this what Bellevue Springs is really about? Shameless murder, home invasions, and rape?

I hate it here, but there's a large part of me that can't force myself to leave.

My eyes drop over my dress. It's tacky, the same cheap dress I wore to Charles' funeral but I can't find the energy to go out and find something new. To be honest, I doubt Maryne would have wanted me to go out and spend what little money I have on a fancy dress.

Besides, this funeral may be in Bellevue Springs, but it's not going to be anything like the last funeral I went to. It's going to be small, private, and filled with only her closest family and friends.

Letting out a heavy sigh, I walk across my room and grab the hairbrush off my dresser and start on my finishing touches. The funeral doesn't start for another hour but the last thing I want is to be rushing around, trying to get ready, and then miss the beginning of the service. I won't do that to Maryne. I know I have a habit of being late for my shifts, but Maryne deserves better.

I put on a little makeup and decide on waterproof mascara, knowing that the emotions are bound to come up and bite me on the ass today. I'd prefer not to look like a drowned rat.

Dropping down on the edge of my bed, I slip on my heels, and check the time. Still forty-five minutes to go. How am I supposed to pass the time?

I've spent the last two days with Colton and while it's kinda been great, it's also been kinda weird. None of the staff have been in and there's been an eerie silence that's taken over the mansion. No one has felt like talking. Harrison has been staring through the back window at Charles' beloved gardens while Mom has struggled not to break.

I've tried to be the glue that holds us all together, but I'm not sure that I possess that power. I mean, for mom maybe, but Colton and I have been together for all of two seconds, and I'm pretty sure Harrison doesn't even like me.

My phone buzzes on the bed beside me and I glance down to find Nic's name flashing across the screen. I pick it up and rub my finger over the screen. Usually, I can't wait to open Nic's messages but right now … I don't know. I'm hesitating and I don't understand why. Maybe it's the guilt that sits heavy in my gut knowing that things between me and Colton are really starting to develop and I know that at some point, I'm going to have to have the dreaded conversation with Nic, letting him know what's going on. It's going to crush him. *I'm* going to crush him, and he's either going to pull away from me or glue himself to my side. There's no in between here. It's one extreme or the next.

Sucking it up, I unlock my phone and glance down at the screen.

Nic - How are you feeling, O? I can be there in twenty minutes if you need me.

I stare at his message and while I desperately want to tell him to get his ass moving and meet me at the church, I find myself holding back.

It's too much. I can't handle it.

Nic has the ability to make me feel, to make me face what's going on, and then forces me to handle it. I don't want to do that, not today. I want to pretend. I want to hide the pain and just make it through the day and if he shows up, my world is going to crumble.

I'm barely holding it together.

I drop my phone into my lap and let out a heavy sigh. "Uh oh," I hear Mom saying from my bedroom doorway. "Did you just ignore one of your boys' messages? You know they're going to come searching you out now just to make sure you're still breathing."

I give her a tight smile and meet her eyes. "Does it make me a bad person that I don't want to have them around today?" I question as tears brim in my eyes. "They're just going to remind me how bad it hurts."

"Oh, honey," she says, walking into my room and dropping down on the bed beside me. She curls her arm around my waist and pulls me into her side. "That doesn't make you a bad person at all. It makes you human. The boys will understand your need for space. They can read you like a book. I wouldn't be surprised if they already knew to back off. You can call them tomorrow and let them know how you are."

My head drops to Mom's shoulder and I let out a heavy sigh. "Are you sure?"

"I'm positive," she tells me, her hand moving to my back and rubbing slow circles. She lowers her voice, trying to keep a soothing tone. "Are you almost ready? I thought we could head down to the church early and offer a few helping hands. You know how crazy these things can get."

I lift my head off her shoulder and try to hold back my tears. "Yeah, I'm ready," I murmur. "I'll go in and grab Colton and then we can go."

"Alright," she says with a soft smile. "I don't want to show up too early and be a nuisance though. We have a few minutes." I nod as she meets my eyes and I find her heart on her sleeve. "How are you doing, Honey? I'm sorry my decision to move here has caused you all this grief. If I had known the things you were going to experience here ..."

"Don't," I tell her. "I'm doing alright. Don't blame yourself for any of this. I know it's been hard but there have also been some really amazing times too, times that we never would have had the chance to experience back home."

"Yeah, you're right."

"Besides, who knows what sort of shit would have gone down at home. We could have been worse off. The Wolves have been making moves against the Widows for months. It's only a matter of time before there's a gang war in Breakers Flats and someone ends up dead."

Mom lets out a loud sigh before pressing her lips into a tight line. "Unfortunately, you're right about that," she says. "Those Wolves have been a pain in the ass for years."

The more talk of the Wolves that passes between us, the more the need to ask that one burning question creeps up on me. I've been holding back on this for days, knowing now really isn't the right time, but I have to know.

Dad was everything to me and if he was hiding something like this, something so big … I'd be devastated. But if Dad was one of them, I can guarantee that all four of my boys knew about it, and not one of them said a word. And if he was, what would that mean for me? If dad was one of them, then by right, I'm a wolf too. Were the years Nic spent at my side just some game to get close to my dad? Is Sebastian even the best friend I've always believed him to be? Is Elijah really my voice of reason? Kairo my protector?

Every little thing that I've known to be true before sitting in that guidance counselors office is in question. I don't know who to trust, what's right and what's wrong. Did Mom know about this and hide it all of these years? Miss Davies could have had a bad case of mistaken identity, she could have had it wrong. It's possible that there was more than one Big Lou in Breakers Flats, right?

Mom's brows crease as she watches me and concern begins filtering through her features. "What's wrong, Honey? What is it?"

Shit. How is it possible for Mom to read me so clearly? Is it impossible to hide anything from this woman?

I look away, not able to meet her eyes as the possibility of learning that she has lied to me all these years begins to haunt me. "I, umm … I had a meeting with the guidance counselor at school the other day—"

"Oh?" she questions, taken back just as I had been. I don't think we even had a guidance counselor in Breakers Flats.

I meet her eyes and just as the words begin to form in my mouth, I pussy out like a fucking bitch. How could I bring up my father just moments before we're due to be heading to a funeral? What kind of insensitive bitch am I? I wasn't raised to kick someone when they're already down. Maybe I belong in Bellevue Springs after all.

"Yeah," I say as pathetic as ever. "She wanted to discuss my future."

"How do you mean?"

"College."

Mom rears back, her lips scrunching in surprise. "College?"

"That's what I thought," I tell her truthfully. "She's been going over my records and grades and she thinks I have potential to be accepted. You know, nothing like an Ivy League like the rest of Bellevue Springs, but a small college. She thinks I can make it."

Mom blinks three times before finally speaking up. "Are you … how do you feel about this?"

I shrug my shoulders. "I really don't know," I say, shaking my head, completely lost on the topic. "She just kinda sprung it on me and then, you know … *that* happened and that was the last I thought about it. I guess I want to know what you think about it."

"My daughter going to college," she muses, her voice rising an octave in her excitement. "I think that would make you the best damn thing to come out of Breakers Flats and if this is what you want to do, then I'll support you completely, but just know, that if you decide against this that I still think you're the best thing to come out of that hellhole."

"I know," I tell her. "It's just the money. I don't have the grades to get a scholarship, not that I'd even know the first thing about applying for one, and from every movie I've ever watched, it's supposed to be ridiculously expensive. I can't afford it, even if I was working full time, and besides, what would I even study? I don't know what I want to do with my life. I've never even had to think about it. I've always learned that to make it through high school without being shot is the main goal."

"Oh, Honey," Mom says, flinging her arms around me and drawing me in. "If money is the only thing holding you back from this then you shouldn't worry yourself. You're my daughter and your education is my responsibility. If you get accepted into college then the financial burden will be on me and you better believe that I will work my ass off to make sure your fees are paid. I will work a second job if I have to, but if this is what you want and you get in, then that's what you're going to do."

I shake my head. "Are you insane? I'm not about to let you pay for this. I don't even know how much it's going to be. Hell, I don't even know if I actually want to go yet."

"Ocean," my mother says sternly. "You listen to me now and you listen closely. I do not care what you want to do with your life as long as you are always striving for success and always being the best possible version of yourself. What I will not tolerate is you letting an opportunity like this slip through your fingers because of your stubborn nature. If you apply and don't get in, then at least you tried, but not trying at all? That is not acceptable. I will take care of the finances."

"But—"

"No. Are you forgetting that Colton doubled my wages? Every week I'll put some aside and by the time college rolls around, we'll be alright."

"Are you sure?"

"I've never been so sure, Honey," she says, cupping my face in her warm hands. "Do you have any idea how proud I am of you for even considering this? I knew you were going to be amazing. You've always had the potential to be so much more. You're going to fly, my sweet baby."

A small smile pulls at my lips and I take Mom's hands in mine. "We're really going to do this?"

"We sure are," she tells me, squeezing my hand before she starts to get all emotional. "You're proof that I did something right."

"Oh, stop," I laugh, pulling her in for the millionth time. "You did right the second I was born. Dad would be proud of how you're handling all of this without him.”

I hear her soft exhale at my ear and she holds me a little tighter before finally pulling back, only when she does, I see the tears welling in her eyes. “Don’t make me cry,” she tells me. “Today is already going to be hard enough without you dropping bombs like that.”

“Sorry,” I grumble. “I think I got carried away in the moment.”

“That’s for sure,” she murmurs, getting up and checking her reflection in the mirror. She runs her hands down her black dress, straightening it out the exact same way that I do. “Okay,” she says, turning back to me. “Now that’s settled, we should head in and find Colton.”

I nod and allow her to pull me up from the bed and twenty minutes later, we’re pulling up at the small church.

Colton takes my hand and helps me out of the car and I can’t help but go over the differences between the two funerals. I haven’t even stepped inside of the church yet and the contrasts are astounding.

This church is tiny and looks as though it could fit a maximum of thirty people inside but there’s something about it so much more personal than Charles’ church. This is perfect for her, it’s exactly what she would have wanted.

Mom steps into my side and the three of us walk towards the entrance. It’s beautiful. It’s been done up with breathtaking floral arrangements that have me looking up at Colton as there’s simply no way Maryne’s family would have been able to afford this. “Did you pay for Maryne’s funeral?”

He nods ever so slightly. “It’s the least I could do.”

My heart swells. I don't know how he does it but every single day I discover something new about him that makes me unbelievably attached. "If you're not careful, you're going to make me fall for you, Colton Carrington."

His thumb rubs back and forth over the top of my hand. "Right back at you, Jade."

I have to tear my gaze away and stop myself from swooning as we step through the entrance of the church, but even had I not looked away, it wouldn't have mattered because the second we get inside and see the marble casket at the front of the church, heaviness settles into my heart.

Harrison stands at Maryne's side, one hand resting over the casket and complete agony on his face as Maryne's family slowly begins to trickle in. "Did you know they were together?" I ask Colton, keeping my voice low so no one assumes that I'm here to gossip.

He nods. "They were together for years."

I gape up at him before looking back at Harrison as all the pieces of the puzzle finally come together. "How could I not know that?"

"They kept it strictly professional," he tells me. "He asked Dad for an advance on his pay just last month. I think he was planning a proposal."

My soul shatters and my steps begin to slow. How could I have not known that about the people I spend every single day with? Am I that shallow?

Colton's arm falls over my shoulder and he pulls me along. "Come on," he tells me, pressing a kiss to my temple and leading me toward the front of the church. "Maryne wouldn't want you falling apart like this."

I let out a shaky breath. He's right. I can fall apart in private when I get home, as for now, I need to be strong for Maryne's family and friends who are no doubt feeling it a lot harder than I am.

With that understanding, I meet Harrison up front and give him a warm hug as I prepare to say goodbye to the woman who was so much more than just a colleague.

CHAPTER 23

I slam my way through the door of Kairo's apartment. "WHERE THE HELL IS SHE?" I yell, marching my ass toward his bedroom and listening to the panicked scuffles coming from within. "I SWEAR TO GOD, KAIRO. IF YOU HAVE ANOTHER GIRL IN THERE I'M GOING TO BREAK SOME MOTHERFUCKING FACES."

"Fuck, babe. Get up, get up, get up," Kai rushes out on the other side of his door, no doubt shaking the girl who sleeps beside him, desperately trying to get her up and out of his bed. "She can't find you in here. She'll fucking kill you."

My fingers curl around the door handle and finding it locked,

I slam my fists against the wood over and over again. "WHY THE HELL IS THIS DOOR LOCKED? WHO IS SHE?"

Kai's voice calls out. "Babe, you've got it all wrong. There's no one here."

There's a panicked feminine wail coming from within the room and I slam my hand on the door again. "KAIRO, OPEN THIS FUCKING DOOR RIGHT THIS GODDAMN MINUTE."

"I'll be there in a sec," he calls back.

"NOW!" I yell, feeling good about actually getting to scream for once even though it's at a wooden door. I bring my foot up and slam it hard, watching as the door rattles on its hinges. It's not the first time I've had to knock this thing down. It's pretty durable. Maybe another three kicks and it'll come flying off its hinges. "I'm getting in there whether you want me to or not."

"Fuck," the girl in the room panics. "You didn't tell me you had a girl. What am I supposed to do?"

"The window," he screeches. "Get your ass out the window. If she gets in here, it's going to be a fucking bloodbath. Trust me, you don't want to mess with this bitch. She's in-fucking-sane."

I hear rattling around the room as the girl hurries to collect her things and I put my face up against the door. "Listen here, bitch. You can fucking have him if you want him but you're going to have to come out here and fight me for him. I haven't cut a bitch in months so I'm really going to enjoy this."

The bedroom window slides open and I slam my foot against the door even harder. "COME OUT HERE," I screech, banging my fists rapidly. "My man ain't going to have some trashy side piece."

There's a high-pitched squeal of terror then Kai's deep rumble. "Hurry the fuck up, girl. The door won't hold much longer."

There are a few loud bangs from within the room and when I kick the door again, it goes flying off its hinges, though not in the same way it would had it been one of the boys kicking it down. I've seen Nic kick a door down when he thought someone was hurting me and that fucker splintered into a million little pieces.

I storm into the room and find a blonde in nothing but a skimpy thong with all her things in her hands. She's halfway through the window and staring at me wide-eyed and terrified.

I start racing towards her. "GET BACK HERE, YOU LITTLE HOMEWRECKER."

She screams and starts moving faster as Kairo dives in front of me, holding me back with everything he's got. His arms curl around me like steel rods and lift me off the ground. I kick my legs out. "LET ME AT HER."

Kai looks back at the escaping girl. "GO," he yells. "HURRY UP."

The girl practically drops out of the window and I look over Kai's wide shoulder to watch as she scampers across the grass. Her thick ass jiggles as she runs and as Kai's eyes drop to mine, we both burst into uncontrollable laughter.

"That was the best one yet," he tells me, relaxing his arms around my waist and turning his hold into a tight, warm hug.

"I know. I figured she'd at least pull her dress on first."

"Can't blame her," he says, shaking his head as the amusement shines in his eyes. "You did come storming in here like a jealous girlfriend ready to tear her ass in two."

"I know, I was feeling a little theatrical this morning."

He rolls his eyes and presses a kiss to my forehead. "I've been trying to get that girl out of here for two days," he explains. "I asked Sebastian to help me out and the fucker just sat back and laughed."

"Then why the hell didn't you call me two days ago? I would have come sooner."

His face twists as he pulls back. "Come on, O," he says, moving around his room and grabbing a shirt. "You and I both know that I wasn't about to call you while you were dealing with another death. That's not fair."

"Trust me, I would have preferred the distraction. I'm getting kind of sick of always having death on my mind."

"Sorry, O," he says, stepping into a pair of sweatpants. "We were all trying to give you space."

"I know," I tell him. "It's fine. I actually really needed a few days just to sit and be sad but I'm feeling alright now. You know, when I'm not thinking about it."

"How's your mom handling it? She was friends with the woman, right?"

"Yeah," I say, briefly looking away not wanting him to see the pain on my face, knowing damn well that if he did, he'd start treating me with kiddie gloves, which would then have the rest of the guys doing the same and I seriously couldn't handle that right now. "We all were. Maryne was the best. She was one of the good ones."

"I'm sorry," Kai says with a deep sigh, walking back across his room and pulling me into his arms. "I didn't realize how fond you were of her."

I shrug my shoulders. "Yeah. There's nothing we can do about it now. She's gone."

Kai scoffs. "Bullshit, O. There's a shitload we can do about it. You know who did this right? They put your life in danger and terrorized your mom and friends. Those other fuckers in Bellevue Springs might be out of our league, but home invasions, trashing homes, and shootings—this is our territory. We fight fire with fire, babe. We'll handle this. I don't want you getting yourself involved."

I shake my head. "I don't want to be involved. For once this actually has nothing to do with me. This is Colton's business shit that his father left behind for him to handle. He says he's going to deal with it and we need to let him. I don't want you guys going down for something that has nothing to do with us."

"Babe," he says, his voice low and warning.

I shake my head and start walking out of his bedroom. "I said no, Kai. So don't even think about it. This is Colton's mess to clean up, not yours."

He huffs and scoffs under his breath. "Try telling Nic that."

I groan as I make my way into the kitchen and scan through his near-empty fridge. I'm not stupid. There's no amount of pleading or warnings that I could give these boys that are going to make them let this go. It just means that it'll be taken care of without my knowledge and I don't know if I should love them or hate them for it.

I grab his orange juice and uncap it before taking a drink and waiting for his slow ass to get ready for the day.

He appears by my side five minutes later and we walk out the door together. "Where are we going?" I question, not having been invited along but going with the flow just as he knew I would.

He scoffs again. "Where do you think? If you're down for spending the day at home, then we're chilling with the boys and for just one day, we can pretend that you never left."

I give him a wide beaming smile and he rolls his eyes before gently nudging me into the wall, silently telling me to knock it off. But what can I say? Kairo is never really one to talk. He's more of a grunt and glare kinda guy but when he's willing to say something sweet, I'm like a sponge ready to soak it all up.

"How's your new boyfriend?"

My face scrunches up. "He's not my …"

Wait. Is he my boyfriend? We've been inseparable for the past few days and he hasn't tried to hide me away when in the public eye, so I guess that means something. I know we're kinda together but is it official? Do I have the right to call him mine?

Kairo shakes his head and gives me a grin. "That's what I thought," he grumbles, his eyes lighting with excitement. "I swear, I will do anything you want if you let me be the one to break it to Nic."

"Oh, hell no," I shriek, my eyes widening in horror. "Do you have a death wish?"

"Not a death wish," he explains. "But I'm down for a good fight. It's been a while."

"Then remind Eli how you slept with his sister last year," I suggest. "He's always ready to go and never knows when to give up, but just leave the brass knuckles out of it, okay? Though, give the kid some fair warning and don't damage his pretty face."

Kairo doesn't respond but the way he sets his jaw tells me that he's actually considering it and I make a mental note to fill Nic's freezer with ice for when they're both sitting on the couch feeling sorry for themselves. Though, if I'm lucky, Kai will wait until I've gone home to pick that fight. It's not like I'm not used to them fighting, it's sexy as all hell but I don't like seeing my boys hurting.

After realizing that I had no choice but to drive one of Colton's car's here, Kairo quickly dives into the driver's seat and leans across to open the passenger's door for me. He holds his hand out while grinning like a damn fool in the black Ferrari. "Keys, please."

Knowing I have no choice but to give up the goods, I toss them toward him and he plucks them out of the sky like a lion diving for a meal. Before my ass has even hit the seat, the engine is revving and Kai is having the time of his life.

I look over at him and he instantly holds a hand up, knowing damn well what I was about to say. "Don't you dare ruin this for me," he demands. "I'm probably never going to get another chance to drive one of these."

I let out a heavy sigh and get comfortable. "Good point," I tell him, "But if you break it, you buy it."

He scoffs and with that, he takes off at the speed of light, leaving all our worries behind.

We reach Nic's apartment building within six minutes and the whole way here, Kai laughed at the way all the people on the streets would stop and stare as we drove past. This car really doesn't belong in a place like this but I was sure to bring the cheapest one in the massive garage. It's probably going to be stolen or stripped for parts by the time I emerge out of here this afternoon, but I need this day with my boys more than I need to worry about a billionaire's cheapest toy.

I've really missed these guys over the past two weeks. They're my security blanket and without them, I've felt so vulnerable, but at the same time, I can't stop questioning if they knew about my dad or if it's even true.

Kai drives right through to the underground parking and blocks in Nic's car rather than parking a Ferrari out on the streets of Breakers Flats.

We get out of the Ferrari and Kai is quick to put on the alarm before he loops his arm over my shoulder and reluctantly hands the keys back. We walk up to Nic's door and before I get a chance to grab the handle, Kai races forward and throws the door wide, letting it rebound against the drywall.

Nic's head snaps up from his phone and his eyes go big. "What the fuck are you doing here?" he questions, kinda shocked but kinda thrilled.

He drops his phone on the kitchen counter and strides toward me. I meet him in the middle and am instantly captured into his warm arms. "Fucking missed you, O."

I pull back and smile up at him. "Missed you too."

He drops his lips to mine, just as he always does, but I pull back before he can kiss me, making us both stiffen. His brow furrows and he watches me with confusion. "What the fuck was that?"

"Nothing," I say, looking away and stepping back from his hold, only to have him come right with me.

He leans in toward me, forcing his stare against mine. "Why'd you pull away? You never pull away."

I shrug my shoulders. "Come on," I scoff, playing it off. "You shouldn't be kissing me anymore. We're not together. Besides, who knows where those lips of yours have been?"

He doesn't give in, just continues to stare when a low groan comes from behind the bathroom door. "Ahhh, fuck. Not again." Sebastion grumbles as I hear the sound of the toilet attempting to flush before he tries again and again. "Fuck me."

The door is ripped open and Sebastian comes out shaking his head. "Bro, I fucked up your toilet again," he says before his head snaps up. He takes one look at me and his eyes widen, horrified by the glimpse he's just given me into his world. "Fuck. O. What are you doing here?"

I give him a blank stare. "What is wrong with you two? Can't a girl just come and chill with her boys every once in a while? What's with the twenty-one questions?"

"It's Carrington, isn't it?" Nic spits. "You're together."

"What? I'm … we're…. no."

"Are you sure about that?" he questions, "Because you don't sound too fucking sure."

"I …" I cringe. "We're not together."

"Yeah," Kairo laughs from the living room. "But you're not *not* together."

I look back over my shoulder and grab the half-filled bottle of soda off the counter and launch it across the room. "Stay the fuck out of this."

"What is it, O?" Sebastian cuts in. "Are you really fucking this guy?"

My glare slices toward him, wishing I had another bottle to throw. "Shut up and go fix the toilet."

Nic grabs my waist, his fingers digging in as he holds me a little too tight. His eyes blaze with fire. "Answer the damn question, O. Are you fucking him or not?"

My brows draw down as anger flares through me. "So what if I am? We already talked about this after Charles' funeral. You said you were okay with it."

"I never said I was going to fucking like it."

I hear Sebastian draw in a breath through his teeth and groan. "So, what's the fucking issue? Are you threatened by him? Insecure about the fact that he makes me happy and hasn't accidentally fallen into some whore's pussy?"

His jaw clenches and he tugs hard on my waist, making me fall into him. His eyes are like pools of midnight and his grip is like a vice, bruising and painful. "You're mine," he roars, anger rolling over him. "You always have been and you always will be. How can you not see that?"

The fuck? He's always been overprotective, but possessive? Hell to the mother fucking no. There's a lot of bullshit that I put up with from my boys but this? No, this is crossing the line.

I slam my hands against his chest and force myself back. "Fuck you," I spit. "I'm nobody's and I'm certainly not yours. You fucked us up, Nic. When are you going to realize that? I'm never coming back to you. We were over the second you decided to be unfaithful."

"Ahh, shit," Sebastian grumbles under his breath.

"The fuck it's over," Nic spits. "You're just toying with him. You'll see. You just need some time to see past the fucking fancy parties and stacks of cash."

My hand slaps hard across his face, leaving my hand stinging as the emotions overwhelm me. "Are you fucking kidding me?" I demand. "After the shitty week I've had you want to hit me with this? Do you not know me at all? Do you seriously think I'm that fucking shallow to sleep with a man to get ahead in life? Fuck you."

I turn and start heading for the door, more than ready to leave this shit behind. And to think I was going to come here to surprise the boys and have a great fucking day. What an epic waste of my time.

"Where the fuck do you think you're going?" Nic demands, stalking right behind me.

I reach the door and grab hold of the handle, tearing it open as I glare back at the prick. "Back to my sugar daddy so I can suck his dick a few times and hope he'll reward me with some buckets of cash. Who knows, if I hit it just right, I might even get some diamonds."

Kai gets to his feet. "Come on, babe. Don't go. He just needs a second to cool down."

I glare at Kai and pull the edge of my shirt up, showing him the marking on my waist that I have no doubt are burning red from Nic's tight hold. "What? You want me to stick around so this asshole can try this shit on me again?" I question, watching as both Kai and Sebastian's eyes go wide. "Hell no. I'll come back once this bastard has learned how to control his goddamn emotions and learns that I'm not his fucking chew toy."

With that, I step out of the door and slam it hard behind me, knowing that Kai is going to get the fight he was looking for after all. I hurry back down the hallway and as I go, I hear the second Kai rushes in to my defense with Sebastian as back up.

Loud scuffles and the sound of flesh being beaten haunt me until I finally get out of the building and hurry into the Ferrari. The engine kicks over and purrs beneath me and as I hit the gas, I find myself actually happy about getting my ass out of Breakers Flats and heading back to the pretentious town that has caused me nothing but pain.

CHAPTER 24

By the time the Ferrari comes to a stop in the impressive garage, my mood has only managed to calm by a mere fraction. My blood boils and every time I even think about what Nic just said, it somehow gets worse. The whole reason for my visit this morning was to fill the void that not seeing them every day brings, and hell, I was even planning on telling them all about the whole college thing, but no. He fucked that up.

Who the hell does he think I am? Does he think he can just bark orders to me like he does to his Widows and that I'll just instantly fall to my knees wanting to grant his every fucking wish?

Fuck him. I'm not his little puppy dog. He can feel me slipping away and that's scaring the shit out of him, but that's not my problem. If he didn't feel the need to wave his dick around, I'd probably be right by his side and Colton wouldn't even be a blip on my radar.

He did this. He forced me against him and he has no one to blame but himself. For the past six months, I've rolled over and allowed him to walk all over me. I allowed him to get away with his dick moves and I've had enough. I value myself too much to allow him to get away with it. There will be no more slipping into my bed to hold me all night, no more flirty texts, no more little slips-ups that end with his lips on mine. No, that fucker lost me when he cheated and it's about time he started to realize that.

I'm sure had I not lost my father the way I did, I probably would have had a little more self-respect and distanced myself from him, but after dad's murder, I needed my boys more than anything and Nic and I just slipped back into those same old roles. But not anymore. I want to be with Colton and if we're going to have any chance of making this work, then Nic needs to back off, and not just claiming that he's okay with us, but actually backing the fuck off and letting me explore what we have together.

I climb out of the Ferrari, still somewhat impressed that I was able to get this bad boy in and out of Breakers Flats in one piece, even if I was only there for less than twenty minutes. That in itself is a huge achievement and Colton should be waiting here for me with a fucking medal.

Making my way into the mansion, I bypass a bunch of contractors, all working hard to get the mansion back in one piece after the DeCarlo brothers destroyed it.

I find mom in the kitchen, madly trying to get everything together. She's been working like crazy trying to keep on top of everything and it makes me feel like a bitch for slipping out this morning. I should have stayed and helped her. What the hell was I thinking?

I was too busy thinking about what I needed to worry about Mom. God, how unlucky was she to have such a selfish daughter? I need to fix this. I'll go and return these keys to Colton, let him know I'm back, and then whatever Mom needs, she gets. In fact, I should take over for her and she should get the rest of the day off.

The second the thought filters through my mind, it's practically a done deal and some of the anger resting on my shoulders begins to lift.

I cut through the kitchen and out another door before taking a wild guess that Colton will be in his dad's office. That's where he always is these days. Long gone are the hours he'd spend chilling out in the den with the boys. He's a different man now, one with the weight of the world resting on his capable shoulders and damn, it kinda suits him.

As I walk down the hall to his office, I find the door open and a smile pulls at the corners of my lips. Charles never had this door open when he was working. It was always closed and I was forced to knock and announce my presence before I barged through here, but not Colton. He's different. He doesn't want to cut himself off from the rest of the world like his father did.

I stop in the doorway and lean against the frame as I look in to find him sitting at his desk, leaning back with the phone to his ear. He notices me the second I appear. "I'm on hold," he explains. "You'd think these fuckers would know who the hell I am. Hold? What the fuck do they think this is? Fuck me. I've never been on hold my entire life."

I suck in an appalled gasp, widening my eyes and showing just how horrified I am on his behalf. "Hold?" I shriek. "Call the cops. Call the FBI. Call the fucking SWAT. A crime has been committed."

His eyes dance with laughter but his straight face doesn't break. "Get fucked."

A grin slips across my face. "Welcome to the real world, Carrington. This is how the rest of us operate."

He shakes his head. "Not when you're dealing with the future of your business," he explains. "This deal is going to be the biggest opportunity they will ever get in their lame existence and they put me on fucking hold. It's a sign of disrespect."

"Well, if it's that big of a deal, then maybe they just needed to shut you up for a moment to do a happy dance."

"A happy dance?" he questions. "You think the CEO of a multi-million-dollar empire stopped to do a happy dance?"

I shrug my shoulders. "It's possible," I tell him. "After all, he's just a little multi-million-dollar corporation, and you, well you're the fucking king in this game. He's talking with the big dogs now." A grin slowly starts spreading across his face as I push off the doorframe and start slinking into his office. "If it was me, I'd want to stop to do a happy dance."

I walk right around his desk and scoot my ass up onto it before sliding across until I'm sitting right in front of him. He leans back a little further and I hook my leg to the other side of his so I have him trapped between my thighs.

He presses a few buttons on the phone and the room fills with the soft hold music. The phone is dropped down on his desk and his hands come to stop on my thighs. "So, this happy dance that you'd do," he starts, his eyes becoming hooded and dark. "What exactly does it entail?"

I lick my lips, wondering when he hell I turned into such a needy whore but when he talks to me like a fucking boss in one of these delicious suits, I just can't help myself. He's so enticing and with those dark eyes that always seem to sparkle with excitement, I'm a fucking goner.

His hands slide higher on my thighs and everything begins heating within me. "Well, I'd start with—"

The hold music cuts off and a deep voice rumbles through the office. "Carrington. I need to go over the figures but—"

Colton reaches forward and ends the call, dropping the room into silence. My eyes bug out of my head and I gape down at him. "Did you just hang up on Mr. Multi-Million-Dollar Empire Man?"

He shrugs his shoulders. "Damn right, I did," he says. "If that fucker thinks he can keep me waiting, then I sure as hell can do the same thing. After all, I am the king of the game, aren't I?"

I roll my eyes, holding back a groan. "You may be a fucking king around here but you're also a cocky fuck," I tell him with a laugh.

"Really now?" he questions, slowly standing until he's hovering over me, pressing in between my legs with his hands coming down on the wooden desk by each of my thighs. He leans into me and I'm forced to lean back against the desk, resting my weight onto my hands. "Tell me, what would a cocky fuck do in this situation?"

Holy fucking hell.

His hand slides around until it's resting against my ass and he slides me to the very edge of the desk until my pussy is pressed right up against the hard column that's overtaking his suit pants. My legs instantly hook around his waist, drawing him closer and grinding against me. "You tell me," I murmur. "A cocky fuck is the kind of man to take whatever the hell he wants, however the hell he wants."

His brow raises and just like that, his hands are on the button of my jeans. They're torn down my legs in seconds and before I know it, he's sinking into me, curling a strong arm around my waist and holding me still so he can freely slam into me over and over again.

Hearing noises from outside the office, my eyes flick to the open door and we both suck in a breath, but he doesn't dare stop.

The brief thought that I was supposed to be asking him something filters through my mind but I can't quite seem to put my finger on what it was, but what the hell. Does it even really matter right now? I'm sure it'll come back to me the second he's finished fucking me into oblivion.

His cock slams against the deepest parts of heaven, slowly torturing me with pleasure. His lips come down on my neck and he kisses me, slowly working his lips up my jaw until they're on my own. His tongue slips into my mouth and I welcome it openly until he's pulling back and meeting my eyes. "Touch yourself. Let me watch you," he says though it comes out as more of a demand and it has me instantly jumping into action, more than desperate to give him exactly what he wants.

My fingers press down against my clit and he pulls back ever so slightly to watch the show. His eyes blaze with desire as his glistening cock slides in and out of my pussy. My legs tighten around him. How is it possible for him to take me from zero to a hundred so damn fast?

My orgasm sneaks up on me and I come hard, my pussy pulsating around him and clenching down on his cock as he refuses to quit moving. I ride out my orgasm and just as I finish, he comes hard with a low growl, dropping his forehead to my shoulder as the intense pleasure slams through him.

"Holy shit," he pants, taking three slow breaths before raising his head and pressing his lips to mine. "Fucking you will never get old, Ocean. Do you have any goddamn clue how perfect you are?"

I bite down on my lip, meeting his eyes as all sorts of emotions tear through me. "Careful, Carrington. I warned you about making me fall for you."

A proud grin tears across his face. "Is it working yet?"

I press down on my lips, thinking over my answer. "It's certainly heading that way," I tell him, giving him my honest truth. "But there's still a lot of shit you need to make up for before that could ever happen."

A seriousness appears in his eyes and his features begin to sober as he nods. "I know, Jade, but you don't have to worry about that. I'll make up for it but it's going to take time. I don't see a strong girl like you completely forgiving me overnight."

I shake my head, completely agreeing with him. "What happened to the douchebag Colton who liked to sneak into my room and watch me? I miss that guy."

"That guy realized that he was being a fucking creep."

"Oh," I laugh. "Good. For a second there, I thought maybe you thought that was fucking normal."

"No," he tells me. "I know it's not, but when you first got here, you threw me. You came barging in with that boss bitch attitude and perfect little body and I didn't know how to cope with it so I did stupid fucking things. I wanted to push you away. I wanted you to hate me and then hopefully, I would have done the same, but you kept coming back for more. The torture got you hot, and fucking damn it, Ocean. I loved seeing you like that."

My brows furrow as I watch him. "You got off on torturing me?"

"No," he laughs. "I got off watching the fire burn in your eyes every time I came near you. You craved it."

"You drove me in-fucking-sane."

He grins wide. "I still do, only now that fire burns so much brighter."

My hand hits across his chest and I push him back a step. "Shut up and get me my jeans before someone walks in here to find me spread-eagled across your desk."

He obliges and as he bends to scoop up my jeans, I jump down from his desk. "I thought you were going to be gone all day," he says fixing his pants before handing over my jeans.

I let out a groan. "You just had to go and remind me about that, didn't you?"

His brows furrow as he watches me. "What happened?"

"Nothing," I groan, deciding not to get into it and ruin the rest of my day. "It's just Nic being his usual asshole self but he'll come running back with an apology so don't be surprised when he breaks through your big fucking gates and shows up outside the pool house."

"That bad, huh?" he questions. "You know, it wouldn't be the worst thing if you just gave it space. Every time you see him lately it ends in some kind of fight." I let out a heavy breath knowing he's right and he steps into me, gently taking my waist, a harsh contrast to the way Nic had clutched onto it this morning. "I want you to be happy, Jade," he murmurs. "And right now, Nic ain't doing that for you."

I meet his eyes, not wanting to admit just how right he is because admitting it would mean that I have to let go of him and I'm not ready to do that, not even close. "Is this a jealous boyfriend thing where you don't want me hanging out with my ex, or are you really just looking out for my best interest."

"Boyfriend, huh?"

My eyes bug out of my head. "Oh, fuck. That just slipped out," I tell him. "I mean, maybe you're not. I guess I don't exactly know. I just assumed ..."

Colton laughs and pulls me in tighter before dropping his lips to mine and kissing me deeply. "I thought you'd never figure it out."

Well, damn. I went and got myself a billionaire boyfriend. How the hell did I manage that?

Butterflies swarm through my stomach and I peel myself away before I go and do something stupid like tell him just how badly I need him in my life. I look back to his desk and start straightening the papers that we messed up while screwing when my eyes scan over a bundle of resumes off to the left of his desk. "Wait," I say, feeling the butterflies in my stomach die and turn to lead. "Did we just fuck beside a bunch of resumes of people who want to take Maryne's job?"

Colton lets out a deep sigh. "Yeah," he says, looking down at the stack. "I've been avoiding going through them. It just feels too final."

I nod, unable to tear my eyes off of them before my plan falls into place. I reach across and take the resumes before striding across his office and dumping them into the fancy as fuck fireplace. "You don't need these," I tell him. "Put Mom in her position. She's been doing it ever since Maryne … you know. If you hire someone else, you're going to have to train them. Mom can do it. She practically did everything with Maryne anyway so she already knows what to do. I'll take over some of the things mom was doing before so everything gets done, but you might need to hire another housekeeper to fill in while I'm at school."

Colton presses his lips together, thinking it over. "I really don't want to replace Maryne," he says thoughtfully. "Do you really think your mom would be down for this? Have you even mentioned it to her?"

"No," I say, "But trust me, planning elaborate parties and making schedules is much more appealing to her than cleaning thirty toilets every day."

"You sure?"

"Yes, I'm fucking sure."

"Alright then," he says with a smile. "I'll tell her this afternoon."

I throw my arms around him and press my lips against his in excitement. "You're the best," I say excitedly. "Just do me a favor and don't let her know that I had anything to do with it. You know, tell her that it's because you see how good she is and that you value how much effort she puts in. That'll make her feel really good."

"Fuck, I love the way you're so selfless when it comes to your mom," he tells me. "But it's true. Your mom is a fucking force of nature. I've never seen someone log as many hours and do such an incredible job. Hell, I don't think I've seen any of our past live-ins actually smile."

"Spend a little time in Breakers Flats and you'll understand how she can be so happy scrubbing toilets. Your family has literally given me and my mom the world."

"Alright," he says, spanking my ass and making it sting in the best way. He's clearly trying to skip the sentimental crap because he doesn't know how to accept a compliment. "Get that fine ass out of here. I have work to do and if you keep hanging around here, I'm going to end up fucking you on every available surface until your pussy is red raw."

I bit down on my lip, more than okay by the idea. "Go," he tells me with a warning.

"Okay," I laugh, slowly backing away before glancing at the fireplace. "Though, can I light them up first? It's only the right thing to do."

His lips lift into a crooked smile and waves a hand toward the fireplace. "Be my guest," he tells me. "But if you're going to burn them, can you burn all this other shit too?"

I let out a groan. I should have known it wasn't going to be that easy. "Yeah, alright," I say, walking towards the big box of papers and dragging it toward the fireplace. "What is all of this?"

He shrugs his shoulders. "Just a bunch of shit that dad was collecting over the years and is now wasting space on my shelves."

I gape at him. "Did you even check any of this? What if it's something important?"

"Anything important would have been filed away or at the main offices, not kept here. This is just his personal shit that he never got around to destroying."

"If you insist," I say, dropping down in front of the fireplace and pressing the magical little button that turns it on. I'll never get used to these rich people's fireplaces. Back home you'd have to sit in front of the fireplace for ages trying to get it to light, but these ones are on and warm with the push of a button.

Just as I wanted, the resumes are the first to go up in flames and it feels so damn good. Maryne will not be replaced today. With Mom taking over her position, things can remain as normal as possible.

I lean back and listen as Colton works while I grab handfuls of papers and throw them onto the fire. I do my best to be a nosey bitch and scan over the papers as I go, though to be honest, I don't understand any of it.

I get halfway through when I grab the next pile to go in the fire and a folder with a familiar,unmistakable mark steals my attention.

"The fuck is this?" I murmur under my breath, quiet enough not to steal Colton's attention away from his phone call. I drop the papers into the fire while keeping the folder on my lap.

The Black Widows mark stares up at me. Why the fuck would Charles have a Black Widows folder?

I tear open the folder in the same breath, desperately needing to know what's in here. Before I've even finished scanning the first fucking page, I'm out the door and racing back to the Ferrari as my blood boils beneath my skin and the rage from earlier comes bounding back twofold.

They fucking know something and this time, I won't be leaving until I have my answers.

CHAPTER 25

I bring the Ferrari to a screeching stop outside the Black Widows clubhouse, this time not giving a shit about what happens to the car. If someone wants to fuck around with it, be my guest. I'm not in the mood right now. This is too fucking big. It's fucking huge and if I find out that Nic and my boys knew about this ... fuck. Things will never be the same.

I storm through the compound and slam my way through the big doors. I've only ever been in here a handful of times and only ever because I had no fucking choice, and one thing is for sure, I've never stepped through these doors without my boys at my back. Walking in here unprotected—fucking stupid.

All eyes fall to me the second the door bangs against the brick wall but I don't fucking care. Let them watch. Let them be witness to me tearing down their fucking second in command because that's exactly what's about to happen.

The folder burns against my skin as I start making my way through the building. It's fucking huge in here, and a fucking mess. These guys live like slobs. There are four cars spread out across the compound, all being taken apart. I have no doubt that they're stolen and the poor people who probably spent their hard-earned cash and most likely couldn't afford insurance will never see them again.

Music blares through the building as guys sit against a bar either drinking, smoking, or counting stacks of cash. No matter what they're doing, their eyes are on me. People don't just wander in here whenever the fuck they want. If you're inside this building it's because you're either one of them or because you've been invited and I can guarantee, not one of my boys would willingly invite me in here.

"Woah," a familiar voice calls, jogging toward me before anyone else can. Elijah catches me around the waist and instantly starts hauling me back toward the door. "What the fuck do you think you're doing?" he spits through his teeth, keeping his voice low, overpowering me, and getting me at least three steps back before I even know what's going on. "Are you fucking insane?"

"Where the fuck is he?" I demand, fighting against Eli's hold.

"I'll get him. Just get the fuck out of here before someone decides that they have a problem with it."

"GET HER OUT OF HERE," a chilling voice booms through the compound. My head snaps up and I find Kian's dark, deadly eyes locked on me and my blood instantly runs cold. How is this guy Nic's father? They look nearly identical but they're nothing alike. Kian is cold, harsh, and practically cut off from everything that makes a human good, while Nic is the whole fucking world ... except for his need to fuck sluts and apparently becoming aggressively possessive like he did this morning. Maybe he does have a few things in common with his father after all.

Eli tugs on me hard and within the blink of an eye, he throws me out the door and the heavy metal slams shut behind us. He keeps me moving, his hard, unimpressed stare never leaving mine as he forces me all the way back to the road and far out of hearing range from the clubhouse.

He doesn't speak a word directly to me, just silently pulls out his phone and holds it to his ear. "What?" I hear Nic's sharp voice snap through the phone despite it not even being on speakerphone, going to prove exactly what kind of pissy mood he's already in after our bullshit this morning.

"Your fucking girl is here and just let herself into the goddamn clubhouse."

"The fuck?"

"We're out front."

Eli ends the call and drops his phone back into his pocket, his glare somehow even sharper. "You're a fucking fool walking in there like that. Are you trying to cause shit for Nic?"

"I couldn't give two fucking shits what kind of trouble I cause Nic. I hope he has the whole fucking world brought down on his ass."

His brows furrow. "What the fuck has gotten into you?"

The door opens with a loud bang and Nic comes striding out looking like the worst kind of guy. The power radiating off him is enough to cut off my response to Eli and I storm toward him, the overwhelming emotions building within me far too great to control.

Anger burns in his eyes and it's not clear if it's from our bullshit this morning or if he's just pissed at the little stunt I just pulled. Honestly, it's probably both.

"Do you think this is a fucking game?" he roars. "What kind of bullshit do you think you're playing coming in here unprotected? Do you know what those fuckers would have done to you?"

"Nothing worse than what I've already suffered through," I throw back at him before holding the papers up at him. "What the fuck is this?"

His eyes flick to the big Black Widow marking on the front and something flashes in his eyes that puts him on edge. The papers are stolen from my hands and he flips it open as Sebastian and Kai appear behind him.

"Tell me you didn't fucking know."

"Know what?" Sebastian asks, stepping into my side so he can peer over the paperwork. "That my father was involved with Charles Carrington."

Sebastian's jaw clenches and just like that, I realize that they all know exactly what's inside that folder. I snatch the papers back from

Nic before he has a chance to finish scanning through them. "Fucking tell me right this goddamn minute what you know or I swear to you, Nic, you will never see me again. I will walk out of here and never look back."

He stares at me and for a moment, Eli, Sebastian, and Kairo fade away, leaving just me and Nic—real, raw, and lethal. He swallows hard and I watch as he mentally goes through his options. He knows damn well that I will follow through on my threat and considering his reaction to the thought of me moving on this morning, I'm going to go ahead and assume that he doesn't want me to walk away.

He lets out a loud breath, realizing that he's backed into a corner and the second he does, the three boys stiffen as admitting that he knows something is admitting that they do too.

"Your father was a Wolf," he starts, his eyes never once leaving mine, and upon seeing the lack of surprise, his brows furrow right along with the rest of them.

"You knew," Kairo says, like an accusation, stepping a little closer.

My eyes cut to his. "Is it such a surprise that I knew something about my own fucking father? Hell, you guys all knew so why shouldn't I? I fucking found out during an appointment at school when someone recognized my father's name. Do you know how fucking stupid I looked sitting there and accusing this woman of not knowing what the fuck she was talking about?"

"Babe," Sebastian says, reaching for me and trying to be that voice of reason that's always been able to calm me during the worst kind of storms.

"DON'T," I snap, stepping just out of his reach and watching his features break. "You all kept this from me. How could you do that? For fucking years. Tell me, did you know from the very beginning? Is that why you guys just suddenly popped into my life?"

"It's not like that," Nic growls.

"You know what? I don't even care about that right now. I want to know if the shit in this folder is fucking true," I demand, hating what I read and refusing to believe it. "I want to know just how low you can get, Dominic."

"Well," he says. "You have the papers in front of you. Read it for yourself."

"I already have read it," I yell at him. "I want to hear it from you. I want you, the guy who's supposed to have my back to tell me that he's always known the very reason why mom and I ended up in Bellevue Springs. I want you to tell me that you've known the answers to the questions that I kept asking and I want you to fucking tell me to my goddamn face that you've lied to me over and fucking over again."

"O–"

"FUCKING TELL ME."

"Alright," he roars. "Your father was a fucking scumbag who stole from Carrington to put food on the fucking table for your ass and he got caught. He was offered two choices. Either pay the money back or lose his life, and that prick decided to pay up, but all he had was you and that fucking prick sold you to Carrington to save himself. You paid off his debt. That's why you're in Bellevue Springs. That's why Charles called you his goddamn property, and that's why I haven't taken your ass out of there. Is that what you wanted to hear? You wanted me to break your precious little heart and tell you the truth about the man who you hold on a fucking pedestal? I was trying to protect you."

I step into him, clenching my jaw. "I don't need your protection. You lied to me. You could have told me from the start."

"How could I have told you? If you knew you were a Wolf, you would have turned your back and walked away from us as some fucked up way to protect us. I wasn't willing to risk that."

"And just like that, you get to make that decision for me? So, every day you put my life at risk by bringing me into your world. You're a fucking Widow and I'm a Wolf. We can't be ... whatever the fuck we are. I can't be anything to any of you, yet every day you risk me like that. If they knew that I'm a fucking Wolf, I'd be—

"Dead."

My eyes whip over to the chilling voice to find Kian striding toward me. My heart races. I've never had this man actually come to talk to me before. I've always had Nic's protection from that, but I don't need him. Not any more. Not if he could hide something like this from me.

I turn back to Nic, not giving a shit about his father right now. "Does my mother know? Colton?"

He shakes his head. "No. Neither of them."

I let out a breath, not realizing how badly those questions had been plaguing my mind since I first scanned through these papers, but now it all makes sense. Why my boys have been so shady about Bellevue Springs, why Charles so suddenly took us in, and why he took an interest in my schooling. I wasn't just staff to him, I was his actual property. Yet in all of this, there's still one question that sits heavy on my heart.

I look back to Nic, feeling as though I could break. "Why didn't he tell me?"

Eli scoffs. "Why didn't he tell you that he sold you? Fuck, O. Why do you think? Hey, Honey, how was school? Oh, by the way, I sold you to a fucking billionaire so I could save myself."

"Fuck you," I snap. "Why didn't he tell me that he was a fucking Wolf, asshole?"

Kian steps into the circle and grabs my chin, forcing my eyes to his as the four boys stiffen, not liking his closeness at all. "You were his little girl and this is no world for princesses like you."

I tear my chin out of his hold. "You can't touch me," I snap. "I'm a fucking Wolf."

He leans in, his eyes brimming with excitement. "As far as they're concerned, you're a traitor. You spend your days running around with Widows. I could do whatever the fuck I wanted to you and they wouldn't do a goddamn thing."

Nic glares at his father. "Back off."

Kian straightens and turns his attention on his son. "What's with this little obsession you have with this girl?" he questions before tracking his eyes up and down my body. "She's certainly nothing special."

My sharp glare cuts to him and he catches my eyes. I raise my chin, trying to appear bigger than my small 5'2, but I know my intimidation techniques would never work on a guy like this. They're more suited to bitchy high school cheerleaders. This is the real fucking world here.

"Back off," Nic warns again but this time, it's not clear if he's talking to his father or me.

Kian laughs. "You think I'm bad," he teases. "Your father was worse."

I shake my head. "You don't know a goddamn thing about my father."

"Oh, really? Because it seems like you're the one who doesn't know anything, Sweetheart. Let me enlighten you."

Nic steps in closer to me and I flinch from his closeness. "Dad. Don't."

Kian ignores him and I find myself listening intently. If someone around here is actually willing to tell me the truth, then I'm ready. I'm done being protected from the ugliness of this world. I'm not stupid. I know my father wouldn't be innocent. No one in this town is, but the question is just how bad could he have been to have a man like Kian Garcia accuse him of being worse?

Kian turns on Nic and grabs him around the throat, pulling him in close to his face. "Why are you still trying to protect her? She's a nobody. She doesn't even live here anymore. Get the fuck over this little fascination you have with her. If she wants to know the truth, then I'm going to tell her the fucking truth like you should have done in the first place. You think you're keeping her safe by hiding this shit from her? All you've done is backed her into a corner, taught her to rely on you instead of being able to navigate her way around this and learn to survive on her own. What kind of bullshit protection is that?"

Kian releases him and Nic looks as though he's only two seconds away from tearing his father apart. Kai puts a hand on his chest, reeling him back in as Kian looks back to me. "Let me tell you a little something about your father," he starts, thrilled to be the one to get to break the news to me. "Your father wasn't just a Wolf, Babydoll. He was second in command and a ruthless asshole. I tried to get him on my side once but he was loyal to his family. He was the best goddamn exterminator on this side of the fucking border."

"Exterminator?" I ask, glancing at Sebastian, knowing he's the only one who would have the balls to step up and offer me an answer.

His face breaks and his heart slips out to be worn on his sleeve. "Hitman, O. An exterminator is a hitman and your father was the best one I've ever seen."

I shake my head. "No, you're lying. My father wasn't a hitman. He wouldn't do that."

Kian scoffs. "Just like he wouldn't sell his only daughter to a rich bastard to save himself? Yeah, Baby, he would. Your father was fucking lethal and could kill a man in seconds."

"No," I say, still refusing to believe it. "Hitmen are supposed to be rich. They do a job and get paid. My father didn't have that kind of money. It's not true. We struggled every fucking day."

A grin lifts the corner of Kian's lips and it's disturbing how much he's enjoying this. "That's what made him so fucking sick. He wasn't a career hitman, he did it for sport because he fucking loved it. He liked the look in someone's eyes as he took their life away. Trust me, it's a fucking rush watching the life fade out of someone under your hands.

He was a fool really. He could have made a killing in the profession, but just like everything else, he fucked that up too."

"So, who killed him then? Was it you?" I demand, wondering if I even care right now. This version of my father doesn't sound like the kind of guy I want anything to do with, but at the same time, he was my daddy. He was the man that came home every day and sat across from me at the dinner table. He would tuck me in at night and turn out my light when I was a little girl and a part of me is desperately holding onto that.

Kian's eyes blaze with anger and he reaches for me. "Listen here, you little bitch," he growls, pulling me in close just like he'd done with Nic but something tells me that he won't hurt me despite the way the boys tense and prepare themselves to dive in. "I had nothing to do with that. None of my boys did."

I slam the folder with his mark into his chest, pulling myself free in the process. "Then why is your mark all over it? Pretty fucking suspicious, don't you think? Your mark is on a folder found in Charles Carrington's office when both he and my father were killed, clearly by the same person. You're the third party in this little triangle, not to mention, there's been a gang war between you and the Wolves for a good six months. Funny how it's been exactly six months since he was murdered. Are they looking for revenge?"

"I had nothing to do with it," he spits. "I won't let you drag me down for this. I've told you what you wanted to know and now it's time for you to fuck off, and now that you know you're a fucking Wolf, don't be so stupid as to come back here."

I take a step back, my chest rising and falling with hard, sharp breaths and just like that, Kian decides we're finished here and turns his back. He starts walking away and I'm left staring at the four boys who hid the fact that my father was a Wolf, hid the fact that he sold me, and hid the fact that I'm the daughter of a murderer..

I meet each of their eyes, leaving Nic's for last and when his fall back on mine, I shake my head, pressing my lips into a tight broken line. "I'm done," I tell him with finality, feeling everything inside of me break.

I turn and start walking back to the Ferrari but a slowing black SUV coming down the road catches my eyes. The two side windows begin lowering and as black shiny metal appears in the open window, Nic's voice rings out loud. "GUN. GET DOWN."

His heavy body slams into my back, throwing me down hard against the concrete. My head rebounds off the ground as my elbows and knees are torn to shreds. Nic's large body holds me down, his arms curling protectively around my head as the deafening shots ring out over and over again.

A low, pained groan is heard behind me and tears instantly spring to my eyes, not knowing which of my boys was hit and despite how much I hate them right now, the thought of one of them being shot makes me sick.

I scream as bullets rain down around us. A second grunt of pain tears through the noise and I scream again, recognizing Eli's groan anywhere.

Shots ring out from behind me and I peer under Nic's arm to

watch Kai shooting back. With the threat of retaliation, the SUV speeds off and I feel Nic relax on top of me. "Are you alright, Baby? Tell me you're fucking alright."

"I'm okay," I say, feeling woozy from the bump on my head.

Nic pulls off me and as he helps me to my feet, I look over my boys to find Eli holding his shoulder with blood pouring out over his fingers, but that's not where my attention stops.

Kian lays on his stomach not moving, just two feet away from the door of the compound with blood pooled around him.

Nic races to his father's aid as the door of the compound is practically pulled off its hinges and Black Widows come pouring out. Nic reaches his father just before them and flips him over to find him barely holding on. "DAD," he yells, slamming his hands down over the wound but he's too far gone. Even if he called an ambulance, Kian's not going to make it.

Sebastian gets on the phone while helping Elijah to keep pressure on his wound as Kairo drops down beside Nic, desperate to help him save his father.

"Who did this?" One of the Widows demands as everyone jumps into action, trying to help where they can.

Nic's sharp gaze snaps up to the men around him. "Wolves," he spits. "Black SUV heading west. I want every last one of those fuckers in my compound in five fucking minutes. I'm going to put each of them in a body bag."

At least ten men run off, climbing onto Harley's and taking off at the speed of light but when Kian starts sputtering and blood comes trailing out of his mouth, my attention falls back to him as he looks up at his son. "I love you, boy," he says, choking on the blood building in his throat. "This is all yours now. Don't let me down."

Nic shakes his head. "Don't you dare say goodbye, you hear me? You're not going anywhere."

Kian's eyes start to grow heavy as tears race down my cheeks. "Tell your mother it was always her. Always."

Nic nods and as tears appear in his eyes, everything inside of me dies. Kian's eyes close and his body goes heavy in Nic's arms. "Dad?" he demands, shaking his father, desperate to hear his voice just one more time. "Dad."

Kai's hand falls to Nic's shoulder and he pries him away. "He's gone," Kai murmurs. "Let him go."

Nic cries out, his voice filled with pain. "NOOOO."

I let out a shaky breath and despite everything we just went through, I find myself moving toward him. I step into his side and as he looks up at me from his position on the bloodied ground, I find a broken man, a version of Nic I've never seen before.

His arms curl around me and he pulls me down into his lap, holding me tighter and crushing me with his strength.

There's nothing but silence as the grief tears through every last person standing around and after five minutes of gut-wrenching pain, all eyes begin to fall on Nic until he finally releases me and gets to his feet.

His chin raises and as he looks around at the Widows before him, every head bows, silently vowing their loyalty, and just like that, a broken, grieving Nic steps up as the rightful leader of the Black Widows.

CHAPTER 26

I sit at the bar in the compound, avoiding the eyes of the Black Widows as they stare at me. Their boss was just murdered and they know I don't belong, yet their new king has insisted I stay, in fact, demanded it. They won't go against him to kick me out, especially considering Kian was Nic's father, but they're certainly not happy about it.

My gut tells me that I should get up and leave. I want to hate Nic. I want to hate all of them. They knew these things about my father and not once did they come clean. How could they do that? I thought we had an understanding. I thought the trust between us was unbreakable, but lately, Nic and the boys have been testing that theory.

Nic silently sits beside me. I couldn't leave him. I should have. I should have gotten back in that damn Ferrari and taken my ass home. It's stupid being within these walls. Men are pacing and despite having Widows out searching for the black SUV, the ones remaining are all searching for someone to blame, and considering I was the reason they were all out front, that blame falls on me.

I've never felt tension like this before. I've just walked right into the firing line of a gang war while technically being on the opposite side. If I was smart, I'd be hauling ass, yet the pain radiating out of Nic keeps me right here.

I watch him as he swirls the amber liquid around the bottom of his glass. He looks devastated and right now, I'm not sure if it's because he lost his father or because of the responsibilities that have just fallen on his shoulders. He didn't have much love for his father. Kian was dark and twisted and not in the romantic kind of way, but in the needs to be locked in prison wearing a straight jacket kind of way. He was dangerous and he made sure that Nic didn't grow up with love, but as Nic grew and it became clear that he was a natural-born leader, Kian couldn't resist reeling him back into his dark world.

What is it with the fathers around here? Is every man over a certain age just automatically a dick. My father had a web of lies and was a fucking hitman for the West Side Wolves, Colton's father was an asshole who abused his wife and children, while Kian was a fucking monster.

I have to give it to the guy, he was the only person in my life who wasn't afraid to tell me the truth and for that, I'm grateful even if it means putting my relationship with my boys on the rocks.

Things will never go back to normal after this. I will never have trust for them again. I mean, I sure as hell trust them to always protect me and always do what they think is right, but I will forever question their loyalty, their motives, and their hearts. It's never a position I wanted to be in, but they've backed me into a corner and I'm left with no choice.

Nic throws back what's left in his glass before slamming it back down on the bar. His cup is instantly refilled and that one goes straight down the hatch too. it's going to be a rough night.

I haven't seen Nic like this since … well, ever.

Not wanting to watch him self-destruct, I slide back off the bar stool and follow the loud grunts of agony until I'm standing before Eli. He instantly grabs hold of my hands as Kai stands at his shoulder with a pair of tweezers that look fucking dirty.

"Give me that," I say, snatching them from his hands and grabbing the bottle of vodka at Eli's side. "You're going to give him an infection."

"This isn't my first rodeo," Kai says as I dump the vodka over the tweezers and clean them off as best as I can.

"Yeah, I know," I grumble, setting my jaw and not wanting to meet either of their eyes. "Tell me, how'd that turn out for you?"

Kai huffs, knowing damn well that I'm talking about last year when he dug a bullet out of Nic's arm and three days later ended up with an infection that had him hospitalized for forty-eight hours.

Confident that the tweezers are as clean as they're going to get, I hand them back and look down at Eli sitting on the bench. His face is white and he looks close to passing out, but the second Kai touches him, it's all going to change.

He grabs hold of my hand, preparing to squeeze the shit out of it while I pick up his discarded shirt, getting ready to shove it into his mouth so he doesn't accidentally break all his damn teeth when he bites down. "Just … wait," he murmurs as I lift it to his mouth, having done this way too many times. "I …"

"No," I say, shaking my head. "I don't want to hear your broken apologies because right now, they mean nothing to me. I stayed because Nic needs me, not because I want to be here. Let's get that straight. Things between us," I say, glancing up at Kai so he knows this includes him, "will never be the same. You guys broke us by deciding not to be honest with me and because of that, no amount of shitty apologies will fix it."

"Come on, babe," Sebastian says, stepping into my side, his arm brushing along mine as he passes Eli a bottle of Absinthe that he instantly uncaps and raises to his mouth, cringing with the movement.

I flinch away from Sebastian's touch and hate the way his face breaks. He's always been one to wear his heart on his sleeve, especially when it comes to me. He's not capable of hiding his feelings.

"Don't. Don't try and change my mind because it's not going to work. You guys hurt me. You betrayed my trust and it's going to take a shitload more than a few smiles and some shitty words to fix it. I just want to make sure that Nic is alright and then I'm out of here."

Eli squeezes my hand but speaks to Kairo at his shoulder. "Let's just get this over with."

All strained conversation comes to an end as Kairo grunts and moves in closer. He gently nudges Eli, prompting him to lean over so he can see better and with a cringe and a quick drink of Absinthe, he does as he's told.

Eli's hold on my hand tightens and I quickly shove the discarded shirt between his teeth before giving him my other hand. He takes it eagerly and it reminds me just how much these guys need me. I hate how much I hate them right now, but I can't seem to pull back on my basic instinct to protect them and offer comfort. They don't deserve it, especially Nic, but at the same time, standing here and watching Eli in pain is killing me.

The tweezers dig into his skin and Eli groans low as his face turns a sickly shade of white. He squeezes down on my hand and I feel an agonizing crack in my left hand.

"Fuuuuuuuuuck," I shriek but don't dare pull my hand away. My eyes fill with tears but he needs this more than I do. He got shot. I think I can handle a small fracture. I've had worse.

"Dude," Sebastian says, looking between me and Eli. "You're hurting her. Let go."

"It's fine," I say through my teeth, looking up at a panicked Kai as Eli lets up on my hands. "Just get the fucking thing out." Kai cringes, realizing exactly what's at stake and digs deeper.

Eli doesn't hesitate, squeezing my hands tighter as he bites down on his shirt in absolute misery. A high-pitched squeak slips from between my lips. "Holy mother of sweet baby Jesus. Tell me you've nearly got it?"

"Nearly," Kai grunts, leaning in closer to get a better look. "It's lodged in the fucking bone. I don't want to do any more damage."

Eli groans, biting down on the shirt harder than humanly possible. "JUST. GET. IT. THE. FUCK. OUT."

Kai glances up at Sebastian, "Get in here with that vodka, man. There's fucking blood everywhere."

Sebastian runs around and takes one look at the back of Eli's shoulder before peeling off his own shirt and using it to help mop up the blood. I roll my eyes. Stupid fucking boys. Do they have no concept of infection control?

The bullet is finally pulled from his shoulder and Sebastian instantly gets in there with the vodka. He presses his shirt over the wound to control the stream of blood and Eli finally lets up on my hands.

I pull the shirt from between his teeth and he lets out a slow breath. "Are you alright?" He questions, still white as a ghost.

"I'll live," I grumble, glancing away.

All three of the boys stare at me and without another word, I turn my back and walk away.

"O," I hear called in perfect unison by all three of them.

I spin around, fixing each of them with a hard stare. "Why the hell did you three just randomly appear in my life?" They all hesitate and the words come flying out of me. "TELL ME."

Sebastian's jaw clenches, the only sign that he's about to talk. He raises his chin, finally ready to give it to me straight. "Kian learned who you were and put us in your life. He wanted to have you watched. He knew that you didn't know who your father really was and he used that against him."

Pain slices through me, right down to my core. "So, it was all a lie? You weren't my friends at all. You were there watching my father and screwing over his daughter in the process."

Kairo nods. "At first, but then we got to know you. You're one of us, Ocean. Who cares how we fucking met? What we have is stronger than that."

"You really think so?" I laugh. "Our whole friendship was based on a lie. We have nothing. Not anymore."

I turn away and don't dare look back knowing damn well that if I did, I'll break. If anything, I've overstayed my welcome, not that I had any in the first place. I'll check on Nic one last time and then I'm out of here.

I start walking back to the bar to take my seat beside him, only he's no longer there. I glance around the large, warehouse-style compound to find him having a whispered conversation with a guy who has a phone glued to his ear.

Nic's eyes flash up to mine and the look within them nearly tears me apart.

This isn't my Nic. The man staring back at me is a complete stranger. This is the lethal, dark version of Nic that could rip a man to shreds with his bare hands. This is the version of himself that he's always tried to protect me from, but something has changed, that need to hide it from me is gone.

I falter, bringing myself to a stop in the middle of the compound. Something screams at me not to take another step, that I should stay away, but as usual, I'm so fucking drawn to him.

I swallow back the confusion and realize the right thing to do is leave. I can't see him like this. I've always known this is a part of who he is. This is his dark side, the side that will have grown men shitting their pants and begging for forgiveness. Seeing him like this ... it's going to crush me.

Nic has always been larger than life for me and while I've always known about this, I've never had to watch him at his worst and I'm terrified of being scared of him, of knowing just how far he can go. Sure, I've seen him beat the ever-loving shit out of a man. I've seen the way he dominates every fucking situation, but whatever comes next ... that's going to change it all.

A hard body presses into my back and as hands claim my waist, Sebastian's low voice sends chills running down my spine. "I've seen that look, Ocean," he tells me, his voice barely a whisper. "You need to go."

I nod and as I go to step around him a guy starts pulling on a thick chain, pulling the roller door up. The only proper door in the warehouse is slammed shut and locked and Sebastian pulls me back into him, clutching onto me tighter. "Fuck. Too late."

The deafening sound of Harley's fill the warehouse as they creep through the roller door, surrounding all sides of the black SUV, the same one that had only rolled past here less than an hour ago with guns hanging out of the fucking windows.

My back stiffens. I really don't want to be here.

The Widows all start to crowd around, at least two hundred of them, all eager to see how Nic is going to avenge his father. This is his first official move as their leader—defending the man who has led them for nearly thirty years. This has to be big. This has to prove that he has what it takes.

This has to send a message—Kian might be gone, but the Widows will live on, stronger, darker, deadlier. They will not succumb to anybody, especially not the Wolves. This will never be forgotten and they will never be forgiven. This war between them just became fucking vicious.

The Harley's come to a stop and the SUV is pulled up between them. The bikers get off and instantly go to the back of the SUV. Other's jump in to help and within moments, three bound and gagged men stumble out of the back and into the center of the warehouse, each one of them terrified for their lives.

Nic strides into the center and the Widows begin chanting his name as the three men glance around in fear, knowing damn well what their fate will be tonight.

Sebastian holds onto me tighter and slowly begins pulling me back into the crowd, trying to protect me from what's about to happen but I don't move a fucking inch. My eyes are glued on Nic and although I know I don't want to see this, something is forcing me to stay, a deep desperation to know exactly who this man is that I thought I knew.

Nic walks behind the three bound men and kicks the back of their legs, sending them all falling to the dirty ground until they're on their knees before him. They shake with fear but if you want to drive by the Black Widows home and kill their leader, this is the price you pay.

They were fools if they thought that they'd get away with this.

Nic stands tall and looks out at his Widows and the massive room falls into silence, anxiously waiting to see what he's going to do.

"These men took our leader's life—My father's life," he says, his tone loud and domineering, demanding the attention of the room. "They disrespected us, came onto our turf, and begged for war."

Nic pauses as his Widows yell for revenge and he pulls a knife from within his jacket pocket, a jacket that is stained with his father's blood. "This will not go unpunished," he roars, making the Widows roar right along with him as my blood runs cold. "If it's a war they beg for, then it's a war we will give them, and we won't stop until every last one of them are buried in our backyard."

I step back into Sebastian's chest and he holds me tighter, knowing I need his support.

Nic steps up to the bound man on the right, his knife glistening in the light above their heads. The man tries to strain his neck to keep an eye on Nic but Nic's not having it. He grabs chunks of the man's hair and tears his head back until his neck is completely exposed.

I swallow hard, my heart racing with fear.

Oh, Nic. Please don't do this.

"Are you their shooter? Did you kill my father?"

"No," the man rushes out, his eyes flicking to the man in the center. "It was Brock. I swear, I was driving. I didn't shoot at anyone."

Nic roars a dark laugh. "So I should just let you go, huh?" he says "I should take the word of a man who so quickly threw his brother under the bus? Where's your fucking loyalty?"

The front of the man's pants become wet as he starts begging for his life. "Please. I'll do anything?"

Nic grips his hair tighter. "What a shame, you're shit outta luck. My tolerance for disloyalty went out the fucking window the second you drove past my clubhouse. The Widows do not grant favors. A life for a life."

With a flash, the knife slices deep across the man's throat, and blood spurts out like a fountain. A loud gasp pulls from deep within me and as the man falls to the ground, Nic's eyes snap to mine.

They widen just a fraction but the darkness swirling within them has him stepping to his next victim, not giving a shit that I've just witnessed him taking a life.

A massive pool of blood begins spreading around the dying man's body, staining Nic's shoes and the knees of the man that he just threw under the bus, but it's as though they don't even notice.

Nic wipes the blade of his knife on the middle guy's shoulder, slicing the side of his neck in the process. "So, you're the motherfucker who killed my father."

"Kian Garcia was fucking scum. He deserved to die and I'll fucking die a happy man knowing that I was the one who had the pleasure of taking him out." he spits, making the whole warehouse erupt in protest.

Some race forward, wanting to end him themselves while others desperately hold their brothers back, knowing damn well that this is Nic's kill.

"I'm going to enjoy this," Nic says, a dark laugh in his tone. "Don't be fooled. I'm going to take my fucking time and it's going to hurt."

A guy steps into Nic's side and hands him a pair of wire cutters and Nic takes them without hesitation. He grabs the shooter's wrist and tears it high above his head for everyone to see, twisting his shoulder in the process and dislocating the joint. He puts the wire cutters around the base of his pointer finger, his trigger finger, and grins wickedly.

"This is going to be framed in my fucking office," he says before pressing down on the wire cutters and tearing the finger free. The guy screams, a loud ear-shattering wail as his finger is cut off.

Bile rises in my throat but I hold it down, unable to look away from the monsters before me. Blood spurts from the shooter's hand, mixing with the blood of his fellow Wolf on the ground as the finger splashes down into the puddle at his knees.

What is this? Is this really Nic? The guy I thought I was in love with? This is a monster, not a fucking hero. I've always known he was capable, but never in my wildest dreams did I think he'd ever be pushed to these limits.

Without warning, his knife slams down over the guy's chest and I'm instantly reminded of the way the silver dagger protruded from both my father's and Charles' chest. The guy attempts to double over with the pain and as the momentum pulls him forward, Nic grabs the top of his hair and tears his head back before slicing his knife across his neck in the same way he'd done with the first guy.

Tears stream down my face and I don't know why. These guys deserve death. It's just the way things are in this world, especially if you make a move like this against the Black Widows, and killing their leader is as bad as it gets. Maybe the tears are for Nic knowing damn well that the old Nic is gone. He won't come back from this and now that I've witnessed it, I'll never be able to look at him the same. He's not even hesitating, just going straight in for the kill without even thinking about it. How dark does one's soul have to be to do something so wicked?

The shooter's body falls heavily to the ground, his blood mixing with the first as Nic disregards them as though they're not even there.

He steps up behind the last guy and just as he had done earlier, cleans off his blade, but instead of doing it over his shoulder, he swipes the knife across his cheek, leaving a red smear for the world to see. It's as though it's some sort of badge—a message.

"I guess you're the lucky one," Nic tells him as he violently shakes, the fear of death rattling him. "You're going to run home and tell your boss exactly what happened here. Tell him how we took their pathetic lives, tell him how my knife sliced across their throats, tell him there's a new fucking boss in town, and tell him that I'm coming for him. You took our leader tonight and we won't stop until we have yours. NOW RUN."

He scrambles to his feet and takes off like a fucking rocket, but Nic isn't about to let him get off that easily. The guy gets through the roller door when Nic's gun rings out loud and clear. The bullet pierces the guy's shoulder, exactly where Eli had been hit. He falls to the ground with a pained groan and we all watch as his desperation has him stumbling back to his feet and running through the pain.

I can't help but look back at Nic with the two bodies lying at his feet and as he stands as the king in his castle, fear sinks into me. I tear out of Sebastian's hold and without looking back, I run out through the roller door and dive toward Colton's Ferrari, hoping to God that I never see them again.

CHAPTER 27

Tears stream down my face as I push the Ferrari to its limits. How could he do that? What kind of monster is he? That wasn't the Nic that I've come to know and love. He's a stranger. The kind of man that nightmares are made of and Kai, Eli, and Sebastian just stood back and watched him do it as though what he was doing was okay, as though he'd done it a million times before.

Has he? Is this the kind of man I allowed into my heart, the kind of man I allowed in my bed?

The Nic that I knew would have had me removed before handling his shit. He would have protected me, but it's as though he didn't even see me when he looked at me. He saw right through me as though the girl he's so used to protecting wasn't even there.

I understand it, I really do. He's a violent guy and was presented with the men who had just killed his father, the leader of the Black Widows. His soul would have been aching. I know the feeling. Losing a parent is the hardest thing that's ever happened to me, but add the pressure he would have been under from his gang to avenge his father, and it would have been torture. But to murder those men in that way … it was brutal. I wonder if he even feels guilt over it or if to him, it's just another Saturday night.

Is this the type of thing he would do before coming and sneaking into my bed, pretending that he's a good guy and touching me with hands that had just dealt death? Don't get me wrong, I was never completely in the dark. I'm well aware that all four of the boys have ended someone's life, maybe many lives, but I've never witnessed it. I've always been protected from it, but the look in Nic's eyes … that was easy for him. He didn't flinch, didn't show a damn sign of guilt, and sure as hell didn't ask himself what the fuck he was doing.

That's not the man I know and certainly not the one I love.

He's a fucking murderer … just like my father.

Mom was right all this time. I should never have let them into my life, but I was young and dumb. There were four incredible guys inserting themselves into my life, treating me like their queen and protecting me with everything they had. What kind of fool could resist that?

Headlights appear in my rearview mirror and at first, I think nothing of it until the car moves right in behind me, too close to be coincidental. My heart rate picks up and my eyes remain locked on the headlights until the car moves in beside me and I recognize Kairo's beat-up shitbox.

I take a breath. Had it been anyone else who had witnessed that, I'm sure the Widows would have been after them. They would have killed them to ensure their silence, and I'm sure had Kian been alive and I'd witnessed him do the exact same thing, he still would have killed me. He would have just gone about it in a way that Nic and the boys didn't know about until it was already too late. But just like the three men who just lost their lives, that's the game you play when you involve yourself with the Black Widows.

My phone blares through the quiet car and my eyes drop to the screen.

Kai.

Great.

I don't know if I can talk to him but history tells me that he'll keep calling until I do. Either that or he'll force me to pull over so he can say what he needs to say. There's no bullshit when it comes to Kai. He's black and white. There's no grey area where he's concerned.

Being shit outta luck, I reluctantly answer. "I'm not in the mood to talk, Kai," I say. "And don't even think about asking me to pull over. I said I'm done. I just want to go home and … forget."

There's a short pause before his raspy, deep tone finally comes through the phone. "I know," he says with a whisper. "I don't want to talk. I just … I need to make sure you get home okay. Just let me drive with you."

My gaze flashes out the window and I meet his concerned eyes through the glass. "Okay," I finally say, turning back to the road. I hear the soft music from his sound system coming through the phone as I drop it to my lap and put it on speakerphone.

We drive side by side for two hours and not a damn word passes between us. Tears silently track down my face the whole way home as the heaviness of my day sits on my heart. I can't stop glancing up to make sure he's still there. I don't know why though. I made it clear that I was done, yet my heart still aches for my boys. I need them in my life, they've been my support system for so long. I don't know how to be without them.

After what feels like the longest drive in history, I finally pull into the driveway of the Carrington mansion. I key in the code and watch as Kai pulls in behind me. The big iron gates slowly peel open and as I speed down the driveway, Kai keeps right behind me. "Whatever you do, wherever you go," he murmurs, his voice coming clearly through the phone. "We love you, Ocean. We always will. Don't you ever forget that."

The tears turn into violent sobs and I hastily end the call, not wanting him to hear just how broken I am, but it might be too late for that. Kai follows me all the way to the top of the driveway and by the time I'm bringing the Ferrari to a stop, Colton is standing there waiting.

I throw the door open and run toward him. His eyes widen in horror, desperately searching my face for some kind of answer as to what has me so messed up. I crash into him, falling into his open arms as I hear Kai's tires on the driveway slowly pulling around the circle.

"Shhhh, Jade," he soothes, rubbing his warm hands up and down my arms as I try to find the willpower to calm my broken sobs.

I don't dare look up but somehow I know Kai's eyes are on me, making sure that I'm well taken care of. I don't doubt that the second he's gone, he's going to have the boys on the phone, giving them the full report and letting them know just how fucked up I was over this.

After the longest moment, Kairo finally hits the gas and I watch as his tail lights disappear into the distance, taking the final piece of my soul with him and leaving me completely empty.

This is it. From this moment, I'll never see them again. It's over. All of it's gone in one fucked-up night.

"What's going on?" Colton asks, his voice dark as he watches Kai's car fade away. "What happened? Did someone hurt you?"

I shake my head, wiping my tears against his shirt as I look up and meet his eyes. There are so many things that I could say, but I find myself searching his eyes, desperate to know one single thing. "Did you know?"

His brows furrow as he looks me over. "Did I know what?"

"That my father was a low-life who sold me to your father to pay off a debt."

Colton's face falls and he gently shakes his head, his face turning white. "You're fucking kidding me? That can't be true."

I nod. "The fucking paperwork is in the car. I'm your property, Colton. You own me."

"No," he says, taking a step back and looking absolutely horrified. "He wouldn't do that. My father was a sick man, but this … no. He wouldn't take it that far. He couldn't have ..."

I meet his eyes and see nothing but disgust within them and just like that I know he's telling the truth.

Colton's hands fall to my waist as his lips press against my forehead. There's a silence between us and it's clear that he's deep in thought, but I welcome it as it finally allows me a chance to calm my raging emotions. "It's true, isn't it?" he murmurs. "That's why you just showed up out of the blue, why you were sent to school, why he welcomed you in like family. He's never done that with staff before and I could never figure it out." I shrug my shoulders and he pulls me in tighter. "Fuck, Jade. I'm so sorry. If I'd have known ..."

"What? What could you have done? Gone back in time and made it so it never happened? There's nothing we can do about it. They're both fucking dead."

"Surely you must know that I don't think of you as property. I never have and fuck knows that I never will."

"Doesn't change the fact that I am your property."

"Whatever you need, Ocean. I'll fucking do it. If you want me to sign some bullshit release then I'll do it, anything. I don't want you to feel like I'm holding you here, but fuck, Jade, please don't go."

"I'll pay it back," I tell him. "Whatever my father's debt was, I'll pay it."

"Jade ..."

"No. I don't care how fucking long it takes," I insist, feeling my eyes begin to well with tears all over again. "It's the only way. I have to pay it back. Every last cent."

"Okay, okay," he says, curling his arms around me again, feeling the desperation creeping up on me. "We can work it out in the morning. Let me take you inside. It's fucking freezing out here."

I glance around and sure enough, there's a light frost over the lawn and I realize that he's right. It's bloody freezing and I hadn't even realized. I allow him to lead me up the stairs and through the front door and by the time he's pulling open the door to lead me out to the pool house, I pull back on his hand. "Please … I just … I." I shake my head, having no idea what I'm trying to say before looking up and meeting his concerned gaze. "I don't want to be alone. I can't. I just … if I was to close my eyes …"

Colton watches me for a short moment before nodding and pulling me back inside the mansion. "You can stay with me as long as you need," he tells me.

We walk back through the mansion until he's pushing through to the den. He leads me to the oversized couch and I drop down onto it. Colton disappears for all of two seconds before returning with a blanket and a bunch of cushions and despite the turmoil my heart and soul are suffering through, I feel a smile tugging at my lips.

Colton collapses down on the couch beside me and stretches out with the blanket. "Come here," he murmurs, reaching for me.

He pulls me into his arms and a sense of comfort finally comes over me and for the first time all day, I finally feel like everything is going to be okay.

Colton is quickly becoming my home and the more time I spend with him, the clearer that becomes. I just wish it didn't terrify me quite so much. His hand rubs up and down my arm and I'm thankful that he's not pushing for answers, he's just content to sit here with me in the middle of the night and hold me until the images in my mind begin to fade, but this time, I don't think his presence is going to be enough to make it go away. Nothing is going to heal this. What I saw … it's not something a girl can simply forget about.

I nuzzle my face into his chest and he instantly pulls me in tighter. "Are you okay?" he murmurs into the darkened room?

I shake my head. "I don't think I'm ever going to be okay."

His lips brush across my forehead and I close my eyes, trying to pull every ounce of comfort out of his touch. "Do you want to talk about it?"

I shake my head yet still feel the words slipping from between my lips. "I don't think I can," I tell him. "The Widows … if they knew I said something …"

"It's okay," he murmurs. "You don't need to tell me what happened, but fuck, Jade. Please explain why the fuck there's a lump on your head and your elbows and knees are all scratched up."

I think over what happened and realize that I want to share this with him, at least the parts that aren't going to put him in danger. He deserves some sort of explanation. One second I was in his office, clearing out a bunch of shit, and the next thing he knew, I was gone.

I curl closer into his side and let out a shaky breath. "I was with Nic and the boys at the Widow's clubhouse asking them about the whole ownership thing. The papers I found today in your father's office had their mark on the front and I had to know—"

"Wait. Your father was a Widow?"

I shake my head. "No, that's just the thing. He wasn't," I tell him, skipping over the deeper truth and deciding to keep myself as distant as I can. "I couldn't understand the connection between the three and I had to know what Nic knew, what all of them knew and it turns out that they've been lying to me since the very start. They knew exactly … they knew it all and they kept it from me."

The fight out front of the compound comes slamming back and I find myself back there, reliving it all as I heard what Kian had to say and I yelled at the boys. That moment is going to live inside my mind, tormenting me until my dying days.

"I was just leaving," I continue. "I'd just told them all to go to hell. I said that I was done and I had every intention of walking away and never looking back. I've never been betrayed like that before and just as I was walking back to your Ferrari, a black SUV came past and opened fire on us."

Colton flinches and I feel his chest stop rising and falling as he captures his breath, holding it in fear of what I might say next.

"Nic threw me down to the pavement, that's how I ended up all cut up. I could hear the bullets zooming past me. I've never been so fucking scared in my life. It was only a few seconds but it felt like it went on forever and when they were finally gone … Nic's dad …"

"Fuck, Jade. Tell me this story doesn't end how I think it does?"

"It's so much worse." Colton holds onto me, just letting me be at one with my thoughts and waiting until I'm ready to go on. "Kian's dead," I finally say, my tone sounding robotic and completely drained of all emotion. "I should have left after that, but I didn't think it could get worse. I couldn't leave Nic when his father's body was still laying warm on the concrete and Eli ... he'd been shot. I just ... I couldn't. I had to make sure they were going to be alright, but then ..."

"Shhhh," he soothes. "It's okay, Jade. You're home now. It's over. You don't ever have to go back. You never have to see them again if you don't want to."

"I don't know what I want. They were supposed to be my family. Nic would always say 'no friends, only family,' and for a while, I believed him. He was supposed to be the one who was always by my side, but he's ... he's a monster."

"Well, that's just the thing about family," he tells me as the memory of Nic's blade slicing across the necks of those men splits through my mind, bringing on the worst kind of headache. "They always have a way of screwing you over, no matter what their intentions."

I've never heard truer words.

Needing the heaviness to fade away, I raise my head and meet his eyes. "You waited up for me."

His eyes flick away and focus on the blank TV screen. "I mean ... I was up anyway. It's not like I was pining for you and waiting by the door."

Somehow he manages to pull another smile from deep within me. "You were waiting for me," I tease.

Colton rolls his eyes and with a heavy sigh, gives in. "Yeah, okay," he says, grinning back at me. "So sue me, I was waiting up for you, but you can't blame me. One minute you're here and the next you were out the door like someone had lit a match under your ass. I was concerned and it turns out that I had every right to be."

"I'm okay," I whisper. "They might not care about betraying my trust, but they'd move heaven and earth to make sure I never got hurt … you know, physically."

"Yeah," he grunts, grabbing my waist and rolling us until he's hovering over me. His lips brush against mine before he pulls back and meets my eyes. "How am I supposed to compete against a guy who saved you from a shower of bullets?"

"Easy," I whisper, being more honest than I ever intended. "There is no competition. Not where you're concerned."

His eyes glisten with joy and I allow his warm smile to light something within me, if only for a second. Colton begins dipping his head and I know that the second he kisses me, this moment of tenderness will wash away and I'll plunge right back into the darkness of my night and I can't allow that to happen, not yet at least. I'm not ready to face it again.

His lips come crashing down toward mine but I stop him with a finger on his lips, wishing so badly that I had it within me to kiss him with everything that I've got and allow it all to fade away.

I shake my head as his face hovers just above mine and I give him a sobering look. "There is a little something I should probably tell you," I say with a cringe, watching as his brows begin to furrow. "You know that whole drive-by shooting I was telling you about?"

"Yeah," he says slowly.

I can't help the grin that tears across my face, knowing damn well that I should be serious about this yet for some reason, I can't help myself. "Your Ferrari might have been parked out on the road and possibly has a few small … holes on the side."

"A few small holes?" he questions.

"Yeah," I say, holding back a laugh. "I take it bullet holes aren't a typical thing around here?"

He shakes his head, his eyes dancing with laughter. "No, Jade. Not even close."

CHAPTER 28

A throat clears and my eyes spring open to find myself wrapped securely in Colton's arms with Charlie, Spencer, and Milo staring down at us.

"Well, fuck," Colton mutters beside me as I pull one of those fugly just woke up morning faces that should have Colton, Charlie, and Nic all reconsidering where they put their interest.

The thought of Nic has a shot of pain storming through to my chest but thankfully I don't get a moment to think on it before Charlie's jealousy cuts through the room. "So, uhhh… is this a thing now or were you two just up late, reminding each other how much you hate the other's guts and then accidentally fell asleep … with all your clothes on?"

Shit. It seems like a lifetime ago that Charlie declared he wanted to pursue something with me, but in reality, it's only been two weeks. How is it possible that so much has happened since then?

In the past two weeks, I've seen five dead bodies, been to two funerals, feared for my life during a home invasion, been shot at during a drive-by, and watched the man I once loved murder two men. Add Colton to the mix and these past couple of weeks have been exhausting.

Perhaps I'm due for a vacation, not that I've ever really had one of those before.

Lifting the blanket, I glance down and check that my tits haven't fallen out of my shirt before sitting up on the couch with a yawn as Colton does the same beside me, though he somehow manages to do it with a bit of grace.

I look up at Charlie with a cringe while ignoring the smirk on Milo's face. "I, ummm—" I cut myself off and glance back at Colton, not sure if I really want to be the one responsible for breaking his friend's heart. I've never exactly been in this situation before. What are the rules? Do I let the guys talk it out like men or do I just dump this shit on them and walk out like a fucking boss?

"Sorry, man," Colton says before I get a chance to screw it up with my awkwardness. "I sorta sealed that deal already."

Charlie narrows his eyes, looking for some kind of confirmation. "Like you fucked her or you're *fucking* her?"

"*Fucking*, bro," he says, giving Charlie a tight smile, hoping he works it out for himself that it's so much more than just fucking.

"No shit," Milo grumbles, stepping forward and giving me a meaningful look that has a cringe spreading wide over my face and making me realize what a shitty friend I've been.

Colton looks up at him and pulls himself to his feet, adjusting his sweatpants in the process. "Sorry, Milo. I didn't mean to steal your girl. I know you guys had … something going on but I assumed it wasn't anything serious."

Milo shrugs. "No, problem, man. It was just a bit of fun to pass the time. I prefer her as a friend anyway." He glances at me and winks and I roll my eyes before he's even started whatever bullshit quip he's going to throw my way. "She's too much drama for me."

The boys laugh but I find myself staring at Charlie who doesn't look quite as amused as the others. He meets my eyes and I pat the space beside me, watching as he slowly makes his way across the den. "Hey Hot Dog," I murmur, keeping my voice low.

"Hot Dog?" he grunts in disgust, rearing back and looking at me as though he's never been so disrespected in his life. "The name is Hot Sauce."

"Oh, shit. That's right," I laugh, pressing a hand over my mouth to try and mask it as best I can. "I'm sorry. That one completely slipped my mind." He rolls his eyes and flops back against the couch and I do the same, keeping my eyes on him. "Are you okay? I know you were kinda hoping for something to happen here."

"Is it real?" he questions. "Or are you just fucking to pass the time and forget all the shit that's going on?"

"It's real, Charlie."

"Are you happy?"

I bite the inside of my cheek and nod.

Charlie looks up, eyeing Colton like the enemy. "Does he treat you well?"

"Like a fucking queen."

He lets out a heavy sigh. "Then I guess that's all I can ask for. I have no choice but to deal with it." He glances back at me and shrugs his shoulders, trying to play it off as though it doesn't tear right through to his soul. "I'll be fine, Ocean. It's nothing the bottom of a bottle can't fix."

"You know I love you, right?" I say, leaning into his side as he puts his arm around me. "You were one of the first alright guys I met here but you and I… I'll destroy you and not in the way you want me to."

"I think deep down I know that," he tells me, watching Milo and Spencer make themselves comfortable in the den. "But I was still hoping. You know your ass is fucking tight, right? I would have hit that over and over again."

Colton grunts on my other side and grabs my arm. He tears me free of Charlie's hold until I'm curled back into his warm side with his arm wrapped around my waist and his fingers flirting with the waistband of my jeans. "Hands off the merchandise, Charlie," Colton warns him. "It's one thing to think about all the things you want to do with my girl but try tempting her with it and you and I are going to have problems."

"Your girl, huh?" Spencer questions. "I don't think I've ever heard you refer to a chick as your girl. Does this mean it's serious?"

Colton nods. "I've spent the last month and a half fucking around and trying to push her away and she's made it damn clear that she's not about to go anywhere, so yeah, it's about time I got on board with the idea. Besides, I have a feeling she would have forced my hand eventually."

I scoff. "Bullshit. It's the other way around, Carrington. You're the one who forced my hand, remember? Or do I need to recap the whole masquerade party and the library?"

"Library?" Charlie asks, peering around me to see his friend. "What the hell happened in the library?"

"The library was nothing," Colton says with a smile in his tone and a heat in his eyes that tells me he's ready to do it all over again. "The shower is where things really took an interesting turn."

"Shower?" Milo shrieks. "What the fuck happened in the shower?"

I glance over at him. "When was the last time you and I spoke? Haven't I told you about the shower yet?"

Milo shakes his head and before he can start cursing me out for depriving him of all the hot and steamy details, Colton's low tone breaks through the room. "Told him?" he questions, looking at me horrified. "Why the fuck would you need to tell him about that? He's your ex."

"Well," Milo grumbles. "I wouldn't classify it as that."

For fuck's sake. This conversation isn't getting us anywhere. It reminds me of all the many nights I'd spent with the boys back home and had them fighting over bullshit things, mostly to stir Nic about his fucked-up relationship with me. It was always fun and left someone with stitches, but we always came back for more. That's gone now and a part of me is happy that I can still have that fun with these boys, but it's not the same. It'll never be the same.

Needing to steer this in a direction where someone isn't going to end up with a black eye, I look around at each of them. "What are you guys doing here? Shouldn't you be sleeping in and enjoying your Sunday morning?"

Spencer raises a brow and scoffs in amusement. "Considering that it's nearly three in the afternoon—no. I'm going to go ahead and say that ship has already sailed."

"Shit," I grumble, leaning forward and searching around for my phone on the soft carpet. "Is it really that late in the day?" My fingers curl around the cool metal and I scoop it up to find my phone battery nearly dead with eighteen missed calls, twenty-three text messages, a bunch of messenger notifications, and even my snapchat going insane. "What the fuck?"

I sink back into Colton's arms and start scrolling through it all. The texts are mostly from the Widows checking in on me. Some from last night after I left and some demanding to know that I'm alright this morning. I ignore them all, especially the ones from Nic. Hell, I don't even open them and read over it, just simply hit delete.

There are calls from them as well but a few of them are from Milo and Charlie from this morning, probably checking in. Then there's messenger which is a whole bunch of shit from Hendrix and Jess, filling me in on last night's party that was so incredible that I should have been there. If only they knew what I was actually doing.

The boys talk among themselves as I get busy texting the girls and allow them to fill me in on the details of their night. I honestly don't give a shit about the party but with my mind continuously jumping back to last night and the way Nic's knife so effortlessly sliced across their necks, I'd do anything to keep myself distracted.

We hang out for hours and it's not until the sun is starting to set that my Mom walks in with at least six boxes of pizza. "I figured you guys hadn't got around to feeding yourselves yet," she says, looking me up and down, the same way she always does when I don't come home at night. "What on earth happened to your head?"

My head? Oh, fuck. The lump. I'd forgotten all about that.

"Shit," Spencer laughs, giving my mom an appreciative smile. "I take my hat off to you, Mrs. Munroe. I've been staring at her head since I first walked through the door but was too chicken shit to come right out and ask. I was hoping an explanation would just get thrown around in conversation."

Mom rolls her eyes. "You'll do well to learn with Ocean, she doesn't just give up information willingly. You have to pry it out of her hands and hope you get the full story."

Colton scoffs beside me. "Ain't that the fucking truth."

"Oceania," my mother warns, realizing that I'm more than happy to let the boys take over and lead the conversation away from my head and to my bad attitude. "Three seconds. Don't make me whoop your ass in front of your friends."

I groan and sit up straight on the couch while meeting Mom's eyes. "You're going to be mad."

"Ocean. Now."

I let out a heavy sigh and try to work out the best way to say this before deciding that getting straight to the point is probably my best option. "I sorta stepped right into the middle of the Widows and Wolves gang war and nearly got shot in the drive-by that killed Kian last night."

Charlie shoots to his feet as Mom gapes. "THE FUCK?"

I cringe but keep my attention on Mom, knowing that she's preparing herself for something. "Oceania Elaine Munroe. How many times do I need to ask you to distance yourself from those boys and now this? I forbid you from going back there. Do you hear me? Those boys have been nothing but trouble since the day they stepped into our lives."

"Mom … I know. I told them that I was done."

She goes to continue ranting and has to physically stop herself before looking back at me. "What?" she demands, confused by my willingness to accept her limits.

"They crossed the line. They've been lying to me all this time and so I told them I was done." My eyes drop to my hands as I feel that familiar ache starting to creep back up.

Milo's broken gasp from across the room draws my attention and I glance up at him to find his heart on his sleeve. Out of all the guys here, he's the one who really got to see the dynamics within my crew and knows just how hard that decision would have been for me to make. He gives me a tight smile while sending a silent promise that we'll cry this out with a bottle of wine until it's completely out of my system.

Mom lets out a shaky breath, trying to calm herself before glancing around at the group of guys in the room. She looks back to me with a relieved smile. "I'm sorry you had to go through all of that, sweety, but I think you'll find you'll be much happier here with these guys. They're not so … tough."

All four of the guys fly to their feet, Charlie being the first to comment. "Tough?" he demands. "We can be tough. We're the toughest mother-fuckers around."

Spencer instantly starts flexing. "Maybe you haven't been around here long enough to know who I am," he says, raising his chin and trying to appear intimidating and to anyone who wasn't born and raised in Breakers Flats, it might have worked but to us, he's like a cute little puppy begging for attention. "I have a reputation. I'm not exactly the kind of guy that parents want keeping their daughters company."

Mom laughs and steps right into Spencer's personal space before clutching his chin like a proud parent. "That's sweet, darling. I'm sure all of you boys are the toughest, manliest men around." She pats his cheek before glancing down at the pizza boxes. "Be sure to eat up, you boys are going to need all your energy to grow big and strong."

With that, she walks out of the room and all eyes fall on me.

"What?" I demand. "I can't help it that my mom thinks you guys are sweet little puppy dogs. You've got to understand that she comes from a town where the 'tough' guys are the heroes of gang war and facing down death every day. This here, despite all the bullshit, this is a breath of fresh air."

"We're tough," Charlie comments. "You know we can handle our shit."

"Oh, yeah. Of course you can," I smile sweetly before glancing at Milo. "You seemed all too quiet during that."

He shrugs his shoulders. "Because I've got nothing to say. I'm not tough and all you fuckers know it. There's no point defending it."

I shake my head. "To be honest," I tell him. "I think you're actually one of the toughest guys I know."

Milo gives me a warm smile before Colton's low voice rumbles throughout the room. "Alright," he says, pressing a kiss to my temple. "Stop fucking with the boys. I have work to do."

"The fuck you do," Spencer says. "You work every fucking day. You're staying right here with us and fucking around. Your work will be waiting for you tomorrow."

He cringes, looking toward the door. "I don't know, man. Do you have any idea how much shit there is to do? I doubt I'll be at school this week either."

Milo drops back down into the couch with a slice of pizza in his hands. "Apply for distance learning. The teachers will just email your work and you submit it before the due date. Easy fix. You'll still be able to graduate and work at the same time. You're Colton Fucking Carrington and your father was on the board, I doubt they're going to deny you."

Relief washes off him in waves and within the blink of an eye, Colton looks a million times lighter. "Huh," he grunts, dropping back onto the couch and dragging me down beside him. "I didn't think of that. It's not a bad idea."

"So, you're going to do it?" I question, leaning forward and grabbing one of the many pizza boxes off the coffee table and putting it on my lap. I cross my legs under myself and get comfortable while Colton steadies the box on my lap.

"Yeah, why not?" he says as Spencer lounges back on the couch beside Milo and turns on the TV. He instantly starts scanning through his options and ends up settling for the Victoria Secret runway show that immediately gains all their attention—though Milo's watching for a completely different reason. "I need everything to go back to normal around here and if I can get on top of everything, then maybe normal might be a possibility."

"I hate to break it to you," I say, "but I don't think your version of normal is ever going to come back. This is the new normal and you just have to find a way to make it work."

He lets out a sigh, not appearing the least bit interested by the beyond beautiful angels strutting the runway in their diamond bras. "I know," he says as he stretches out on the couch and turns to give me his full attention. "But for everyone who's in business with Carrington Incorporated, all they see is uncertainty. They think I'm just some unqualified eighteen-year-old kid taking over and not knowing what the fuck I'm doing. I have to get this back on track before I lose them and destroy everything my father built."

I purse my lips, trying to figure out some way to help him out when it hits me. "Have a party."

Colton bites back a laugh as Charlie gapes at me. "Okay," he says, turning his stare at Colton. "I take it all back. You can keep her, man. I don't have room for that kind of crazy in my life."

I flip off Charlie before focusing back on Colton. "I'm not fucking crazy. Just hear me out," I tell him. "Your dad did it when your mom left and the world saw him as a stronger man, so why can't you do the same? Invite all the biggest names in the business and every A-lister in your contact list, dazzle them with dancers, alcohol, and a good time then prove to them you're the fucking boss and the only rightful heir to Carrington Incorportaed. Prove to those mother-fuckers that you're it, that you're the one who's about to lead a revolution, and if they don't climb on board now, they'll fucking regret it. Have them eating out of the palm of your hand. Don't let them want you, make them need you."

"Do you think that would really work?"

"I saw you during that board meeting, Colton. I know it will work."

Colton looks across at the TV screen but the faraway look in his eyes tells me that he's really considering this. When he finally looks back at me, his lips pull into an interested grin. "A party, huh?"

"Yeah," I say as an excited grin stretches wide across my face. "What's your take on Gatsby?"

CHAPTER 29

My silver gown hangs heavily from my body with the stunning fringe tickling my knees. Who would have known that all this beading, feathers, and pearls would weigh so much? It's worth it though. This dress paired with my dark hair and plum lips just hits differently. It's not like the other gowns I've worn which were slimming, elegant, and beautiful—this dress is wild. This dress screams for fun, it demands respect, and it tells everyone who looks my way to watch the fuck out.

This dress is a fucking boss.

I lean into the mirror and fasten my headpiece, laughing at the feathers that stick high above my head and the line of pearls that trail across my forehead. This couldn't be real. I don't even look like me. How the hell did I get accepted into this world and am now attending my third party? My high school prom wasn't even going to be this good. Hell, I'm sure prom would have just been a cheap DJ in the school gymnasium and some tacky decorations. Everyone would have left after an hour and got wasted in the park.

"Hey, I found something for you today," Mom says, stepping into my room and blowing me the fuck away in a strapless, floor-length, black and gold, beaded gown, hugging her body just right. I've never seen Mom like this, not even her wedding dress was anything close to being so spectacular.

Mom couldn't believe her ears when Colton extended her an offer to attend the party. She nearly collapsed on the spot and then burst into tears of happiness which only made me well up too. Though, the moment was completely ruined when he destroyed it by offering her his credit card to purchase a gown. I could have ripped his handsome head off. I might be the type to jump at the opportunity to spend what isn't mine, but not mom. She would have seen it as a charity she didn't need.

She thanked him and respectfully declined his offer to pay which is how we spent all of Thursday night going from store to store until we found the perfect dresses. They're rented of course, but so worth it. I'd do anything to be able to keep this baby hanging in my closet until my dying days but it's just not meant to be. Maybe one day I'll be able to actually afford stuff like this, until then, I could really get used to this renting thing. I didn't actually know we could do that, though it certainly explains how some of the girls back home were walking around with Prada bags. I never actually stopped to think about it, just always assumed they were either whoring themselves out, had a knock off, or stole it from some unsuspecting housewife.

My eyes scan over Mom's dress and while I saw her quickly try it on during our shopping trip, it's not the same as seeing her completely dolled up with her hair done, makeup looking flawless, matching headpiece and black gloves that stretch past her elbows. "Mom," I breathe, staring in wonder. "You look stunning."

"Oh, stop honey," she says, her cheeks blushing the softest pink at my compliment. "You're going to embarrass me and then I'll never find the nerve to actually walk into that ballroom."

"Don't be ridiculous," I tell her. "You look amazing and you should know it. Walk in there with your head held high, have a few glasses of champagne, and actually enjoy yourself for a change. You've never had the chance to enjoy yourself like this. Take advantage of it, and hell, maybe even find a rich man to flirt with."

Mom's eyes bug out of her head. "I will do no such thing," she says, looking horrified. "Most of these men are going to recognize me from working at the other parties. Not that I'm interested anyway, but they wouldn't even dare show me any attention. I'm just a lowly housekeeper and they're well aware of that."

"Geez," I tease. "What happened to all those times you've told me not to sell myself short?"

"Oh, Ocean. Cut it out. I'm not interested in having an affair with some man who wouldn't know the first thing about taking care of a woman from Breakers Flats so it doesn't matter anyway."

"Uh-huh."

Mom rolls her eyes and steps in behind me in the mirror so she can look me over, just as I had been doing before she walked in. "This dress really is something," she tells me. "It's a shame we're going to have to give it back."

"I know," I sigh. "I was just thinking the same thing."

Mom raises her hands over my head and as she lowers them back down, a long pearl necklace is placed around my neck. It droops low between my cleavage, following the plunging line of the dress. "I found this in the store this morning and thought it would go perfectly with your dress."

I run my fingers over the pearls. "It really does," I whisper, feeling as though it completes my outfit for the party. "How long can we keep it for?"

"This is yours, Ocean. I bought it for you."

My eyes bug out of my head as I spin around to face Mom. "What? You couldn't have. What do you mean you bought it?" I go to start pulling it free from my neck. "This is too much."

"Stop," mom demands, forcing me to release the pearls until they're dangling back between my breasts. "Colton has been throwing promotions at me left, right, and center. It's fine. The necklace was half off and really not as expensive as you're picturing it to be. Consider it your birthday present. You'll be eighteen in a few weeks and when I saw it, I just knew you had to have it. It can be the start of your very own collection."

Tears well in my eyes and I do my best to hold them back, not wanting to ruin my makeup. "Thank you," I whisper, throwing my arms around her and holding tight. "This is the most precious thing I could have ever gotten. I swear, I'll look after it with my life. Thank you so much. I love you."

"I love you too," she whispers. "Now, what do you say we go and leave our mark on this party?"

"Nothing could make me happier," I tell her, pulling back to find a warm, loving smile spread wide across her face. The excitement brims in her eyes and just like that, I know she's going to have the best night of her life.

I slip into my borrowed heels and as Mom loops her arm through mine and leads me out of the pool house, I can't help but feel that this is the best possible ending to another long week. I don't know how I did it, but somehow I went a whole week in Bellevue Springs without my world exploding into a million tiny pieces.

I'm not going to lie, distancing myself from my crew has been the hardest thing I've ever had to do. Can I even call them my crew anymore? I guess not, that's not who we are anymore. They're just the guys who I spent years idolizing and trusting, but now … nothing.

I've dodged at least one hundred calls during the week and deleted twice as many texts. I meant it when I told them that I was done. I don't have room for betrayal in my life. They've always boasted about how we're a family and will always have each other's back, but what happened to having my back when it came to being honest? What happened to having my back when it came to telling me about my father? Did their words not matter then? Because they sure as hell mattered to me. I trusted them to always be truthful and right now, I don't know if their betrayal stings more than learning my father was the best hitman this country had ever seen, and not only that, that he did it for sport, not because he was good at it.

My father was a cold-blooded murderer just like Nic. I'm sure dad would have been proud to learn that I'd been spending all my time with a man who was just like him. Lucky me. I don't think I've ever been so happy to be out of Breakers Flats.

Bellevue Springs still isn't my home, not by a long shot, but at least it's away from them, away from the horrors I've left behind. I truly have a chance to start over, even if I never get into college or find a proper job, I'm confident that I'll never move back there. I'll find a way to make it on my own.

Apart from avoiding the boys, I finally got a real chance to settle in at school and properly get to know some of the girls there and to be honest, they're starting to change my perspective on bitchy high-school chicks. They're not all bad, but don't get me wrong, some of them are just plain awful. I've had to learn to give them a chance before instantly judging them based solely on the fact that they're female.

I spent Tuesday with Miss Davies in her office, filling out a million college applications and crossing my fingers that they'll be accepted. Every single one of them were past the submission deadline so there's a good chance that I won't get it, but I can always hope.

Colton's application for distance learning was accepted within the space of two hours so he was able to fall into his own routine while keeping up on his studies and also kicking ass in the office. I'm not going to lie, it also opened up a little extra time for him to spend with me and I feel as though every extra second spent with him was well worth it.

He's capturing me in a way that Nic never did and it kills me to admit that I always thought Nic was the real deal, but I was blinded. Colton has my full attention and for once in my life, I'm wanting to better myself, I'm wanting a future and not just assuming that I'll have Nic to catch me when I fall.

Colton is so much more than that. He encourages me to stand on my own two feet and while he's more than happy to hand over a credit card and make all my problems disappear, he's also the first person to push me to make the change for myself. What more could a girl need? The fact that he does it with a sexy as sin grin on his face is just the added bonus.

I always knew climbing into bed with Colton Carrington was going to be a dangerous game, I just never knew how dangerous it could be. Not only am I at risk of letting someone in, my heart is at risk of being torn to shreds. He's reeled me in and now I'm terrified that he might let me go. I never intended on giving him that power, but day by day and smile by smile, he unintentionally takes it, leaving me wide open and more vulnerable than I've ever been before.

Is this what it feels like when you're falling in love? It didn't feel like this with Nic. I still clung tightly to my power with him, but with Colton … I don't know. This just feels like something so much more—something massive … something astronomical.

It's as though we've finally moved past all the bullshit and now have this chance to actually start living our lives and what better way to celebrate than having an epic party?

Mom starts pulling me toward the backdoor but I lead her around the house. I cut through the backdoor when going to the first black and white party and I've always regretted it. There's just something so incredibly magical about walking through the front and being welcomed in as a valued guest and having your name marked off. When I snuck through the back, it felt like I was some delinquent teenager slipping into a party I wasn't meant to be at.

Mom reluctantly agrees and when we finally reach the front door, that reluctance instantly fades away as she becomes dazzled by the sight before her. We've spent most of yesterday and today helping set this all up so it's not exactly like we haven't already seen the amazing decorations but with the sunset and the room lit up with lights and music, it's like walking into a dazzling, crystal version of wonderland.

Jazz music fills my ears and the smile that spreads across my face is as real as it's ever going to get. Champagne flutes are put into our hands and I pull mom deeper into the party. "Are you ready for this?" I question, glancing across at her to see the excitement filling her eyes.

She takes a quick sip of the expensive champagne and holds out her glass to clink against mine. "I was born ready."

Within three seconds, I lose mom in the crowd and I roll my eyes, knowing that she's out there making friends in this crazy new world we live in and having a good time just as she deserves.

Not wanting to waste a single minute of this party, I walk into the crowd and get halfway across the dance floor when I find him.

Colton Fucking Carrington.

My eyes roam greedily up and down his large frame as he talks to an older gentleman while looking like the most important man in the room, but truth be told, he is. He wears a suit that looks as though it was taken straight from the 1920's—Blue dress shirt, tie, and vest covered with a cream suit that somehow makes his hazel eyes stand out. He has the attention of every woman in the room yet his eyes are focused solely on me.

I walk toward him but am sure to keep my distance as he wraps up his conversation with the older man beside him. After all, this party was put together solely for the purpose of proving to the Carrington business contacts that Colton is the fucking star of the show and I refuse to do anything that will jeopardize that.

"Wow," he says, walking toward me and meeting me in the middle of the dance floor as I take a sip of champagne. "You look breathtaking."

His arm slips around my waist and just like in the movies, he takes the champagne flute from my hands and places it on a passing waitress' drink tray before effortlessly sweeping me around in a dance. "Everybody is watching," I warn, reminding him that although we've gone public with our relationship to our friends, we haven't exactly announced it to the world and perhaps a party with all of his business contacts in attendance isn't exactly the best idea.

"I hope they are," he tells me. "I'm not hiding this. You and I … we're doing this. I'm serious about being with you and if they have a problem with it, then they can fuck off but they're going to regret it, because in this fucking game, I hold all the cards."

I smile up at him but before I get the chance to say exactly how much I appreciate his comments, his lips are pressing down on mine. "What was that for?" I question when he pulls back.

"Don't take this the wrong way, Jade, but you have a habit of fucking up sentimental moments with ridiculous sarcastic comments to hide the fact that you don't know how to respond. So, I kissed you because I'd prefer to savor the moment before you go ahead and fuck it up."

I purse my lips and grin up at him. "For the record," I say. "I was going to remind you that you're a fucking boss and not only do you hold all the cards in your hands, but you hold mine too."

His brow raises and he looks at me as though he's seeing a stranger. "Wow, I thought I'd have to torture you to get a little emotion out of you."

"Look who's throwing around sarcastic comments now," I laugh. "And quit acting like I'm some kind of robot. I have a heart buried in here somewhere. I just don't like to admit it sometimes."

"I know," he murmurs, pulling me in tighter. "I'm just teasing you."

I roll my eyes and let him move me around the dance floor and with each step he takes, he completely sweeps me away. The song changes and we dance again until a waitress walks by with a food platter and steals my attention.

"Come on," he says. "Let's get you fed and then I have to sweet talk Milo's dad into signing a new contract that will make him an extremely wealthy man."

"Isn't he already a very wealthy man?"

"He is, but this is …"

"Next level?"

"Exactly."

I push up onto my toes and brush my lips over his. "Then what are you waiting for? I can take care of myself. Go and show them who's boss."

Colton grins wide and within seconds of his arms falling from around my waist, Charlie and Spencer are at my back, ready to pour shot after shot down my throat and truly welcome me into their group.

CHAPTER 30

The chandeliers rattle above as the party rages into the early hours of the morning. Colton dominated with every single contact he could get his hands on and somehow managed to get a shitload more business in the process so I think it's safe to say that the party has been an absolute success. At least, I know Mom would agree seeing as though she spent a good portion of her night dancing with Hendrix's father and drinking more than she has in years.

I couldn't stop watching her. Seeing her being so carefree was refreshing, though I don't know how she's going to feel in the morning. I don't think she's even had a sip of alcohol in years so I'm sure she's going to wake up with a killer hangover. I might be the one on bacon and eggs duty tomorrow.

Most of the older people have gone leaving only the spirited ones here to party with us, and by spirited, what I mean are people like Milo who have stripped off most of their clothes and are running around the party in nothing but a 1920's hat, suit pants, and suspenders. He looks insane but the smile on his face is infectious.

The old jazz music has been swapped out for something we can all get down to and it pulses through the mansion, rattling the chandeliers and sending vibrations through the floor to ceiling windows.

A lot of the girls from school are here and mixing with all the guys I knew from BSA. It is honestly the best night of my life. I've never enjoyed myself like this and felt so damn welcome. Since the second his last business contact walked out the door with his drunk wife, Colton hasn't moved from my side and he's made sure to show me the best damn time of my life while constantly flashing me that perfect smile that has everything inside of me melting.

I'm a fucking goner where this guy is concerned. If I'm not careful, he's going to drown me in a world that I don't belong in and I may never find my way out, but then a part of me doesn't want to get out. I want to stay right here and drown in his love, succumb to his touches, and falter under his deep words.

Spencer steps into my side and hands me another shot glass. "Do you think you could handle another?"

I grin up at him and take the shot from his hand as Colton murmurs something about tonight being a messy night. "Please, do you even know who you're talking to? My bra matches my panties. That is not a trait of a woman who can't handle her liquor."

Spencer smiles wide and holds out his own shot. "Then what are you waiting for?"

Our glasses clink in the middle and just as the cool liquid burns down my throat, Charlie comes running in with a shot of his own. "Me too, me too, me too." He throws his shot back and the movement has him tripping over his own damn feet and slamming hard against Spencer.

The two of them go down like a sack of shit and I hold onto my stomach as I howl with uncontrollable laughter.

Colton shakes his head, probably thinking about which couch to let them crash on and how much of a hassle it's going to be when they inevitably hurl all over it, but either way, he lets them go, not one to ruin their fun.

Milo comes bounding back into our circle and slips an arm around my waist before literally picking me up and removing me from Colton's side. "Come on, bitch. We're dancing."

Well, who the hell am I to say no? Though, I have to admit, I'm surprised these guys haven't figured out that Milo's gay yet ... or bi. Who knows? God knows he doesn't.

I let him pull me away and as I turn to hurry toward the dancefloor, I crash into a hard body and come to a startling stop. "Oh, sorry," I rush out, laughing but the man's grip on my arms has me glancing up and meeting his eyes.

I suck in a harsh breath as his familiar smell wraps around me and makes my head spin.

Nic.

His stare bears down on me and I'm instantly jolted back into the Black Widows clubhouse to where he stood behind those men and so effortlessly took their lives. Desperation cuts through me. I've been avoiding his calls all week and I can guarantee that hasn't sat well with him. I try to tear out of his grip. "Let go of me."

"Time to fucking go," he spits before moving his hand down to my wrist and spinning on his heel. Nic gives me a hard tug and I stumble after him as my heart begins to race.

"What the fuck do you think you're doing?" I demand, desperately trying to pull back on his grip as for the first time in my life, being held by him really isn't as thrilling as it's always been. My head spins from the sheer amount of alcohol pulsing through my veins and my attempts at freedom become laughable. "Dominic," I yell over the music, knowing damn well that the bastard can hear me. "Let me go. I have nothing to say to you."

He tugs me harder and I slam into his back, my stumbling not stopping until we're out of the ballroom. He leads me right out into the cool night and I feel my wrist beginning to bruise.

Nic starts for the stairs and I panic, knowing damn well that I'm in no shape to navigate my way down them, especially in these heels, but the thought doesn't even seem to enter his mind as he pulls me down the first one. I struggle to keep up with his pace, focusing with everything that I have on putting my foot on each step before taking the next.

We get halfway when he decides that I'm not moving fast enough and tugs me harder, sending me toppling over the next step. I fall to my knees but his momentum has me falling and slamming my chest hard against the concrete steps.

I suck in a pained breath as my chest begins to ache and my knees that had only just healed get scratched up all over again.

Nic groans in frustration. "Look at you," he snaps, pulling hard on my wrist and hauling me to my feet before grabbing me and throwing me carelessly over his shoulder. "You're fucking pathetic. You're fucking wasted and can't even stand up."

"Yo," a familiar voice calls from the bottom of the steps. "Ease up, Nic. You're fucking hurting her."

"She's fine," he snaps back at Sebastian, making me wonder if all the liars are here or just these two.

I slam my hand hard against his back and get an odd pleasure out of the loud slap against his skin. "Put me the fuck down. I'm not going anywhere with you, especially when you're like this."

Nic finally gets to the bottom of the stairs and puts me on my feet where I find all four of the boys but my attention is solely on Nic. My hand lashes out and it slaps hard across his face. "What the fuck is your problem?" I yell, desperate to hit him again and again. "How dare you put your hands on me. Who the fuck are you? It's like I don't even know who you are anymore."

Nic turns on me as the boys crowd around. "Me?" he demands. "Look at you prancing around that fucking party as if you own the place. You're a complete stranger. Do you even remember where the fuck you come from because it sure as hell seems like you don't."

"Fuck you," I snap. "How dare you come at me for wanting something better for myself."

"Better? You're whoring yourself out in there, showing off your body, and throwing back shots with those cocky fucks."

"Dude …" Eli warns but gets instantly ignored.

"You're acting like a fucking idiot in there. You should be embarrassed for yourself. I'm taking you the fuck home. I'm done with this bullshit."

My hands slam up against Nic's chest. "I'm not going anywhere with you," I yell at him, my throat instantly hurting from the raspy anger that shoots out of it. "Maybe you've forgotten that I watched you slice a fucking knife across those bastards necks. You're a fucking monster, Nic. You're not the guy I knew. It's like your father died and you went right along with him. You don't have to be a monster to lead, you know. You don't have to be him."

Nic grabs the pearls around my neck and yanks me in close. "You don't know what the fuck you're talking about."

I raise my chin, refusing to give in. "You need to leave. All of you do. I told you on Saturday night—I'm done with you. You're fucking no-good gang members who have lied to me since the beginning of fucking time and I'm not sitting around and letting it happen again. Now, leave."

Nic's jaw tightens and I see the refusal on his lips when a deep rumble comes from behind me and instantly calms my racing heart. "Get your fucking hands off her."

Nic's gaze snaps up to Colton's and it's darker than I've ever seen before, darker than when he was staring down his father's murderers. "I'll put my hands wherever the fuck I want," Nic growls low, his tone a nasty warning that Colton should back off. "She's mine. Always has been. You're a fucking phase."

"Phase or not, she asked you to release her, so I'd suggest you do it now before I make you."

Nic throws me behind him and I slam into Kai's chest as he gets in Colton's face. "The fuck did you just say to me? Do you have any idea who I am? The kind of influence I could have over you?"

Colton's hazel stare flashes back at me and takes in the red mark across my chest and my scratched up knees. He scoffs as he looks back at Nic. "I know exactly who you are," he taunts, making every one of my nerves stand on edge. "You're a fucking loser who just put his hands on my fucking girl because he's pissed that she chose me, chose a life away from you, and chose to have something better for herself. Do you honestly think she'll ever go back to a man who throws her around like a fucking ragdoll, who drags her down the stairs, and constantly leaves her bruised? No fucking chance. I don't care if she doesn't want me, but I will make sure that she never goes back to you."

Without warning, Nic's hand curls into a fist and it cracks across Colton's face. I run out of Kai's arms, ready to check on him when a low laugh sounds through the silence. Colton rubs a hand over his jaw before spitting a mouthful of blood down onto the concrete. He holds his arms out wide while grinning back at Nic. "Is that all you've got, fucker?" And with the speed of light, Colton throws a punch that has Nic falling back a step.

I stare in shock. No one has ever landed a punch on Nic, it's simply something that I've always believed to be impossible and the way that Colton stands before him in victory speaks to the devilish goddess living inside me. I've never been so fucking turned on.

Nic runs back at him and just like that, it turns into a fucking brawl. I've always known Nic to be larger than life, the toughest guy on earth who could take anyone down with a single blow, but against Colton, it's a fair fight. He's holding his own and it's the most impressive thing I've ever seen. I wouldn't be surprised if Colton had been trained in martial arts, it seems like the kind of thing that Charles would force him into at a young age.

No matter the reasons for why he knows how to fight, what matters is that he's taking the upper hand, proving to Nic that he underestimated him.

Not wanting their leader to lose, Kai, Sebastian, and Eli dive for their guns, ready to end this, but I'm not about to let that happen. They'll never hurt him. A punch-up is like child's play to them and now that I've seen exactly what these guys are capable of, I'm not about to let them get involved.

I turn on the boys, staring each of them in the eyes as I listen to the sound of flesh being pummeled behind me. "You're going to have to shoot me to get to him," I warn them, watching the hesitation in each of their eyes and taking note of the way their guns lower away from my chest.

"Come on, O," Kairo says. "Move out of the way. I don't want you to get hurt."

I hold up my bruised wrist and show off my red chest. "You didn't give a shit about me getting hurt when he dragged me down the fucking stairs, now back the fuck off. If Nic wants to come here and step into Colton's territory to start shit, then Colton has every fucking right to defend what's his."

"You're not his. You're one of us."

"The hell I am," I insist. "You lost me. All of you did. Now get your fucking leader and get the fuck out of here. I never want to see any of you again."

Sebastian takes a hesitant step forward. "O."

"No. Please … just go. All of you. I can't do this anymore."

He lets out a breath before finally nodding and cautiously stepping around me. He walks right into the boys' fight and hooks his arms around Nic, hauling him away from Colton. Nic resists and tries to fight him off but the fight has worn him down. "Let's go," Sebastian urges. "She doesn't want us here."

"I'm not leaving without her," Nic spits. "She doesn't belong here. She belongs with us."

"I know," Sebastian says, "but today is not the day. We'll come and sort it out once you've calmed down. She's never going to come back like this. You know that. We need to earn her trust back."

"How is that going to happen when she won't fucking talk to me? To any of us?"

"Time, bro," Eli says, meeting my eye. "She just needs time."

I walk over to Colton and look him over before watching as Kai gives Sebastian and Nic a hard shove to get them moving. "This isn't over," Nic says, looking back at me and wiping blood off his face while making all sorts of guilt come rushing in and sit heavy in my gut. "I'm going to come back for you. You don't belong here."

I shake my head, watching as the hurt seeps into his eyes but surely he must know that he stood no chance after the bullshit on Saturday night and then storming in his like a fucking raging bull and making demands. Hell, my fucking wrist is going to be sore for days. "Just go home, Nic."

He clenches his jaw and as Colton's hand slips into mine, he finally turns around and walks away.

CHAPTER 31

There's a long beat of silence as we stand out in the night, watching my crew disappear up the long drive before Colton pulls me into his side. "Come on," he finally says. "Let me get you back inside."

I keep my eyes on the boys, unable to look away and watch how each one of them glances back to look at me with longing and regret filling their deep gazes. I know they're all hurting, but surely they can understand how wrong this is. Nic's behavior … I've never seen anything like it from him. He's always been so put together, cool, calm, and collected. This possessive wildness isn't him. I understand that he has a lot on his plate with becoming the new leader of the Black

Widows and trying to fill his father's shoes but he can't keep going down this destructive path. He's screaming out for help, but it can't be from me. He needs to learn how to let go.

As for the others, they should have been smart enough to reel him back in. How could they think that coming here tonight was a good idea? Clearly, they're all aware that I don't want anything to do with them otherwise I would have responded to their constant calls and text messages. They all need to back off and give me a chance to catch up with everything that's been going on.

With a heavy heart, I let Colton lead me back up the stairs and as his arm slips over my shoulder, I listen to the soothing tones of his deep voice. "Are you alright?"

"I should be asking you the same thing," I murmur. "How the hell did you learn to fight like that?"

Colton scoffs. "You don't grow up as a Carrington without learning a thing or two about defending yourself. But I wasn't asking about you physically? They're just bruises. You're strong and they'll fade. I'm asking about on the inside. Are you alright?"

I shrug my shoulders. "I honestly don't know. Nic is supposed to be my best friend. He's supposed to be the guy who has my back and always wants what's best for me, but over the past few weeks he's become a stranger."

"He'll come around," he promises me. "It's a guy thing. He'll realize that he's fucked-up and he'll make it right. You just need to give him the time to figure out how to do that and work up the courage to admit that he was wrong."

"And when that happens?" I question. "Are you going to get jealous and force him away?"

"Why would I do that? You've already told me how much he means to you. If having them in your life makes you happy, then that's where they need to be. But don't get me wrong, they're going to have to make up for their bullshit and don't expect me to let them anywhere near you until they've magically earned your trust back, but we're going to have fucking problems if they can't get on board with you and me being together because I'm not about to give you up."

I stop at the top of the stairs and turn to look up at him. "You really mean that?"

"Yeah," he says. "I want you to have the world, Jade, and if I have to kick each of their asses to make it happen, then I will."

I press up onto my tippy toes and brush my lips over his and as someone opens the front door and walks around us, we hear the music pouring out from the ballroom. "Do you want to go back to the party?" he asks, pulling away only a fraction.

I shake my head. "I'm not exactly in the party mood anymore. Nic killed my vibe."

"Okay," he says. "Should I take you back to the pool house?"

I shake my head again, meeting his eyes, and just like that, his hand slips into mine and he leads me back inside the mansion. We walk through the long hallways, listening as the music from the party gets quieter and quieter the further we walk.

Colton leads me upstairs but when we pass all the bedrooms, I find myself looking up at him and hating the redness on his jaw from

Nic's punch. "Where are we going?"

The corner of his lips twitch into a small smile and when he looks back down at me, I see nothing but awe shining down at me. "I want to show you something," he murmurs, gently squeezing my hand and making the butterflies soar in my stomach.

My brows furrow but my curiosity is too great and I allow him to pull me along until we reach two massive double doors on the top floor at the opposite end of the house to the library. Colton pushes through the wide doors and I stare in wonder at the open living space with floor to ceiling windows the whole way around.

The room looks over the front of the property and I can see for miles, looking over the whole of Bellevue Springs. "Woah," I say, walking into the room and taking it in. "How have I never been in here before?"

"Dad liked to keep this room private. I had the den downstairs and he had this."

"Geez, I don't blame him. If this was my place I'd keep this all to myself as well."

Colton chuckles under his breath before taking my hand and pulling me along. "You haven't seen the best part." He leads me over to the window and just like downstairs, presses a few buttons, and watches as the windows sink back into the main part of the house and open to a wide balcony that spans nearly the whole length of the mansion.

"Wow," I breathe, walking right to the edge and peering over to get the best possible view. I look out and watch as people walk down the massive drive to their cars after having an incredible night. I watch the moonlight sparkle in the many pools and watch as the soft evening breeze sweeps through Charles' prized gardens. "This is incredible."

Colton's hand drops to my lower back and I find myself turning into him. "Thank you," I whisper. "I really needed this."

"What's that?"

"A reminder that there's still beauty in the world."

Colton's lips drop to mine and gently brush over them before he meets my eyes, looking deep into them and saying all the things we refuse to say out loud. "Trust me," he whispers. "There's plenty of beauty in this world. I look at it every fucking day."

I raise my chin and kiss him again, feeling all sorts of emotions begin to overwhelm me and pulse heavily through my veins. His arms curl around my waist and he pulls me in tighter against him and for a brief moment, I'm scared that Nic might have done some damage and one wrong move could have him dropping in pain, but as he deepens our kiss and tightens his hold on my body, I realize that a little pain isn't going to stop him.

Colton's hands drop to my ass and he gently lifts me off the ground then takes me back into the private living room, leaving the glass windows wide open. The cool breeze brushes across my skin as he lays me on the soft couch and comes down on top of me. He never once breaks our kiss, his lips always moving against mine and our bodies never breaking apart.

The desperation creeps up on us and I slip his suit jacket down his strong arms until the soft material is crashing against the carpeted floor. He untangles the headpiece, pearls, and feathers from my hair and tosses them aside before replacing it with his fingers, guiding them deep into the back of my hair and holding me still.

Our bodies grind against one anothers and when his other hand finally reaches down between us and tugs the beaded dress up over my hips, my eyes begin rolling into the back of my head.

I never knew I could need him this bad. Need his touch, his kiss, his love.

My thong is torn down my legs as I reach down between us and release him from the confines of his suit pants. His cock springs free and as he guides himself to my entrance, I hook my leg around his hips and draw him in, needing it more than I could have imagined.

Colton presses up into me, thick and heavy, completely filling me and I feel my world explode around him. It's exactly what I need, what my body craves and desires. How is it possible to be this good? But fuck, when he actually starts to move … it's like arriving at wonderland and being told that you get to go on *all* the rides.

He moves in and out of me, filling me over and over again and as his lips come back to mine, he untangles his fingers from my hair only to lace them through mine and hold them tight. The connection intensifies between us and something becomes so much … more. It's raw, real, and honest. It's not just two people getting it on and fucking for a good time, it's two people becoming one, coming together and making something beautiful, finding a connection and holding onto it for dear life.

He takes me hard, increasing his speed and giving me everything he's got until I push him back and straddle his waist, needing desperately to be the one to take control.

With me sitting up, he tugs the dress up over my head, leaving the pearls around my neck and tossing the borrowed dress aside. My strapless bra is undone and dropped to the carpet just moments before his mouth comes down over my aching nipple.

His tongue swirls over it and I tip my head back as I ride his cock. His hand tightens on my hip, holding me close, and refusing to let me stop. "Fuck, Jade," he groans low, the torture, need, and desire in his voice doing so much more to me than anyone else ever could.

I feel my orgasm building and as his hand slips from my hip and reaches around to my ass, I know I'm not going to last much longer. He squeezes my ass with a firm grip and I clench my eyes, feeling myself just moments from falling over the cliff into a blissful, earth-shattering orgasm.

"Don't you dare come, not yet, Jade."

"I can't," I breathe, clenching down on him so fucking tight and doing all that I can to ride this out. "I can't hold on."

His hand squeezes my ass again and I groan knowing there's not a damn thing I can do about it. The devil could come and take my soul and I'd happily hand it over just to feel this moment with Colton.

Knowing I'm just moment's from falling off the edge, Colton grabs my hips and holds me still. He slams up into me, holding onto the same rhythm and sending my world into a complete tailspin. "Holy shit," I pant, grabbing hold of his shoulders and squeezing them tight.

My head drops to his and he instantly collects my lips in his, never once slowing his movements. Colton's hand drops down between us and he finds my clit with the softest pinch and my head gets thrown back. "Fuck, Carrington!"

He does it again before adding pressure and rubbing over it, the sound of his desired chuckles filling the room. "That's right, Jade."

I clench down around him even tighter and he groans with need. "I'm going to come," I say, almost frantic, breathing heavily as he slams up into me and teases my clit with his magical fingers.

Colton grabs my jaw and forces my eyes back to his and I see his whole world, so close on the edge. His eyes are dark and stormy and without a doubt, he's about to come undone. "Let me see it. I want to watch you come."

His words tear me apart and within seconds, my orgasm rips through me. "Fuck," I yell, digging my nails into the warm skin of his shoulders. He doesn't dare stop moving, even when his own orgasm comes up and threatens to paralyze him.

His hands dig into my skin and we both ride out the high together, intense and so fucking powerful.

My breath comes in quick, sharp pants as I come crashing down into him. He holds me against his chest, both of us still reeling from that incredible ride. "Holy shit, Jade," he whispers into the cool room. "I could do that every day for the rest of my life and never be done with you."

I lift my head and meet his eyes. "I'm counting on that," I tell him, laying out all my cards and letting him see just how serious I am about this thing between us.

Colton's hand travels up my body until his fingers are brushing over my jaw. "Good," he finally says, his eyes boring into mine and holding me captive. "Because I don't plan on ever letting you go."

I crash back into him, my lips crushing against his and devouring him and just like that I feel him hardening between my legs, more than ready to prove it all over again, and as he slowly starts to move, I realize more than ever that I'm not just falling for Colton Carrington, I've already fallen and fuck, it feels good.

CHAPTER 32

I push the broom through the silver confetti littering the ballroom floor. I don't know whose stupid idea it was to have confetti bombs go off when Colton officially announced that he will be taking over for his father and running Carrington Incorporated indefinitely.

Oh, shit. That was my stupid idea.

I can't deny that it was fun and watching the surprise on his face after the announcement was pretty fucking incredible. The cleanup … not so much. This shit is like glitter. It goes everywhere. Even after the cleanup, I'm going to be finding little confetti pieces for months.

I hadn't exactly cleared this with Mom or Harrison so I wasn't surprised when the job got dumped on me. It's not a big deal though. The cleanup crew have been here since six this morning and have done an incredible job of packing away the party so considering it's after one in the afternoon and I'm only just getting started, it's really not as bad as I thought it was going to be. Though, having said that, it's still not going to be a five-minute cleanup job. I'll probably be here for a good part of the afternoon.

People hurry around me, dismantling tables, pulling off table cloths, taking down decorations while others scatter around collecting discarded champagne flutes and making a pile of lost clothing items which I'm sure all belong to Milo. Though there are a few too many hats in there but I'm sure Milo will claim them all anyway.

Wanting to get this over and done with, I push my broom around the ballroom and do my best not to miss a damn silver sparkle, though after finishing the floors, I quickly realize that my job isn't even close to being done. Confetti litters every tabletop, every chandelier, every statue, and every floral arrangement.

I'm going to be here forever. At least I learned a lesson though—don't fuck with Mom and Harrison's plans.

I get stuck into it and have to put up with Colton as he constantly walks past and laughs at my punishment. The confetti might have been a slight surprise for him too but it's not as though I let off fireworks inside the room. I'll save that great idea for the next one.

By five in the evening, the staff is gone and the ballroom is mostly put back together. I stick around to do the finishing touches, the ones Maryne used to do herself. She liked the ballroom set up a certain way when it wasn't in use, just in case Charles wanted to show it off to his guests—because he always wanted to show it off.

Once it's absolutely perfect, I walk out of the ballroom and peer back through the open doors. Last night was crazy amazing. The last two parties I've attended here have been incredible but both ended in a shitty way. Last night though … it was perfect and I can't wait to do it again. Well, assuming Nic can keep his stubborn ass away.

Stepping back, I close the door and officially bring an end to the most incredible night of my life. I turn around and as I start pushing the cleaning cart back toward the staff quarters, noise from the foyer catches my attention.

I let out a frustrated sigh. I'm so not in the mood for guests.

With Mom busy in the kitchen and Harrison taking the afternoon off, I'm left to go and welcome these people in. I start making my way toward the foyer and with every step I take, I become more and more on edge. There was no buzzer for the gate and no knock at the door. Whoever these people are, they just welcomed themselves into Colton's home as though they had every right.

That realization has me picking up my pace. The last time people just ran in here, the house got shot up and Maryne ended up dead. I can't risk that again. Whoever these people are, they need to take a back seat and realize that they can't just live life however the fuck they want, and if I was smart, I'd be running the opposite direction.

What kind of idiot rushes into situations like this? I should be scrambling away and letting Colton know that someone just barged their way through his doors again, yet something keeps me moving. If these people were dangerous, I feel like they would be making more noise. Dangerous people seem to be loud, you know, with the whole intimidation thing they've got going. These people are just talking among themselves in a snappy, bitchy kind of way.

I break out into the foyer at a pace too fast for my feet to handle and I come to a screeching stop by slamming my hip into the hallway table. "Ah, fuck," I grunt, making the three women in the foyer whip around.

My gut instantly sinks.

Laurelle Carrington and her two bitchy twin daughters, Cora and Casey with bags upon bags of luggage.

Just fucking great.

"I… uhh." Shit. What the hell am I supposed to say? 'Welcome home, bitches?' No. I don't see that going down well.

"Ugh," twin one says, looking me up and down as her face scrunches in distaste. "You're still here."

"Who's still here?" Laurelle asks, stepping forward and looking me over in a similar way that her daughter had, yet unlike her daughter, something has me stepping back. This woman is batshit crazy. It was only two weeks ago that she stormed into her ex-husband's funeral and lit his ass on fire while wearing six-inch stiletto heels. This is the real MVP of revenge, not someone who should be messed with.

The other twin lets out a sickening laugh. "This is the girl we were telling you about. The one who let all those gangsters into father's wake and assaulted us. She works here."

Laurelle's eyes snap to mine. "You work here?"

I swallow back, unsure why the hell I feel so terrified of her.

This shit hasn't happened before. I make a fucking point not to be scared off by over-privileged bitches like this. "Where the hell is your uniform?"

"I, uhhh … I don't wear one."

"Unacceptable," she spits. "From now on, you show respect to your hosts by wearing your appointed uniform. Is that clear?"

"Umm … Colton hasn't requested that I wear a uniform and Charles never asked me to."

Laurelle's eyes flame with rage. "Do I look like Charles? I am the lady of this house and I have requested that you wear a uniform. If you cannot respect my rules, then you will be asked to leave. Is that clear?"

The twins grin as they watch their mother roast me and I shamefully nod my head, wishing to be anywhere but here. "Yes, that is clear."

"Good and while we're at it, you do not address my son by his given name. He is Mr. Carrington to you, nothing more and nothing less."

I raise a brow and decide that if I allow her to walk all over me now that I'll be setting a standard that I simply won't accept, and God fucking knows that Colton isn't going to accept it either. I suck up my pussy attitude and raise my chin. "That's more than fine," I say with a sickly sweet smile before taking a step toward them and watching as the three of them grow wary, the twins clearly remembering exactly what I'm made of. "And what shall I call him when we're fucking? Cause he kinda likes it when I scream his name."

Laurelle sucks in an appalled gasp as the twins mimic her shocked tone. "Oh, shit," I say with a cringe, sarcastically placing my hand over my mouth and sucking in a gasp of my own "I think I cracked my halo."

Laurelle steps into me and I watch as her hands begin to shake with rage. "You better start packing your things, missy. I'm going to have you out of here so damn fast."

The twins snicker behind her as my lips pull up into a wicked grin. Maybe the twins weren't quite forthcoming enough when recapping their stories to their mother. I don't take kindly to threats. "You see, that's just the thing," I tell her. "I may be 'the help' but I'm also your son's girlfriend and seeing as though he owns this property, I guess that kinda makes me the lady of this house. So I guess you're the one who's going to have to watch herself."

"You don't want to start a war with me, young lady."

"Oh, you see. I think I really do. You're a crazy bitch who lit her ex-husband on fire and you're also the bitch who walked out of her son's life. You didn't even stay for him after his father died," I look over her shoulder at her daughters. "None of you did. You all stuck around long enough to see what you could get your hands on. You're all greedy bitches and the only reason you're here now is to try and sink your nails into Colton, but guess what? It won't work."

Laurelle grins at me, her white stiletto heels making her tower over me. "Oh, really?" she says. "Have you ever met a man who wouldn't move heaven and earth for his mother? Colton is hurting. He's still emotional from losing his father and what he needs right now is his mother and trust me when I say, it will only take a click of my fingers to convince him to be through with you. My son is a Carrington. He will not stain the family reputation by being with someone as lowly as you. This is a phase and he will be moving on. Carrington's don't associate themselves with trash."

With that, she steps away and heads for the grand staircase as the twins continue to stare at me. "Now," she says, looking back over her shoulder and indicating to the massive pile of suitcases. "Be a darling and deliver our belongings to our rooms. I expect dinner at seven and a glass of Moet from Charles' personal cellar."

She disappears up the stairs and I feel the rage beginning to burn through my veins but bitch one and bitch two aren't quite finished yet. "Listen here," the braver of the two says, making me think it must be Cora, considering our past run-ins. "Things are going to change around here. You're not the fucking princess of the mansion anymore. Bellevue Springs is our town and as of now, we're taking it back."

"Mom's right," the other says, stepping into me. "You're done. Especially after the bullshit you pulled at father's party. We're taking the mansion, we're taking the girls, and we're taking the fucking school. We're going to make your life a living hell and only once you think you can't possibly take it any longer, we're going to destroy you."

"You can forget about Colton and you can forget about Bellevue Springs," the bitchier of the two states. "You're going back to where you came from, slumming it with the other trash. Now, if you don't mind," she continues, slapping on a fake smile. "We have to go and tell our beloved big brother how excited we are to be home."

They run off, skipping up the stairs two at a time with their laughter flowing behind. "Be a darling," one calls, mimicking their mother. "Fetch our belongings."

What. The. Actual. Fuck?

What just happened right now? His bitch mother and bratty twin sisters are back. For good and desperate to make my life a living hell.

Fuck my life. I won't stand for this. I'm going to run these bitches out of here so damn fast. They won't take him away from me and if they're serious about wanting to be in his life for the right reasons, then they're going to have to get used to the fact that we're together because I'm not going anywhere.

As for their fucking luggage … they can deal with it themselves. I'm not their personal slave. Fuck them. They got the bags up the first sixty-six steps, I'm sure they can manage the last grand staircase by themselves. Just think how accomplished they'd feel achieving that all by themselves.

I go to walk away when it hits me—how is this going to look to Colton? I want him to see his mother and sisters for the bitches that they are, not me. If he thinks I'm making matters worse, he might just push me away. After all, I can guarantee that his mother is going to be in his ear about finding an appropriate girl to be with and not staining their precious reputation.

Fuck. I don't want to lose him. I can't. Things only just got good between us. I don't want to risk losing him because his mother wants to play mind tricks and take everything from him. I can't even go and complain to him because his sisters are just moments away from offering to suck his dick for attention and I have no doubt that they're already telling him about the beyond awful experience they just had with the help.

I look back at their stupid luggage.

I have no choice.

Heaviness sinks into my stomach and I find myself dragging my feet as I move toward their bags. I'll just deliver their stupid bags and get the queen bitch her wine, and then I can go and find Colton and explain that I was being a perfect angel. Sounds like a solid plan to me. If anything, I can consider this my yearly dose of exercise.

With that, I curl my fingers under the handle of the first bag and get my ass moving.

By the time I've delivered the final bag and have dropped down on the final step, my calves are aching, but it's not over yet. I still need to get Laurelle her stupid glass of … wait. What did she want? Actually, I don't give a shit. She'll get what I give her and should hope that I don't accidentally trip and ruin her white blouse with red wine in the process.

I make my way back into the staff quarters and after quickly glancing around and not finding Mom anywhere, I pull out my phone and give her a quick call. "What's up?" she answers almost immediately.

"Do you know where Charles' personal wine cellar is?"

"Huh?" she grunts as I hear the buzz from the vacuum cleaner in the background. "Why do you need his personal stash?"

"Haven't you heard? Laurelle and the twins are back, and she's insisting that I fetch her wine from his personal cellar. Either he keeps the good shit down there or it's just another way she can make him roll in his grave."

Mom lets out a heavy sigh. "Yeah, I noticed they were here. Laurelle has already had a quiet word with me about my misbehaved daughter. She would have had to say something good to get a reaction out of you that warrants a mother to mother conversation."

"She was … very pleasant."

"Oh, honey. Please don't cause any issues. I'm sure she'll only be here for a while before they move on again."

"Hope so," I grumble.

Mom lets out a sigh and I listen as she turns off the vacuum cleaner. "Do you want to call it a day and I'll grab the bottle of wine?"

"No, it's alright. You have enough on your plate already, and besides, I have a feeling that if I don't jump to her every command, she's going to figure out a way to make me regret it."

"I hate that I think you're right," she mutters. "Just remember to smile and be polite and then we can bitch about that witch behind closed doors."

"Alright, but I'm not making any promises."

I can practically hear Mom roll her eyes before she lets out a little huff at having to deal with her delinquent daughter. "The cellar is down past the back staircase. There's a small door that leads down into it. You can't miss it. Just be careful. The stairs leading down into it are very narrow. I don't want you to fall."

"Kay, thanks. I'll be careful."

Mom ends the call and I get to it, letting out a frustrated groan in the process and I just happen to be on the complete other side of the massive house. Hell, maybe she didn't request I go to this wine cellar to fuck with Charles, maybe she was fucking with me.

I find the door exactly where Mom had explained and as I push it open and look down into the darkness below, I can't help but feel like this is some kind of creepy dungeon.

Not able to find the light switch, I step down into the wine cellar and within a second, the room floods with light. I shake my head as I continue down the narrow steps. Of course, Charles would have motion sensor lights in here. Only the best for his personal wine cellar. I wouldn't be surprised if this room was also temperature controlled.

I get down into the main part of the cellar and glance around. It's kind of beautiful in here. I'm not going to pretend that I know a damn thing about wine, but I can tell that this shit is freaking old. Half of it is in locked, glass cases or up on fancy stands with spotlights showcasing it. It's kind of ridiculous but clearly these are his prized possessions.

I walk around. There must be at least two thousand bottles down here and the thought of ruining his collection to satisfy his ex-wife starts to irk on my nerves. Colton told me that Charles used to hit her and I totally understand her wanting to fuck with him, but using me to do it? Charles was a douche, but this isn't exactly a position I want to be in.

I wonder if Laurelle would notice if I grabbed a bottle from the main cellar and left this alone. She can get her revenge on her ex herself. I don't want anything to do with it. Besides, I don't need to give her more ammunition to use in her grand plan of getting me away from Colton. She can get her own hands dirty. I'm not going to be her little errand girl.

I start heading back toward the stairs when a soft rattle grabs my attention and I spin around, nearly knocking over a prized bottle in the process.

What the hell was that?

I search through the room before giving up and shrugging it off. It's got to be my mind playing tricks on me.

I start for the stairs again when I hear the same noise, only this time it wasn't so soft and I'm damn sure that shit wasn't my imagination. Shivers run down my spine and I find myself creeping through the wine cellar.

Please be a rat, please be a rat.

"Hello?" I call. "Is someone down here?"

I get no response and find myself curling my fingers around the closest bottle of wine, gripping it tightly and preparing to use it if I have to.

My mind instantly takes me to the DeCarlo family. It's only been a little under two weeks since they stormed through here. What are the chances that one of them has been hiding out down here, waiting for the right moment to strike? Colton declared that he will get them back so I don't doubt that they're on edge. He's that powerful that he could destroy their whole legacy with just the click of his fingers.

I instantly shrug that thought off. I doubt someone is going to wait down here that long. It has to be something else.

I turn a corner and come to a standstill as I find a big metal door that looks like the kind of door that banks would use to guard their safe. This door means fucking business. This door means secrets.

What has Charles been hiding down here?

I should be walking away. I should take the stupid bottle of wine and run yet something has me walking toward it. I need to know what's on the other side, I need to know what Charles has been hiding.

My hand curls around the big metal lock and I give it a hard pull while hearing the rattle louder on the other side. The lock slips out of place with a loud bang and my heart races.

I let out a shaky breath and grab the handle while readying myself to run. The door is heavy and I give it a hard yank, trying to prepare myself for what's on the other side.

The room is in darkness but as the door slowly swings open, the light from the wine cellar seeps in and lights it up.

A loud gasp travels up my throat and my hand tightens around the wine bottle as a grinning, malnourished, and beat Jude Carter stares back at me.

"Well, well," Jude says, yanking on the thick chains that keep him locked in the room. His eyes travel up and down my body as he licks his lips. "I guess Colton finally decided to deliver me a little gift after all. Why don't you come over here and let me finish you off."

His voice sends chills sweeping over my body, reminding me of the way he touched me, the way he violated and raped me, and I can't allow that to go unpunished.

I have to do something.

A darkness seeps into my soul, a darkness I wasn't aware that I possessed and for a brief moment, I feel for Nic as I finally begin to understand him, understand the bloodlust, and the need to take justice into my own hands.

It's been three weeks since he raped me and three weeks of people desperately searching for him. If I was to let him go, I risk him coming back and I risk him telling people where he's been. I can't allow that to happen. I can always go to the authorities but just like the poor girl that came before me, she was called a liar and he got away with it without even a slap on the wrist. I'd rather die than let that happen.

There's only one thing for me to do—I have to kill him. I have to end this.

I raise my chin and step into the secret room, realizing that this isn't Charles' dirty little secret at all, it's Colton's. He's kept him chained down here for three weeks, lying every time someone asked him if he knew what had happened, lying when he told me that he had no idea where he was, lying, lying, lying. Just like Nic. Just like Sebastian, Kairo, and Elijah.

I'm done listening to the men in my life decide what truths they want me to know. I'm done being the pathetic girl who lets a man walk all over her. I'm done waiting for revenge and I'm done having these men dictate my life.

My time is now.

I make my decisions.

My hand curls tighter around the neck of the wine bottle and I slam it against the metal door, listening to the sweet sound of the glass breaking and leaving me with nothing but jagged, sharp edges, the perfect weapon to slice across his neck, the same way Nic had done with those men in his clubhouse.

My eyes meet Jude's through the darkened room and I don't care how much Colton has beaten and tortured him over the past three weeks, it will never be enough. I have to do this, not only for me, but for the other girl he hurt.

All sense of right and wrong leave me and as I take another step deeper into the secret room, a sick, twisted smile spreads wide over my face and I watch as Jude realizes just how far I'll go to protect my sanity.

"Time to say your prayers, fucker. Your time is up."

<u>Rejects Paradise Series Playlist</u>

Game of Survival - Ruelle
I'm Gonna Show You Crazy - Bebe Rexha
Nightmare - Halsey
Never Tear Us Apart - Bishop Briggs
Bird Set Free - Sia
Helium - Sia
Dusk Till Dawn - Zayn feat Sia
Heaven - Julia Michaels
Graveyard - Halsey
Bad Bitch - Bebe Rexha
Love Drug - G-Easy feat Halsey
Hurricane - Tommee Profitt
Unloveable - Delacey
Power - Isak Danielson
Cruel Intentions - Delacey feat G-Easy
Not Afraid Anymore - Halsey
Unstoppable - Sia
Monsters - Tommee Profitt
Can't Help Falling In Love - Tommee Profitt
Angel Cry - G-Easy feat Devon Baldwin
Bad At Love - Halsey
Creep - G-Easy feat Ashley Benson
In The End - Tommee Profitt
Wicked Game - Daisy Gray
Haunted - Beyonce
Gasoline - Halsey
I Feel Like I'm Drowning - Two Feet
Twisted - Two Feet
Wild Horses - Bishop Briggs
The Fire - Bishop Briggs
Killer - Vallerie Broussard

426

Thanks for reading!

If you enjoyed reading this book as much as I enjoyed writing it, please consider leavinge a review.

www.amazon.com/dp/B08C4XKL1V

For more information on Rejects Paradise, find me on Facebook or Instagram –

www.facebook.com/SheridanAnneAuthor

www.instagram.com/Sheridan.Anne.Author

<u>Other Series by Sheridan Anne</u>

www.amazon.com/Sheridan-Anne/e/B079TLXN6K

<u>Young Adult / New Adult - Romance</u>

The Broken Hill High Series (5 Book Series + Novella)

Haven Falls (7 Book Series + Novella)

Broken Hill Boys (5 Book Novella Series)

Aston Creek High (4 Book Series)

Rejects Paradise (4 Book Series)

<u>New Adult Romance</u>

Kings of Denver (4 Book Series)

Denver Royalty (3 Book Series)

Rebels Advocate (4 Book Series)

<u>Urban Fantasy - Pen name: Cassidy Summers</u>

Slayer Academy (3 Book Series)